PRAISE FOR

BEFORE YOU KNEW MY NAME

"A brave and timely novel which will fuel the debate on women's rights to walk safely through our streets. I raced through the pages, anxious for resolution, yet at the same time not wanting this beautiful writing to finish."

—Clare Mackintosh, author of *I Let You Go*

"Unflinching and heartbreaking; powerful and empowering, the story of Alice and Ruby is our story, the story of every woman, everywhere. I know I'll be thinking about it—and them—for a very long time to come."

—Carole Johnstone, award-winning author of *Mirrorland*

"*Before You Knew My Name* will make you cry, make you angry, make you think. Jacqueline Bublitz pushes the boundaries of crime fiction in all the right ways. It's a deeply moving, deeply original, story that, hands down, is one of the best novels of the year."

—Alex Finlay, author of *The Night Shift*

"The most wonderful book. Unusual, beautiful, feminist, gripping, deserves to win prizes. I loved it so much."

—Marian Keyes, internationally bestselling author of *Grown Ups*

"A really remarkable book—so fresh and original. I've never read anything quite like this."

—Laura Barnett, author of *The Versions of Us*

"I fell head over heels in love with this heartbreaking, beautiful and hugely important novel. Jacqueline Bublitz's prose is luminous and the up-all-night, just-one-more-page plot is brilliantly clever and original. Everyone should read this book."

—Rosie Walsh, author of *The Man Who Didn't Call*

"I was mesmerized by this exquisitely written, heartbreaking, lyrical story of friendship from beyond the grave."

—Jane Corry, author of *My Husband's Wife*

"An astounding debut novel that every woman will feel in their bones. At last, a whodunit, where the victim is the front and center of the story. Beautifully written, real, feminist and properly haunting, it deserves all the awards."

—Lizzy Dent, author of *The Summer Job*

"An unputdownable debut—striking, moving, gripping throughout and so sharp on the things that unite us."

—Elizabeth Kay, author of *Seven Lies*

"Fiercely topical and full of compassion, *Before You Knew My Name* starts where many thrillers and news stories do: the murder of a young woman. But instead of a hunt for the killer, this novel explores the personhood of the victim—who she was, what she loved, all the years that were stolen from her. It's a story about female agency and value in the face of male violence, and also about resilience, about memory, about how love adapts and survives."

—Julie Cohen, author of *Together*

"The murder of an attractive young woman is the foundation on which many crime novels are built. . . . But in her unique first book, Australian writer Bublitz turns that traditional construct on its head with fierce compassion and a welcome dose of feminist outrage. . . . This is undeniably a crime story, but Bublitz's creativity, affectionate descriptions of a New York City she obviously adores, and strong character development make this novel stand out in a crowded genre. A unique, feminist take on the suspense genre and our fascination with violence."

—*Kirkus Reviews*

"A touching and compelling read . . . a moving story of two women connected through more than an act of violence, but through heart and spirit."

—PopSugar, "Thriller and Mystery Books That'll Keep You Hooked from Beginning to End"

LEAVE
THE GIRLS
BEHIND

ALSO BY JACQUELINE BUBLITZ

Before You Knew My Name

LEAVE THE GIRLS BEHIND

A NOVEL

JACQUELINE BUBLITZ

EMILY BESTLER BOOKS

ATRIA

New York   London   Toronto   Sydney   New Delhi

EMILY
BESTLER
BOOKS

ATRIA

An Imprint of Simon & Schuster, LLC
1230 Avenue of the Americas
New York, NY 10020

First Emily Bestler Books/Atria Paperback edition October 2024

EMILY BESTLER BOOKS/ATRIA PAPERBACK and colophon are trademarks of Simon & Schuster, LLC

Simon & Schuster: Celebrating 100 Years of Publishing in 2024

For information about special discounts for bulk purchases, please contact Simon & Schuster Special Sales at 1-866-506-1949 or business@simonandschuster.com.

The Simon & Schuster Speakers Bureau can bring authors to your live event. For more information or to book an event, contact the Simon & Schuster Speakers Bureau at 1-866-248-3049 or visit our website at www.simonspeakers.com.

Interior design by Ritika Karnik

Manufactured in the United States of America

1   3   5   7   9   10   8   6   4   2

Library of Congress Cataloging-in-Publication Data
Names: Bublitz, Jacqueline, author.
Title: Leave the girls behind : a novel / Jacqueline Bublitz.
Description: First Emily Bestler Books/Atria paperback edition. | New York : Emily Bestler Books/Atria, 2024. | Summary: "The acclaimed author of the "tour de force" (The New York Times Book Review) Before You Knew My Name returns with a fresh suspense novel about a woman haunted by a serial killer and the ghosts he left behind"—Provided by publisher.
Identifiers: LCCN 2024024299 | ISBN 9781982199050 (trade paperback) | ISBN 9781982199074 (ebook) | ISBN 9781797185422
Subjects: LCGFT: Thrillers (Fiction) | Novels.
Classification: LCC PR9639.4.B83 L43 2024 | DDC 823/.92—dc23/eng/20240604
LC record available at https://lccn.loc.gov/2024024299

ISBN 978-1-9821-9905-0
ISBN 978-1-9821-9907-4 (ebook)

For HW, who saw them before I did.

No herring so red but I raise my voice and give chase.

—NGAIO MARSH, *DEATH IN ECSTASY*

Down, down, down into the darkness of the grave
Gently they go, the beautiful, the tender, the kind;
Quietly they go, the intelligent, the witty, the brave.
I know. But I do not approve.
And I am not resigned.

—EDNA ST. VINCENT MILLAY,
EXCERPT FROM "DIRGE WITHOUT MUSIC"
FROM *COLLECTED POEMS*

*I*n her own bedroom, she has a night-light shaped like a star. It turns off when she is sleeping, because she doesn't need it to stay on all night. Only when her eyes are still open. It's not really the dark that she's afraid of, anyway. It's not being able to see where all that darkness ends.

Her teacher said the stars don't actually go away; it's just that sometimes the sun makes it too bright to see them. And when you can't see the sun anymore, that's not because it's gone, either. You've just been spun away from the light.

There are no suns in this room. Unless you count the three blue ones scribbled on the wall. She saw them when he first brought her here. Back when there was still a little light. Now there's not even a crack under the door.

Who drew those suns? Was it the girl she can hear through the wall? The one who's been singing the same song over and over? That girl sounds too grown-up to draw blue crayon suns on somebody's wallpaper, but maybe those scribbles have been here for a long time already.

Like she has.

She likes being sung to when she can't sleep. But not by the girl on the other side of the wall. Because that's not the right song. This is not the right room, or the right bed. She is not supposed to be here.

She's been spun around and around. And now she can't see anything at all.

AMITY

ONE

New York, May 2015

R uth-Ann Baker is having an unremarkable day.

For the twenty-six-year-old New Yorker, *unremarkable* looks something like this . . .

She gets out of bed before 10 a.m. She does not worry excessively about her dog, Ressler, dying (she just worries a small, helpful amount). She does a quick tidy-up of her apartment and eats the right food at the right times. A bagel for breakfast, a salad sandwich for lunch. She drinks three coffees, none of which make her overly jittery, and she does not grab at her stomach when looking in the mirror, or hate any part of her body excessively. She completes the requisite amount of steps for herself and for Ressler, and she does her breathing exercises. Talks briefly to her uncle Joe on the phone. Ignores a call from her mother and communicates with her father exclusively through emojis. She watches a half-hour documentary on climate change at 5 p.m., and times her wallowing after. Ten minutes to worry about the state of the world, and then she puts her hair up in a messy bun and gets ready for work. The walk to Sweeney's Bar will take her ten minutes, the way it always does. Meaning she'll be right on time for her shift, the way she always is.

There is nothing remarkable about her day at all, no cause for concern.

Until.

Her cell phone begins to beep loudly, just as she drops it into her bag. Living in Manhattan, Ruth is used to wailing sirens, to honking horns and sudden booms that make you jump, but the noise emanating from the bottom of her satchel has a different tone; there's an insistent, high-pitched urgency to it. She scrambles to retrieve the phone, her fingers brushing over the tiny stun gun disguised as lipstick and the can of deodorant that's really mace, until she finds it, just as the beeping stops. And now she understands why that sound seemed to reverberate all around her. She has been sent an automated emergency alert, one that would have echoed throughout the city and beyond.

Ruth feels her stomach drop. It's a notification about a child abduction. She knows that AMBER Alerts can be sent directly to cell phones these days, but it's still a shock to receive one right here in her apartment.

Taking a deep breath, she reads over the truncated details, each line causing a little earthquake that makes her hand—and the phone—shake.

AMBER ALERT Hoben, CT
VEH DrkBlu Van
CHILD 7F 4ft 45lb
SUSPECT White M 30–40 yrs
CHECK MEDIA

Less than ninety characters of information, but Ruth can see through the gaps. A little girl has been taken from the town of Hoben, Connecticut, by a man with few identifiers, outside the blue van he was driving—possibly across state lines, given the alert has been sent as far as New York City.

A child has gone missing. An adult male has driven her away.

Ruth tries not to think about what that man did next.

Or the town he took the little girl from. Where so much has already been lost.

———————

"It's a real one tonight, Nancy Drew!"

Owen Alvin greets Ruth with his favorite nickname for her, and the feverish glee that comes from finding his little bar improbably busy for a Monday. Most nights, Sweeney's—full name Sweeney Todd's Sports Bar—attracts a small, dedicated crowd, who come for the endless loop of Stephen Sondheim soundtracks and/or the latest playoffs screened on the three muted television sets mounted on the back wall. But tonight, Ruth's workplace is packed with patrons, most of their faces unfamiliar to her. Sweeney's must have featured in another one of those "Secret places only New Yorkers know about" articles, she thinks with a grimace, as she joins her boss behind the bar.

Owen appears to mistake her expression for a smile, as he beams at her.

"Let's do this!" he half shouts over a cranked-up version of "Losing My Mind" from the last Broadway revival of *Follies*.

Accurate, Ruth thinks dourly. Her mind is somewhere else entirely.

CHECK MEDIA, the AMBER Alert had said.

Even as she read this, back at her apartment, Ruth knew she had to resist. When it comes to missing girls, she's made a promise *not* to check media, and she has every intention of keeping her word. But that doesn't stop her thoughts from returning, over and over, to the little girl. To that town. Old, familiar fault lines have started to quiver under Ruth's skin, and it's only loyalty to Owen that keeps her from faking a migraine and asking to go home. She wouldn't do that to him on a busy night like this.

This tiny neighborhood bar has been her sanctuary for five years now, ever since Owen hired her as a favor to her uncle Joe. Back in 2010, Ruth was a twenty-one-year-old college dropout with a chasm where her future used to be. She'd been studying forensics; the plan, for as long as Ruth-Ann Baker could remember, was to become a criminal profiler. But all that changed, thanks to the episode. She went abruptly from being top of her classes at her city college to living with her uncle and Gideon, Joe's then-new husband, on their then–newly purchased hobby farm in the Hudson Valley. It wasn't an official term by any means: "the episode." But that's what they called it, Ruth, Joe, and Gideon. And Officer Canton, back in Hoben, although he likely had many names for what she put him through that winter. When she came out the other side in the spring, Joe suggested she move into his recently vacated apartment on the Upper West Side. It would save him having to find a new tenant, he told her.

Before the episode, Ruth had lived in a small Morningside Heights apartment with her parents, or rather, her mom, because her dad had already moved out. Living by herself felt like a much-needed reset button, and it helped that Ruth knew Joe's building and the neighborhood well; she and her parents had stayed with him for a full year when they first moved to New York, in the fall of 1996. Any concerns Ruth's family had about her living alone were eased when Officer Canton, who they'd known for years, showed up at the farm with Ressler. This, too, was framed as a mutually beneficial proposition. Despite his pedigree, the loving but recalcitrant bloodhound was failing spectacularly in his designated career as a K-9 with the Hoben Police Department, where Canton had his hands full with new canine recruits. If Ruth could just look after him for a while . . .

(Of course, Ressler, all droopy, one hundred pounds of him, ending up looking after her.)

Owen knows very little about that time in Ruth's life. When Joe introduced the two of them, Ruth had met Owen's requirements for bar staff: thanks to her uncle, she had a solid appreciation for the world of musical theater and an unwavering respect for the pride flag that hung out front of Sweeney's. Whether Ruth could pour beers was irrelevant, as was her history before she walked in the door—although her new boss did have a particular fascination with Ruth's former field of study, which she'd shared in her (very informal) interview, because Joe said she didn't need to lie about her past.

Just tell small truths, Ruthie, her uncle had advised her. *Then no one thinks to go looking for the big ones.*

"You know, Ruth-Ann," Owen said at the start of her first shift, "they say a bartender has as much chance of predicting a person's behavior as a fully trained criminal profiler. So consider this job a continuation of your studies!"

"I'll be on the lookout for any dubious pie makers," she'd replied, the reference to *Sweeney Todd* cementing their friendship just like that.

On her second night at Sweeney's, Ruth had walked in to find a large glass jar behind the bar. Inside was a glossy photograph of Len Cariou from the original Broadway production of *Sweeney Todd*, along with a pink disposable razor.

"I got you a Kill Jar," Owen explained proudly. "Anyone gives you demon barber vibes, you can take their credit card from that little tab folder I showed you yesterday and drop it in this jar instead, and I'll know to keep an eye on them for the rest of the night. How does that sound, Nancy Drew?"

She'd nodded, feeling alarmingly close to tears.

Since then, Owen has seldom called Ruth by her own name. It's either Nancy or whatever other fictional female detective he's encountered while flipping through old television shows at 3 a.m. And they've rarely needed to use the Kill Jar. But she's remained quietly committed to its purpose, because she's always on the lookout for demons.

That said, she's too distracted to profile anyone tonight, suspicious or otherwise. In fact, she probably couldn't pick any of Sweeney's current patrons out of a lineup; they could all be the same person, so blurred is her normally keen vision. Her attention has been fixed on those three silent televisions mounted on the wall. She's been hoping to catch a news ticker running along the bottom of the screens, some kind of update on the missing girl. Because it wouldn't be breaking her promise if information about the little girl's disappearance came directly to her, would it?

It's not like she asked for that AMBER Alert, either.

But there are no breaking headlines from Hoben, Connecticut, scrolling beneath the *Monday Night Baseball* broadcast that Jan, Sweeney's barback and most committed Major League fan, has playing across every screen. If it wasn't for the memory of that shrill alert she'd received back at her apartment, Ruth might think she'd imagined the whole thing. Conjured up a missing child after she'd realized the date. Because this unremarkable Monday in late May has long been designated Missing Children's Day, here in the States and around the globe.

Was that alarm simply another one of Ruth-Ann Baker's infamous delusions, brought on by her aversion to this date? She could ask Owen if he, too, received the AMBER Alert. Or maybe check with Jan, whose phone is always buzzing with sports scores and sure bets she'd placed the night before. But Ruth can't think how to frame the question casually enough that they won't see the glitter of her panic.

Hey, guys, did you see a kid just went missing from my old hometown?

What if they say no?

What if they say yes?

Ruth is not prepared to have either of those conversations. She busies herself with work instead, losing herself in the mundanity of pouring beers, refilling popcorn bowls, and forcing smiles.

Finally, right at 11 p.m., the bar clears out. Soon, there are only two customers left. A couple of old regulars, sitting on one of the ratty couches down the back, drinking bourbon and arguing about who should be allowed to run for president.

"Time to go," Owen shouts down the bar, before asking Ruth if she'd like to join him and Jan for a post-closing nightcap, which she knows is code for heading to a club in Chelsea, where she'll sit in a booth minding their bags and the drinks while they dance until sunrise.

"Gotta get home to Ressler," she answers, faux apologetic, and Owen seems to buy this excuse, because he tells her she might as well finish for the night then. The two quarreling regulars haven't even left yet as Ruth races out the door, before her boss can change his mind.

Walking home, Manhattan's calm, spring air is at odds with her mood. Without Sweeney's to tether her, Ruth is beginning to feel those tremors again. And now she has her own safety to worry about too. It's something she has to consider after every late shift. How to navigate streets that change shape in the dark. Ruth knows that if you regularly walk alone at night, you should probably mix up your route a little. Tonight, after leaving the bar earlier than usual, she makes a quick calculation. If she heads south on Amsterdam, she's guaranteed to see other nocturnals exiting the twenty-four-hour CVSs and Duane Reades dotted along the way, all those harried people with their plastic bags full of painkillers and diapers and hopeful, last-minute contraception. At this hour, in this neighborhood, there's always someone needing something, and she'd like to be noticed by them. So that if someone is ever asked, *Have you seen this girl?* they just might remember her.

As a young woman living alone in a big city, she has to think about these things. A year ago, a teenage girl was murdered down in Riverside Park, and for weeks no one could figure out who she was. Most people were shocked by the whole thing, but not Ruth-Ann Baker.

"You act like this is Times Square before the Marriott moved in," Owen teased her once, when he saw the self-defense kit she carries in her bag. The lipstick stun gun in particular had amused him.

On the walk home tonight, she slips that little stun gun into her pocket, next to her keys.

When she reaches her uncle Joe's co-op on West Eighty-Sixth, Ruth looks left, right, left again before heading through the first of the building's two security doors. Despite her eagerness to get upstairs, she waits until the second door has clicked shut behind her before she races across the gleaming lobby to the elevator.

She keeps her right hand in her pocket, fingers smoothing over the stun gun, as she takes the slow ride up to her floor. Before exiting into the shared hallway, she closes her eyes briefly, listens for the sound of footsteps or breathing, and then she walks purposefully to her apartment's front door. Stepping inside, she barely has time to fix the three internal chain locks before Ressler gambols toward her, perpetual drool dripping from his jowls.

"Hey, big guy," she croons, bending down to scratch the folds of his ears.

Ressler responds with his own scratch against her leg, a sign that he needs to be let out, ASAP. Ruth reaches for his harness, hanging from its hook in the entranceway. She might have been desperate to get home, but now that she's here, taking Ressler for a walk suddenly feels like a welcome postponement. Because what comes next seems alarmingly inevitable.

Out with her hound dog, Ruth can be brave in a way she wishes she could bottle. This must be what it's like, she often thinks, to roam the streets at night as a man. Still, she turns Ressler around before they reach Riverside Drive, because not even her dog would make her feel safe in that park when it's dark.

When they get back to the apartment, Ruth stands frozen in the entranceway, unsure which direction to move in. For the first time in a very long while, she has a strong desire to check all the cupboards, even the ones only a contortionist could hide in. Then there are the thick curtains, all those folds a person could conceal themselves behind. And the two shower recesses, with their tinted screens. Not to mention the walk-in robes. There are two spare bedrooms, the doors to which she keeps closed. As Ruth looks toward the closed door of her own bedroom, she thinks of how hard her uncle had tried to make that room feel welcoming to a seven-year-old, back in 1996. The walls painted in bright colors and hung with cheery posters. The pretty pillows, and the newly purchased queen bed that Ruth secretly hated, because it was positioned under a window she was certain her new neighbors could look right through. Most nights that first year, if someone checked on little Ruthie, they would find her asleep on the room's polished wood floor.

Joe doesn't know that the grown-up Ruth still sleeps on the floor sometimes. Neither do her parents. Cynthia Baker has taken a year out to "find" herself—in Italy, mostly. And Ellis, who lives with his second wife in New Jersey, hasn't known where his daughter sleeps for years now.

Not this again, sweetheart, he'd probably say if he did know.

Ruth's parents have never been good with what they both still refer to as her "quirks."

Her therapist does know about her sleeping habits. But Courtney is on maternity leave until early August, and Ruth never really clicked with her male replacement, so she hasn't had a session in months. With her old geology metaphors coming thick and fast tonight, she regrets not trying harder with the new guy. It would be nice to be able to contact him, tell him she's started thinking about the lithosphere again.

She could call Officer Canton, ask him about the missing girl. But Canton specifically told her not to call him after-hours anymore, not unless it was an emergency. *Even then, you should call 911, Ruthie.* Besides, this isn't an actual emergency. The cracks caused by that AMBER Alert. Only Bill and Patty Lovely would understand why she feels so unsteady. She can just imagine the soothing calm of their voices, the way they'd say, *Are you okay?* and really want to know the answer. But the Lovelys don't deserve to be woken by a ringing phone this late at night. If anyone should be left to sleep like the dead, it's them.

Shuddering at the idiom, Ruth takes a step toward the door to her room and opens it.

It is only a small shock to see Beth Lovely sitting primly on the bed. Deep down, Ruth had known she'd be there, but it still causes a jolt.

"You came back," Ruth says from the doorway.

"Of course," Beth responds softly. "How could I not?"

"Are the others—"

But Ruth doesn't need to finish her question.

"They won't come unless you ask them to. A promise is a promise, Ruthie."

And with that gentle assurance, Beth is up and across the room, arms outstretched.

"I missed you," Ruth says as they embrace.

"I missed you, too," Beth sighs against her cheek, her breath a cool breeze that causes Ruth's skin to dimple all over.

Her dead best friend has always had this effect on her.

TWO

On the afternoon of May 15, 1996, Beth Lovely disappeared from the children's playground directly across from Hoben Heights High School, in Hoben, Connecticut.

Her tiny, dead body was found eleven days later, buried in a shallow grave in the woods behind Longview Road, some six miles from where she'd been taken. She was only seven and a half years old.

Ethan Oswald, the thirty-one-year-old music teacher who murdered her, was arrested the same day.

Back then, as it is now, Hoben was a predominantly middle-class town just off Interstate 91. Longview Road was situated in North Hoben, where the nicest houses were. Big old Colonials, set back from the road down tree-lined, circular driveways and surrounded by woods and walking trails. No one thought they'd find Beth Lovely in this part of town, during those painful days it seemed like everyone was looking for her. Just like no one thought to suspect Ethan Oswald, the high school's popular new teacher, who also led the choir at the town's largest church.

Bill and Patty Lovely attended that church. They loved that choir. Their only daughter, Beth, did too.

If the Lovely girl's disappearance had shocked the residents of Hoben, her murder was more like a numbing. How could that nice man, that considerate, churchgoing teacher, do such terrible things to a child? It made no sense, not then, not now. To this day, some townsfolk still find it incomprehensible that Ethan Oswald murdered Beth Lovely. They refuse to accept his guilt. Not that it matters in anything but principle, because Oswald has been dead since 2002.

Which means he can't be responsible for the disappearance of another little Hoben girl all these years later, in 2015.

But there is no denying the eerie similarities. That's what Ruth has been trying to push down all night, ever since receiving the AMBER Alert. With Beth by her side, she no longer needs to pretend she can't see those similarities. She doesn't need to pretend she can't see *her*.

The first time Beth showed up in her bedroom, seven-year-old Ruth had only just moved with her parents to New York City. By unspoken agreement, the two girls never talked about what happened back in Hoben. They simply played together, had fun together, the way any little girls would.

Like an imaginary friend? a child psychologist once asked, when Ruth hadn't yet figured out she shouldn't answer such questions.

No, because she's real, she'd said at the time, which prompted a whole new round of tests, most of which felt like tricks.

Those tests didn't stop Beth coming back, they just taught Ruth not to tell anyone about her visits.

Five years ago, it was Ruth herself who asked Beth to leave. Even though this was the last thing she wanted, it had to be done.

But now Beth is back.

"Are you sure you want to do this?" she asks. She is sitting next to Ruth on the bed. They have Ruth's laptop open in front of them, search bar ready.

"It won't be like last time," Ruth answers, and they both fall silent. Thinking about blue vans, and springtime, and the town neither of them ever returned to.

It can't be Ethan Oswald.

But that doesn't mean they shouldn't know who *she* is.

———

The missing girl's name is Coco Wilson.

She disappeared from her front yard, where she had been playing after school. Coco and her family—mother Ivy, father Leo, and fourteen-year-old sister Maya—only recently moved to Connecticut from Leo's home state of Louisiana. At this early stage, they have not been put in front of any news cameras, but according to local reports Ivy grew up in Hoben, and the family returned this spring to be closer to her ailing parents. Little else has been shared about the Wilson family, but Ruth knows that will change if Coco isn't found soon. Parents are among the first to be scrutinized in missing children cases—not just by the police, but by the public too.

The early reports that Ruth reads focus on a physical description of Coco. Her light, curly hair, her brown eyes, and the gap in her front teeth. The *Star Wars* tee she was wearing and the color of her sneakers. Ruth pushes through the repetition of these heart-rendingly specific details, looking for—what, exactly?

"Something that everyone else has missed," Beth says. "That's what you were always good at, Ruthie."

Ruth reads on. She notes that a search team, including Hoben's K-9 squad, was mobilized around 4:30 p.m., after a frantic Ivy Wilson alerted the police. Several witnesses have come forward;

according to local media, somewhere between 3:45 and 4 p.m., a number of Hoben residents saw a blue van speeding away from town, with a little girl matching Coco's description sitting in the front passenger seat. In addition, an elderly neighbor of the Wilson family, a Mrs. Coralea Michaels, looked out her parlor window at 3:33 p.m. to see Coco talking to a young woman walking her dog. Coco was still in her own yard, and the blond, ponytailed girl, her back to the near-sighted Coralea, was standing on the street, the small, white dog at her feet.

I was baking an apple pie, and the timer went off just as I looked out the window. That's why I remember the specific time, a distressed Coralea is quoted as telling the police.

"That poor woman will be feeling so guilty," Ruth says. "In hindsight, people always realize they could have done more."

"What about the girl with the dog?" Beth replies, frowning. "How come they're not saying much about her?"

"Sometimes the police hold back key information," Ruth reminds, but even as she says it something prickles at her skin. A memory that isn't hers, exactly. More like a story someone told her, or a song she used to listen to.

Officer Canton—technically Sergeant Canton these days—would know about the ponytailed girl with the small dog. He'd know all the things you won't find in an official news report right now, or maybe ever. Information you have to *really* look for. There's a place online where Ruth could probably find these things for herself. But she's not ready to go there. Not yet. Right now, her promise feels only half-broken, and she'd like to keep it that way.

Checking her watch, Ruth sees that it's nearly 2 a.m. Coco Wilson was last seen more than ten hours ago.

In most cases, if a child is taken by a stranger, they'll be dead within three hours.

An anonymous person has just posted this comment under one of the latest news articles about Coco. It's not a statistic the girls need to be told.

Ruth snaps her laptop shut, just as Beth says she should go.

"Get some sleep, Ruthie," she says hopefully, as if she knows her sudden reappearance has made that unlikely.

"You'll come back?" Ruth asks.

Beth nods, before adding softly, "For as long as you'll let me."

Ruth does indeed struggle to fall asleep. Restless, she reaches under her pillow to find the small ring she keeps hidden there. Slipping it onto the pinky finger of her left hand, the only place it still fits after all these years, she twists the small band around and around, thumb and forefinger of her opposite hand worrying the five blue petals and yellow eye of the delicate flower raised at its center. This was Beth's ring, a forget-me-not given to her by her maternal grandmother on her seventh birthday, and nobody knows Ruth has it—not even Beth's parents.

Ruth can understand why Bill and Patty might want their daughter's ring back. But she lost so much of herself when Beth—and the others—went away. It would break her heart to lose the ring too.

She gets down from her bed to lie on the floor with Ressler, where his head rests on a pile of dirty clothes. The revving motor of his snores calms her own breathing, and soon Ruth, too, is sleeping like the dead. Or with them. Because when she opens her eyes in the middle of the night, the others have come back after all.

They stay just long enough for Ruth to note that the little girl is not there among them, but not long enough for her to ask them if they know where on earth Coco Wilson might have gone.

"Did you hear about the little girl from Hoben?" Joe asks on the phone the next morning, when Ruth is back in her bed.

Although his tone is casual, Ruth knows immediately this is the real reason her uncle called. Ostensibly, he wanted to tell her about some new, vegan, organic food that his new, vegan, organic neighbor in Gardiner had just recommended for Ressler. Ruth is used to Joe and Gideon treating her dog like a favorite nephew; under normal circumstances, the recommendation would be welcomed. But she knows that, up in the Hudson Valley, Joe would have received the AMBER Alert last night too.

"Yeah, I did hear about her," Ruth answers, attempting to match Joe's light tone.

A rare silence hangs between them.

"It's not the same," Joe says finally.

"I know that," Ruth responds quietly.

Don't I?

"Oswald is dead," Joe says firmly, as if he can hear his niece's thoughts.

"I know that," she repeats.

Ethan Oswald died in prison less than seven years into his life sentence for the kidnapping and murder of Beth Lovely. It wasn't a shiv, fashioned by a vengeful cellmate, or the electric chair, or a self-made noose. He died a regular death, from pancreatic cancer, the same way Ruth's high school librarian died, and the nice old man who ran the bodega down the street died too. Oswald took his last breath in a hospital bed, soothed by pain medication, with music playing and a priest on call. Or so Ruth read a few years later, when she knew how to find such things online.

"Are you going to be okay, Ruthie?"

This time, Joe doesn't try to mask the concern in his voice.

"Yep."

"You'd let me know if you weren't okay, right?" Joe pushes.

And maybe it's because he's not coming right out with it. Maybe it's because he can't actually say the words, the way no one ever seems to be able to say the words when it comes to Ethan Oswald, but for the first time Ruth hears more judgment than concern in her uncle's tone. The same creeping frustration that her parents can never seem to hide from her.

Not this again, sweetheart.

You can add *sweetheart* to any sentence and make it sound like you care.

What if it is this again? she wants to ask Joe. *What would you do then?*

But instead she tells her uncle not to worry, before making an excuse to hang up.

"Ressler needs to pee."

"I should get going, too," Joe responds with a sigh. "Gideon wants to buy an alpaca this afternoon, and we haven't finished arguing about it yet."

After he ends the call, Ruth leans back on her bed and pats the covers to let Ressler know he can come up beside her.

"Your uncle Joe worries because he cares," she says to her dog.

And Joe is one of the most caring people she knows. A man who lives large, and loves large, and adopts every stray he comes across, because he cannot stand to see any animal—or person—in pain.

Beth was always very curious about Joe. She couldn't understand why a grown man would be so kind to a little girl if he didn't have to be.

A grown man had only pretended to be kind to Beth, just so he could hurt her.

Is that what happened to Coco Wilson too?

Ruth is wavering.

She should just leave it alone. Let the experts do their work, like they're actually trained to do. Hadn't she learned that the hard way, last time around?

But Beth came back. That has to mean something.

And the others came back when she was sleeping; she is sure of it. *A promise is a promise*, Beth said. Does that mean Ruth wanted them to return?

Them: the *other* dead girls. The ones who first came to Ruth on her twenty-first birthday. When they wanted her to prove that Ethan Oswald had murdered them too.

THREE

*T*he less dead.

Five years ago, on the morning of her twenty-first birthday, Ruth was sitting at the small desk in her bedroom working
through the assigned reading for her victimology class later that
day. She was scanning a journal article about modern victim
precipitation theories (victim-*blaming* theories, she called them
in her head) when she encountered that term for the first time:
the less dead. It described how certain serial murder victims were
considered "less dead" than those victims whose lives before their
deaths had been assigned a greater societal value. Ruth was well
aware of the hierarchies of victimhood that determined whether
you might be considered an "innocent" victim or one who had
somehow contributed to your own demise (not unlike the com-
mentary on social media, she's often thought). But this was the
most explicit way of saying it.

Only some deaths matter.

Beth's death had mattered. Ethan Oswald had targeted a
sweet little white girl from a middle-class neighborhood in Middle America, and that made her the perfect victim. What had

made him think he could get away with it, this man who was later found to be of so-called sound mind? There were so many other targets he might have chosen. Girls less visible. Less—dead.

Something niggled at Ruth then, a forgotten splinter working its way out. A quick online search for Dr. Steven Egger, the esteemed professor who'd coined the phrase "less dead," reminded her that she'd come across his research many times before. Just last semester, she'd attended a lecture on unsolved serial killer cases, where she'd been introduced to another of Dr. Egger's particularly lucid terms: *linkage blindness*, the phenomenon by which law enforcement officers sometimes failed to recognize a pattern of serial killings in their jurisdiction because they mistakenly viewed each murder as an isolated incident. They failed to connect the dots.

Ethan Oswald was only ever convicted of one murder. He had no record, no priors for even a minor incident in his past. If he—and the criminal justice system that convicted him—were to be believed, he simply woke up one morning and committed a spontaneous, heinous act. One that might have long gone undetected, if not for an anonymous phone tip about a little girl's shoe spotted out on Longview Road. (The police never did recover the shoe that Sunday morning, but Officer Canton's K-9 squad picked up Beth's scent in the very spot the anonymous caller had described, before those highly trained noses followed her scent farther along the road to a house that made the dogs howl.)

What Ruth realized, as she considered this on the morning of her twenty-first birthday, was that serial killers often flew under the radar. They were the good guys, the *nice* guys whom neighbors had no idea about. A teacher, a choirmaster . . . Was Ethan Oswald confident enough to take Beth because he'd done it before—and gotten away with it? Had he used other girls as practice and, because they were "less dead," the police had failed to see these dots, let alone connect them?

Had they missed a serial killer right under their noses?

It made sense in a way nothing had ever made sense to Ruth before. She knew, even before she returned to the unsolved crimes database she'd used recently for a class project, that she'd find it: the pattern everyone else had missed. And there it was. There *they* were. Rhea, Leila, and Lori. Three girls who, over the course of eight years, had disappeared, never to be found. They had lived within a sixty-mile radius of each other. Within a sixty-mile radius of where Beth Lovely was found. They were older than Beth, yes, but each victim was younger than the last. As if the perpetrator had been counting down.

Ruth was so intent on finding everything she could about these Connecticut cold cases that she missed her afternoon lecture. Every new piece of information only added to her conviction that their mysterious disappearances were a trial run for Beth's abduction. There was Rhea Mullins, who was considered a runaway for the first two weeks she was missing. Leila Kalb, whose young parents were always in trouble with the police—initially, no one took that report seriously, either. And Lori, who had just moved into her grandmother's trailer, while her mother was in rehab. These girls existed at the margins, and their disappearances barely made a ripple.

Ruth had found her less dead. So, she was now convinced, had Ethan Oswald. But it would be difficult to prove it, as there was no record of Ethan Oswald having ever been in Connecticut before January 1996. Not in 1983, when fourteen-year-old Rhea was last seen at a gas station just off the I-91. Not in 1985, when thirteen-year-old Leila disappeared walking home from the local swimming pool, or six years later, in 1991, when eleven-year-old

Lori Gill vanished after checking out six books from the mobile library on her grandmother's street.

But it didn't matter, Ruth reasoned. Oswald was a teacher. All three girls went missing in the summer, when school was out for him too. He *could* have been in Connecticut. After all, some of the worst serial killers were known to cross state lines.

And to have their favorite hunting grounds.

That night, out with her parents for dinner at an Italian restaurant in Lincoln Square that her family always went to on special occasions, Ruth was distracted. She knew it would take more than a hunch, and a database tabulation, before she could take her theory to the Hoben Police Department. Especially if they knew about Beth, and all the times psychologists had told young Ruth she couldn't see her when she actually could.

She was used to not being believed.

Maybe, she mused as she pushed pasta around on her plate, she should take some time off school to concentrate on building her case against Oswald. It would probably help her studies in the long run. She was weighing up how this would work when her father cleared his throat and her mother let out a kind of noisy breath that suggested she'd been holding it for some time. Ruth looked up from her dinner and finally noticed how uncomfortable both her parents looked. At first she presumed they'd been fighting again; newly separated, Ellis and Cynthia had not yet discovered how to be on easy terms. But then she saw that her father was holding out an envelope. Odd, Ruth thought as she reached for it, given she'd already opened her (separate) presents from both of them.

Inside was a typed letter, and a check made out in Ruth's full name. For the sum of $100,000.

"What—?" Ruth started, but then she saw the names at the bottom of the letter. Bill and Patty Lovely. Beth's parents.

"They thought it might help with your studies," Cynthia said, looking like she was going to be sick.

"We told them we couldn't possibly accept this," Ellis added, "but they insisted, Ruthie. So what could we do?"

It sounded like an apology.

Ruth looked at the check in her hand and felt dizzy.

"Please," she said weakly. "I just want to go home."

———

She was lying in bed later that night, twisting the forget-me-not ring around with her thumb and forefinger, when Beth came to sit beside her.

"Happy birthday, Ruthie," she said. She nodded at the envelope on Ruth's bedside table. "They added me to their life insurance policy when I was born. It was just meant to make it easier for me to get my own insurance when I was older. But you know . . ."

Ruth did know. After getting home from the restaurant, she'd read that letter from Beth's parents over and over. How Bill and Patty had always intended to gift their daughter's death claim payout to Ruth when she turned twenty-one. Maybe Ruth could do something with the money to honor Beth's memory, they suggested—though, the letter stressed, she was under no obligation to the Lovely family whatsoever; Bill and Patty simply wanted what was best for Ruth, and she could use the money in any way she chose. She didn't even have to thank them. In fact, they'd prefer Ruth didn't make a fuss about it.

"That's because your birthdays make them sad," Beth said, with uncharacteristic bluntness. "It reminds them that you're still alive and I'm not."

It was the first time Beth had drawn a line between the two of them so starkly. She got up and left the room then, without saying anything else.

And when she returned just before midnight, she wasn't alone.

Unlike Beth, the three young girls she brought with her hadn't aged since they'd disappeared. They looked exactly like they did in the photographs Ruth had found of them online. Which is how she immediately knew who they were.

"They insisted on coming." Beth sighed, but she was smiling. Whatever dark mood she'd been in earlier seemed to have passed.

Eleven-year-old Lori, sitting cross-legged at the end of Ruth's bed, was the most excited. She kept giggling behind her hand, which appeared to annoy Leila.

"Don't scare her off by being a freak," the thirteen-year-old said from her seat next to fourteen-year-old Rhea on the floor.

"Too late," Rhea had said, smirking, before giving Ruth a long look. "What can we do to help you find the man who killed us?"

———

Five years later, Ruth still remembers every detail of that first meeting. The girls were so funny, so smart, and so sure she could help them. As Ruth read over every available case note for each of the girls (there weren't many), they made their own observations about what the police got right—and what they got wrong. She wrote down everything they said, and Beth watched on, as proud as a sister.

"I thought it would help us stay close," she says now, pulling Ruth out of her reverie. "But that sure backfired, didn't it."

"It wasn't your fault I lost the plot," Ruth says, shifting over on her bed so that Beth can lie down next to her.

"Your uncle is right, though, Ruthie. This thing with Coco Wilson—it's not the same. Maybe you should stop before you . . . well, before you can't stop."

"She's only seven years old," Ruth answers, staring at the

ceiling, because if she looks at Beth she might cry. "Doesn't she deserve every bit of help she can get?"

"Of course she does, Ruthie. But I don't see what we can do."

Ruth sits up. "You said yourself that I used to be good at seeing things other people missed. I know I failed to prove that Oswald was a serial murderer, but I still believe I was right. I saw the pattern when no one else could, so isn't it possible I'll be able to see something here? Something that might get overlooked otherwise?"

Her uncle's voice is fading to nothing now as Ruth jumps off her bed and reaches underneath it for the bag she's never been able to throw away. She pulls out the smallest of the journals inside. The very first notebook in which she'd written down what the girls had told her. Flicking through page after page of scrawled verbatim quotes, Ruth waits for something, anything, to jump out. And then she sees it, right near the back of the book.

He didn't seem like a stranger.

Five years ago, Ruth had underlined this comment six times. So hard, on that last stroke, her pen had ripped right through the page.

FOUR

She's had the talk about strangers.

   "You do know, don't you, pumpkin? Never to talk to strangers."

   How do you know if they're a stranger? *she wanted to ask. Because it was confusing. Being told to smile and say hello and be polite to everyone she meets. Then being told it would be okay to kick a person in the shins if they tried to take her away.*

   Take me where?

   That was another of her questions. At seven years old, she knows about villains. They wear masks and speak in scary voices. They try to steal your voice so they can use it for themselves, and they let your father fall over a cliff so they can take over the pride. But aren't the people who rescue you often strangers too? The ones who find you when you're lonely and lost and say, Hey, why don't you come with me? I can help you!

   Do the good guys want to hurt you too?

   Her mommy and daddy never warned her about that.

   They must be getting worried. It's hard to say how long she's been gone, because it's only ever dark in here. The window above the bed has been covered over with the kind of paper that teachers write big words on, and it seems like something has been pushed under the doorframe.

The door is too far away for her to reach, anyway. She can move her arms a little, but the chain that has attached her left wrist (she only just learned left from right) to something sticking out of the wall is not long enough for her to touch even that papered-over window. He put something cold and hard around her ankles too.

Then he disappeared. After he clicked that last cuff shut, he walked out of the room without looking back.

It's quiet now. She sometimes thinks she can hear muffled sounds on the other side of the door, but inside this room it feels like that time she held her breath under the waves in the ocean. Something between a hiss and a roar.

What if he just leaves her here?

Is her mommy calling for her? Did her daddy come home from work yet? Maybe they're angry with her. Because they really did tell her not to talk to strange men. Which means they'll be so mad when they find out what she did. How she followed him across the road. How she got into his van. He was still being so nice then. He even offered her a stick of gum. She could smell the mint on his breath as he helped her up into the front seat. It was like he'd just brushed his teeth.

He stopped being nice so fast. After he went around to the driver's side and got into the van too. When she'd reached for the door handle, he'd leaned across to hit her hand away. Not hard enough to hurt, but it made her cry anyway. Her parents had never, ever smacked her.

"Don't be a baby," he said as he started the van.

She had the briefest flash of her yard, the open front door to her house, before she squeezed her eyes shut to stop those tears.

"Good girl," he told her, back to nice again.

And then he spun her away.

FIVE

Ruth makes a brief list of the things she'll do differently this time around. So that she doesn't inadvertently trigger another episode.

For a start, she won't contact Officer Canton, not unless she has concrete proof. And she definitely won't reach out to Coco's family (the memory of Rhea's sister calling her a *crazy bitch* down the phone still smarts). Nor will she make assumptions. She will simply use the tools available to her and keep an open mind. Like any decent citizen detective would do.

Ruth used to belong to an online community full of those detectives, and when she reactivates her account today it's clear not much has changed in the five years she's been gone. The home page of *What Happened to Her* still displays the same depressing stats around declining homicide clearance rates, and missing person cases, and the disproportionate impacts of violent crime on marginalized communities.

And it still flashes that same hopeful message underneath.

YOU could be the one to make a difference.

This site was one of the earliest to leverage crowdsourcing to help solve cold cases. It was started by Watson from Wichita, who, by his own admission, was obsessed with the unsolved murder of his third-grade teacher twenty years before. Within the space of a year, *What Happened to Her* grew from Watson's dedicated blog into a dedicated community of online sleuths, all willing to pay the site's private membership fees in exchange for being able to bring their own obsessions to the group. It wasn't cheap to join, but that was the point. *What Happened to Her* (and, later, *Him* and *Them*) was a place where people who were dead serious about true crime could meet other like-minded citizens and really get to work.

When Ruth joined after her twenty-first birthday (the only time she spent a dime of Beth's death money), she immediately added cold-case profiles for Rhea, Leila, and Lori. And then she added Ethan Oswald to the database of serial killers that Watson from Wichita scrupulously maintained. *Suspected*, Ruth had selected from a drop-down box, before sharing her theories on how the girls' disappearances might be connected to Beth's abduction. Bringing up Ethan's profile page now, she goes over the timeline she painstakingly created back then: the map of his movements from Minnesota, where he graduated high school the year Rhea disappeared, to the private music college he was attending in Boston when Leila went missing two years later (that, at least, put him in New England). In 1991, when Lori was taken, Ruth had traced Ethan back to the Midwest, where he was teaching music. Last stop, a high school in Ohio, before he moved to Connecticut in January 1996.

That qualifier, *Suspected*, has never been updated.

"Aren't you supposed to be looking for Coco?" Beth asks, frowning at Oswald's profile. "There's nothing to see here. Nothing's changed."

"The whole point of keeping a database like this is to look for similarities between perpetrators," Ruth shoots back, sounding more defensive than she'd intended. She hadn't come here to look at her old research, but there's no denying there was an immediate pull to Oswald as soon as she logged in. This place, as familiar to her as Sweeney's, was once her only lifeline. The one place she didn't have to hide her obsessions, because everyone had their own fixations on this site.

After the episode, logging out of *What Happened to Her* was part of Ruth's promise to leave the girls behind. But she's always wondered if anyone tended to them in her absence.

"I just want to check one thing," she tells Beth. "And then I promise we won't come back to this page."

Ruth clicks through to the *Known Victims* link on Oswald's profile. And there she is.

`Beth Lovely, 7 yrs old, 1996 (Hoben, CT).`

Proof is currency on *What Happened to Her*. Ruth never was able to get the other girls' names added to this list.

And then she gasps. Because a new name *has* been added, right below Beth's.

`Amity Greene, 14 yrs old, 1995 (Herald, OH).`

According to this site Ruth trusts more than any other resource out there, Ethan Oswald had another known victim. He *did* hurt another girl, a year before Beth was murdered.

And Ruth never even knew she existed.

"*Enough*, Ruthie."

That's what Officer Canton said when he showed up at her door in early March 2010.

Standing in the entranceway of that apartment in Morning-side Heights, he looked and sounded—weary. Wary. And sad. For over a month, Ruth had been calling him constantly. Day, night, it made no difference to her by then. He was the only person she wanted to talk to, outside her new friends on *What Happened to Her*.

Officer Canton, whose K-9 team found Beth's body.

Officer Canton, who burst through Ethan Oswald's door.

When she'd first started seeing the girls, Ruth just wanted to let him know that there might be more to Oswald's story. Even if the best law enforcement officers in the state had thoroughly investigated him, even if Oswald himself had categorically denied having any other victims, wouldn't Canton at least *consider* what she'd discovered?

He'd been patient with her at the start. Sympathetic. Curious, even. But then she began contacting the girls' families, and Officer Canton's patience ran out. By the time he came to Ruth in New York, he was even a little angry with her.

"I've got families threatening to sue the Hoben Police Department for malpractice, Ruthie. And Rhea's sister—she wants to sue *you*. She says you've been harassing her."

"I just wanted to help."

Canton had sighed. "I know that," he said. "But Ruthie, you've been giving these families false hope, and at the same time making it look like the police didn't do their job. *Their* job, kid. Not yours. I know you feel really strongly about Oswald, and believe me, if we could tie that bastard to other cases, we would. But there's just no proof."

Ruth had opened her mouth to protest, but Officer Canton had held up his hand.

"Ghosts don't count, Ruthie."

Now, as she stares at the new name on Ethan Oswald's *Known*

Victims list on *What Happened to Her*, Ruth feels the shame of that day shift toward vindication. Because there was another girl after all.

And this time, her intel is not one bit reliant on the dead.

———

Because Amity Greene is not dead.

In fact, her life is on full display for anyone to see.

According to her Instagram profile, Amity lives in *New York, New York*, and her occupation is *Muse*. She had an acai bowl for breakfast yesterday. Got bangs cut on the weekend, after vowing never to do that again, and has given up coffee—also again. As Ruth scrolls through post after post, taking in the slick selfies and the requisite amount of self-affirmation (*If you can't handle me at my worst, you don't deserve me at my best* appears to be a favorite quote), she wonders if she might have the wrong woman. But Ruth has done her due diligence, and this does seem to be the only Amity Greene from Herald, Ohio, who was fourteen in 1995. Which makes her thirty-four now (*Shhh*, Amity said on her last birthday post. *Let's just pretend I'm 29!*).

The one odd thing Ruth can identify, when she has scrolled back far enough, is the absence of any online content, on any of Amity's social media accounts, from January 2013 to June 2014, when she returned with a post featuring one white word against a plain black background.

Hi.

Amity Greene's rebrand since then has not exactly been subtle. Before January 2013, she regularly posted pictures of her various body parts at New York hotspots. Her lips up against a cocktail glass. One smoky eye peering out from behind impeccably curled blond tresses. Long, tanned legs in the kind of vertiginous heels Ruth has never seen anyone actually wear in real life.

But after coming back online in the middle of last year, Amity appears to be intent on positioning herself as part stylist, part self-help guru. Her feed is now full of earnest entreaties to live one's best life. In Louboutins, of course.

It's amazing what you can ascertain from an open social media account. Ruth keeps digging.

She finds it late that afternoon. The reason for Amity Greene's extended break from social media. There might have been nothing more than her unlinked name on *What Happened to Her*, but over on *Stranger than Fiction*, the true crime website Ruth had been trying to avoid until now, Amity appears in dozens of search results. This fringe site hosts the kind of online community where people stay up all night debating which celebrities belong to satanic cults and which world leaders are lizards in disguise; there isn't any major mystery or minor conspiracy you can't find an opinion on here, and when Ruth first entered Amity's name, a slew of hits came up, mostly from the site's *Cold-Blooded Killers* subforum.

Holding her breath as she clicks on the top search result now, Ruth expects to see Ethan's name appear too.

But she encounters a different murderer entirely.

Eric Coulter. *The Socialite Strangler*. So named by a salivating press on New Year's Day, 2013, after this son of two fixtures on the Manhattan social scene was arrested for the murders of four young sex workers across as many boroughs. His intended fifth victim had just escaped a New Year's Eve party he'd hired her to strip at; this wily teenager from Staten Island was the one who got him caught.

Amity Greene, according to various commenters on *Stranger than Fiction*, was married to him at the time.

Ruth had been on her own hiatus when the news of Coulter's arrest was all over the front pages. Still, it was impossible to avoid the case completely. After his arrest, the media couldn't get enough of the scandal—it was top-shelf clickbait. Who wouldn't want to read about a wealthy playboy UNDONE BY HIS IMPULSES, as one headline blared. As if strangling young, vulnerable women was nothing more than a neural misfire, a little glitch in Coulter's otherwise platinum-plated pathways.

Even with her self-imposed ban on true crime, Ruth was aware of Eric Coulter. But she cannot remember any mention of a wife in those feverish stories after his arrest. Surely that wife would have been worth a few headlines at least? Once again, *Stranger than Fiction* fills in the blanks. In the 2013 threads dedicated to Coulter's shock arrest, followers of the case, some of whom seemed oddly complimentary of the accused, were initially split on whether Amity Greene was indeed his wife, or just some hanger-on he liked to party with in the early 2010s. As proof of the latter, someone uploaded a series of social page pictures of the couple arm in arm at various events, where Amity was only ever referred to as Eric Coulter's *lucky date*.

I know for a fact they were married in Vegas in 2012! one commenter kept protesting into the void, right before Coulter was convicted. Post-conviction, that same ardent community member declared that Amity had just annulled their marriage.

That bitch!! came the first reply to this post. *Jumping ship when he needs her most.*

Yeah, well, trash is as trash does, another member posted in response, attaching an image and three vomit emojis to their comment. *You should see where she came from.*

"Maybe we—" Beth starts, but it's too late. Ruth has already clicked on the attachment.

They both stare at her laptop screen as the image slowly loads.

———

It is a 1994 junior varsity choir portrait. Amity Greene would be easily spotted in the front row of the yearbook photo even if someone hadn't drawn a big red arrow above her young head. She must be thirteen in the shot, but she already has the long limbs and delicate prettiness Ruth has seen in photographs of the grown-up Amity, that unusual symmetry that draws you to a face out of fifty, even if you can't quite pinpoint what makes it so pleasing. Ruth is wondering how this image of the teenage Amity, smiling in her white tee and denim overalls, is supposed to represent trashiness, when her breath jags in her throat. It is the second time Amity Greene has made her gasp.

At least five students in the picture are wearing sweatshirts with *Tilden Tigers* emblazoned across the front.

Tilden Tigers. The football team at Tilden High School, Ohio. The school Ethan Oswald taught at for two years before he moved to Hoben, Connecticut, at the start of 1996.

Ruth's heart is a stopwatch ticking down as she returns to Ethan's case file on *What Happened to Her*, before toggling back and forth between his profile and that yearbook image. Between evidence that Amity Greene attended Tilden High School in 1994 and the presence of her name underneath the list of Ethan Oswald's known victims on *What Happened to Her*.

Here is incontrovertible proof that the woman she's been online-stalking all afternoon *does* have a connection to Ethan Oswald. This choir portrait proves she was a student at the very last school he taught at before moving to Connecticut. A *music* student.

Does this mean Ethan was her teacher? More importantly, what happened to make Amity his victim? One who *survived* him? Ruth's head is swimming, in large part because she has no idea how Amity came to appear on *What Happened to Her* in the first place. Information on that site is always verified; Ruth understands this better than anyone. If she's listed as a *Known Victim*, it's because someone knows that to be true. But who?

And why is the only murderer whom Amity's been publicly tied to not in fact Ethan Oswald, but an infamous serial killer from New York City?

For all that she's just uncovered, Ruth feels utterly lost. Dimly, she can hear an alarm sound. A warning to step back before it's too late.

This is when she feels a cool hand on her cheek. The soft, familiar reassurance that only Beth can bring.

"Maybe she's the missing link."

Ruth cannot turn away from that.

———

At Sweeney's that night, Ruth feels both exhausted and strangely euphoric. She keeps bumping into things, as if she's lost her depth perception, and eventually Owen asks her if she's high.

"I haven't seen you this animated since . . . since . . ." Owen trails off; they both know he's never seen her act this way.

"I wouldn't come to work *high*," Ruth insists. "I'm just tired. I didn't get much sleep last night."

It's not a lie, but this only seems to make Owen more suspicious.

"Something's up with you, Veronica Mars," he says, pursing his lips, but any further conversation has to wait. A rowdy group of regulars has just walked through the door.

Ruth feels a sense of relief at the distraction, though she's surprised to find a taint of disappointment at its edges. If anyone was going to understand what Ruth did this afternoon, right after finding Amity Greene's yearbook picture, it would be him. Her boss, who also understands obsessions and second acts, and—what's he always calling those songs that he loves? *I Want* numbers. That's it. The moment in a musical where the protagonist reveals what's been missing in their life. The thing they want so much and finally have the courage to pursue.

Ruth imagines how that conversation with Owen might go.

You know how we got that AMBER Alert last night? About that little girl, Coco, who's gone missing? Nineteen years ago, my friend went missing too. She was murdered by a man who everyone thought was a nice guy. The kind of man who wouldn't hurt a fly. No one saw it coming. They couldn't believe it when he was arrested. Which I just don't get. Because this wasn't a crime of passion, Owen. It wasn't an accident, what he did. People kept telling me I was wrong to fixate on a case that was already solved. Like—how lucky were we that this man was caught so quickly. He only killed one girl!

But I've never thought it was just one girl, Owen. And today I found proof that I was right. So here's the big number, Owen, what I want is—

Ruth stops short. This was supposed to be about finding Coco Wilson. And she *does* want that, of course. But it would be only a small truth to say that it's the missing girl she's decided to pursue.

Excusing herself to use the bathroom, Ruth closes the door to Sweeney's single, unisex stall and takes out her cell phone. She does a quick search of Coco Wilson's name first. There was a press conference a few hours ago, where a bewildered Ivy stood, weeping silently, a dazed Maya next to her, while Leo pleaded with whoever took his baby daughter to bring her home. Ruth sees that the Wilson family's first appearance in front of the cameras dominates any news stories about Coco; this can only mean the media has nothing else to report.

Next, she turns her attention to Amity Greene, who in the last hour has updated her Instagram with a picture of a lush spring bouquet, tagging a famous Upper East Side floral atelier in the post. *Who needs to pay rent?* the caption says, with a winking emoji after.

Distaste, like a brittle metal, settles on Ruth's tongue.

She rereads Amity's response to the DM she spontaneously sent this afternoon. That first message contained a lie, but Ruth will deal with the consequences of this later. Putting her phone back in her jeans pocket, she leaves the cubicle, and in the fractured mirror above the bathroom's fissured sink, she catches sight of herself. It does indeed look like she's high. Glittering eyes, flushed cheeks, the joker smile pulling up the corners of her mouth. She bares her teeth and lets that smile crack wide open before heading back to the bar, telling herself that she's got this.

She can perfect her *I Want* number later. For now, it's enough to have started the show.

SIX

The lie Ruth told was simple enough.

She told Amity Greene that she was producing a new true crime podcast about the wives and girlfriends of serial killers, and she wanted Amity as the first special guest.

The idea came to Ruth courtesy of an ad she'd seen on *Stranger than Fiction*. A banner promoting a new podcast hosted by a former FBI agent, something about solving cases so cold they might as well be considered freezing. This tagline was supported by a cartoon pistol with icicles hanging from the barrel; Ruth had rolled her eyes and scrolled on. Still, as she struggled with how to introduce herself to Amity, that pistol popped back into her head.

She could have been up front about her interest in Ethan Oswald. But for all Ruth knows, Amity isn't even aware her name has been published on that *Known Victims* list. *What Happened to Her* is a private, members-only site, after all. Maybe what happened with Oswald is something she seldom talks about, or straight-out refuses to discuss. Leading with a potentially buried trauma from when she was fourteen years old might have scared her away.

And Ruth did not want to scare away this living, breathing connection to Ethan Oswald. So she told the lie, and Amity came back within an hour, saying she was intrigued. And now, less than twenty-four hours later, they are minutes away from meeting each other for the first time.

Waiting for Amity, Ruth is trying to remember why she thought this was a good idea.

She hadn't expected everything to move so fast. Finding this woman. Reaching out to her. Amity's immediate response, and her willingness to talk to Ruth, as if she had been hoping for such an invitation.

I'm staying on West 57th. I can meet you for lunch tomorrow. Anywhere close by suits xox

Amity had signed off her message as if they were already friends.

For their lunch date, Ruth chose the Italian restaurant she and her parents had dined at on her twenty-first birthday, and many other family occasions. The Lincoln Square location worked for both women, but more importantly, it felt like familiar territory for Ruth, when nothing else about this situation did. Walking in, she'd been greeted enthusiastically by the longtime floor manager, Nico, but if his welcome eased her nerves, the relief was temporary. Now, sitting near the door (always seat your interrogation subjects in a place they feel they can escape from, she once read), Ruth tries to do her breathing exercises. Somehow, at this table set for two, she's forgotten how to breathe in and out at all.

"Water," she croaks to a passing waiter, grateful that Amity appears to be running late.

When Amity Greene does arrive, she stops in the doorway of the restaurant to check something on her phone. This affords Ruth a close-up look at the woman she's been zooming in on all over social media. There's no doubt that she is beautiful, strikingly so. Like that ill-fated actress Sharon Tate, Ruth realizes, wondering if Amity knows this. When she looks up from her phone, Amity beams at Nico, who has just approached her, before leaning close to whisper something in his ear. He turns and points to Ruth, watching from her seat, and now that megawatt smile is directed at her.

"Hellooooo!" Amity breathes, approaching the table. "I'm so sorry I'm late. *Traffic*, you know."

Ruth is pretty sure Amity walked here like she did, since she's only a half dozen blocks away, but she smiles in sympathetic agreement as Amity sits down across from her in a waft of powder and perfume.

"I'm Amity," she adds unnecessarily, extending a diamond-heavy hand.

"Thank . . . thank you for agreeing to meet me," Ruth stutters, holding out her own (bare) hand, before suggesting they order a drink.

The truth is, Ruth was totally unprepared for how this would make her feel. Sitting across from a woman who, as a girl, had known Ethan Oswald. And then somehow grew up to marry a serial killer. It makes her laugh unexpectedly. Because how *does* one prepare for that?

"What's so funny?" Amity asks.

"I'm just really glad to meet you," Ruth responds, a little startled now, because she means it.

It's the first truth she's told Amity Greene so far.

———

"*Did you really have no idea?*"

After mimicking the accusatorial tone of a person pretending to be a friend, Amity rolls her eyes and sighs. "That's all anyone wants to ask me, Ruth." She narrows her eyes. "But you seem different. Which is why I agreed to meet you."

"Different how?" Ruth asks, sipping at her wine. Amity is already on her second glass of champagne.

"Well, for starters, you have zero social media presence. I checked. And I like that, because you have no idea how many people want to talk to me just to make themselves look good."

Ruth nods silently because, in the last half hour, she's learned it's best to just let Amity talk. Her run-on sentences and swift turns inevitably end up taking them somewhere interesting. She has this habit of stopping to tap her manicured forefinger to her veneered front teeth, which signals that a revelation is on its way. It's almost hypnotizing.

Not to mention, her staccato verbosity has saved Ruth from having to build on her lie about the podcast. Yet.

As if reading her mind, Amity lets out another sigh.

"I have been asked to do other podcasts, but no one wants to talk about *me*. It's all about Eric. As if he doesn't have all the attention already." She frowns. "Don't get me wrong," she adds. "I totally feel sorry for those whor—those *sex workers* he murdered. And if I had known about it, of course I would have said something. Anyone would, right?"

Ruth nods again.

"But I didn't. I had no fucking idea."

Amity takes a gulp of her champagne before turning the glass in her hand, examining it. She appears to be weighing something up.

"I'll do your podcast, Ruth. As long as you don't make me look bad. And as long as you don't lie to me. I'm sick of being surprised by people. It's never good."

It's suddenly hard for Ruth to swallow. This is the moment she should come clean. Ask about Oswald and dispense with the whole podcast ruse. She opens her mouth to say something, anything, honest, when Amity leans forward.

"Exactly how far back do you want me to go?" she asks. "Because it's not like Eric was the first guy to hurt me."

Nail against front teeth, tapping.

"Uh, whatever . . . whatever you consider the starting point," Ruth answers, her resolve vanishing just as the hard *r*'s of Amity's Ohio accent reappear.

"I blame Julie Jordan."

"Julie Jordan?

"Yes, Ruth. Julie Jordan. From the musical *Carousel*."

Amity stops to sip at her third champagne, then peers over the lip of the glass at Ruth.

"You know it?"

"A little," Ruth answers.

"Good. Because let the record show that my life was ruined because of Julie *fucking* Jordan."

"How so?" Ruth asks, confused.

"You wanted to know where my life started going wrong, yeah? Well, it was when I got the role of Julie Jordan in our high school production of *Carousel*. Everyone was all mad about it, because I was only a sophomore, but Mr. O said I was better than every senior in that class."

Ruth tries to keep her face neutral. "Mr. O?"

"Yeah, the senior music teacher. He was the music director of the show. That was, you know, his thing. He freakin' loved *Carousel*, because some old neighbor showed him the movie when he was a kid. And I loved it because of him."

Amity pauses to tap at her front teeth again. As Ruth watches her prepare to launch into another story, inspiration strikes.

"Do you mind if I record this bit on my phone?" she asks.

Amity shrugs. "Fine by me. Although it's not about serial killers."

If only you knew, Ruth thinks. But she smiles and tells Amity that if it's about an important experience in her life, then it's important to the podcast too.

"I want to know where you came from," she says.

"Cool," Amity answers with another shrug.

Trying not to let the shaking of her hands show, Ruth sets her phone down on the table, opens the voice memo app on the home screen, and hits record.

———

Mr. O was all about trust. He was always saying that. "I'm big on trust, Ami. And you need to trust me, if you want to be as good as I know you can be in this role."

He was the teacher, Ruth. I was fourteen. So—I trusted him.

We start having private lessons after school. Singing, breathing, movement. At first it was in the music room where we took choir most days, but then he invited me to his house, where we practiced at night instead of directly after school. My parents knew; it wasn't considered weird. Not to them. Not to me. I just wanted to be a good Julie Jordan. Because I felt like I knew her, you know? This young woman stuck in a shitty, small-town life on, like, an actual carousel that was going nowhere. Plus, I wanted to stick it to all those bitchy seniors who thought I wasn't good enough to have the lead in their fancy fall production.

We got pretty close, Mr. O and me. I was learning a lot from him, and my voice was getting so much stronger. Everything was normal between us. And then it wasn't. Because one night, while we were practicing the bench scene, he slapped me across the face—just out of the blue—and it fucking hurt. When I started to cry, he said I needed to know what it felt like, if I wanted to be Julie Jordan. He said he'd done this with other girls he'd coached, and it always worked. After that, he hit me every time we were alone together. Mostly slaps, but once a sort of punch. I remember him holding me after and kissing me. First my forehead. Then my nose. And then my mouth. My first proper kiss. Despite what people said about me, I'd never even pecked a boy's cheek before that. It was disgusting. I can still remember the feel of his fat tongue, and the way he tasted like minty eggs. The first time you have sex, it's supposed to be bad, right? But not your first kiss. That's supposed to be amazing. And once you hate kissing—which I did after that—well, there's not much hope for anything else, is there?

Fucking Julie Jordan.

Anyway, my English teacher saw the bruises. There were a lot by then. So I told her what was happening in my private lessons. And then all hell broke loose. I got hauled into the principal's office, and he called me an attention seeker. He said I was promiscuous and asking for trouble. I didn't even know what promiscuous meant. I had to look it up! And then a member of the school board came around to our house. "These are very serious allegations," he told my parents. "And they could have serious consequences for your daughter, blah, blah, blah . . ."

So, of course, my folks freaked out. My own parents said that no one was going to take my side, because everyone loved Mr. O, and that it wasn't like he'd, um, you know, raped me or anything. They told me I should say I made it up, that nothing actually happened, and let the whole thing die down. So I did. I took it back.

And then he went and killed a kid. Mr. O, I mean. She was the same age as my little sister.

But it's not like I could have known that would happen.

And who would have believed me, anyway?

When Ruth first played Amity's words back on her phone, she thought she might be sick. Listening to her calmly describe what

Ethan Oswald did to her, and how people reacted after, made Ruth so angry she could barely function.

All she's been able to do since then is lie on her bed staring at the ceiling, replaying Amity's words over and over. It hurts to move.

"Just don't be mad at *her*," Beth says from her usual perch at the end of the bed.

"I'm not mad at Amity," Ruth says defensively, but she supposes she might be, a little. Maybe a lot.

She sits up. "I need to take Ressler for a walk before work," she tells Beth.

Which might be true. But there's something else. A part of the recording Ruth is not yet ready for Beth to hear. She needs to listen to it one more time on her own, first. Because sharing it is bound to change everything.

"Come on, boy," she says to her dog, picking up her phone and headphones and heading for the door.

When they'd said goodbye at the restaurant, Amity was definitely tipsy.

"That was *fun*," she said, as if they hadn't just been talking about the worst moments of her life.

"We'll do it again soon," Ruth had assured her, but that felt like a lie. She'd already decided there was no point in carrying on with the fake-podcast angle. And it wasn't like they could be friends. Not when Ruth had listened to Amity's stories about Ethan Oswald and never said a word about her own connection to that man.

They were on the street, ready to go their separate ways, when Amity ducked her head, unexpectedly demure.

"I left you another recording," she said, not meeting Ruth's eyes. "When you went to the bathroom. It's something I never told anyone, but it felt good to say it out loud. You can judge me if you want to, but . . . I really hope you don't, because I like you, Ruth. And I could use someone on my side."

Her face had been so hopeful then, it was like seeing her for the first time.

Ruth had taken her time in that bathroom, splashing her face with cold water and doing her breathing exercises over again. She'd been trying to steady herself after what Amity had just told her about Mr. O.

Turns out, she'd also given Amity the space to make a confession.

Walking Ressler toward the park, Ruth returns to that secret recording, her heart thumping as if it's the first time she's heard it.

I knew Mr. O had a thing for kids. Well, I suspected it, because he was always asking me to bring my little sister to rehearsals. The ones at his house, I mean. And he was always asking questions about her. What movies did she like, what was her favorite animal, that kind of thing. Gemmy's a twin, and he said he was fascinated with mixed twins, because he used to live next to a pair, who he said made him an honorary triplet. But he never asked anything about my little brother, you know? Mostly I paid no attention, but then one time he wanted to know what size underwear Gemmy wore. I stopped answering his questions after that, because that was definitely weird, and when he kept asking me to bring her over I made excuses not to. Anyway, that's not the bad bit. Well, it is, but this next bit is worse. Don't hate me, Ruth, okay? I was just a kid. But after he moved to Connecticut, he used to write me. A lot. He said I was one of his Julie Jordans, which meant I could never give up on him. And I wrote him back. Even after he went to jail. I knew what he'd done, and I still didn't tell him no. It was like he had some kind of power over me.

So it shouldn't be any surprise I ended up with a serial killer, hey. I'm just that kind of girl.

SEVEN

We're missing something."

Beth, who has been pacing Ruth's bedroom, stops suddenly. Asks to hear Amity's confession over again.

Ruth hadn't managed to keep it from her for very long.

She'd come home from her shift at Sweeney's tired and distracted, and Beth had immediately intuited that something was up. So Ruth had relented, playing her the second, secret recording Amity made at the restaurant. Where she'd admitted all those things she couldn't say to Ruth's face.

"*It was like he had some kind of power over me,*" Beth repeats this morning, her face a frown of concentration. "But that's no surprise. Men like Ethan Oswald can be really charismatic, right?"

"And very manipulative," Ruth says, thinking back to the serial killer typologies she'd studied in college. "But they don't often hurt people in their own families."

"Isn't that only because they don't want to get caught, though?" Beth replies. "Besides, Amity wasn't family."

"No, she was just his Julie Jordan." Ruth rolls her eyes, but then they grow wide. "*One* of his Julie Jordans, Beth. *One of them.*"

"Do you think he was abusing other girls?" Beth's eyes have widened too.

"That would be bad enough," Ruth says, feeling as if she's driving through fog and is nearly out the other side. "But what if he asked other students to groom their little sisters?"

Ruth and Beth stare at each other as the realization dawns.

"Like the girl from the playground," Beth whispers.

"Exactly," Ruth responds, but there is no triumph in her tone.

———

Ruth once asked Beth why she could remember what happened to her, but Rhea, Leila, and Lori had no memories of how they died.

"I *don't* remember," she'd answered. "My last memory is talking to an older girl at the playground about my poppy, who was sick in the hospital. After that—it's just blank. But every detail of my death is out there, Ruthie. Even the coroner's report. I *know* what happened to me because those blanks have all been filled in. It's different for the other girls. They don't even know where their bodies are buried.

"When you disappear like that," she'd added, "there are some things you need people to remember *for* you."

People like Ethan Oswald. Unfortunately, he'd taken most of his memories to his own grave.

But now they have Amity Greene.

She said Ethan wanted her to help him build a relationship with her little sister. All the questions, all that information gathering about Gemmy. He clearly didn't want to seem like a stranger when they met.

This puts Beth's last actual memory in a very different light.

"That girl in the playground asked you a *lot* of questions, right?" Ruth confirms now as Beth nods.

Swallowing hard, Ruth returns to an early news article about Coco's disappearance that she'd bookmarked. The one with the neighbor, Coralea Michaels, describing how she'd seen a young, ponytailed woman talking to Coco right before she disappeared.

Ruth points at her computer screen. "*This* is the pattern, Beth. We've found it!"

"She wouldn't have—" Beth starts, but Ruth cuts her off.

"You think females don't do that kind of thing? There are definitely women out there who have helped men hurt kids, Beth. Especially when that man is in a position of power. Like, if he was her teacher."

Beth shakes her head. "Are we talking about Ethan Oswald now, Ruth? Are you saying he had an *accomplice*?"

"It's possible, right? Because you remember that girl asking you questions, and there were things he just knew to say, and . . ." Ruth trails off. Now she can't seem to swallow at all.

Beth glances at the news article about Coco and the pony-tailed girl, then back to Ruth.

"And now there's some copycat out there?" she asks. "With the same . . . what do you call it? MO?"

It's Ruth's turn to shake her head. "I don't think it's that."

She'd learned about copycat killers in class. Men obsessed with some sort of promise of shared infamy. Like Eddie Seda, the New York Zodiac Killer, or Martin Torrent, who drove around the Midwest in a Volkswagen Beetle thinking he was Ted Bundy. As copycats, they wanted people to know what they were up to; they wrote taunting messages to law enforcement and the media, and Torrent even gave himself a nickname: TBK. The Babysitter Killer. Men like that wanted the notoriety their predecessors had.

Oswald, for all the damage he'd caused, just doesn't seem famous enough to emulate.

"What if . . . ," Ruth says slowly, the idea forming as she speaks it. She stops to make sure, then starts again. "Amity might have refused to give Ethan what he wanted, Beth. But what if another girl, another one of his Julie Jordans, *did* help him? And what if *she's* still out there—helping someone else?"

Thursday afternoon, Coco Wilson has been missing for three whole days. Online, people are suddenly paying more attention. A case file has been opened on *What Happened to Her*, and over on *Stranger than Fiction* people are enthusiastically sharing their theories now that they have a genuine child abduction at their fingertips.

For many commenters on *Stranger than Fiction*, Coco's father, Leo, is the number one suspect. Statistically, as one community member points out, a child is most likely to be murdered by someone they know (since when do people on this site care about stats? Ruth thinks uncharitably). Fuel was added to that dumpster fire earlier today, after it was revealed that, technically, Leo is not Coco's father. Not biologically, at least. Fourteen-year-old Maya is Leo's daughter from an earlier relationship, and he adopted Ivy's daughter, Coco, when she was an infant.

I didn't want to be the one who said it, Ruth reads in one accusatory thread. *But Coco doesn't exactly look like she'd be his daughter, right? Maybe he wanted to get rid of her. Start again with one of his own.*

"People are horrible," Beth sighs. "That poor, poor family."

The euphoria of their recent discoveries has faded, and now they are stuck with the problem of what to do with them. Amity might have fallen into their lap. But if Ethan Oswald really was recruiting young women to help groom his victims, finding *them* seems like looking for the proverbial needle in a haystack. He'd worked at a lot of schools across the Midwest, and he also gave private lessons. Who knew how many students he'd taught over the years?

Or how many high school productions of *Carousel* he'd managed to stage.

Ruth lets out another one of her gasps. "Beth! Oswald ran the drama program at Hoben Heights High!"

How to check if her latest hunch is right? An image of Amity standing with the junior varsity choir pops into her head, and she realizes she knows where to look for answers.

They have a few false starts.

The first copy of the 1996 Hoben Heights High School yearbook that Ruth downloads includes portrait pages from only the freshman class. The next one is mislabeled—it's actually from 1976, which is like flicking through a scrapbook from a different universe.

Then, on a genealogy site promising to help New Englanders find answers to questions about themselves they didn't even know they had, Ruth sees an ad offering full yearbook downloads for only ninety-nine dollars a copy.

"Third time's a charm," she says to a concerned-looking Beth as she enters her credit card details.

A file arrives in Ruth's email inbox within five minutes. And then it stops feeling like a game. Hoben Heights High is the school she and Beth would have attended together if Ethan Oswald had never come into their lives, and it's sobering to consider how no single student graduating in 1996 had any idea what was coming so soon after they were handed copies of this very yearbook. The shocking arrest of the popular new music teacher at the end of May. The media that descended on the town, and the dark cloud that would settle over all the student club dinners and open houses, and the muted graduation ceremony that followed.

It wasn't just the girls' lives that were changed that spring.

Steadying herself, Ruth opens the file. Immediately, it's clear from the scribbled comments on the inside cover that she's purchased a copy of someone's personal yearbook. She skips over pages of colorful writing and messy drawings, heading straight to the book's Clubs & Activities section. A few extra clicks, and there it is. A photo montage of the school's musical that year, mounted right before spring break.

Carousel.

Among the montage of photos showing the set being built and earnest students working tech, there is an image of a slight brunette clutching a bright bouquet of flowers. A man's arm is slung about her shawled shoulders. His face has been scratched out, but the girl's nervous smile and wide eyes have been left unmarked.

Our Julie Jordan, Annie Whitaker, the caption below the photo reads. *And our Music Man, Mr. O.*

Ruth can hardly breathe as she scrolls back through the pages of student portraits, looking for the girl. She's not a freshman or a sophomore, like Amity Greene was. Not a junior either, but there she is, in the seniors section. Annie Whitaker.

Future Prime Minister of New Zealand is printed underneath her picture.

Most likely to marry a murderer, someone has scribbled in red ink beneath that official caption.

According to the Hoben Heights High yearbook, Annie Whitaker was a visiting exchange student from New Zealand, who joined the class of '96 at the start of the school year. She appears four times in the yearbook's pages. There's her senior picture: a headshot in which she's smiling with her lips closed. And that photograph of her with Ethan Oswald, on the page dedicated to *Carousel*. In the International Students Club group shot, she's sitting in the back of four rows, her head turned away from the camera, so that Ruth can identify her only by reading the names and countries listed at the bottom of the page, and the brief paragraph detailing how she came to be at Hoben Heights High.

By contrast, Annie is sitting in the middle row center of the senior choir photo. Still with that uneasy smile, but staring straight at the camera this time.

Julie fucking *Jordan*, Ruth hears Amity say.

On impulse, she sends Owen a text.

What kind of girl was Julie Jordan, boss?

He comes back within a minute.

A masochist.

Thirty seconds later, he sends a link to a video clip. Ruth clicks on it, bringing up what looks to be a live, bootleg recording of a *Carousel* number called "What's the Use of Wond'rin'." In the clip, a woman stands center stage, clutching at her shawl, while a group of younger girls crowd around her. Ruth hits pause, before the first line can be sung.

"Beth," she says, looking at those young girls watching, waiting. "I miss them."

"I know you do. . . ."

There is a question at the end of Beth's sentence that she doesn't ask out loud. Ruth nods as if she heard it anyway.

———

"Yuck."

Leila, arms folded across her chest, hasn't changed a bit. Neither has Rhea; she is just as poker-faced as Ruth remembered. Only Lori, nestled next to Beth on the bed, seems younger, somehow.

Maybe that's because Ruth feels so much older, now.

"What took you so long?" Leila had asked her, when she got home from Sweeney's tonight to find the girls waiting in her bedroom.

The reunion came with a tumble of questions from the girls, mostly about whether Ruth had missed them (*of course*), and whether she really thought Ethan Oswald was connected to Coco's disappearance (*maybe*), and how long they were going to be able to stay this time (Ruth had no answer for that).

They wanted to hear all about Amity and about the Julie Jordans (*You found two already!* Lori had cheered, clapping). And they all said they would try hard to remember if anyone had ever seemed especially interested in them right before they disappeared.

"You'd think we'd have noticed someone actually giving a shit," Rhea said, which made the others laugh.

And then they asked Ruth to play Julie Jordan's song, "What's the Use of Wond'rin'."

"Yuck." Leila is not impressed. "She's basically saying it's okay if a man treats you bad."

"No, she's not," Rhea says, surprising Ruth. "She's saying that sometimes you like someone so much, you'll pretty much let them do anything. Even mean stuff."

"Why would you let them do that?" Lori asks, looking like she might cry.

"Because most people aren't all good or all bad," Rhea answers, reaching over to ruffle the younger girl's hair. "And it can be hard to give up the good bits."

Leila frowns. "It shouldn't be. Should it, Ruthie?"

"No," Ruth says quietly. "It shouldn't."

For years, Ruth has wished she could take that Kill Jar from Sweeney's out into the world, bottle up all of the terrible things a person could do to another human being, then screw the lid on tight and hide that jar away.

What she needs to do now is open that jar. Hold it up to the light and examine all the ways a person becomes a predator. Not just the bad stuff they do, but the *good bits* too. The constancy. The thoughtfulness. The attention. The ways of making someone feel like they are finally understood. That's a heady proposition for most people, especially an impressionable young woman on her own in another country, like Annie Whitaker seems to have been.

Narcissists know exactly who to prey on. What had her college professor once called it? A dyadic dance. Oswald tried to lead Amity, but she ended up betraying him by telling someone what he was doing. That must have made him really mad. Mad enough to find another dance partner, in another state, and teach her all the same moves? Ruth wonders.

Mad enough to take that choreographed routine further this time around?

Everyone knows what happened to Beth Lovely in 1996. But what happened to Annie Whitaker, once Ethan Oswald had her in his sights?

There are just so many ways, Ruth thinks, for a girl to disappear.

EIGHT

The dark is different now.

The light must have changed outside. Is it dinnertime? She's hungry. Thirsty. And wet, where she accidentally peed herself again. When he comes back, he'll probably be angry about that, because she can feel that it's gone all the way through to the mattress. The sensation had been warm, pleasant for a moment. The relief of letting go. And then she had been mortified. Seven-year-olds are not supposed to wet the bed.

He had told her not to be a baby. Back in the van, when she knew something was wrong, only just a little, and then a lot. He was driving too fast, and then he was humming under his breath, the way her dad did when he thought he was alone in the house. It was like she wasn't even there.

Does anyone know where she is?

She's never not been home for dinner. Even when she's played outside for longer than she was supposed to, which is easy to do in a town where everyone's front yards are big enough for sprinklers and slides, and some people have backyards that run right into the forest. Wild woods where, someone at school said, if you're quiet enough, you might see a black bear. She's been wanting this to happen forever, but it never has.

Part of her wants him to come back. The man who gave her an egg sandwich and a glass of water at his kitchen table, before he said, "Come with me," and that's how she ended up in this room. Stuck on a mattress she's peed on, just like a baby after all.

The other part of her, the not-baby part, knows that it's better if he stays away. That she's safer if he's gone. Which he must be. Because there's not even a shuffle through the walls anymore. Just that darker darkness, and the hiss and roar in her ears.

"Please," she shouts, just to be sure. Banging on the wall with her free hand. "I want to go home."

Nobody answers. But then she hears the sound of tires on gravel, right outside that covered window. The slam of doors. She can feel the vibration.

And she hears the click of a lock. Footsteps. Whispers. Laughter. He's come back from wherever he was. And he has someone with him. A girl.

She bangs on the wall again, and that's when the laughter stops.

Music starts to play instead. Louder than his laugh, and nicer. She closes her eyes and pretends she's in her ballet class. Her new teacher says dancing can make you happy even when you're sad, because it gives you something called Indoor Fins, which must be what dolphins have, because they always seem to be smiling.

She dances to that music now. Faster and faster. Spinning out of these chains, off this wet, stinking bed. Leaping through the air like those happy dolphins. Free—

And then the music stops.

Laughter. Whispers. Footsteps. The click of a lock. Slamming doors and tires on gravel.

All her sad comes right back. Because she wasn't really dancing at all.

NINE

Most likely to marry a murderer.

The next morning, Ruth wakes up with these words in her head.

After taking Ressler down to relieve himself (and apologizing for being a very distracted dog mom this week), Ruth comes back to her bedroom, which is beginning to feel like her whole apartment. When she's remembered to eat, it's been at her desk or on her bed. Anything she's watched or read, it's been done in this room too. Only Sweeney's and Ressler have lured her away.

Yep, everything's a-okay down here, she'd texted Joe yesterday, promising to call him on the weekend.

It's Friday, the beginning of her work weekend. The girls left in the early hours. They'll be back soon enough, but for now, Ruth has no plans outside of showing Ressler a little love. She might take him to Riverside Park, or maybe for a meander uptown.

But first, Ruth opens her laptop and types Annie Whitaker's name into a search bar sitting below a series of animated doughnuts, each with a single bite taken out.

After a brief pause to wonder how on earth people ever found each other before the internet, Ruth turns her attention to the search results on her screen. Or, rather, the lack of them. While there is no shortage of Annie Whitakers out there, none appears to be a match for the girl from the Hoben Heights High School yearbook. As Ruth clicks through a series of images and social media bios, no one even remotely resembles the serious, dark-haired girl who once played Julie Jordan.

It's only when she stops to make herself a coffee that Ruth has her first coherent thought of the day. While faces don't usually change that much (Botox and fillers aside), names often do. Especially if a woman gets married. It's been nineteen years; this woman could be Mrs. Annie Anyone by now. And she could be anywhere.

Ruth starts with the most likely place. Annie Whitaker's home country, New Zealand.

Looking up New Zealand's population, Ruth is surprised to see that it currently sits at around four and a half million people, significantly less than the population of New York City. Maybe that will make tracking down Annie Anyone easier, she thinks.

Half an hour later, Ruth has to concede that it's much harder to find someone in New Zealand; when it comes to personal data, the country seems to have significantly fewer tools for hire.

Frustrated, she types, *How do you find someone in NZ?!!!* into the search bar. She should have acknowledged her limitations from the start (that being no knowledge of New Zealand whatsoever, outside those Conchords guys Joe and Gideon find so funny). Because someone has already done the work—the *mahi*, they call it in their blog article—on how to find old friends online. *Kiwi* friends. Clicking on the first recommended link the blog author has so helpfully provided, Ruth is taken to a social networking site with a busy home page, one that looks like it hasn't been updated since its proclaimed launch at the start of the 2000s.

Lost & Found.

Everyone's looking for someone, Ruth thinks, as she starts her search for Annie Whitaker all over again.

She can't find any matching profiles, which doesn't surprise her. Unlike Amity Greene, this woman doesn't appear to have cultivated an online persona. But there are four pages of posts from people seeking former classmates with the surname Whitaker. Near the bottom of the third page, Ruth sees an old post with the heading *Exchange Student Reunion!*, and she feels that familiar prickle at her skin. The vibration that tells her she is on the cusp of a new discovery.

Sharing this everywhere I can, the post from someone called Sez Hocking starts. *I'm trying to organize a fifteen-year reunion of all us kids who went to the States in 95–96. Anyone know where I can find . . .*

Ruth can't see an Annie Whitaker on the list of names Sez has included in her callout. But in the dozen or so replies to her post, people keep adding their own names and queries.

Ruth stops. Reads over one of the last comments again.

Anyone know what happened to Roseanne Whitaker? I sat next to her on the plane from Auckland to LA. Always wondered if she made it to Broadway!

Have you been living under a rock, bro? someone named Kat Malone responded.

No, just in Arizona, Clinton Browne came back, adding a series of question marks.

Here you go then, Kat replied, sharing a link to an online news article from 2009.

If she thought the revelations about Amity Greene's past were shocking, nothing prepares Ruth for what Ethan's *other* Julie Jordan grew up to be.

The year after her high school exchange, Roseanne "Annie" Whitaker did indeed marry a murderer.

Or a man who became one. In 2009, Annie's husband of twelve years, Peter Mulvaney, was arrested for a horrific double homicide in their hometown of Marama River, New Zealand. Peter's two daughters were just eight and eleven when the local farmer murdered the girls' teenage babysitters, Kelly Parker and Nichole Morley, on the banks of the town's eponymous river. According to multiple news stories from the time, it was a crime that shocked this small, rural community, situated on the west coast of New Zealand's North Island. Ruth can see why. The murders were brutal. Peter Mulvaney strangled seventeen-year-old Kelly, and when her cousin Nichole, who had just turned fourteen, tried to intervene, he beat the younger girl unconscious with a rock before weighing both girls down in the river. That would have been awful enough, but the subsequent discovery of Kelly's diaries also strongly suggested the then-thirty-nine-year-old married man had been sexually abusing her—though some in the media insisted on calling their relationship an "affair"—for at least two years prior to her death.

It reads like the kind of crime that would have been turned into a TV movie in the States, but it would seem the people of Marama River, New Zealand, closed ranks. After a trial that resulted in a life sentence for Peter Mulvaney, it's like the story just went away. Try as she might, Ruth can find very little public discourse about Peter or the girls.

But she has found Annie Whitaker.

Even if she goes by the name Rose Mulvaney now, Ruth has little doubt this wife of a convicted double murderer from New Zealand is another of Ethan Oswald's Julie Jordans. She's not as thin, her hair is lighter, and she is nine thousand miles from her old high school in Hoben, Connecticut. But in the few Mulvaney family photographs rotated through the media when the crime was still in the news, the adult Annie—*Rose*, Ruth corrects herself—has the same tight smile, the same wide-eyed stare as her teenage self.

This woman couldn't look any more different from the vibrant Amity Greene. But it appears they both graduated from Ethan Oswald to their very own murderers. The reality of this is so stark, Ruth can't fully comprehend it. One of Ethan's Julie Jordans growing up to marry a killer would be shocking enough.

But *two* of them?

"My dad always used to say you shouldn't put the horse before the cart," Beth says, reaching for Ruth's trembling hand.

She hadn't even noticed the girls come back.

"You're assuming this Rose had the same kind of relationship with Ethan that Amity did," Beth continues. "We can't know that for sure, Ruthie."

"You could always ask her," Rhea says dryly. "Instead of being so Nancy Drew about everything."

Beth shoots her a look, and Rhea shrugs.

"The Ruth I know would be all over this shit. *Real* leads for once, right there in front of her." The young girl waves her hand around. "Not just dead girls like us."

———

Amity calls at 9 p.m.

"I went to your bar," she tells Ruth breathlessly. "But they said you weren't working tonight."

It almost sounds like an accusation.

"Anyway," she rushes on, "I'm in your neighborhood, and I wondered if you wanted to get a drink?"

"Uh . . ."

Ruth is still in the sweatpants and tee she wore when she

took Ressler for a brief walk, hours ago. She hasn't even brushed her teeth. Mostly, she's been searching for, and finding nothing about, Rose Mulvaney.

It occurs to Ruth that she could ask Amity if Ethan ever mentioned Annie Whitaker in those letters he sent her. And so she says yes to the offer of a nightcap, thinking this will please Rhea, at least. As far as Ruth can tell, Nancy Drew didn't make a habit of questioning her sources at bars.

The two women meet up at a dive bar two blocks from Ruth's apartment. There's an old guy in a Yankees cap out front with his even older-looking dog, and immediately Ruth wishes she'd brought Ressler along. Not that she needs protection from Amity, but it does feel odd to be meeting on the other woman's terms this time around.

Amity is already sitting up at the bar, wearing what appears to be a man's white shirt as a dress, and sipping at a glass of something dark.

"Bourbon," she says, waving her glass at Ruth, then leaning in for a hug. Her breath smells like one of the cloths they use to wipe down the tables at Sweeney's.

They don't know each other well enough (or at all) for Ruth to ask Amity if she's drunk, but it certainly seems like she might be. Ruth sits down next to Amity on a wobbly bar stool and wonders what she's doing here.

"I thought of some things about Eric," Amity tells Ruth, after she's ordered both of them a drink. "You can record me if you like."

This is another perfect opportunity to come out with it. Admit that Coulter is not the man she's interested in. But once again, Ruth cannot bring herself to come clean. Not to a maybe-drunk Amity who seems like she's got more things she wants to get off her chest.

So Ruth swallows her questions about Oswald and Annie, opens her voice memo app, and sets her phone down on the sticky bar. Telling herself this is what a real investigator would do.

(Don't lead the witness. Isn't that the rule?)

"He wouldn't even let me use the bathroom in the middle of the night," Amity starts, talking directly at Ruth's now-recording phone. "In case, you know, the drip of a tap woke him."

For the next hour, Ruth listens as Amity blithely recounts the many ways her husband used to control her. *Microaggressions*, she calls them, but they sound pretty big to Ruth. The rough sex. The bank accounts she couldn't access. There was a time she wasn't even allowed to have her own key to their apartment.

So when people started asking her if she'd had any idea about him, and she said no? That was kind of a lie. This is what a definitely drunk Amity says now, as she leans in close to Ruth's phone once again.

"Let the record also show that he was a complete and utter prick from the start."

When she turns her attention back to Ruth, Amity's eyes are glassy. "Stay away from Aries men," she says, nodding at her own sage advice. "They're *all* about aggression." She narrows those glassy eyes. "You're what? An Aquarian?"

"What makes you say that?" Ruth asks warily.

"There's just something . . . *kooky* . . . about you, Ruth. And, like, a bit remote. My grandma always said that's because Aquarians are from a different planet. When's your birthday anyway?"

"January twenty-fourth."

Amity taps her nail against her front teeth, then waggles her finger at Ruth.

"Same day as Ted Bundy was executed," she says, as if this explains something.

Ruth is surprised she would know that, and her expression clearly shows it.

"What can I say?" Amity's shrug is more like a shimmy. "I have a thing for serial killers."

Ruth feels as though she's just swallowed all the ice in her water glass. "What—"

But Amity is already off on another tangent. Something about how being an impulsive Sagittarian always got her in trouble as a kid. Like the time she—

Ruth doesn't hear the rest of the story. It's almost like her brain is actually clicking pieces together again; the sound in her head reminds her of fingers snapping.

When Amity takes a breath, Ruth takes her own quick breath and jumps in.

"You know, some people think your old teacher, Mr. O, was a serial killer too."

"Mmm," Amity responds, as if this is not news to her.

Ruth does her best to sound casually interested in this next bit. "Did he ever say anything about that in those letters? The ones he wrote you from jail?"

Before Amity can answer, Ruth offers to buy her another drink.

It was a complete misemployment of her bartender training. The way Ruth ensured Amity was intoxicated just enough not to care about what she said next, but not so drunk she couldn't speak at all.

And maybe it was guilt about this totally irresponsible behavior, more than how genuinely confused Amity seemed about where she might be sleeping tonight, that made Ruth bring her back to the apartment and put her to bed on the living room couch. Because the last thing she'd actually wanted was to have this woman in her home.

This woman who never told on Ethan Oswald again, after that first time. And might still be protecting him now.

"What kinds of things did he talk to you about?" Ruth had asked at the bar, but Amity insisted she couldn't remember anything Ethan had said to her. As if she'd forgotten her recorded confessions.

"What about a girl named Annie Whitaker—did he ever mention her in his letters?"

When Ruth asked this on the walk home, Amity had answered, "Who's that?" before loudly singing "Tomorrow" at a random man they passed on the sidewalk, making him jump.

"The letters are gone now, *Ruthieeeee*," she'd singsonged in the elevator up to the apartment. "I sold them all last year to some weirdo collector. Ten thousand dollars for the whole lot. But don't tell anyone about that; it was meant to be a secret."

When Ruth had tucked a blanket around her on the couch, Ressler watching from the doorway, Amity had briefly grabbed her face, pulled it close.

"I'm a terrible person, Ruth." She'd stopped then, shaking her head slightly. "But *shhh*—that's a secret too."

Seconds later, Amity Greene was sound asleep. Soon, she was snoring.

Ruth sits on the living room floor all night, watching her.

TEN

If Amity is embarrassed to wake up sprawled on Ruth's couch, she doesn't show it.

Sitting up, wearing nothing but a black lace bra, she stretches her arms above her head before accepting the coffee Ruth hands her.

"Thanks for looking out for me last night," she says through a stifled yawn. "I'm usually much better at holding my liquor."

After a sleepless night on the floor, Ruth's guilt has faded; she barely feels the pang.

"No problem," she says with a faux shrug. "I was just as bad, believe me."

What's one more lie between them now?

As Amity starts hunting for her clothes, Ruth feels a surge of adrenaline course through her. Being awake all night, she's had hours to practice this next question, but she's still nervous about getting it right.

"We got some great material for the podcast," she begins carefully. "And I'm sure I'll have some more questions for you. But just one for now, Amity. . . ." Ruth steadies herself. "That collector who bought those letters from you—I could use that kind of money myself, and I have a few things they might be interested in. You wouldn't happen to have their contact details, would you?"

Amity's right eyebrow shoots up at this request.

"Don't worry," Ruth assures her. "That part is completely between us, I promise. I wasn't even recording by then. It's just, this place"—Ruth sweeps her hand around the living room—"belongs to my uncle. I'm totally living off his goodwill, and he could kick me out anytime. So if there's a way to make some money . . ."

Amity taps at her teeth again. "I never knew his real name. It was some guy who found me online and had me drop the letters off at a rented mailbox. Once the money was transferred, he disappeared."

Standing up, she reaches out to give Ruth a farewell hug.

"Good luck finding him," she says brightly. "And thanks again for looking out for me last night."

She is at the front door when she turns around to look back at Ruth. "What's your podcast going to be called, anyway? I've been meaning to ask."

Ruth glances at her closed bedroom door. "*The Other Girls*," she says, after a beat.

Amity frowns. "It's okay, I guess. But what about *The Other Women* instead? It's a little more grown-up, don't you think?" She beams at her own suggestion. "People will think that it's about serial killer side chicks, but really—it's about the women he *couldn't* kill."

———

If Ruth thought she'd been ricocheting off the walls these past few days, careening from one hypothesis to another, it's nothing compared to the way she starts spinning as soon as Amity leaves.

"Write it all down," Beth suggests. "There's too much going on right now for you to see how it all fits. Writing it out might give us a different perspective."

Beth's right. Mapping their discoveries of the past five days can only help.

They start with the indisputable. Last Monday, a seven-year-old girl went missing from their old hometown. Witnesses saw a man driving her away. And one had seen an unidentified young woman talking to Coco right before she disappeared.

Also indisputable. Amity Greene met Ethan Oswald when he directed her in a high school production of *Carousel* the year before Beth was murdered. Another teenager, Annie Whitaker, an exchange student from New Zealand, met Oswald the same way, just months before he killed Beth.

According to Amity, Oswald regularly abused her during rehearsals for the show. He also displayed an unhealthy interest in her little sister. When she told another teacher about the abuse, no one believed her, and Oswald went unpunished, allowing him to move from Ohio to Connecticut with no blemishes on his record. Later, he started writing letters to Amity, and she wrote him back. Years later, an anonymous person purchased Oswald's half of their correspondence for a significant sum, and those letters might now be considered lost. But is any of Amity's story actual fact? They have only her word to go on.

And they have no words at all from Annie Whitaker. From *Rose*.

What *can* be said about those two teenage Julie Jordans is this: they both grew up to marry men who murdered young girls.

As for Ethan Oswald's letters to Amity, a quick online search showed that not even Ted Bundy memorabilia sells for that much. Which means someone must have wanted those letters badly enough to pay well over market value for them.

Investment? Ruth writes in her notes. *Or insurance?*

Surely Amity wouldn't have handed them over if anything he wrote incriminated her. But what if they pointed the finger at someone else? Might that person be willing to pay a lot of money to get them out of circulation?

Oswald's correspondence could very well bolster the girls' growing theory that he had a young accomplice, whom he tasked with grooming his even younger victims. But without any proof, they're back where they started. Because they've never been able to prove their original hypothesis either. That Ethan Oswald was in Connecticut well before he officially moved there in 1996. In 1983, 1985, and 1991 specifically. When Rhea, then Leila, then Lori, disappeared.

All they really have to go on right now are the stories of a woman who, by her own admission, has *a thing* for serial killers.

"She was just a girl when she met him," Beth reminds Ruth. "Whatever you think of Amity, she was only fourteen. And he was harming her."

"I know that." Ruth frowns, though she knows she shouldn't be annoyed at the reproach in Beth's tone. The truth is, she does need to be reminded of that sometimes. Amity Greene is not always easy to feel sorry for.

Sighing, Ruth gets down on the floor, where Ressler has been sleeping all morning, periodically lifting his head to watch her pace the room. Apologizing again for how distracted she's been, she buries her face in the folds of his neck.

"Your life must have been much more fun before you moved here," she says into his fur. "Roaming around actually looking for people, instead of being cooped up in this apartment with me."

Ruth has sometimes wondered if Ressler retained any memories of his failed K-9 career in Hoben. Or whether he, too, has a blank space where that town used to be.

Ruth can't even remember what the main street looks like.

Bringing her laptop down to the floor, she pulls up a map of Hoben on her screen, before plugging in her old address on Canyon Road. The street view makes it look like a movie set. All those white, double-story houses with dark shutters. The wide front lawns and rosebushes, neatly trimmed. It's all familiar in an uncanny valley way, and Ruth can't bring herself to zoom in on her old house; instead, she types in another address. One that's been in the news an awful lot this past week.

Coco Wilson was taken from the front yard of a modern Cape Cod on Pinewood Drive. Along that street, the houses are close enough together for neighbors to wave from their windows. Or look out through the glass and see a little girl talking to a young woman with a dog.

Burying her face in Ressler's neck again, Ruth inhales the comforting corn chip smell of his fur before she types in another address, mapping the distance from Pinewood Drive to 1279 Longview Road. To that set-back-from-the-road, hidden-from-view house where Beth was murdered. Before her body was buried in the dense, dark woods behind the property.

When she brings up the street view for this address, the effect is seismic. Ruth's insides lurch so spectacularly, she nearly throws up. It's still there, that house. Still standing. When she would have had it razed to the ground.

Who lives there now? Do they have any idea what happened in that house nineteen years ago?

In America, you can find almost anyone for a fee. It doesn't take long for Ruth to bring up the property ownership records for 1279 Longview Road. She reads that the current owners have been there since December 2001. They bought the house from a family who had lived there since January 1997. The owners before them had maintained the property for fourteen years. Since 1983.

"Beth," Ruth calls out, but it sounds more like a croak.

Beth.

The house Beth was murdered in was sold the year after her death. Ruth had never stopped to consider that Ethan had only ever been a tenant. Why hadn't she wondered how a high school teacher could afford to buy a house in one of the most exclusive parts of Hoben? Especially when he was said to have come from a working-class town in Minnesota, and records showed he relied on scholarships to get through college.

Whoever his landlord was, they'd owned the house for fourteen years. Since 1983—the year Rhea went missing. Did Ethan already have a relationship with the owners when he started renting their Longview Road home in early 1996?

Had he been in that house before?

The deed in front of Ruth lists the owners over that fourteen-year period as Mrs. Helen, Miss Louise, and Mr. Magnus Torrent.

Something about these names is familiar. And when the connection finally comes to her, Ruth wonders if she really might be losing her mind now.

The copycat killer. TBK. The Ted Bundy wannabe. He might have called himself the Babysitter Killer, but his real name was Martin Torrent.

His wife was named Helen. And his children were called Louise and Magnus.

Opening another tab, Ruth looks up the TBK case for the first time since they did a deep dive into his pathologies in one of her criminal psychology classes.

It's as bad as she remembered. From 1979 to 1982, Martin Torrent had roamed the Minnesota–Wisconsin border, preying on young girls who had advertised their babysitting services in the area. Torrent murdered twelve of those teenagers, across five counties, before he was caught, thanks in large part to the letters he'd sent the police, taunting them. Like Ethan, he died in jail, a decade after receiving a life sentence for his crimes. But unlike Ethan, he was a family man. An engineer with a wife and two kids, also teenagers. *Twins.*

Louise and Magnus Torrent. After his arrest, Louise and Magnus disappeared from public view with their mother.

If Ruth felt queasy before, it's like she has a fever now. Ressler shifts away from her, as if she really is hot to the touch.

"Sorry, boy," she whispers. "But do you know what this means?"

Unlike Ethan, Martin Torrent is high up in the annals of true crime. Which makes it very easy to find out where he came from. Within minutes, Ruth knows where the Babysitter Killer was born, where he grew up, and, most importantly, where he lived with his family until his arrest in late 1982.

Linnea, Minnesota. A small town in Carver County, on the banks of the Minnesota River.

This time, Ruth really does throw up. Making it to the bathroom just in time, she heaves into the sink. There's so little she knows for sure about Ethan Oswald. But she does know that he was born in Carver County, Minnesota. This was an easy find, years ago, when she tracked down his birth records. Everything is adding up now. The twins Amity mentioned. Ethan leaving the Midwest around the same time Torrent's wife and kids went off the radar. The fourteen-year ownership of that terrible house in North Hoben, Connecticut.

And all those young girls going missing along the I-91, starting in the summer of 1983. Right after the Torrent family had moved to town.

Ethan Oswald *was* in Hoben long before 1996. With everything Ruth has just uncovered, surely this, too, can be considered indisputable.

"Beth," she calls out again. "Beth!"

But her friend has long since left the room.

ELEVEN

Maybe he's a magician.

Maybe he's performing some kind of trick. A disappearing one. She saw a man lock a lady inside a box, once. And when he opened the doors again, she wasn't there. The lady was wearing a sparkly dress, and she came back eventually. That part of the trick is fuzzy now. How did she come back? And more importantly, where was she all that time she was gone?

How long has she been here? Is it days now? It takes a whole year to go around the sun, her teacher said, but nothing moves in this room. Will she still be here when it's Christmas?

She heard a telephone ring earlier. It rang for a very long time, and nobody answered. That's happened three more times. She's been counting. But now it's very quiet. Everybody must be sleeping, even if it's a little bit lighter now. As if it's nearly morning. She was supposed to start work on her art project, whenever tomorrow morning actually is. Her daddy was going to show her how to make a papier-mâché volcano using baking soda and something else she can't remember. They've already collected a stack of newspapers and a soda bottle to make the mountain. He said they could add red food coloring, and the lava would actually be red.

"It'll be a neat trick," he said.

Thinking about building that volcano with her daddy makes her even sadder than when the music suddenly stopped in her head.

Her stomach gurgles loudly. Her whole life, she's never been this hungry. Or this sad. It's like all her happiness has been boxed up, sealed with that packing tape her mommy uses when she puts away their Christmas decorations.

"So the mice can't get in," she always says. It takes a sharp knife to open those boxes up again the next year.

And now she's thinking about how they put dead people in boxes. That's what happened to her daddy's parents, before she was even born. They were put inside coffins, and then they went up to heaven. But they must have known how to get out of them, otherwise heaven would be a very strange place.

She needs to use the bathroom again. He's going to be so mad when he comes back. She's wet the bed so many times.

Trying to roll away from the mess she's made, her fingers graze something solid under the bedcovers. She rolls it toward her, slow and careful, so it doesn't go the wrong way. Finally, it's close enough for her to grasp.

It's a blue crayon. Her third-favorite color, after yellow and red. She brings it up to her nose, smells the waxiness, and then she takes a big bite out of it, snapping the crayon in half. But it doesn't taste like blue should taste, and she spits it straight back out, crumbled pieces dripping down her chin.

It was supposed to taste like sky. Or the sea. Yellow, she thinks, should taste like the sun.

She doesn't want to know what the color red would taste like.

TWELVE

The general consensus is that Helen Torrent changed her name after her husband's arrest and subsequent conviction. And then she vanished. Possibly to Northern Europe, where her family was from originally.

Or she disappeared to a quiet town in Connecticut, USA, with her eighteen-year-old twins, Louise and Magnus.

And their honorary triplet, Ethan Oswald.

Is this enough to take to Officer Canton? Ruth can just hear his sigh. Knowing the family of a serial killer doesn't make *you* one, he'd probably say. Or definitely say. Right now, any link Ruth has found between the Torrent family and Ethan Oswald is purely circumstantial. As for Annie Whitaker, there's even less to go on. Amity might have said there were other Julie Jordans, but she didn't seem to recognize Annie's name when Ruth mentioned it. She could be lying about that, however.

Ruth needs to be careful. Especially if she *wants* Amity's story to be true.

A doctor once suggested Ruth was prone to apophenia, that she was excessively concerned with making patterns, even when none existed. He said she couldn't recognize her own cognitive bias and took things too far. Officer Canton had seemed to agree, when he showed up at her apartment and said, *Enough.*

We've turned over every stone, Ruthie, believe me, he'd said, right before telling her this was, in fact, an intervention. Two days later, her parents had sent her to live at the farm with Joe and Gideon. That's how much everyone thought she needed help.

But the police can't have turned over every stone, Ruth thinks now. If they had, Canton would already know that Ethan Oswald grew up next to a serial killer. He'd know that the family of that killer owned the house Beth was murdered in, and he'd know that Mr. O liked to spend time coaching his teenage Julie Jordans in more than just their musical roles.

Those girls who could never give up on him, no matter the terrible things he did.

Ruth is the one who's discovered these things. Because she takes things just far enough. It's always been clear that people have never understood how she sees the world. The way she *knows.* That nothing is random. Nothing is coincidence.

Which means even the most terrible things might be prevented—if you could only see them coming.

———

Where to start? *Who* to start with?

Ruth now has three women in her sights. Three wives of notorious murderers, all of whom have undeniable ties to Ethan Oswald. She could keep pushing Amity about the content of those letters. Or she could find a way to contact Rose Mulvaney. But what about Helen Torrent, Ethan's neighbor-turned-landlord? Should she investigate this relationship first?

"Why not do it all?" Leila asks, late Saturday evening. "Don't you have friends who can help with that kind of thing?"

"Maybe you should get some sleep instead," Beth interjects. "You didn't sleep last night, when Amity was here, and now you seem a little . . . wired."

If Ruth didn't know better, she'd think Beth was trying to discourage her. There's been a change in her demeanor ever since Ruth found out about the house on Longview Road. Or maybe it's Rose Mulvaney that's got her acting so skittery.

When they'd looked at those press photographs of the New Zealand woman, Beth was definitely uneasy.

"She *could* be the one I remember from the playground," she'd said, chewing at her lip. "But wouldn't I remember if she had an accent? I mean, she wouldn't exactly sound like us."

An obvious point that hadn't occurred to Ruth.

"I'll go to bed soon," she assures Beth now, before turning back to Leila, who is lying on the floor, her head on Rhea's lap. Lori hasn't come with them tonight.

"I'm not sure I'd call them *friends*, Leila. But you're right: I do have some acquaintances who are very good at finding people."

Specifically, people who don't want to be found.

There is a section on *What Happened to Her* where you can rally the troops. Call in any experts in their field to help you solve a particular problem. Ruth goes to that forum now and creates a new post.

Calling any TBK experts out there! Does anyone know what happened to Martin Torrent's wife, Helen? I'm also interested in any info on the wife of Peter Mulvaney, the Marama River killer. I believe she now goes by the name of Rose and lives in New Zealand.

It can't do any harm, Ruth thinks. On this members-only site, it's not like Rose or Helen will see her request.

Ruth pauses to tap at her front teeth, Amity-style. She should probably stick to her story, though. It's not like she needs an alibi—but it's always good to remember your lies.

I want to interview these ladies for my new podcast on the wives of notorious murderers, Ruth quickly adds, underneath her initial post. *I'm already talking with the wife of the Socialite Strangler, which has been super interesting. Any help tracking these other two women down would be much appreciated. Thanks in advance for your help!*

As various members start liking the post, adding their thumbs-up and spyglass emojis, Ruth feels the validation. That this is a perfectly normal thing to be doing.

All she needs now is for one of those thumbs to point her in the right direction.

———

She really should ask for help more often.

Right before she's due to leave for work on Sunday afternoon, Ruth checks her post on *What Happened to Her* and sees that she's received a promising response.

Check your messages!! @RoderickAlleyn has written. Ruth remembers him from last time; no one uses their real name on this site, but they do happily promote their credentials, and this retired private investigator from London was always up for a challenge. It would seem not much has changed for him these past five years, either.

It's good to see you back in these parts, @RoderickAlleyn continues in his private message. We missed you!

(Ruth's own moniker on *What Happened to Her* is @DrBurgess96. As for her credentials, when she joined the site, she simply listed herself as: Friend.)

@RoderickAlleyn goes on:

> I'd not heard of the Marama River killer. Thank you for bringing that one to my attention, especially since I have a particular interest in down under crime. Here

is the most recent email address I could find for Rose Mulvaney—it seems she once offered private music lessons, and though her website is no longer active, perhaps this email still works. Do let me know!

Now, when it comes to Helen Torrent, the best I can tell you for now is that she is thought to be living in Oslo, Norway. You know I like a challenge, and I'm currently laid up recovering from double knee surgery (everything fell apart at once!), so if you're patient with me, I shall see what more I can find for you.

All my best,
RA

As a former private investigator, @RoderickAlleyn appears to have found this information effortlessly. Ruth thanks him profusely, and then she takes her time formulating a message for Rose Mulvaney, crossing her fingers that her retired London sleuth will come through with details for Helen too.

She hopes it's soon, because a plan is starting to form. She can see the shape of it already, as improbable as it seems.

THIRTEEN

Four days later, Ruth's plan has gone from improbable to very, very possible. And now it's time to share it.

The redacted version, at least.

Sitting up at the bar with Owen after closing, she can't help but be amused by his reaction to her announcement. The way he gazes to the left and scratches at his chin. Life, for Owen, is one long stage direction.

"A podcast, you say?"

"Yep." Ruth tries to keep her voice light. "A serialized one."

"And you want to go to *New Zealand* to record it?"

Owen says this like Ruth has announced a solo expedition to Antarctica.

"Yep," she repeats. "*New Zealand*. One of the women I'm going to feature lives there."

She can't blame Owen for being bewildered. When Rose's reply to Ruth's unsolicited email came through, she'd been confused herself. She still hasn't quite got her own head around the fact that Rose Mulvaney has agreed to talk to her. In person.

"I don't get it," Owen says. "A true crime podcast?"

At this point, Ruth's small truths are verging on big lies. But there's no turning back now. It's not like she can tell him what's actually going on. Instead, she sticks to her story.

"You've heard of *Serial,* right?" she asks. "It's a podcast that was massively popular last year. Total cultural phenomenon. So now true crime podcasts are really taking off, and I thought, why not put all those wasted years of college to use. Produce a podcast of my own. One that looks at *all* the people impacted by a murder—not just the perpetrator, which is what most everyone else seems to focus on. I think I could do something really different."

Turns out, the more people Ruth delivers her made-up spiel to, the more believable it sounds.

"Will it make you famous?" Owen asks.

"Maybe," Ruth says, pretending to think on it. "I might even win a Peabody."

This has the desired effect. Owen claps his hands at Ruth's newly found confidence, before adopting an air of concern.

"Listen, Laura Holt. When you showed up at my door, I promised your uncle that I'd keep an eye on you. Is what you're planning dangerous in any way? Do you even know this woman?"

This woman. Rose Mulvaney. Who, like Amity Greene, thinks Ruth wants to interview her for a podcast. Wants to talk to her about what it's like when you discover your husband is a brutal killer.

"*She* never murdered anyone," Ruth answers. "And her husband is in jail. So I'm sure I'll be fine."

"She's not going to turn out to be a Mrs. Lovett or anything?" Owen persists. "Because, you know, many people consider her to be the actual villain in *Sweeney Todd.*"

"That's because people *love* to blame the woman," Ruth responds.

And that's not what I'm doing, she adds silently, even as her stomach tightens.

"Fair point." Owen nods, then gazes off into the distance again. "I once flew twenty-two hours to see Bernadette Peters sing at the Sydney Opera House," he muses.

He looks like he's about to launch into a monologue about that journey, when the door to Sweeney's jangles open, and a tall, lean young man walks in.

"We're closed for the night," Ruth calls out, at the same time as the guy says, "Shit, sorry!" as he evidently realizes his mistake.

With the bar's main lights off, his face is mostly stubble and shadow, but his smile has clearly caught Owen's attention.

"We open again at three tomorrow," her boss says in his best come-hither voice. "We'll take care of you then, I promise."

Another broad smile, accompanied by a "Thanks, mate," and the interloper is gone.

Owen lets out a low whistle as the door closes behind him. "Where has *he* been all my life!"

"Australia, I'm guessing," Ruth says, rolling her eyes.

"Yes! The accent was a dead giveaway. Speaking of the dead . . ." Owen's eyebrows return to their high arch.

"If there's a Mrs. Lovett among my podcast subjects, you'll be the first to know," Ruth promises. "That is, if you let me have the time off to find out."

Two weeks, that's all she needs. And the timing couldn't be better, because Amity has just announced she's off to Paris for a month. With a "friend." Ruth has lost her only source in New York, and it's time to cast her net wider.

"Fine," Owen says. "You can have your time off. Just promise you'll be careful, Cagney. I'm too old to come rescue you."

"Duly noted, Lacey," Ruth responds.

She slides off the bar stool, kisses his cheek, then heads for the door. She is reaching for the handle when Owen calls after her: "How did you get her to agree to talk to you, anyway?"

"Beats me, boss," Ruth answers over her shoulder. "Maybe . . . maybe nobody else asked."

———————

Ruth does know why Rose Mulvaney agreed to talk to her.

If using a made-up podcast as the lure to get Amity talking was Ruth's first brilliant idea, leveraging that lie to get to Rose Mulvaney has been her pièce de résistance. The way she played into the fears of this obviously private woman. Suggesting she knew of other podcasters, less scrupulous ones, who had recently expressed interest in covering the Marama River murders. The kind of podcasters who like to blame women for men's behavior. They were already digging around in Rose's past, Ruth had implied, and they would have no compunction about telling Rose's story without her. Ruth never even had to mention Ethan Oswald. She'd guessed that if Rose was hiding her earlier connection to yet another child murderer, she'd be alarmed at what all that supposed digging would uncover.

Maybe she'd even want to get in front of the story.

Other lies came easily to Ruth after that. Like when she said she was going to be in New Zealand this month for "work," so she could just "swing by" Marama River. She knew she'd get more out of Rose if they were in the same room.

"I'll be able to tell if she's lying about anything," Ruth said to Beth, to justify her own lies.

"Won't she be able to do the same with you?" Beth had shot back.

Things have been tense between them ever since.

"I just don't see how flying across the world is going to help

Coco Wilson," Beth repeats tonight, after Ruth gets home from her chat with Owen.

"If Rose *is* the girl you remember from the playground," Ruth explains, "then maybe she'll admit that Oswald put her up to it, and I can persuade her to tell the police in Hoben. It'll be a new lead for them. It might help."

"Help Coco's case?" Beth asks. "Or ours?"

She sweeps her hand about the room, as if the other girls are there too.

"Coco's been missing for ten days," Ruth says in exasperation. She's getting tired of defending herself. "*Ten*, Beth. Imagine if someone had clutched at just one more straw for you after ten days."

It's a low blow, but Ruth's not sorry.

She doesn't want to fight with her best friend. And the truth is, she has no idea whether she's doing the right thing. For Coco or anyone else. But it has to be better than doing nothing at all.

What Beth can't see. Won't see, ever.

There is responsibility in being the one who didn't die.

That night, unable to sleep, Ruth lies awake wondering what it would be like if the whole podcast thing were true. If she really was doing research for *The Other Women*, like she keeps claiming. What would it be like to have no connection to the material you were investigating, outside morbid curiosity? What kind of person would she be, if her own interest in murder was nothing more than macabre fascination, the way some people get obsessed with freak accidents or natural disasters?

When she was little, Ruth's favorite possession was an old atlas that had belonged to her mother as a child. It was a dusty, cloth-covered tome that, propped up, was almost as tall as she was. It had a double gatefold in the middle, three panels that opened out to display a map of the earth's tectonic plates. Ruth loved running her fingers over the puzzle pieces those plates made, and the continents that fit within their borders. This was before she knew that, much like those shifting plates, everything on the earth's surface was precarious too. How easily borders could be redrawn, so that even the surest thing, something printed in a million books, could one day become obsolete. Back then, she thought it took a million years for things to become unrecognizable. She couldn't imagine the world could change so fast. That entire countries could disappear in a day.

Thinking about that old, green atlas now, Ruth wonders if she might have grown up to be a geologist. If things had turned out differently.

"You do like your geology metaphors, mixed as they are," her therapist once commented.

Ruth had been embarrassed when Courtney said this. She'd shrugged and said at least she didn't imagine herself to be a giant insect (she was reading Kafka at the time), and this led to a whole new discussion about why she felt the need to imagine herself as anything at all.

———

Whatever sleep Ruth might have clawed back in the early hours is interrupted by a phone call from her mother, currently living on Central European Summer Time.

When Ruth mentions the time difference in New York, Cynthia is mildly apologetic.

"Sorry, sweetheart," she crackles down the phone from a seaside village on the Italian Riviera. "I know you work late, and I didn't mean to wake you. I just can't seem to keep all these time zones sorted."

All these time zones. That would be two, total. Ruth tries not to roll her eyes, even though her mother wouldn't see it.

"It's all good, Mom," she says. "I was awake anyway."

"Why are you awake so early, Ruth?"

Despite the staticky line, Ruth can hear the change in her mother's tone. The quick stab of worry sharpening her words, so that the question comes out more like an accusation. Classic Cynthia. Afraid to ask directly if anything is wrong.

Ruth defaults to her usual excuse—"Ressler needed to pee"—before changing the subject, asking her mother to describe all the delicious food she's been eating. She pretends that the descriptions make her mouth water, when the reality is, Ruth's stomach has become so knotted, she can't remember the last time she actually enjoyed a meal.

The call ends with Cynthia once again inviting her daughter to join her for the summer, and Ruth promising once again to think about it. Another lie, but she's stopped keeping track by now.

A little over an hour later, at the more civilized time of 7:30 a.m., Joe calls.

"Just checking in, kid," he says, and Ruth immediately knows the reason why.

"What did Owen say to you?" she asks.

"He said you wanted some time off to go traveling," Joe replies without missing a beat. "What's up with that?"

"I thought I might drive up tomorrow and explain it to you and Gideon in person," Ruth tells him. "But honestly, it's nothing to worry about."

They both know she's said that last part before. Back then, it was as a big a lie as any she's ever told.

FOURTEEN

Despite her tendency to see patterns in other people's lives, great swaths of Ruth-Ann Baker's own memories are bright, shiny postcards with nothing written on the back.

There are facts she can line up in a row. Like moving from Hoben to New York a few months before her eighth birthday. She remembers the carpet at Radio City Music Hall, where her parents took her to see the Christmas Spectacular that first winter in the city. Eating burgers in Herald Square after visiting Macy's with her uncle. But she can't remember the name of her third-grade teacher. She can recall her very real fear that Patience and Fortitude, those majestic marble lions stationed outside the New York Public Library, might suddenly come to life and make their way uptown to her uncle's Upper West Side apartment—but she has no memory of where her parents did their grocery shopping after they moved to Morningside Heights. Or how she got to school, who she sat next to in class, or what she ate for dinner. Her parents made forgetting their family's foundation; after they moved to New York, they avoided looking back at their old life in Hoben, even if that meant losing the surrounding months and years too.

The only person who ever helped Ruth fill in the blanks was her uncle Joe. But if Joe helped Ruth remember parts of her life in Hoben, he was even better at helping her forget. Joe turned New York into a playground; he made moving to the city a game. When Ruth was with her uncle, she had no time to think about Beth and everything else she'd left behind in Connecticut. In New York, her uncle taught her how to be a kid again. How to trust that the world wasn't always a dangerous place.

At the center of Ruth's kinship with her uncle, there is an undeniable, unbreakable bond. But she can't help feeling that five years ago, she failed him. When the episode happened, it was as if all that effort he'd put in had been for nothing. She was still that messed-up kid he'd had to pick up off the floor. She was still the girl he had to take care of, when his sister and her husband seemingly had no idea how to relate to their own child. Ruth's parents never knew what to do with a traumatized seven-year-old's "quirks," let alone a twenty-one-year-old who started talking about dead girls. Joe opened more than his home to Ruth, in a way her parents couldn't; he always made space for her. That kind of unwavering support makes you want to live up to a person's best idea of you.

Is she about to fail her uncle again?

All Ruth knows for sure is that she doesn't want to lie to him. But she has to tell him *something*. On this bright Saturday morning, Ressler lying in the back seat of the old Mercedes she's borrowed from Owen, she is navigating the roads to Joe and Gideon's farm as slowly as she can, hoping inspiration will come as she drives. A light bulb moment, somewhere before the town of Gardiner, that will help her explain her travel plans without looking like she's lost the plot all over again.

When the farmhouse does come into view, Ruth still has no idea what to say. If this were a regular visit, she would stop a minute to take in the majesty of her surroundings, this place she retreated to in March 2010 and emerged from so much stronger. The place where Officer Canton pulled up in his truck a few weeks after her arrival, a four-year-old bloodhound sleeping next to him in the front cabin. The very dog now pawing at the door of Owen's car, desperate to be set free. But Ruth's pause today is not about the stark beauty of the Shawangunk Mountains rising behind the farmhouse, nor the deep green of the spring-fed pond shimmering beyond the adjacent barn. She needs to steady her breath before getting out of the car because so much depends on her getting this right.

If she does tie her upcoming trip to the podcast, she'll be lying to Joe, no different from the way she's currently deceiving Amity and Rose. And if she so much as mentions her quest to find Helen Torrent, she'll eventually have to come clean about her landlord theory. Which he'll see through straightaway. Her uncle will know that all roads lead right past Amity. And Rose, and Helen. All the way back to Ethan Oswald.

When she's supposed to have left him behind too.

"Are you staying?"

"Just the one night," Ruth answers, deliberately casual, as Joe pours each of them a glass of wine. "Got to be back for my Sunday shift. 'Sunday Sundays,' you know. Where we play Owen's favorite Mandy Patinkin records all night."

"That Owen is a crack-up," Gideon says, his six-foot-six frame filling the kitchen doorway. "We wish you could stay for longer, though, Ruthie. We miss having you around."

"Plus, you haven't met the alpacas yet," Joe adds. "And yes, I said alpacas, plural. We ended up getting two."

"The more the merrier." Gideon winks before excusing himself to go finish some work in the barn.

Despite the circumstances they met under in 2010, Ruth and Gideon have always been firm friends. He and Joe had been at the farm for only a few months when they took Ruth in. She recovered from the episode in the company of this gentle giant, who had swept her uncle off his feet when they met in Boston the year before. The UK-born Gideon was visiting family, and Joe was there for work, and her uncle likes to say they were both only passing through that city to find each other. He firmly believed the universe had conspired to introduce them. In a state that would sanctify their marriage, no less.

From her first days with them at the farm, Ruth understood why Joe would think there was something fated about his love for Hamish Gideon. Her new uncle was as solid as the surname they called him by, and as kind a person as Ruth had ever met. He never once complained about the feverish houseguest he inherited from his husband that terrible winter. If anything, Gideon was better than Joe at sitting with Ruth's sorrow. Letting her feel it.

"You don't need to be *fixed*," he told her early on. "You're not broken, Ruthie."

Another night, he said something no one else ever has.

"If those girls are real to you, that's all that matters."

If there is anyone Ruth could admit her plans to now, it would be Gideon.

She has to resist calling him back to the kitchen, using him as a crutch for what comes next. She looks at Joe, sitting across from her at the marble counter, and takes a deep breath. Grateful at least for the presence of Ressler sleeping at their feet, his legs twitching with the memory of running through the fields earlier.

"*So.*"

Joe stares at Ruth over his wineglass. Sipping at her own, she reluctantly meets his eyes. In her uncle's features, Ruth can see the faint trace of her mother, the way you can sometimes see remnants of your breath on cold mornings. She wonders if Joe can see anything of himself in her face too. Gideon has always said that they look alike, but the truth is Ruth barely recognizes her own reflection. She sees something different in the mirror every time she looks.

"What's going on, Ruthie? Owen said something about a podcast and you flying to *New Zealand* next week?"

Of course her boss had forewarned him. This feels like a betrayal; Owen is supposed to be her friend too.

"Don't be mad at Owen," Joe says, as if she has voiced this frustration out loud. "He's just looking out for you, Ruthie. He might not know everything, but he's not stupid, either."

Ruth's hands suddenly feel slippery, and she sets her wineglass down on the bench with a clatter.

"What do you mean by that?"

Joe's hand is up in the air. "Calm down, kid. Your secrets are safe with me. But Owen knows *something* is up with you." Joe lets out a deep breath. "You could just tell him, you know."

Joe's voice is gentle as he says this, but Ruth processes it like a shock.

"You helped Mom and Dad pretend like it never happened," she retorts, her back teeth pressing hard against each other.

"And I sometimes wonder if that wasn't the worst thing to do," Joe responds quietly. "We didn't know anything about childhood trauma, Ruthie. Not really. And I think we might have listened to the wrong people sometimes."

"The wrong people?"

"Do you remember all those specialists you were dragged to?"

She'd thought of them as the Clipboards. She nods.

"There were one or two who were adamant all you needed was a change. That moving would help you forget what happened. We didn't think to ask where those memories might go."

There's something in her uncle's face that Ruth hasn't seen before. *Guilt.* And this is the last thing Ruth would ever want him to feel.

"I'm sorry," they both say at the same time, and then the moment passes. Where they might have followed the knifepoint of those memories all the way back to Hoben, Connecticut, in 1996.

Instead, Ruth tilts her half-empty glass at Joe.

"So, *New Zealand*," she says, mimicking her uncle's earlier emphasis. "I leave on Tuesday. I'll be back in time for Pride weekend."

"Priorities," Joe responds with a small smile.

He pours them both another drink, shaking his head slightly.

"Are you at least going to tell me what this trip is all about? Why this particular woman, Ruthie? Owen said her husband is in jail for killing two young girls, but I don't get the connection from there. New Zealand is a long way from New York, and there are plenty of murders a lot closer to home."

Although you're supposed to be staying away from any murders, she can hear Joe thinking.

Tell a small truth, Ruth realizes. It was her uncle who taught her this, after all.

"I think Rose Mulvaney used to live in Hoben," she says.

Joe's eyes widen, then narrow just as quickly. His next question is as big as the room.

"Did she know that prick Oswald?"

Ruth swallows. "It would be a massive coincidence if she did, Uncle Joe."

This isn't exactly a lie.

Now Joe asks Ruth the question she knew they would get to eventually.

"Does this have anything to do with that little girl who went missing last week?"

"Kind of." Ruth shrugs, giving her uncle another small truth to hold on to. "I can't deny that her kidnapping got me thinking. About all the things I didn't fully understand back then. And I thought"—here comes the lie, easy enough—"that I might do something a little more healthy with my questions this time around. Explore them via a podcast, you know? And I am actually already talking to a woman here in New York. Rose is going to be my second guest."

Looking at her uncle's concerned face, Ruth grasps for one more small truth she can offer him.

"I really think," she says, "that there's more to these women's stories than we ever get to hear. And with my background, I could be the one to change that."

———

Not everything from Ruth's past has been erased. Some memories are filed away in the back rooms of the Hoben Police Department, where Officer Canton still works. Xeroxed copies of conversations sit on shelves at the Connecticut Department of Children and Families, where some of those Clipboards she was forced to see probably still sit at their same desks too.

Like much of what she remembers from her life in Hoben, Ruth is never sure how many of these memories are real. But there are things that really did happen, she's sure of it.

Small truths, big lies. Maybe the only difference is which part of the story gets told.

———

Later, Ruth and Joe walk down to the pond, stopping to stare across its viridescent surface at the sun setting over the Gunks. On such a warm, still evening, it is hard to imagine the starkness of winter in this place, the frozen water you could skate on, the stripping of the surrounding trees, and the meadows turned to slush. Ruth arrived at the farm at the end of one such winter, but it is spring she remembers best from that time. The thawing. Now, on this cusp of summer, she wonders just how much of winter she will bring back with her from New Zealand.

She must have sighed, because Joe turns to her now, asks if she's sure. That she can keep her grip on reality this time around. That she won't start filling her room—and her head—with dead girls.

Ruth has long given up on convincing people like Joe that they weren't in her head. According to the round of specialists she'd acquiesced to sitting down with afterward, Ruth's infamous episode when she was twenty-one was a break with reality. A clinical example of unexamined trauma manifesting as a series of hallucinations. In the form of murdered girls.

Now she smiles her practiced smile at Joe, the one she's been perfecting ever since Officer Canton showed up at her apartment five years ago and said she needed help. "I'm past all that," she assures her uncle.

These days, she knows how to make it seem like the episode was simply a glitch. Just a little aftershock that went on a bit too long.

"I stopped seeing dead people"—she raises her fingers to put air quotes around the phrase, making a joke of it—"a long time ago, I promise."

Hoping that the inky darkness between them hides the way she crosses those fingers on the way down.

———

Ruth is packing up the car the next morning, trying not to think about leaving Ressler for so long, when Gideon comes up beside her.

"I made you something last night," he says. "To take on your travels."

Ruth stares at the intricate, bronzed metal object he presses into her hands.

"It's a triskelion," Gideon tells her, pointing at the three inter-connected spirals in her palm. "And because I know you like to go looking, Ruth, you'll find this symbol has significance across many ancient cultures. But I'd suggest you focus on the Greek goddess Hecate."

When she gives him a puzzled look, Gideon simply shrugs and says he just has a feeling: Ruth-Ann Baker and Hecate will get along.

FIFTEEN

W elcome back, Olivia."

"Pope or Benson?" Ruth asks as she joins Owen behind the bar on Sunday night.

It is her last shift at Sweeney's before she flies to New Zealand next week. The reality of her impending journey feels no less precarious than when the idea first occurred to her. But there's no denying she's also excited. Given how easily it's all happened these past few days (*Too easily?* Beth had inevitably questioned), you could even say the universe has conspired to help her for once.

Taking Gideon's triskelion from the back pocket of her jeans, Ruth traces its three spirals. One for each of the women she's investigating. That has to be a sign.

"Celtic, right?" a deep voice says, making her jump.

Lost in her thoughts, Ruth hadn't noticed someone sit down at the bar, directly in front of her. She blinks this man into focus, observing the strong slope of his nose, the sun-kissed skin. And his eyes, so light they remind her of sea glass. He has a cloth-covered notebook next to him on top of the bar, and he is staring right at her.

"That talisman you're holding . . ." He nods at the triskelion. "It's Celtic, yeah?"

The accent is vaguely familiar.

"My uncle said something about it being connected to the Greek goddess Hecate," Ruth responds, surprising herself. Why did she feel the need to share this with a stranger?

"Ah, the triple goddess. Cool!"

He holds out his hand across the bar. "I'm Gabe, by the way."

"You're Australian," Ruth replies, realizing he was the guy who'd come in after closing the other night.

"Guilty," he responds with a grin, dropping his hand. "Although I'm an honorary New Yorker for the summer, if that makes a difference?"

He re-extends his hand.

When Ruth still doesn't take it, his grin widens. He appears to be flirting with her.

Which is the last thing she needs right now.

"That really is a cool piece," Gabe tries again, indicating the triskelion. "I used to be obsessed with the chthonic deities as a kid."

"What's a chthonic deity?" Owen asks, coming up next to Ruth.

"They're the gods of the underworld," Gabe answers, squinting as if he's trying to recall lines from an old textbook. "If I remember correctly, Hecate is a goddess of thresholds; she has three heads or something, so she can see in all directions. And she's all about avenging wrongful deaths."

He quickly types something into his phone and gives a self-satisfied smile at whatever comes up on the screen. "Yeah, that's right. She was the leader of the restless dead."

Well, that's not exactly subtle, Gideon, Ruth thinks, but she feels a small thrill as she returns the triskelion to her back pocket. She cannot wait to get home to find out more about Hecate.

Even if that thrill might also have been caused by something— by someone—else.

———————

He is from Melbourne, although he grew up all over. After spending the last semester on an exchange program at U of M–Ann Arbor, he's come to New York for the summer before heading back to his law degree in Australia. He's funny. Articulate. Interesting. They've been chatting easily, all night.

And she is definitely not going to sleep with him. With everything else going on, she cannot afford the distraction.

Besides, Ruth isn't someone who goes on casual dates. She knows that approximately five people are murdered in Australia per week. This is the kind of fact she can readily retrieve from her archives. She also knows this number is closer to six murders a week here in New York City, but from a much smaller population base. This might suggest people are less murderous where Gabe comes from, but she's still not going to offer him her phone number. She never gives it out, which is something that confounds Owen. She can see her boss watching her now, though he's pretending not to. Nothing would please her boss more than if she took this handsome stranger home tonight.

Setting a napkin and a glass of water down on the bar, Ruth suddenly feels like the indoor heating has been turned up to November.

"Last drinks," she says sharply.

Ruth-Ann Baker, modern-day chthonic deity, already has a date lined up with her demons. No need to fill up her dance card any further.

Ruth spends Monday morning checking for any news on Coco Wilson. She finds only one important update to her case. A reward is now being offered: $10,000 for information that might lead to Coco's safe return. She once read that monetary rewards are sometimes offered when investigators already have a suspect in mind. They consider the money as bait, a lure, encouraging someone close to that suspect to come forward. Especially if they're currently financially reliant on the perpetrator.

Something Ruth has never been able to answer: Who phoned in the anonymous tip about a child's shoe that led Ressler's canine grandfather, John Douglas, to that house on Longview Drive?

No reward had been offered back then. If it's a strategy being employed by the Hoben Police Department today, does that make it more or less likely that Coco's own family had something to do with her disappearance? Because all that initial finger-pointing has shifted to outright accusation now. It doesn't help that Coco's adoptive father is considered an outsider in Hoben. A Black man in a predominantly white neighborhood, who showed up from out of state not long before Coco disappeared. It's obvious to Ruth that most of this online chatter about Leo Wilson is racism, dressed up as concern. And so many of the accusations are wildly outlandish. Some insist that Coco never even made it to Hoben when the family moved from Louisiana, despite concrete proof that she attended the town's local elementary school in the weeks before she went missing. Her new classmates have even created a little shrine to her at the entrance to the school. Teddy bears, flowers. A Princess Leia doll. And a hand-painted sign. *Come home soon, Coco!*

Ruth wonders how Bill and Patty Lovely feel when they drive past that shrine. There used to be a memorial to Beth at the playground she was abducted from. A swing set painted her favorite colors. And a plaque with her name and the short span of her life engraved on it. Ruth remembers when it was unveiled, right before she moved to New York. Brand-new and shiny at the time, but what does that tribute look like all these years later? She has no idea how long a swing set is designed to last.

If Coco never makes it home, how long will those teddy bears and that doll be left out front of the school? Ruth can't imagine they'll still be there by summer. Memory-keeping is a full-time job, she knows, and most are not up to the task.

This makes her think about her own parents. How they have no idea of her current plans. If forgetting is her family's foundation, omission might be considered the roof over their heads. This is how Ellis managed to quietly pine for his coworker for three whole years, waiting until Ruth turned twenty to ask his wife for a divorce. This is how Cynthia planned her sabbatical in Italy, without advising anyone until after she'd left town. Some omissions are bigger than others, of course. But they've all sprung from the same tacit agreement: the three of them will do anything to avoid causing each other unnecessary pain. And if that means only ever being a family at a distance, so be it. Arm's length is still within reach of each other.

Ruth is considering that distance when her phone buzzes. She half expects it to be one of her parents, but it's a text from Owen.

Hey, Dana Scully. Crocodile Dundee left something behind you might be interested in . . .

I'll come by this afternoon, she messages back.

Ruth justifies this quick response by telling herself that she needs to pass the day in some kind of fashion. It's better than sitting here dwelling on memorials and memories.

This Gabe from Australia might be nothing more than a distraction. But she has to admit that he's a very good-looking distraction. And if Ruth recalls correctly, even Special Agent Dana Scully had a weakness for men who looked good.

Owen is deep in a phone conversation with an errant rum supplier.

Ruth sits across from him at one of Sweeney's two outside tables, eyes closed, her face turned toward the midday sun. In just a few weeks, summer will have officially arrived, and half the year will be gone. Ruth has never been able to define her relationship with time. She has always imagined herself to be lithologic, a series of layers. And if the strata of her body delineate the significant events of her life, she has trouble seeing these moments in relation to time itself. Five years since her retreat to Joe and Gideon's farm. Nineteen years since she moved with her parents to New York City. Go back a few months from there, and you would reach the hours and days that seemingly no longer exist. From her therapist, Ruth learned that a seven-year-old lives at the boundary of something called childhood amnesia. Around this age, memories of infancy and early childhood start to get hazy, harder to retrieve. A predictor of how completely they retreat from view? Whether an event is continuously talked about, whether it becomes calcified through repetition. It's no wonder she so often feels like a blank slate when it comes to whole years of her childhood.

Mostly, Ruth feels like she exists in a liminal space, perpetually at the threshold of what is remembered and what is forgotten. This makes her think of Gideon's ancient Hecate, whom she started reading up on overnight. As a liminal goddess, Hecate moved smoothly between these spaces, between times, between states of being, when all Ruth feels is stuck at the edge of things. Does that make what she is about to do a leap—or her next fall?

Unsettled by these ruminations, Ruth opens the cloth-covered notebook Owen delightedly handed over when she arrived. Gabe's notebook. The one he'd set down on the bar last night. Owen found it on the floor, under the bar stool Gabe had been perched on. Brushed aside somewhere between first drinks and that abruptly announced last call.

Flicking through it, Ruth sees that the first few pages are filled with schedules. Flight numbers, their dates and times. Then a series of addresses, some of them recognizable as being from New York, Brooklyn mostly, along with a string of cell numbers with initials noted after each one. Girls he's met here, Ruth immediately assumes, before telling herself that it's none of her business. Still, she keeps turning the pages. Next, she encounters a few short passages that read like diary entries. Gabe's take on New York, which offers little that others haven't said about this city many times before. How busy the streets are, how impatient and indifferent people can be. How friendly. How dirty and smelly and shiny and sanitized it all is, and could he live here?

Probably not. Unless I win the lottery.

Ruth tells herself to stop reading. It feels intrusive, now that she can see him right there on the page. But then she sees *herself*. A pencil sketch of her face that, despite the simple lines, is immediately recognizable. The way one of her eyebrows is shorter than the other. The three holes in her left ear versus the single piercing in her right. The ever-present crinkle between her eyes, and the messiness of curly hair that had been pulled up then taken out of its topknot too many times last night. Because when she'd talked to Gabe, she'd found herself unsure of where to rest her fluttering hands.

When had he drawn this? When she took a late dinner break, leaving him alone at the bar for all of fifteen minutes? Having someone draw your portrait without you knowing feels like an uninvited intimacy, like being watched through a window.

Hastily scanning the rest of the notebook, Ruth sees only blank pages, and this somehow makes it worse. The anomaly of seeing herself in the middle of this man's diary—and then nothing. She feels her heartbeat quicken, the *3—2—1—Go!* of panic rising in her chest, but as she closes Gabe's notebook and puts it face down on the table, she tells herself she should feel flattered. That it's supposed to feel nice to be seen.

Isn't that what everyone wants? Those who have nothing to hide, at least.

Owen appears to be wrapping up his call; he is mouthing something at her to suggest as much. With the sun still warming her face, Ruth feels her desire to run subside. Perhaps this whole podcast ruse is making her bolder. As Owen hangs up on the rum supplier, she does the most un–Ruth-Ann Baker thing with her discomfort. She picks up Gabe's notebook, opens it to that sketch of her face, and writes her cell number underneath. Then underlines it three times.

"Make sure Gabe gets this when he comes back in," she says, pushing the notebook across the table at Owen.

She'll soon be nine thousand miles away. Ruth has always valued the physical safety that comes with distance.

If only her mind worked the same way.

———

The Ancient Greeks had a name for the ghosts of girls who died too young. They called them the aōroi. The untimely, unfinished dead. Excluded from the underworld, but no longer at home on earth, these restless spirits found their salvation in Hecate. The goddess of both night and light, and a gifted necromancer, Hecate not only spoke to the dead, she could compel them.

Flanked by her faithful hounds, Hecate lived at the boundaries of our worlds, and she frequently crossed them—bringing her dead girls with her.

It was three in the morning when Ruth came across these words in an essay dedicated to Gideon's goddess, Hecate. It made her wonder if her uncle knew more about her plans than he'd let on.

All Ruth can say for sure, as she prepares to leave for New Zealand, is that the more she learns about Hecate, the more it feels like looking in a mirror . . . and finally seeing her own reflection in the glass.

ROSE

SIXTEEN

It has taken Ruth just over twenty-eight hours to get from New York City to Marama River, New Zealand.

She has no idea if she's tired. At some point on the journey, one that involved three flights, interminable waits in airport lounges, and the half sleep that comes with never fully tuning out your surroundings, tiredness became moot. Ruth has maintained enough lucidity to get from one place to the next, but not enough to hold on to any coherent thought. She left the last of those somewhere over the Pacific. Dozing through the box set of a comedy series that wasn't as funny as she'd remembered, Ruth woke up on the descent into Auckland, thinking about sea-glass eyes. One bumpy domestic flight along the west coast later, and she was getting picked up at the regional airport closest to Marama River by an elderly, kind-faced man with a name tag reading *George Morehu*.

He's just told her the Mulvaney farm is coming up, next on the left.

Ruth is grateful for the confirmation. All the road signs are in kilometers, and her cell phone lost reception soon after the shuttle van turned inland from the small, coastal airport where she was George's only customer on this Thursday afternoon, New Zealand time. From there, the serpentine path to Marama River has taken Ruth over an hour's worth of miles, along a road bordered by dense native bush on one side and steep sandstone cliffs on the other. On the flight down from Auckland, the hills and valleys far below had made Ruth think of a reclining woman, draped in a verdant robe; from her small plane window, she had traced the jut of hip bone, the curve of spine, and felt humbled by this ancient, rolling beauty. On the ground, the landscape slithers past; up close, it seems more reptilian than recumbent. And because George has kept his driver's-side window down the whole ride, Ruth can smell the just-rained rot of felled wood, the mossy damp of slick rock and sodden earth, in the air. It is all so abundant, so Jurassic, she wouldn't be surprised if a dinosaur came lumbering through the trees.

"They know you coming, girl?" George asks over his shoulder, interrupting this thought.

As one of the few sentences her driver has spoken since helping load her bags into the van, Ruth can't tell if the old man is joking. At the airport, holding up a sign with her name on it, he told her that New York was his favorite city he'd never been to, which gave them two minutes of conversation, tops. On the drive itself, he'd put on an old Stevie Wonder album, turned up just loud enough to prevent them from speaking any further.

"Uh . . . ," she responds, wondering why he thought to ask that.

"The Mulvaney family don't get many visitors," George continues, after turning back to face the road. Ruth can't see the expression on his face.

"I've got your pickup booked for Sunday morning. But you let me know if you need me to come get you sooner, eh."

Sooner than Sunday? She is only spending three nights with

Rose. It wouldn't even be one night, if not for the fact that, in her haste to organize this trip, Ruth had underestimated just how far from anywhere the Mulvaney farm is. She's since discovered that Marama River isn't actually a town. Technically, it's a rural settlement; the "village" off the main road consists of a church, a recreation hall, and a cemetery, but there is no main street, and there are definitely no hotels nearby; no motels or handy homestay options, either—if you don't count Rose Mulvaney's own house, where, at Rose's invitation and against her better judgment, Ruth will now be spending those three nights.

Which George seems to think is too many.

It's less than seventy-two hours, Ruth keeps telling herself. And a real podcaster would no doubt jump at the chance to have that kind of access to, that kind of intimacy with, their interview subject.

Still, Ruth feels a small panic dislodge, flap its wings in her chest, just as the van turns off the main road into an unmarked driveway. Tall, leafy trees lining the road on both sides block any view of the Mulvaney farm's rolling fields and the mountain range presiding over them; Ruth knows these hidden details from maps, just as she knows there is a river that carves its way down from those ranges, through the fields, and then out to the sea.

A river upon whose wintry banks two teenage girls were murdered. One strangled, the other beaten, before both of their unconscious bodies were pushed into the icy waters of Marama River to drown. Did Peter Mulvaney march his young victims through these very trees six years ago, herding them to their death? Ruth wishes she could ask the branches tapping at the roof of the van what they saw. What they remember. It seems to her there must be forests and lakes and fields all over the world aching with the memories of a girl's last moments.

George's shuttle van takes one final bend, loose gravel flying from its tires. As the view opens up, the Mulvaney farmhouse emerges from a tangle of overgrown grass, dotted with the carcasses of discarded tools. A field roller with missing tires. A rusted rotary tiller and a snap-toothed excavator bucket, tipped on its side. Ruth recognizes this equipment from her time with Joe and Gideon, though most of her uncles' machinery still looks like it's just arrived via a John Deere catalog. Likewise, their neat, well-maintained farmhouse in Gardiner looks nothing like the Mulvaney homestead. Ruth can feel George's eyes on her as she steps out of the van to take in the peeling wood of the single-story house, the dangling gutters, the dilapidated porch, and the way the whole structure seems to sag with an unseen weight. Next to the front door, Ruth can see a jumble of muddy boots, below three all-weather coats hanging from a horizontal beam. Three, where there used to be four. That fourth hook is still there.

"Let me help you," George says, as if Ruth hasn't simply been standing there, silent and staring.

He brings her suitcase from the back of the van, deposits it next to her, then nods at the house.

They know you coming, girl?

Those wings beat harder in Ruth's chest as she contemplates this kind-faced man driving away, leaving her here.

"Maybe—" Ruth starts to say, when the front door opens and a woman appears in the frame. Makeup free, with gray hairs speckled at her temples, she's wearing leggings and an oversize jumper that swamps her small frame. She has a thin smile. Wide eyes.

Rose Mulvaney. Annie Whitaker. *Julie Jordan.*

Flustered, Ruth turns to thank George for his help, but he has already returned to his van. He starts the engine and pulls away from the Mulvaney house even before Rose has stepped down from the porch.

The two women stare at each other across the driveway.

"Thank you for agreeing to meet me," Ruth says finally, holding out her hand.

There is a pause before Rose takes it.

"I'm glad you made it," she says, and Ruth can already hear the lie.

———

For dinner, Ruth is served warm bread and homemade minestrone, the bones of something meaty still floating in the pot.

"You're not a vegetarian, are you?" Rose asks Ruth, setting a steaming bowl down in front of her.

"Not tonight," she jokes, with a smile that isn't returned.

As Rose silently takes her own place at this battered kitchen table, Ruth flushes at the clear rebuff. Ever since Rose led her inside just over an hour earlier, she has been trying to find some spark in the woman. Some proof of life. Her host has been polite and hospitable, in the sense of clean towels for the bathroom and dinner served. But she seems—barely here.

It's unnerving. And the last thing Ruth wants to feel is unnerved by Rose Mulvaney. Here in this house, on this farm, where there is no cell phone reception and, apparently, no Wi-Fi either.

("They keep saying it'll come one day," Rose said when Ruth asked. "But we tend to get forgotten all the way out here.")

For what feels like the tenth time since George disappeared down that driveway, Ruth reminds herself that she has no reason to be afraid. Even if this *is* the girl Beth remembers talking to in the playground nineteen years ago, that doesn't automatically mean she's dangerous. As Beth herself had pointed out, Ruth has no idea what kind of relationship Ethan Oswald had with the young Annie Whitaker. And even if it was similar to how Oswald treated Amity, wouldn't that make this woman one of his victims too? She was only seventeen at the time.

Ruth suppresses a sigh as she looks over at Rose, then around the room. This kitchen, like much of the interior of the farmhouse, has the feel of something unfinished. As if a renovation was halted halfway. It's not just the paint-stripped cupboard doors and the naked, dangling curtain hooks above the windows; Ruth senses an absence of intention, like the Mulvaney home is permanently on pause. What plans for this house, for this family, were abandoned when the police knocked at Rose Mulvaney's door?

(Something Ruth has never been able to decide. Are you most yourself right before a terrible thing rearranges you? Or is it what happens next that makes you who you are?)

She puts down her spoon.

"Is it true that you lived in Hoben, Connecticut, as a teenager, Rose?"

She nearly called her *Julie*.

Rose visibly stiffens, but does not look up from her dinner.

"I hated that place," she says quietly. "My parents never should have let me go."

"It's very young to go halfway across the world on your own," Ruth agrees, hoping she sounds like the sympathetic, yet curious, podcaster she's supposed to be.

Rose meets Ruth's gaze across the table.

"Lots of Kiwi kids do it. They're keen to get out there and see the world," she explains. "And I was no different. I had dreams of bright lights and Broadway. But I got sent to small-town USA instead."

Staring back at Rose, Ruth struggles to reconcile the pale, plain woman sitting across from her with a young girl who thought she was destined for the stage. She turns this incongruity around, examines it. Pricks her thumb on a thought.

What if the way Rose seems as downtrodden as her farmhouse is simply a performance she's putting on for her guest?

"I know Hoben," Ruth presses on. "Why did you *hate* it there?"

Rose shrugs.

"It just wasn't the right place for me."

"*Why?*" Ruth repeats, and even as that single syllable slips from her mouth, she understands her mistake. The plea in her tone, making it sound like this is the most important question she has ever asked.

Like she has no clue what the answer will be.

It's immediately clear that Rose catches this. There's something about the way she looks at Ruth now; her expression is not triumphant exactly, but something akin to relief flickers across her face. As if she realizes that, whatever her secrets might be, the woman who's come from New York to interview her doesn't know them all.

For the first time, Rose shows her teeth when she smiles.

"It's been a long day," she says across the table. "For you especially, Ruth. Why don't we save the questions until tomorrow. I promise to give your podcast my full attention then."

She definitely looks like a different person now. Less shrunk into her clothing. Sharper at her edges, somehow. It makes Ruth think about how some animals play dead in the presence of a predator. Tonic immobility, it's called. When prey becomes unresponsive to stimuli in order to prevent further attack. It's obvious, watching Rose lean back in her chair, that something has just changed between them.

It's like she no longer perceives Ruth as a threat.

Which means she did see her as a threat, before that slipup. This makes Ruth's desperate *why* worth it, she decides. Because if Rose is performing for her tonight, if she did think, even for a moment, that Ruth was the dangerous one, it can only mean she really does have something to hide.

———————

Rose suggests they get a little fresh air before bed. Most of the farm has now been leased out, she tells Ruth, but she's held on to a few fields—*a couple of paddocks*—behind the house. She grazes three goats and her four horses there. It's always nice to go say good night, she says.

"Were you born in New York, Ruth?" Rose inquires as they get up from the table. "So few people seem to be, these days."

"I grew up there," Ruth answers.

"Well, then you were a lucky girl. But there's nothing like the night sky in this part of the world. Especially if you've always lived in a big city."

Through the long kitchen window over the sink Ruth sees an ink-black sky with nothing—no streetlights, no other houses—to lift the stain of darkness.

It's just a walk, she tells herself. There's nothing to be afraid of.

It's early winter in New Zealand, and Rose advises Ruth to "rug up" against the cold. She leaves the kitchen to retrieve her puffer jacket from her suitcase, set down in a bedroom that clearly belongs to one of the two Mulvaney daughters, currently boarding at a Catholic girls' school a two-hour drive away.

"Be careful," Beth starts as Ruth zips up her jacket, but Ruth brushes her worry aside.

"It's *horses*, Beth. I'll be fine."

"Something isn't right with that woman," Beth tries again, but Ruth has already pulled a beanie down over her ears.

"There's only one way to find out," she says, before heading back to Rose Mulvaney, waiting at the front door.

All four of Rose's horses are rescues. Kaimanawa, named for the mid–North Island ranges these wild mares once roamed, before getting caught up in an annual muster. Rose adopted a mother and her foal soon after Peter went to jail, and a year later she took on two additional fillies. It's something she'd always wanted to do, she told Ruth, as she directed her along a gravel path behind the house. Left on the farm alone, it felt like the perfect time to make this long-held dream come true. Especially since every other dream she'd had for herself had shattered.

When Rose said this, there was no trace of self-pity in her tone. As if having your world fall apart was just a fact of life.

"I was going to be a Broadway star," she scoffed, shaking her head. "But I became a music teacher to a bunch of country kids and married a farmer, instead. And life certainly had other plans for me after that."

On that walk, it was like being with a different Rose, again. She was self-deprecating, forthright. Ruth could only wonder which version of the woman she was going to get next.

The two of them are now leaning against a metal gate, waiting for Mamie, Honey, Kiki, and Belle, Rose's beloved rescues, to amble over from the other side of a large field. As Rose calls out to them, almost crooning, Ruth gazes up at the canvas of bright, beautiful stars now visible above them, and finds herself thinking about Kelly and Nichole.

Was this the kind of sky they looked up at from the riverbed, the night they died?

It is unfathomably brutal, Ruth thinks. The scale of Peter Mulvaney's violence that night.

And yet Rose stayed in Marama River, even when her parents packed up and moved to Australia; they had also funded their granddaughters' escape, Rose explained, by paying the boarding school fees she could not have afforded on her own.

"I wanted to keep a home for my girls," she'd said, when Ruth asked if she ever thought of leaving too.

"My daughters are my world," Rose says now, her gaze fixed on the approaching horses. "Any mistakes I've made are mine alone to carry."

Mistakes.

Just how many has she made? Ruth wonders.

"I don't want them involved in this podcast," Rose adds, just as the horses arrive in their little herd, sniffing at the gate. Kiki, the smallest of them, immediately reaches over the fence to mouth at Ruth's jacket, finding the zip and tugging. Hard.

Rose stifles a laugh. "She's testing you," she says, pushing at Kiki's neck until the horse lets go of Ruth's jacket and comes to sniff at her rescuer's pockets instead.

"Horses are hierarchical creatures," she continues, as if she hadn't mentioned the podcast at all. "They like to see who they can bully. What they can get away with."

"I know a few humans like that," a voice says loudly behind them, and it's not only Ruth who jumps as the speaker emerges out of the dark.

It—she—is a long-legged girl in a school uniform, her neat outfit and prim ponytail at odds with the feline glow of her eyes.

"Juno!" Rose exclaims. "You scared me half to death." She shakes her head as if not quite comprehending the girl's presence. "What are you doing here?"

"I wanted to meet this special visitor all the way from New York City," Rose Mulvaney's eldest daughter says, looking from her mother to Ruth and back again.

"Come on then," Juno adds, reaching for Rose's arm. "Let's go back to the house before she freezes to death out here."

SEVENTEEN

Peter Mulvaney left the engagement party when it was in full swing.

It was nearly midnight, and despite the ongoing revelry, the girls' babysitters needed to get home. They had an interschool netball tournament the next day, over an hour's drive from Marama River. As team captain, seventeen-year-old Kelly needed to be on the road by 7 a.m.; the first game was at 9:30 a.m. Fourteen-year-old Nichole, ever faithful to her older, more athletic cousin, was tagging along to take care of the refreshments. Orange slices and chilled water. Chocolate bars from the canteen when the players needed a sugar rush. Nichole loved helping out in any way she could.

To read the crime reports, it would appear Nichole Morley died trying to help her cousin too. From the defensive wounds on her body, it seems she fought, not just for her own life, but for Kelly Parker's too. Peter Mulvaney told the police that Nichole attacked him first; that when he beat her unconscious with a large rock from the riverbank, it wasn't just an accident—it was self-defense.

Nobody believed a word he said.

What he said was this. When he got back to the farmhouse on the night of the party, he'd offered to make two trips. It was always his intention to take Kelly home first, then come back for Nichole. With Rose still at the party, he didn't want to leave eleven-year-old Juno and eight-year-old Minnie alone in the house for too long. Juno had recently started having vivid nightmares that caused her to wake up and scream the house down. She was so disorientated after, she needed someone to rock her back to sleep.

On the drive to Kelly's house, Peter said, she asked him to stop at Marama Bend before dropping her home. She wanted to spend some time with him down at their "special place" by the river. They fooled around. Things got a little rough. But Kelly liked it that way. Nichole must have followed on foot, taking a shortcut across the farm. When she saw him play-fighting with Kelly, she flew at him, attacked him. He defended himself. He said that things got out of hand.

He said.

What he didn't say: Nichole's injuries were the most severe. Peter Mulvaney reserved his rage for the girl who fought back.

Because the deal had always been supplication.

Kelly Parker understood the brief. She had been compliant for two whole years, ever since she turned fifteen and her nearest neighbor, the father of the two children she so often babysat, first put his hands on her thigh and said, *Doesn't that feel nice?*

Doesn't that feel nice? Kelly Parker never answered this question in the pages of her diaries, the ones that were used as evidence in the murder trial. Diaries that proved Peter Mulvaney started abusing her two years before he murdered her. It seems they spent a lot of time in that "special place."

"You've read the diaries, I assume," Juno says to Ruth now. "I know there are still copies out there."

The three of them are sitting at the kitchen table. Rose drinking a glass of pinot noir, Ruth sipping at a sauvignon blanc, and Juno, all of seventeen, holding a tumbler of whisky in her hand. This had surprised Ruth, the casual way Juno poured herself an alcoholic drink when they arrived back at the house. There was no trace of defiance on her face when she sat down, either. As if drinking hard liquor in front of her mother was something she did all the time.

In the light of the kitchen, Ruth can see that feline gleam she'd noted down at the horse paddocks is a product of the metallic gold slash of Juno's heavy eyeliner, turned up into a bold cat's eye. The school uniform she'd been wearing when she first arrived—the classic tartan skirt and white shirt, the knee-high socks and solid shoes—has been discarded in favor of black tights and a sweater with a large NYU logo on the front. The neat ponytail is still in place; Ruth suspects the young girl knows the severity of the hairstyle draws even more attention to her startling eyes, but in the way of the most self-possessed teenage girls, she has mastered the act of pretending not to care.

Walking back to the house, Ruth had listened as Juno blithely explained to her mother that she'd hitched a ride home with Pauly, her PE teacher, whose girlfriend lived nearby. *Yes*, the Matron knew she'd left the hostel. *No*, she wasn't missing any important classes tomorrow. And *no*, Minnie hadn't wanted to come home tomorrow night. She was going to stay with her friend Pania for the weekend, as per their original agreement. Juno seems to be entirely in control of whatever this agreement might have been.

In fact, she seems to be in charge of all things. It was Juno who suggested they sit down in the kitchen to talk, and Juno who deftly turned the conversation to *The Other Women*, Ruth's supposed podcast, not long after first drinks were poured. She advised Ruth that she was taking a communications class—media studies, she called it—at school next term, and the students would be required to produce a podcast of their own. She was thinking about doing hers on a real-life murder, she told Ruth. Though she hadn't decided which one yet.

"So when Mum told me you were interested in featuring her on your true crime podcast, I knew I had to meet you," Juno explained. "You can even interview me, if you want. I *was* the kid Kels and Nic babysat, after all."

"Juno!" Rose had scolded then, her first show of actually being the parent in their relationship. But this hadn't seemed to faze her daughter.

"Whatever, *Mother*. I'm just trying to help."

By then, jet lag was wreaking its havoc, making Ruth feel as if she might topple backward from her hard-backed dining chair. It seemed easiest to go along with Juno and worry about her real questions for Rose tomorrow. She had said Ruth would have her full attention then, after all.

So she'd set her phone down on the table and opened up her voice memo app.

"You're recording a podcast with *that*?" Juno had asked incredulously, which made Ruth glad she'd gone to the trouble of buying proper recording equipment to bring on her trip. It meant she was able to answer honestly that tonight was just about taking notes. She was saving the good stuff for tomorrow.

As Ruth nods at Juno's latest question, saying that yes, she has read copies of Kelly's diaries, Rose looks from her daughter to her houseguest.

She sets down her wineglass.

"Young girls lie," she says quietly.

"So do old men," Juno shoots back.

"Your father—" Rose starts, but Juno cuts her off.

"Yeah, yeah. I've heard it all before, Mum. Dad was the *adult*. The grown fucking man. No matter what you think of Kelly."

"I'm going to bed," Rose announces abruptly, before Ruth can ask what she *does* think of Kelly Parker.

As Rose leaves the kitchen, Juno pulls a face at her mother's retreating back.

"Why'd she even invite you here if she's not going to say anything? So bloody typical."

Ruth has no idea what is typical of Rose Mulvaney. She can only shrug and suggest they call it a night too. The temptation to keep Juno talking is strong, but she resists. Despite all her posturing, Juno is still a kid; her youth makes the ethics of extracting information from her, especially under false circumstances, feel ambiguous at best. Outright devious, at worst.

"Do you even know where you're sleeping?" Juno asks, clearly annoyed at being dismissed for a second time. "Because I saw your bags in *my* room, Ruth."

Ruth opens her mouth to say she's happy to sleep on the couch, when Juno sighs.

"You can have it. I'll sleep in Minnie's bed. It's my old mattress, anyways." Another sigh. "We're not big on new around here, as you can probably tell."

A few minutes later, Ruth finds herself settled in Juno's single bed, a fresh, soft sheet between her skin and a pile of heavy, scratchy blankets. She's grateful for their warmth if not their texture; the temperature outside must be near freezing, and there does not appear to be any central heating in the house. She shivers as she switches off the bedside lamp. The immediate darkness of the room is thick, soupy. Like Ruth could scoop up handfuls of it, though when she tries, her fingers slice through the air without any resistance. She can barely make out her own extremities, and the rest of Juno's room has disappeared into the black. The poster of the lone resister in Tiananmen Square, facing down those tanks. The framed quote Ruth didn't recognize, something about *Risk!* and not caring for the opinion of others. The stack of books in the corner, a precarious tower of summer reads and at least five of those tomes they say you must read before you die. And the pile of folded washing on an armchair that looks like it's been there for weeks. A *teenager's* room, Ruth thinks, albeit missing the usual fingerprints: the goofy photographs of friends and random assortment of souvenirs that so often assert a burgeoning identity. Juno has left very few traces of herself in this room.

Ruth contemplates this evening's surprise guest. It's not that she hasn't given any thought to the offspring of men like Peter Mulvaney. She's read and watched a ton of interviews featuring grown children grappling with the sins of their murderous fathers. And their pain is always obvious, no matter how much time has passed. It makes Ruth glad she didn't push Juno for more information just now. Thanks to her father's appalling behavior, the girl has a heavy burden to bear.

If anything, Ruth should be trying to protect Juno Mulvaney. She makes a promise to do better in that department. And then— it must be because the jet lag has made her woozy—Ruth finds herself thinking about Gabe. His sea-glass eyes briefly flash in front of her like a beacon, before her head drops to the side, and she sinks through the bed, down into the promise of dreamless sleep.

Outside, a mournful bird hoots its sorrows. On the bedside table, the glinting spirals of Gideon's triskelion are no match for the darkness.

Mercifully, the dead girls stay quiet tonight.

EIGHTEEN

There was never any sign. People always want there to be a sign.

"They don't ever believe me, or they think I wasn't looking hard enough. But Peter wasn't living some double life that I completely missed. He just made a very bad decision that became a series of bad decisions. It was out of character, what he did that night. I mean, he could barely euthanize a dying calf. Ask anyone. Or ask anyone back then, at least. They'll all tell you: Peter really was one of the good guys."

Rose, over coffee the next morning. Talking into the newly unboxed voice recorder Ruth set down on the kitchen table. Her daughter across the room, leaning against the sink as she listened to her mother's speech, despite being asked to leave. In the playback, Ruth can hear Juno's snort of derision when Rose calls Peter a good guy.

All Ruth really wanted to do, when they sat down together after breakfast, was return to Hoben. Take Rose back to that town, after coming so close last night. But with Juno always there, she knew she had to wait. And wait, and wait. Because the girl has barely left her mother's side. Right now, Juno is taking a shower while Rose is in her bedroom getting dressed after her own shower, and Ruth, sitting on the bed in Juno's room, could make her move. But that feels too much like an ambush, and Ruth knows she can't afford to upset Rose or make her feel uneasy. Not when she's out here in the middle of nowhere, with no way of contacting George Morehu to come pick her up if she was asked to leave.

This might be the longest Ruth has ever been offline since she first got a cell phone. She can't even text Joe or Owen, or tell the Lovelys where she is. Nor can she hunt for updates on Coco Wilson, or see how Amity is faring in Paris (no doubt she will have posted endless updates from her time in the City of Light), let alone check whether @RoderickAlleyn has made any progress on finding Helen Torrent. She has push notifications set up for that, but she has no way of receiving them here.

"Is it worth it?" Beth asks. "Spending all that money, and now you can't *afford* to piss Annie Whitaker off?"

Is that what's got you so bothered? Ruth wants to ask. Is it the fact that she's used some of that life insurance payout to fund this trip? It seems unlikely, but then again, they've never been in this position before. Outside of funding her membership on *What Happened to Her*, Ruth had previously refused to touch Beth's death policy money. It's been sitting in her account, gaining interest, for years. A tainted benefaction. Until now.

"Why so serious?" Juno asks from the doorway, and when Ruth doesn't immediately answer, she comes into the room and starts rummaging through those folded clothes piled on the chair. "Can't spend the day in this," she says over her shoulder, indicating the rough-looking towel that is wrapped around her body. "Do you *mind*?" she adds, which Ruth takes as her cue to exit Juno's bedroom and leave her to get dressed.

Wandering back to the kitchen, Ruth finds Rose has resumed

her regular seat at the table, her eyes closed to the slant of winter sun coming through the window.

She opens her eyes as Ruth approaches and then narrows them briefly.

"Is my daughter bothering you?" she asks.

"Not at all," Ruth says hastily. "It's nice to be around someone so . . . *sure* of themselves. I'm not sure I was like that at seventeen."

"I most certainly wasn't," Rose says. "But Juno's always marched to the beat of her own—well, her own entire orchestra, really."

Like that slant of sunlight, Ruth senses the slim band of opportunity in front of her right now.

"When you were seventeen—" she starts, just as Juno bursts into the room.

"Quit talking about me like I'm not here, Mother," she says, before swooping in to give Rose a kiss on her cheek.

Wearing combat boots and a leather jacket over some kind of black catsuit, Juno looks, in this moment, like a real-life superhero.

"We should go get coffee," she tells Rose, before turning to Ruth. "Sound good?"

"Sure," Ruth answers, trying not to dwell on her latest lost moment. She still has forty-eight hours at the Mulvaney farm, she reminds herself, which means there's plenty of time to get Rose alone.

Although there is something she wants even more than a decent coffee.

"Can we go somewhere that has Wi-Fi?" she asks, and her obvious desperation makes Rose and Juno laugh the same laugh, so that for a split second, their two faces morph into one.

———————

Their chosen coffee shop turns out to be in the nearest actual town, twenty minutes' drive away. Maybe even longer, but for

Juno's lead foot. They take a series of back roads to get there, speeding over hills as vertiginous as Ruth has ever seen, the sensation from the back seat not unlike being on a roller coaster. And she hates roller coasters. They make her dizzy.

After one particularly steep ascent, the car momentarily airborne over the crest of the hill, Ruth's cell phone begins to buzz in her bag. At last, reception! But no matter how badly she wants to look at her phone, trying to read at this speed would surely add to her dizziness. Reaching into her bag, resting her hand on the warm comfort of the phone's vibrations, Ruth tells herself a few more minutes of this digital detox can't hurt.

Soon they are traveling down a two-block main street with four pedestrian crossings. Juno has finally slowed down, and Ruth can see colorful baskets of flowers hanging from the awnings of a secondhand bookstore, a bakery, a thrift shop. A three-story pub takes up one entire corner, while at the end of the main street, beyond an ungated railway crossing, the pavement gives way to giant lots with high, barbed-wire fences and signs advertising timber, car parts, every kind of steel. The café that Juno points out is just over the tracks, which seem to divide the country town into two distinct parts.

When they enter the café, Juno strides confidently to one of the few empty booths, near the back of what appears to once have been a church. The trio sit beneath a stained-glass window featuring the Three Wise Men and a series of barn animals, before Juno and Rose both excuse themselves for the bathroom. Alone, and stationary, Ruth finally gets to check her phone.

We miss you! A selfie of Joe, Gideon, and Ressler on the couch.

Message when you can. All good here. Are you?? A follow-up text from Joe.

Nancy Drew! The boy was in here, asking after you. Owen, part one.

Tell. Me. Everything. Owen, parts two, three, and four.

Hey. An unknown number.

Then a second message, sent the same minute, and three more after that.

It's Gabe. You probably need to know that part.

So, hey. It's Gabe.

The creepy guy with the notebook.

The NOT creepy guy with the notebook who can explain everything.

Timestamps show a break of six minutes before Gabe's final text.

Owen said you're in New Zealand. How cool. Anyway, if you get this and you're not too weirded out by my (cough, cough) artistry, shoot me a message back. Gabe.

"Whoa! Who's got you smiling like that?"

Juno, back from the bathroom, stands above Ruth, smirking.

"A boyfriend back in New York?"

I don't have a boyfriend, Ruth goes to answer, but she stops herself. This kid doesn't need to know about her private life. And what would she say about Gabe, anyway? *Oh, I met this cute Australian at the bar I work at, and he drew this weirdly accurate picture of me, and that maybe means he likes me. But it could also mean that he's a potential stalker who will one day try to kill me. So I don't know whether to be charmed or alarmed, and—*

Ruth sets her phone face down on the table. There's no need to go into any of that. She sees Juno raise her eyebrows at the gesture before turning her head to look at her mother, currently standing near the café's front counter. No words are exchanged, but Juno suddenly stiffens.

"Come on," she says quietly. "We'll go somewhere else for coffee."

Ruth doesn't have time to ask what is going on as Juno picks up her cell phone and shoves it at her before striding to her mother's side. Arm around her shoulder, Juno steers Rose from the café. Following them, Ruth watches as both Mulvaneys hold their heads high until they are outside and halfway back to the car. Only then, scrambling to catch up, does she see the way the two of them slump against each other. A brief collapse, before mother and daughter separate, straightening their shoulders and reasserting the distance between them.

"They make shit coffee anyway," Ruth hears Juno mutter.

———

It happens all the time. Being told they're not welcome somewhere. It's just never happened there until today.

As it turns out, Nichole Morley's third cousin started working at the (lamely named, Juno scoffs) Church Café a few weeks back. If they'd known, they never would have gone in the first place, Juno huffed, as she drove them home. Though that might have been the last place the Mulvaneys could get served between here and bloody Australia, she'd added.

Rose remained silent the whole car ride back. When Juno parks back at the farm, her mother wordlessly exits the car, walks straight past the house, and disappears behind it.

"She'll go hang with her horses for a bit," Juno says. "That's what she does when she's upset and doesn't want to show it." She scowls. "I hate this place," she continues. "I can't wait to leave for good one day and take Minnie with me."

I hated that place, Ruth hears Rose say about Hoben, Connecticut.

"I bet you're a wonderful big sister," she tells Juno, because she wants to say one true thing to this girl.

"Yeah, well. I don't know any different." Juno shrugs. "When we were kids, I used to pretend I was an actual goddess. Like, not just in name. And my power was being able to reflect people's anger back at them, so that anytime they tried to hurt someone, they'd just hurt themselves instead. Minnie, my little Minerva, was all about extracting rage, morphing it into something better. Me, I just wanted to turn it back on the person. Make them destroy themselves in the process. My sister and I are different that way." Juno juts her chin. "If I can be the hard-ass, Minnie has a better chance of staying sweet. *Soft*. One less life hardened up by this shit, you know?"

Then, as she has done so often in the short time since they met, Juno recalibrates.

"Fuck it," she says. "Do you want to go on a tiki tour of this shitty place? I can show you where Kelly and Nichole died."

Ruth had been about to ask if there was some other place she could get phone reception. She has texts she needs to respond to. Requests she wants to check in on.

But those needs dissolve the second Juno makes her offer.

"Let me grab my voice recorder," Ruth says quickly, as something like triumph flickers across Juno's young, brutal face.

"So, what's your hook?"

"My hook?"

"Your hook," Juno repeats as they turn from the Mulvaney driveway onto the main road, before taking a sharp left onto a descending, unsealed path that eventually plateaus at the edge of a dense woodland. The foliage of the majestic trees marking the entrance to these woods has the effect of a velvet curtain; Ruth can see the smallest gap of light between the heavy, swooping branches.

"Private entrance," Juno says by way of explanation as she parks the car at the side of the road and turns to face Ruth.

"Like I told you, I'm taking media studies next term, and I know a few things about podcasts already. What I'm wondering is, what's your podcast actually trying to do? It's obviously not about solving a big mystery, not if you're including my father's crimes. Everyone already knows he's guilty as sin. So what's it about? A bunch of women blabbing away about their poor relationship choices can't be it, either. No offense, but you don't seem like the kind of chick to care about that."

Before Ruth can respond, Juno gets out of the car. Ruth does the same.

"This way," Juno says, pointing to that small gap between the trees. "Pretend it's Central Park," she adds, catching Ruth's hesitation. "And don't worry, I'm not going to kill you." She smiles that brutal smile of hers. "I'd never get away with it around here."

Managing a hollow laugh, Ruth follows Juno, thinking that Amity Greene was a breeze compared to the tornado that is Juno Mulvaney. Within twenty-four hours, Ruth had extracted more from Amity than she'd learned about Ethan Oswald in nearly as many years. One day with Rose and Juno, and she's seemingly forgotten why she came all this way in the first place. First, Rose shut down any conversation about her year in Hoben. And now Juno has her heading deep into the backwoods to show her the place where two girls who Ruth is only pretending to be interested in were murdered.

And the most confusing part? Ruth *is* interested in what happened to Kelly Parker and Nichole Morley. The same way she can't stop thinking about Eric Coulter's victims. Even if this feels like the ultimate betrayal of Beth and the girls.

As if the only dead girl worth following is the one right there in front of you.

Ruth considers Juno, stalking into the woods ahead of her. The teenager is obviously trying to impress her by adding a little menace to her already abundant attitude. Not realizing this doesn't actually make her seem tough—just young. A self-proclaimed goddess, unaware that Ruth can see her posturing for what it really is. Armor like that is familiar to Ruth.

She catches up with Juno just as they approach a small, half-hidden sign. *Marama River Reserve.* Below that, a small, carved arrow: *Marama Bend—this way.* Dense bushland, bright with winter-blooming flowers, rises on either side of the track that opens up beyond the sign; immediately, Ruth can hear the soft, shushing sound of flowing water.

Leading Ruth forward, Juno appears to have dropped her line of inquiry about the podcast. The distant sounds of the river meld with the crunch of their feet on the gravel, accompanied by the intermittent squawk and caw of unseen birds in the surrounding trees. It is eerie, no doubt, but also beautiful.

As they walk, the weight of the triskelion sits heavily against the lining of Ruth's jacket pocket. It makes her think of Juno's desire for a supernatural power that could direct people's actions back at them. What might Hecate, with her school of restless girls, make of young Juno Mulvaney?

They walk another five minutes before Juno stops and issues another of her sudden commands. "This way." Ducking beneath the bare branches of a row of large cherry trees, Ruth sees how they'd concealed a steep, natural staircase carved into the earth. Careful to avoid the exposed roots and loose stones that make up the tread of each step, Ruth gingerly descends behind her guide. The sound of the river is a loud hiss now, and when she follows Juno through a wall of fern and bracken at the bottom of the stairs, they emerge onto a small, pebbled beach.

The *special place.*

The riverbank where Kelly and Nichole died so violently is currently dappled in sunlight. Up close, the river looks like a ribbon of fine, jade silk. Just ahead, the flowing water unfolds over, around, a scattering of large, mossy boulders, before twisting out of sight.

Marama Bend. Here, right in front of them, the river is calm. Wide like a smile. A place for floating, and for dreaming.

Not for drowning.

"We used to come here all the time as kids," Juno says as Ruth walks in a small circle, taking it all in.

When she turns back to face the river, Ruth has a desire, despite the winter chill, to wade into the water. She imagines slipping under that shimmering surface, and immediately has the strangest sense of having been here before. Of sinking to the bottom of Marama River, looking up at the blurred sky above her as she digs her fingers into the silty riverbed beneath her. She can feel the fine fragments of stone and shell and bone sifting through her hands, before she breaks the surface, gasping, laughing, at the shock of cold air waiting.

When Ruth tries to shake this sensation away, it rolls through her again. The feeling is more solid than déjà vu, which, for Ruth, has always had the consistency of smoke, a memory disappearing the moment you reach out to grasp it.

"You feel it, don't you?" Juno says as she sits down on the cool sand at the water's edge and motions for Ruth to join her. "You feel *them*."

Juno squints out at the water, hugging her knees to her chest.

"Kels and Nic used to bring Minnie and me here in the summer," she continues. "It's deep out there in the middle, so they'd take one of us each on their backs and we'd have water fights, or we'd swim between their legs. We'd bike here, or sometimes cut through the paddocks, and when Kels got her license she'd drive us down to the entrance on the other side of the bend. I loved that. It felt so grown-up. This used to be my happiest place in the world."

"Did the police ever talk to you about coming here with Kelly and Nichole?" Ruth asks, only to be rewarded with a withering stare as Juno turns her gaze from the water to face her.

"I was a kid, Ruth. I don't exactly remember what I told the police."

Then, unexpectedly, Juno puts her head in her hands.

"And the things I do remember, I wish I could forget," she adds, her voice muffled by her cupped palms.

"I know what you mean," Ruth says, too fast.

Juno removes her hands at this and tilts her head at Ruth.

"What do *you* remember from your childhood?" she asks.

"I'm not entirely sure." This is an honest answer, at least. "Whatever I think I remember from that age, it could just as easily be a story somebody else told me."

Juno nods. "I get that. Like, if you remember something *too* clearly, did it actually happen? Maybe it's just something you kept hearing about, and it's not even real."

She stops, bites her lip.

"But I do remember coming here. That's real. Like, I can feel what it was like to brush up against Kelly's legs as I swam between them. Wondering if she was going to close them around me, like she did this one time, trapping me under the water. It must have only been for a few seconds, but that's my first clear memory of knowing I could die. Ironic, huh? That the first sense of my own mortality came from the girl my father murdered."

They sit in silence for a while after this. Juno asked if she could feel the girls here, but as Ruth closes her eyes, it's not the restless dead she thinks about but a tiny Juno, held under the water, so sure she was going to drown. She imagines Kelly Parker scooping her up that split second later, laughing and apologizing, promising not to scare her like that again. But of course, it doesn't work that way. You can't take back what you teach someone. Kelly was the first person to show Juno how little it takes to subdue a girl.

"Do you think you could kill someone?"

Still staring at the water, Juno's tone is flat as she puts this question out there.

Ruth swallows. "I've thought about that a lot," she admits. "And I can't say for sure. But I don't think so. I just can't imagine what it would take out of you."

"I can," Juno responds, turning her gaze from the river back to Ruth. Her eyes are wet. "I think I could really hurt someone. If I had to. Like, if it was to protect my family."

She quickly wipes at her eyes before standing up, offering her hand to Ruth.

"Got what you need from here? Because I've had enough of this place. Let's go visit the girls' graves, instead."

The two headstones are set side by side at the top of a hill that looks down on the reserve. The cemetery is small, no more than ten rows and maybe a hundred plots, filled mostly with the names of men and boys from the late nineteenth and early twentieth century.

"A bunch of old colonizers and some local boys who died in the war," Juno tells Ruth over her shoulder as they walk up the hill to the crest where Kelly and Nichole are buried.

Six years on, the girls' graves appear very well tended. Semi-fresh flowers sit in jars on either side of the two headstones, with a collection of trinkets scattered at the base of each little monument. Rain-matted teddy bears. Burnt-down candles. Rose quartz and a rainbow of other crystals. Etched into Kelly's headstone is a star, along with the words: *Our shining light*.

On Nichole's, a heart, and the words: *Ever loving, ever loved*.

"Do you believe in ghosts?"

Another of Juno's questions, shot like an arrow.

Standing by the graves of Kelly and Nichole, Ruth is still considering her answer when Juno shakes her head, lets out a brittle laugh.

"More importantly, do you think they *haunt* us?"

Up here, on this hill above the reserve, Ruth can hear a distant roar of waves, that endless back-and-forth of the ocean declaring its simultaneous arrival and departure. She could tell Juno about existing in that liminal space. The border she straddles between life and death. She could tell Juno about the dead girls who showed up in her room on her twenty-first birthday, and about Beth. But would she call any of that a haunting?

"Not like in the movies," is all Ruth can think of to say.

"You're very weird," Juno responds, her fingertips resting on top of Kelly Parker's headstone. "But yeah; the movies always get things wrong." She pats the granite under her hand. "Especially when it comes to murder."

NINETEEN

Juno laughs and calls Ruth a city girl.

"I thought the rule was never go to the second location," Ruth huffs in response, struggling to keep up as the younger girl leads her across a field of damp, ankle-deep grass. "No one said you had to watch out for the third."

"Oh, if I wanted to kill you, I'd have done it already," Juno says breezily over her shoulder. "Relax. I'm taking you somewhere nice and pretty this time."

They are trespassing on private property. A sign nailed to the first fence that Juno made Ruth scramble over said as much. Behind them, the car had been deposited at yet another roadside, after they'd left the cemetery and driven at least ten minutes down an unsealed track with a sign that said *No Through* at its entrance.

. Having navigated a second boundary fence, Ruth is now following Juno through a wide field, dotted with large black-and-white cows, many of whom raise their heads to observe their uninvited guests warily.

"Shit," Ruth says as she steps right into the cracked, gooey mess one such cow has left behind.

"Sure is, *city girl*."

"I'll have you know I was born in a small town," Ruth retorts. "Surrounded by woods and black bears, which are slightly scarier than cows."

"Bears? Cool! Whereabouts?"

"Connecticut," Ruth replies to the girl's back, before she can stop herself.

If she had hoped Juno wasn't really listening, the way the girl suddenly stops and wheels around tells Ruth otherwise.

"Mum lived in Connecticut."

"I heard that," Ruth says, trying for nonchalance.

"Yeah. She went to high school in some place called Hoben. But she doesn't talk about it much. No surprises there, right? She doesn't talk about *anything*. I think it wasn't great for her over there. Her host parents were really strict, and her host brother, Chip—how *American* is that—was awful. He pretended to be this sweet kid, but really he was a little psychopath. And there was this creepy teacher . . ." Juno stops. "But there's *always* a creepy teacher, right?"

"Seems like that whole town is creepy," she adds, without waiting for Ruth to respond. "Last month a little girl was kidnapped from there. I've been reading all about it online."

Standing, facing each other, the early afternoon light gives Juno a kind of dented halo, and Ruth dimly recalls that the girl's namesake, the ancient goddess Juno, was known as the protector of women.

"I heard about that, too," Ruth responds, hoping the sudden red to her cheeks gets mistaken for her simply being unfit.

"She's probably already dead, right?" Juno says, squinting at

Ruth, before spinning around to resume her march across the field.

At this point, Ruth is struggling to keep up in more ways than one. It shouldn't be surprising that Juno knows about Coco Wilson's disappearance; Ruth is hardly the only person interested in missing girls. It also makes sense that she'd be curious about the American town her mother lived in. But just how much does she know about Rose's time in Hoben? And about that "creepy teacher" in particular?

How much does Ruth *want* her to know?

When she does catch up to her enigmatic guide, Ruth finds herself at the edge of the world. Beyond one last wooden fence is a steep path that drops well over a hundred yards to the Tasman Sea below, where deep blue-green water meets an expanse of dark, glittering sand. Wordlessly, Ruth mimics Juno's shimmy through the slats of the fence, before carefully following her footsteps down the sand and reed track. Her feet lose traction a few times, but she manages to stay upright, and when they finally reach the beach, Ruth lets out her breath in what sounds more like a gasp.

Sun-flecked black sand stretches out in front of them like a night sky, gleaming. In the distance, the ocean rolls with waves that seem to fold into, rather than crash against, the shore. Behind them, exposed limestone cliffs glint amber and gold in the early afternoon light, rising back up to the grassy plateau from which Ruth so gingerly descended just now.

"My god, Juno."

"Yeah."

Ruth sees pride tug at the corners of Juno's mouth, before she rearranges her expression into one that gives nothing away, and they set off down the beach.

Walking side by side, Juno tells Ruth that with the tide this far out, they don't have to worry about all the little inlets formed by the jutting rocks that make up the cliffside of the beach. If the tide was all the way in, these inlets would be filled with rushing water by now. She adds casually that there are very few ways to access this beach; for most of this stretch of the west coast, it's just cliff face and ocean.

"So, what happens if the tide comes in while we're down here?" Ruth asks.

"We'll be fucked," Juno says sweetly, which makes Ruth laugh.

As they continue along the beach, fine black sand seeping into Ruth's sneakers and warming her feet, Juno points to a series of rock stacks rising out of the sea, and explains that there used to be four of them, a mother, father, and two children. *The family*, these pinnacles were called.

"But one of the stacks, the tallest of them, gave way a few years ago. Slowly, and then all at once. Until it got washed away completely. Now it's just the mother and her two daughters. The dad couldn't hack it. Funny, hey?"

This feels like an invitation.

"Do you miss your dad, Juno?"

Overhead, two wide-winged seabirds swoop and squall, performing a kind of noisy sky ballet.

"I'm mad at him," she answers, after a long pause. "I'm so mad that he fucked everything up for us. All because . . ." Juno's voice catches now. "For what, actually? That's the part I don't understand."

"Do you have any idea why he took it that far?" Ruth asks, imagining that tallest stack finally giving way, disintegrating into the ocean after resisting so long.

Juno shrugs again. Ruth can see her attempt at nonchalance takes effort this time.

"There was a rumor Kelly was pregnant. Everyone was talking

about it. It wasn't like anyone guessed it was him. But it must have gotten back to him, and he freaked out. 'Cause that would have messed everything up. Like, my mum would have left him, for sure. And he would have lost us and . . . well, he lost us anyway, so what was the point?"

"I don't know that there is a point," Ruth suggests.

"Then why are you here?" Juno shoots back.

Ruth recognizes the tactic; the girl is masking sadness with anger.

Juno sweeps her hands toward the remaining pinnacles. "I mean, what's the *point* of your little podcast, Ruth?" Her voice is unnaturally high now. "If it's just what men do? Girls get murdered. They get *kidnapped*. Why even bother talking about that shit, if there's no meaning to any of it?"

"Because there's a truth that's bigger than one person's terrible decisions, I guess," Ruth answers, wondering why it's hard to lie to Juno, when it's become so easy with everyone else.

"Juno, your dad acted in a way lots of men have," she continues carefully. "He's part of a long line of males who have tried to solve their problems the exact same way: by taking them out on other people. A big part of talking to women like your mom is trying to understand how an otherwise normal guy"—Ruth uses air quotes on the word *normal*—"could do such terrible things."

Narrowing her eyes, Juno appears unsatisfied with this answer. As if she senses its incompletion.

"Who else are you talking to for the podcast?" she asks. "You've never said."

Ruth tries for a casual smile. "This whole thing is still so new," she says. "But I promise that as soon as I know more about my other interview subjects, I'll tell you what I can."

(So she *can* lie to Juno just as easily after all.)

Juno wrinkles her nose, then nods. "Okay," she concedes, before declaring they should head back, because the tide is sure to turn any minute now.

———————

It's late afternoon by the time they get back to the farm. As Juno parks in front of the house, Rose comes onto the front porch, hand on her hip.

"A message about where you were might have been nice," she says, frowning at her daughter as Juno and Ruth get out of the car.

"That reminds me . . ." Juno turns to Ruth, ignoring her mother's admonishment. "The house is a total black spot, but if you stand over there"—she points to a small rise to their right—"you'll get two bars on your phone, at least."

"When Peter and I took over this place from his parents, we knew it was isolated," Rose says as Ruth and Juno follow her inside. "But we had no idea what was coming down the line. Or, rather, what lines we would miss out on by living here. That's part of the reason the girls board in town. My old encyclopedias from high school don't quite cut it when it comes to school projects. Though they do keep promising a new cell tower is on the way."

Ruth wonders if it pains Rose to mention Peter in an anecdote from their old life. She has already noted that he's missing from the various framed photographs around the house. There are plenty of pictures of Juno and Minnie, but none of the girls with their father. There aren't many photos of Rose on the walls, either, and none at all from when she was a young girl herself.

The history of this house is full of gaps.

Ruth pushes down her desire to check her phone and accepts Rose's offer of a glass of wine, joining her at the kitchen table as the sky grows dark outside.

It has started to rain, heavy drops playing a symphony on the kitchen's tin roof. Candles, in jars that Juno lined up along the windowsill, flicker down to their waxy ends. In charge of atmosphere tonight, the teenager has also been playing DJ via her phone. Most of the local music she plays for Ruth has a melancholy feel to it, even when the beat suggests dance floors and all-night parties. The lyrics speak of home, of land and belonging, and when they're sung in te reo Māori, the effect is even more poetic. Even Juno seems moved, despite her instance that she can't wait to leave this place.

Ruth lets herself feel an ache for New York. The intensity of today has her yearning for Sweeney's, and for Ressler. His specific corn chip smell. His beautiful, droopy ears, and the way he overextends his neck when he howls. Knowing that he is safe and happy with her uncles should also make Ruth happy, but it somehow makes her feel even more alone here.

Maybe it's the music.

With the songs and the candles, and the rain, the house feels different tonight. There is a beauty to its remoteness, its flaws, and it transforms Rose too. In the candlelight, Ruth can finally see a glimmer of the girl she might have been. There is something compelling about her face that Ruth had missed until now. An intensity, as Rose sways to the music, her eyes closed, that makes her almost—beautiful.

She says she wasn't like her daughter when she was younger. Could she have been just as fierce if she'd never gone to Hoben Heights High?

It takes only one man to unravel a girl.

And what happens when the next man finds her, so soon after? Rose married Peter Mulvaney just one year after she returned from Hoben. He was twenty-seven and she wasn't yet nineteen.

When Juno excuses herself to take a shower before bed, Ruth knows this is her chance. Rose, three-quarters of a bottle of red wine staining her lips, has started scrolling through her daughter's phone, looking for music she used to like "at that age," and it feels like a door has creaked open. Now all Ruth needs to do is give it a push.

"You had eclectic tastes as a teenager," she says, smiling at Rose as a frenetic Red Hot Chili Peppers song gives way to an early Mariah Carey ballad.

"I did," Rose agrees. "Music was my life back then."

"Juno said you have a good voice," Ruth lies. "Like, *really* good."

"She said that?" Rose looks stunned. "It's not often my daughter gives me compliments."

"Well, she's a teenager." Ruth broadens her smile.

"She's Juno," Rose says, shaking her head. "She makes *me* feel like the teenager."

It's time for Ruth to push a little harder.

"What were you like back then, Rose? What was the dream? Other than being on Broadway, I mean."

"Not this," Rose waves her hand around the room. "My daughter thinks I don't understand, but all I wanted was to get out of here too. I made it as far as Connecticut . . . and then I bounced right back."

"I know you didn't like where you ended up over there. But did you like being an exchange student, at least?"

"Not particularly," Rose answers, moving her fingers in time to the music, as if she can see each note in the air. "I was lonely most of the time."

"But you had music."

Fingers still tapping at the air, Rose closes her eyes again. Something terrible crosses her face, a memory that clearly causes her pain.

"I was supposed to audition for performing arts schools in New York, Boston, Chicago," she says, without opening her eyes. She switches to an impeccable, if hokey, American accent. "That was the dream, kid. But, gosh darn it, it was not meant to be." Rose blinks her eyes open. "Those who can, do," she continues. "Those who can't, teach."

That accent, how well she has captured its cadence, is surprising.

"I know Ethan Oswald was *your* music teacher, Rose." Ruth says this quickly, because it really does feel like now or never. "I found an old yearbook, where you were the lead in his production of *Carousel*," she rushes on. "And I know he killed a little girl just a few weeks later."

There is only rain on tin, the faint hiss of a running shower, and the melisma of a young woman singing about her vision of love. Rose remains silent against this background score. When she finally opens her eyes, she stares straight at Ruth.

"Well done," she says. "You found out my big secret. Good for you."

Sarcasm was definitely not what Ruth expected. Or, worse, scorn. Because Rose seems to be looking at her with a slight sneer now.

"You are not the first person to be interested in my relationship with Ethan Oswald," the woman continues, leaning forward across the table. "I went through hell in Hoben, thanks to all the ugly things people want to think about a seventeen-year-old girl. Ethan was my *friend*. He was going to help me get into theater school. That's all there ever was between us. I was surprised as anyone when he—"

Only now does Rose falter. She sits back, elbows on the table, and briefly puts her head in her hands. A small shake, and then she looks back up at Ruth.

"I left Hoben a very sad and confused young girl. And when I got home, Peter swooped right in. He might have been a *good guy*, Ruth. But he definitely saw me coming."

"How so?"

"Men like damaged girls, Ruth."

In the background, Ruth can hear the shower turn off. She knows that she has time to ask one more question of Rose, two at most, before Juno returns.

"Does anyone here know about Oswald?" she asks.

"God, no!" Rose's response is lightning quick, as if she, too, is aware that Juno could come back any second. "Which is why this subject is absolutely off the record."

"But you didn't do anything wrong. So why hide it?" Ruth tries not to sound incredulous. If she really were doing a podcast, there's no way she'd stay quiet about this.

"Come on, Ruth. You know how things work. If you didn't, you wouldn't be here. It's bad enough that apparently I somehow 'let' my husband murder two young girls. Now imagine people knew that I used to get a ride home from school every day with a child killer. It didn't go down well back then, and it certainly wouldn't go down well now."

"But if you didn't *do* anything . . ."

Rose outright scoffs at Ruth now.

"Since when does that matter? Never let the truth get in the way of blaming a woman, right? And I *am* guilty, when you think about it. I made a very stupid mistake by not seeing how dangerous it can be when a grown man takes an interest in a teenage girl."

Is she referring to her husband and Kelly Parker here? Or her own relationship with her high school teacher? Ruth opens her mouth to pursue this, when Juno comes back into the kitchen, frowning.

"We ran out of hot water again," she huffs. "God, this place is falling apart." She sits back down at the table with an exaggerated sigh.

Within seconds, Juno reclaims her phone from Rose, and starts playing a new song. Something jangly about a woman loving a man like her own mother did.

"For you, Mama," Juno says, winking at Rose before turning to Ruth. "True story," she says over the music. "Mum was once such an emo loser, she came home from her exchange early. Technically, she didn't even make it to graduation."

"And my daughter thinks this means she should be able to drop out of school, too," Rose says, pouring herself another glass of wine. "But that is *not* going to happen."

"Just trying to take after you, *Mom*," Juno responds with a grin.

She holds out her hand, and Rose takes it. Ruth can only sit back in silence, as mother and daughter rise and begin to dance around the room.

If Rose is acting the part yet again, who exactly does she think her audience is? Is this show of domestic happiness just for Ruth? Or is Rose trying to fool her daughter too? So that Juno thinks she has at least one parent looking out for her. A mother who dances her around the room. Fast enough to blur any secrets she's been hiding.

It's not like you can erase them completely, Ruth wants to tell her.

Because the girl you once were can never be fully left behind.

When she's sure the others are asleep, Ruth wraps herself in one of those heavy blankets from Juno's bed, before tiptoeing on socked feet out of the house. She stands on the front porch, looking up at the night's vast, clear sky, the stars above her glimmering like those sunlit specks of sand on the beach today.

She goes over everything Juno told her down by the water. And before, when they were trespassing through those fields. The references to Rose's host family and her awareness of the Coco Wilson case. Where does a kid like Juno get her information? she wonders. And when it comes to Hoben, how far back do her sources go?

Ruth shivers, pulling the blanket tighter around her. Beth's murder is old news, she reminds herself. Ethan Oswald is dead and buried. The less Juno knows for now, the better, she decides. That girl has more than enough to deal with already.

And so does she.

Murdered girls. *Kidnapped* girls. All of them lost.

Ruth stares up at that night sky and feels her heart constrict.

"Where are you, Coco?" she whispers, before she turns and quietly pads back inside.

TWENTY

*H*ere Comes the Sun."

That's the song her mommy always sings to her when she can't fall asleep. That's the right song. It's by those beetle guys her parents love so much, even though they're quite old now, and two of them are even dead. Sometimes her mommy gets sad about dead people she doesn't know. There was a man who was her favorite singer, and she cried a whole lot when he died. She even cries when a person dies on a TV show. Or a dog. But that is sad, when you think about it. Even if it's not a real dog, it can make your chest feel funny.

How sad is her mommy feeling right now? Maybe lots more than about her favorite singer, because it seems like you'd be much more sadder about your own dead daughter. Not that she's dead. At least, she doesn't think she is. But there's no way to be exactly sure. One time, she heard her grandmother talking about a baby boy that died. How he went to— what's that game with the stick called again? Limbo. The baby boy went to limbo, and that wasn't the same place as her other grandparents went, which was heaven, obviously.

Limbo was somewhere else, but she wasn't exactly sure where.

Somewhere in the middle, it seemed like her grandmother was say-

ing. Is that where she is now? Stuck where no one can find her, like that little baby boy. Like—a ghost?

Is she a ghost now?

Is that why the girl on the other side of the wall can't hear her? The one who keeps singing the wrong songs.

Is that why no one is coming to take her home?

Or at least up to heaven.

Here comes the sun. . . .

She closes her eyes and tries so hard to hear her mother's voice.

But she hears a whole other voice, instead.

TWENTY-ONE

Rose sleeps through half of Ruth's last full day in Marama River.

"She's totally hungover from last night," Juno says, when Ruth asks if her mother is okay. "Nothing that Panadol and sleep can't fix."

It's still pouring rain outside. With little to do but wait for Rose to get up, Juno suggests they play cards. Her game of choice is poker; halfway through their fourth round she puts her hand face down on the kitchen table and sighs.

"Please don't make my mother look bad for this. She doesn't usually drink so much. I think she was just nervous, and it all got a bit much, you know?"

"I wouldn't make her look bad—" Ruth starts to protest, but Juno cuts her off.

"She's *not* a bad person. And she tries to be a good mother. Even I have to remember that sometimes."

Before Ruth can respond, Juno has picked up her cards again.

"Come on, Ruthie," she says imperiously. "Let's see if you can beat me this time."

When she does reveal her cards, the girl has four aces in her hand. She spreads them out in front of Ruth and grins.

Proud of herself, like she's just pulled off a trick.

———————

When Rose does finally emerge from her bedroom around 1 p.m., she blinks at Ruth as if she is surprised to find her still there, sitting at her kitchen table.

"I'm done with your podcast," she says, as if they were already halfway through a conversation about it. "I retract my permission to be recorded. Take me off your list and get someone else."

"Mum!"

Juno is clearly surprised by this turn of events. She looks from her mother to Ruth and back again, then lets out a low whistle.

"Did something happen after I went to bed last night?" she asks. "Because this seems rather—dramatic."

"Cut it out, Juno," Rose says sharply. "You've had far too much to say for yourself lately."

If she's taken aback by her mother's mood, Juno doesn't show it. Instead, she pulls a face at Rose's back as she stalks back to her bedroom.

Juno turns to Ruth. "I swear that woman has a split personality sometimes. Sorry about that."

Ruth manages a little shrug, trying to hide her dismay. Rose pulling out of her podcast means more than Juno could know. The podcast itself may not be genuine, but her reason for wanting to keep Rose talking very much is. She's not sure if she believes any of what she's been told so far. Not by Rose, and not by Amity, either. But there have been times both women have seemed on the verge of admitting—*something*.

How dangerous it can be when a grown man takes an interest in a teenage girl.

Isn't that what Rose said last night? Dangerous enough to lead to the abduction of a child? Exactly how culpable would that make a teenage girl, if she didn't stop him? Or if she didn't ever tell anyone else about it? Let alone if she actually helped carry out his plan . . .

Ruth looks at Juno now. This seventeen-year-old girl, the same age as Rose was when she lived in Hoben. She came right out and asked Ruth not to make her mother look bad. Which, come to think of it, is exactly what Amity asked of her too.

Is she supposed to see only the good in them?

Most people aren't all good or all bad, Rhea had said the other day. And yet we so often insist they be one or the other, Ruth thinks. We don't like contradictions, even if they are the truest thing about a person. Was it a relief for Amity and Annie to have Oswald see their duality and not only like it, but teach them how to use it?

What *did* he see in his Julie Jordans?

This is what Ruth needs to find out.

"Do you want to watch a movie?" Juno asks, interrupting Ruth's ruminations. "Or maybe go for another drive?"

Ruth tries to ignore the hurt on the girl's face when she says that she's got some work she needs to do instead (what she really needs to do is sit and *think*).

"No biggie," Juno sniffs, as if she couldn't care less. "I should probably do some homework too."

As she leaves the kitchen, she mutters, "There's nothing else to do in this hellhole. But what do you care about that."

———

Tomorrow morning, George will come in his shuttle van to take Ruth back to the airport. From there, she will fly back to Auckland and spend the day at the airport hotel before catching a late-night flight home to New York. Her time in Marama River will be done.

Beth had asked her if it was worth it. Tonight, as Ruth gets into Juno's bed after yet another long and strange day, she cannot say for sure. On the one hand, she could never have got the measure of Rose if they'd just talked online. On the other, Rose has presented so many versions of herself these past few days, it's hard to say exactly what Ruth has learned about her. The best part, undeniably, has been meeting Juno Mulvaney. A girl even more mercurial than her mother, but she's kept Ruth on her toes, at least.

They did end up watching a movie together, late this afternoon. A local film about a boy who loves Michael Jackson and makes up outlandish stories to cope with the many ways his formerly incarcerated father lets him down. Ruth is sure she caught Juno crying at least twice during the movie. Rose had silently joined them halfway through, bringing a conciliatory bowl of popcorn. If she cried, too, Ruth didn't see it.

They had an early dinner soon after, with no mention of Rose's prior outburst. Instead, the three of them ate grilled cheese sandwiches—toasties, Rose called them—while Juno asked Ruth a dozen questions about New York, insisting that one day she was going to live there herself.

After that, their conversation, like last night's candles, seemed burned down to the wick.

Preparing to turn the light off and go to sleep, Ruth looks over to see Juno standing in the doorway again. She has a strange look on her face.

"Would it be okay if I messaged you sometime?" she asks, stepping into her bedroom.

"Of course," Ruth responds, sitting up. And she means it.

"Cool," Juno says, coming to sit on the edge of the bed.

"What's that?" she asks, reaching over to pick up Gideon's triskelion from the nightstand. Later, Ruth will regret how she shot her own hand out to stop Juno from touching it. In the moment, the gesture is automatic.

Clearly surprised at the rebuff, Juno reels back. "Whoa, okay. I wasn't going to break it."

"Sorry," Ruth says, picking it up and holding it out to Juno. "It's a gift from my uncle. A talisman he made to keep me safe."

Tentatively taking the triskelion from Ruth, Juno runs her fingers over its three spirals, her face inscrutable.

"What's it supposed to protect you from?" she asks.

"I think it's mostly to protect me from myself," Ruth answers. She must be exhausted, because she adds, "I need help with that sometimes."

If this resonates with Juno, she doesn't show it.

Handing the triskelion back, she stands up and sighs. "You're lucky, Ruth."

"Lucky?"

"Yes. You get to leave. I'd give anything to go with you."

"I still lived with my mom at your age," Ruth starts, but Juno frowns.

"In New York *City*, Ruth. Not some hick place where everyone hates you."

"They don't hate you?"

Even Ruth can hear that it comes out as a question.

"They do. Thanks to what my dad did, my whole family is trash around here. My mum's only friends these days are horses."

Juno turns for the door, then stops.

"She can't really afford to keep them, you know. But she keeps rescuing them. Like, that's the person she would have been, if men had left her alone."

She furrows her brow.

"Anyway. Thanks for saying I can contact you. I know we're not friends or anything. But maybe I can convince Mum to give your podcast another chance. I'll see what I can do."

"That would mean a lot to me," Ruth responds, wishing she could offer more to this girl.

"No probs." Juno shrugs. "You're the most exciting thing that's happened to me in a long while, Ruth-Ann Baker. Everything is going to be so *sooooo* boring once you're gone."

The next morning, Ruth is back at the region's domestic airport, waiting for her flight to Auckland. And back to compulsively checking her phone.

There's no denying that being cut off from civilization (aka the internet) at the Mulvaney farm had its benefits. Being able to focus on one thing at a time, for a start. But as soon as her phone started beeping again, partway through the shuttle ride back to the airport, Ruth had felt an immense sense of relief. Even that little rise outside the house, the one Juno had directed her to, had only given Ruth enough coverage to text Joe and tell him everything was fine. Her emails wouldn't load, nor would *What Happened to Her* or *Stranger than Fiction*. Standing on that small hill, she was still, essentially, marooned.

But now she had the world at her fingertips once more.

"Somebody missed you, eh?" George had said from the driver's seat of the van, listening to those beeps. "You got a fella back home, girl?"

(He was much more chatty when driving away from Marama River.)

"Just my dog," Ruth had joked, but she had let herself think about Gabe then. Those undeniably cute messages he'd sent, just very much at the wrong time. The ball was in her court with that one, it seemed. She could either ignore his texts or take a swing back.

Now, at the airport, she still can't decide.

There are so many other things that require her attention. Like the fact Coco Wilson has seemingly dropped out of the news cycle since Ruth's been offline. Nearly three weeks have passed since the little girl was abducted, and Ruth fears she is about to go missing for a second time. Right now, the news is full of stories about Hillary Clinton, who has just officially launched her presidential campaign in New York, and all the men who want to run against her. Ruth knows that people's attention spans contract at the best of times, and she can only hope at least a little space is reserved for a child who still needs people to look out for her.

And then there's Amity's social media. Surprisingly, there have been no shiny, new posts from Paris since Ruth last checked, which seems very un-Amity. Instead, her latest post, from just a few hours ago, appears to be taken from a rooftop bar in Brooklyn with a view of Manhattan. It's very strange, Ruth thinks, because Amity definitely said she was away for a month. Maybe Amity's "friend" has asked her to keep their trip to Paris on the down low, and that photo was a decoy? Ruth will have to ask her when they both get home.

She's standing in line to board her flight when her phone beeps yet again. This time, it's a push notification from *What Happened to Her* saying she's received an update from @RoderickAlleyn. Heart thumping, Ruth clicks through to the message, trying not to knock into her fellow passengers as they progress toward their waiting plane.

"You'll need to put your phone away while you cross the tarmac, ma'am," the young woman checking her ticket says.

"Sorry," Ruth replies, looking up from the screen. Waiting until she is seated on the small plane to read it again. Checking that nothing has changed in the time it took her to buckle up for the flight. That she hasn't misunderstood what @RoderickAlleyn had to say.

It seems her retired private investigator from London has found Helen Torrent. Helen *Halvorsen*, @RoderickAlleyn corrects, because that is the name she goes by now. She is indeed residing in Oslo, Norway. And if Ruth will just give him one more day to make sure his information is unimpeachable, he has something rather interesting to share about exactly what the wife of the Babysitter Killer is doing there.

Stay tuned, the message ends. Because I think you're going to be just as surprised as I was!

HELEN

TWENTY-TWO

At times like this, Ruth wishes she liked to swim.

If her life were a TV show, this is the point where the harried female investigator would put on her goggles and do some laps. She'd tumble-turn her way through everything she'd learned so far, trying to make sense of it, while staying fit and slim in the process.

In the movies, she'd probably go for a run.

Instead, Ruth is stuck staring at the ceiling of the hotel room she's rented for the day, directly across from the international terminal at Auckland Airport. Her flight to New York doesn't leave until 11 p.m.

All she really needs to do right now is—wait.

In twenty-four hours, apparently, she will receive that promised reveal about Helen Torrent. *Helen Halvorsen*. A generic online search for that name hasn't brought up anything to help Ruth guess what @RoderickAlleyn might be alluding to. What he did share: Helen took her grandmother's maiden name and moved to Norway around 1997—the year she sold her house in Hoben. Ruth even has the address of her apartment in an area of Oslo called Grünerløkka, a neighborhood described in online travel articles as *hip* and *funky*. Oslo looks to Ruth like someone turned a fairy tale into a city. But if she knew next to nothing about New Zealand when she came here a few days ago, she knows even less about Norway. From this distance, it's impossible to say just what that address reveals about Helen's life, other than how far it is from where she started with Martin Torrent in Linnea, Minnesota.

With the answers to her questions still eluding her, Ruth is feeling restless. On the flight to Auckland, she could at least distract herself by analyzing her send-off in Marama River. The way Rose had seemingly shrunk into herself again, not even mentioning her decision to pull out of the podcast as she said goodbye. How Juno had hugged Ruth, all bony shoulders and feigned apathy at her visitor's departure, when George pulled up in his van.

"I hope it was worth it," she'd sniffed, unknowingly echoing Beth, as Ruth got into the back seat. "Coming all this way, for my mother to be such a pain."

As George took off down the driveway, Ruth had turned back to see Juno and Rose on the porch of the farmhouse, their heads together. It looked as if they were arguing with each other. And then they were gone.

But Ruth knew, in that moment, she would see the Mulvaneys again. That's the way unfinished business works. She's done her reconnaissance trip. When she gets back to New York, she'll just have to find a new way to get Juno's mother talking.

For now, she needs to focus on Helen Halvorsen. This mysterious woman, tantalizingly close.

So close, in fact, that were she in Oslo, Ruth could walk right up to her door.

Booking a last-minute flight at the airport is made to look a whole lot easier in the movies. Ruth is sent to three different counters before a frazzled young woman regretfully advises her that tonight's flight back to New York is nonrefundable.

"You'll lose your seat. And it's *business class*, ma'am."

"I didn't pay for it," Ruth assures her, because the woman looks so worried. It's easier than explaining how she's been spending Beth's death money so carelessly these past few weeks because the sooner it's gone, the better.

Turning her attention to Ruth's original request, the airline representative begins to type at great speed on a keyboard Ruth cannot see from her side of the counter.

"We can get you good seats on a flight via Singapore and London, leaving tomorrow morning"—*clack, clack, clack*—"if you are prepared to spend a night in Melbourne along the way. That will get you to Oslo late Tuesday morning, local time. It's, um, not cheap, though."

"Done," Ruth says, without checking the cost.

The thing about spontaneity, she'd realized back on her bed at the airport hotel, is that you have to run with an idea when it comes to you. And she *had* practically run across the road to the international terminal when inspiration struck.

Why *not* knock on Helen Halvorsen's door? By the time Ruth arrived in Oslo, she'd likely know what @RoderickAlleyn wanted to tell her. And if not, she could find out about this woman for herself.

Her sense of physical security has always been intrinsically linked to knowledge, she realizes. Her whole adult life, she has disarmed potential threats to her safety through learning as much as she could about a person's behaviors and motivations. Whenever she leaves it to others to do the work something inevitably gets missed.

"Tell us about it!" the girls say. Her less dead, whom no one ever seems to look for anymore. They seem invigorated by this latest adventure. Even Beth, so wary these past few days, is excited. Mostly for Ruth to be leaving New Zealand.

"I didn't like that woman," she tells Ruth. "At least in Oslo, you'll be far away from her."

———

A few hours later, Ruth is half-heartedly looking over the hotel's room service menu, when her phone makes a series of dings. It's Owen, seemingly incapable of sending a single block of text when he has news to share.

Nancy D! Your boy was just in here. AGAIN.

He's cute.

VERY cute.

He wanted to know when you are back.

When ARE you back?

It's 11 p.m., Saturday night in New York. Ruth allows herself a satisfied little smile as she realizes Gabe is not out on a date (Owen would surely have mentioned that important detail). Perhaps it's time to respond to those messages she received back at the Church Café.

But unlike conversations with dead girls, when it comes to Gabe, she still can't think what to say.

TWENTY-THREE

Melbourne is colder than Ruth expected an Australian city to be. Wetter, too, with the kind of stop-start rain that feels like it's always, and only, right over the top of her. She has, however, been pleasantly surprised on this layover to discover how cosmopolitan this city is. Whenever she's thought of Australia, she'd imagined scorching heat. Bronzed lifesavers. Deadly animals. But all three are conspicuously absent in Melbourne.

What it does have are great cafés. A bustling downtown district. And more dead girls.

They are all over the front pages of the local papers on those café counters. Two sisters—fourteen-year-old Gina and seventeen-year-old Ari—murdered last week by their father, Brant, in what the media is calling an act of revenge against his estranged wife. The circumstances of this crime are both disturbing and heartbreaking. A father shooting his own daughters, then setting the family's inner-city home on fire. The mother, Lara, coming home from work to find her ex-husband standing in front of that burning house, holding a gun to his own head.

He made sure she knew what he'd done to their daughters before he pulled the trigger.

In the five days since the murder-suicide, more details have emerged about the man's reign of terror against his family, including just how many times his wife's pleas for help were ignored by everyone from her in-laws to the police. Melbourne, it seems, is a city reeling from its failures. Ruth reads pages and pages of articles dedicated to examining the epidemic of family violence not just in this city but across the entire country. The data is horrifying; at least one Australian woman a week is murdered by an intimate partner.

Ruth already knows how dangerous a woman's own home can be, but alone in Melbourne for twenty-odd hours, this stark reality bothers her more than usual. The idea that you're not safe on either side of your front door.

Infuriatingly, she can also see that a small, angry faction has already turned on the girls' mother.

This is what happens when you keep children from their fathers, someone insists on a comments thread under one of the latest news articles about the crimes. And far too many people seem to agree with this distorted view of cause and effect.

Way to go with the victim-blaming, you piece of shit, one commenter has protested, at least. *No one is responsible for what Brant did except Brant himself.*

If Ruth wholeheartedly agrees with this comment—and she does—then what was that all about back in Marama River? Her driving need to uncover the relationship between Annie Whitaker and Ethan Oswald? She feels a slow creep of shame wind through her as she considers that she might be inadvertently absolving Oswald in some way. Even harder to reconcile is how she knows that's not actually going to stop her pursuit of Rose.

What does that say about her own line between good and bad? Evidently she is full of contradictions herself, these days.

Unsettled and overcaffeinated, Ruth takes a walk through the city's botanic gardens, just as Melbourne's clear skies of the last hour begin to darken again. She stops to sit on a bench across from a small, decorative water fountain. As she closes her eyes to the gentle gush of the rising and falling water, Ruth imagines sifting all her competing thoughts through her fingers, to see which ones might stick.

Something obvious lands, like a raindrop in her palm: spend too long in your own head, and *any* thought is possible. Even the ugliest ones.

She takes her phone out of her pocket and tries to get out of her head.

I'm in your city.

It'll be midnight in New York when Gabe receives this text, so Ruth doesn't expect a response, but she's barely put her phone back in her pocket when it dings.

Hey.

A minute of those telltale dots. The ones that suggest words typed out then deleted, over and over. Or a forthcoming essay. She waits, real raindrops hitting her head and shoulders, to see which of the two it will be.

It was an essay. An apology wrapped up in self-deprecation. Sitting on that bench in the rain, Ruth learned that Gabe felt like a *total wanker* for getting so drunk at Sweeney's that he'd left his notebook at the bar. He was just nervous, he said. Wanting to make a good impression on her. And his art clearly wasn't going to do that.

Turns out Gabe is funny. Articulate. Interesting. And good at apologies.

Ruth signals her forgiveness with a question.

Do you sketch every woman you meet?

And now it's early evening in Melbourne. She's in yet another hotel room, sitting cross-legged on a king-size bed, a scattering of emptied minibar bottles around her, and talking to Gabe as easily as she had that night at Sweeney's. It hadn't taken them long to switch from text to a phone conversation, before moving, with only slight hesitation, to a video call. That was Gabe's idea. As long as Ruth didn't mind seeing what he looked like in the morning, he'd joked. She'd quickly touched up her makeup in her hotel room's small, beautifully lit bathroom and wrapped herself in one of the plush robes hanging in the closet, before joining him on-screen. She didn't want to look like she'd tried *too* hard.

Gabe had seemed genuinely embarrassed when Ruth made him explain what his deal with the portrait was. She learned that, while he might be studying contract law, Gabe had been obsessed with graphic novels ever since he read *Maus* by Art Spiegelman as a boy. For as long as he can remember, he has been creating a visual diary of his life, turning his experiences into panels that he rarely shares with anyone. Instead, when something catches his eye, he tries to capture it in pencil form as surreptitiously as he can.

The official term for what I'd like to be able to call myself is a graphic memoirist, he'd further explained. *But that's probably a stretch for what I'm capable of. I'm just capturing what I see in this city so I don't forget it.*

When Ruth asked to see more of Gabe's work, he'd reluctantly sent her something he'd been working on this past week, a series of frames showing the same subway seat, filled by different New Yorkers as the day progressed.

After that, he asked her about the podcast. Owen had clearly filled him in on the reason for her travels, though it would seem her boss had exaggerated her qualifications. According to him, she was halfway to that Peabody already.

"It's still early days," she insists now, when Gabe asks where she sees the podcast going. A small part of her, the raided-minibar-soaked part of her, wants to tell him that it's all a scam. No, not a *scam*; that would make her sound terrible. A bait and switch. A neat trick. He's off-screen at the moment, making himself a coffee, and it would be easy enough to make a confession to a view of his rented Brooklyn apartment instead of his face. Then, if Gabe was disappointed in her, she wouldn't have to see it.

But when he reappears on the screen, coffee in hand, the moment passes. Ruth decides she doesn't want to sully this one lovely thing in her life right now.

"I'll know more after I get to Oslo," she says, before unscrewing a tiny tequila bottle with her teeth and trying not to show when it hurts.

"Tell me more about this woman you're trying to track down," Gabe says, stifling a yawn. "She doesn't even know you're coming, right?"

"Not exactly."

Not at all.

Initially, Ruth had figured this made her sound ambitious, the way she'd impulsively gone all the way to New Zealand to meet Rose, then booked a spontaneous ticket to Norway instead of heading home. Now she wonders if it doesn't make her sound a little unhinged. Haring off after a person she cannot say for sure is the *right* person. Or exactly why she wants to catch her in the first place.

Thankfully, Gabe doesn't seem alarmed, just a bit confused, like he was when she first told him about Oslo.

"So, she's the ex-wife of a serial killer, who has been in hiding for years," he repeats slowly, "and you want to bust her cover—why? Sorry, Ruth. It's after 4 a.m. here, and I'm a little slow on the uptake at the best of times."

Ruth takes a swig of tequila and smiles. Her logic would be hard to follow at any hour of the day.

"You ever heard of the serial killer TBK?"

Gabe appears to think on it, then nods.

"The guy who killed all those babysitters, yeah?"

It's Ruth's turn to nod.

"I saw a documentary on him, I think," Gabe says. "One of those really painful ones, where they play super-ominous music and zoom in on pretty young actresses pretending to look terrified as they reenact being brutally attacked. I've never understood why they do that."

"The actresses?"

"No." Gabe laughs. "The people who make those documentaries. Like, you don't need to dramatize what happened. At some point it becomes mockery. Or exploitation."

Ruth likes that he's smart. She likes that he's not just interesting but *interested* too. Maybe he could help her with what comes next.

"There's actually this whole other girl—" she starts to say, when Gabe looks away from the camera at something, then pulls a face.

"Shit, Ruth. I have to go. I'm supposed to be meeting a mate from Oz for breakfast, and I should probably get some sleep first."

"Go, go!" Ruth says, laughing, because they've been talking for hours. And because she wasn't really sure how much she'd intended to say.

Gabe's smile is almost bashful as he asks if it would be okay for them to have a drink *in person* when she gets back to New

York. He tells her that he'll be out of town himself for the next few weeks, but back in New York at the start of July. And he promises not to bring his notebook along on their date.

Their *date*.

"You'd better go," Ruth says, smiling.

The goodbye that follows is hasty, awkward. Gabe appears to start blowing Ruth a kiss, before thinking better of it; his fingers go to his lips and stay there a beat too long, then drop out of view. Ruth tries not to show her cat cream smile until he's ended the call.

But once Ruth is sure Gabe can no longer see her face, she lets that grin split her incredulous, minibar-drunk joy wide open. Allowing herself to entertain the wildest possibility of them all: that a person can be good *and* true.

And that she might have met him at last.

———

In the morning, as she repacks her bags for Oslo, Ruth's head is cloudy from last night's demolition of the minibar. Somehow, her clothing seems to have expanded, maybe even multiplied, since she last tried to close her suitcase. Pulling things out and refolding them, she is on autopilot, until she lifts a small, silk camisole from her suitcase and it floats in her hand, when she knows it should feel heavy.

Her triskelion. She had wrapped it in this camisole back in Marama River. But it's gone. It takes Ruth three frantic checks of her entire bag to accept that it's not here. Her talisman. This link to Hecate that was supposed to accompany her along this entire journey. Did she take it out of her suitcase when she was in Auckland? She has no recollection of doing that, but then again, she has been very distracted these past few days.

A new fear lurches in Ruth's stomach. She races to the bathroom, where she pulls everything out of her makeup case, not caring where it lands. Relief comes out in a gasp when she finds the small velvet pouch with Beth's forget-me-not ring tucked safely inside.

Taking off the gold chain she's wearing, Ruth loops Beth's ring through it before putting the necklace back on. The little flower now sits at the hollow of her throat. A small, satisfying pressure, to tell her it's still there.

She will send a message to the airport hotel back in Auckland. Maybe housekeeping picked up the triskelion, and they'll send it to her in New York. It *can't* be lost. That's not how these things are supposed to work.

But at least she still has Beth's ring. She's not sure she'd be able to get on the plane without it.

————

In the airport lounge, waiting to depart for Singapore, Ruth uses her cell phone to book herself a room at a boutique hotel in Grünerløkka that looks to be close to Helen's apartment. She is still holding the phone when it buzzes in her hand. It's Gabe.

Safe travels, his first message says. He's obviously sped up his typing, because the next message comes through almost immediately.

I looked up the wife of TBK this afternoon. Holy hell, how did you manage to find her? I am seriously impressed with your detective skills, Nancy.

Maybe it's the missing triskelion. Maybe it's the hangover, or the reality of what she's about to attempt, but instead of being happy to hear from Gabe, Ruth feels—irritated. Annoyed at his eagerness, and at herself for oversharing. She never should have told him the extent of her plans, because now he clearly feels like he's part of it. That's her fault, not his, and she knows she's being unfair, but the last thing she needs is for some man she barely knows to sidetrack her. She knew from the start he had the potential to become a distraction. Why hadn't she left their flirtation at the bar like she was supposed to?

Dimly, Ruth is aware that she's turning on Gabe, the same way Rose inexplicably turned on her the other morning. As if something had fundamentally changed in the sober light of day.

Boarding now, she texts back, even though the flight has not yet been called.

She can only hope that by the time she's returned to the Northern Hemisphere, she'll know how she really feels about this man who wandered into her life. Gabe, with his sea-glass eyes. And really bad timing.

In another life, he might have been the one she was chasing.

TWENTY-FOUR

Something Ruth never knew: you can yearn for the dark.

In mid-June, Oslo doesn't have nearly enough of it. It's 10 p.m., and the sun is still hovering just below the horizon—and it'll be back over it again by 4 a.m. tomorrow. This city is not far enough north for the hazy blue light slinking through her hotel room curtains to be considered the region's famed midnight sun, but it's certainly not night as Ruth knows it.

The endless dusk is making it hard for her to fall asleep, despite the fact she cannot remember ever feeling this tired. It's as if her head and body are in different hemispheres, and her vision is as hazy as the light outside. Which is understandable, given all the time zones she's crossed to get here.

Frustrated with her body's lack of compliance, Ruth gets out of bed, wandering into the living room of her spacious hotel suite. She goes to the room's small balcony, peering through its ornate iron balustrade to the Akerselva, the river that winds its way through Oslo. Out of sight, from this vantage point, are the cobbled streets of Grünerløkka she'd wandered this afternoon, taking in the vintage clothing stores, the fountains and statues, and the busy restaurants, where the waitstaff switched seamlessly from Norwegian to English whenever she ordered a coffee.

It's probably all that caffeine keeping her awake, cocktail-mixed with the anxiety that's been twisting her stomach ever since she got off the plane at Oslo Airport. *Nothing to declare.* That felt like a huge lie, but nobody pulled her out of the customs line. She made it through those gates and was able to take an express train to the city, with no one running after her, saying: *Wait! Why exactly are you here?*

Immigration forms never give you the option to say: *I still haven't figured that out.*

Ruth allowed herself today, this Tuesday in Norway, to transition more than just her body clock. She'd wandered those little streets of Grünerløkka, and the nearby city center, without once checking her proximity to Helen Halvorsen's apartment. Walking along the waterfront promenade in Aker Brygge, taking in the deep blue beauty of the Oslo Fjord, Ruth tried to unknot that tangle of stress in her belly. Telling herself that nothing bad could happen somewhere this beautiful. Immediately remembering what did happen in 2011, just a short ferry ride away, on the island of Utøya. Sixty-nine people shot dead at a summer camp, so many of them teenagers. And another eight victims murdered here in the city on that same terrible day.

It is inconceivable, the scale of terror one man can unleash on a city. And incongruous with the feel of *this* city, seemingly so safe, even late at night. Standing on her balcony, Ruth can sense how all that extra daylight invigorates the streets below. She imagines walking home from her late shift at an Oslo bar instead of Sweeney's, not having to carry her lipstick stun gun or her can of mace, because there wouldn't be nearly as many shadows along the way.

What a difference just a few more hours of light would make.

Ruth will make use of *all* her hours tomorrow—if she could just go to sleep right now. She needs to feel well rested. Clear-headed. Because she plans to show up at Helen Halvorsen's door tomorrow morning. Where she'll knock, and say—

Ruth might know what to say, if @RoderickAlleyn had actually come through for her like he promised. It's been over twenty-four hours now, and the only follow-up message he's sent is to say he needs a little more time.

I got in a little trouble with something very similar last year, he'd explained cryptically. And I'm not sure my lawyer has forgiven me for that debacle yet. I just want to be 100% sure before I tell you. I assure you it will be worth the wait.

But Ruth is not going to wait. She marked enough time back in Marama River, and she got next to nowhere for it. With or without @RoderickAlleyn's big reveal, she's planning to meet Ethan Oswald's former landlord face-to-face. She'll just have to use the podcast as her calling card and hope it works a third time.

Ruth is finally drifting when her silenced phone buzzes from the nightstand. Bleary-eyed, she reaches over to check the screen. *Gabe*. Always with the timing! Still, she sits up in bed to read what he has to say, six hours behind her in New York.

Hey Nancy D! It's so warm here today—I'm typing this from Rockaway Beach, which I never even knew existed (I'm guessing you did, ha). Will definitely have to come back here in the summer. How is Oslo? Paid 50 bucks for a glass of wine, yet??? More importantly, did you meet up with TBK's wife? Man, your life is so much more exciting than mine!!!

Ruth leans back against the bed's pleated headboard, gently knocking the back of her head against it as she weighs up her options. It's *nice* to receive messages like this. They make her feel like she's a normal person doing normal (and, yes, *exciting*) things. Plus, she hasn't heard from anyone else back home today. Probably because they all think she's stayed in New Zealand a few extra days to "explore." Which makes Gabe the only person who knows exactly where she is right now.

That young girl who was murdered in Riverside Park. Alice Lee. She suddenly pops into Ruth's mind, just as she stops tapping against the headboard. There was a really interesting piece about her life and death in the *New York Times* for the one-year anniversary of her murder. Something from that essay comes back to Ruth now. It had taken so long for people to realize Alice Lee was missing because no one knew where she was meant to be.

I'm going to see Helen tomorrow morning, she impulsively texts Gabe back. *So if you don't hear from me . . .*

Ruth finishes with that ellipsis, hits send on her message, then puts her phone in the nightstand's drawer.

"Do you really want to drag him into this?" Beth starts as Ruth lies back down. "He seems very . . . uncomplicated."

"I'm not *involving* him," Ruth answers defensively. "I just thought it would be nice for at least one person to know where I am."

Burying her face in a pillow to block out Beth's frown and that persistent blue light, Ruth remains awake until well after midnight. Thinking about dead girls. About New York. Marama River. Melbourne, and Oslo.

And how any place can feel safe—until it's not.

———

When she wakes the next morning, Ruth sees that the flower ring on the chain around her neck has left an imprint at the hollow of her throat.

Reaching up, she can feel the grooves of the petals, and the round of the ring's tiny band, under her fingertips. As if Beth had been pressing that forget-me-not hard against her skin all night.

Helen Halvorsen lives on the third floor of an elegant apartment building set across from an old church. It stands close to the Ankerbrua, known colloquially as the Fairy Tale Bridge, thanks to the bronze sculptures at each of the bridge's four corners, inspired by Norwegian fairy tales. Crossing the bridge this morning, Ruth stops to take in one of the most striking of the large sculptures: a naked girl, half straddling a wild bear. At a separate corner, another girl grips at the horns of a large ox, her feet suspended in the air. She has no idea what fables these young girls represent. But she does find it comforting that neither one of them looks particularly bothered by her beast.

Fortifying herself, Ruth approaches the street entrance to Helen's building. The stone facade, painted sunshine yellow, is punctuated with small balconies, laden with potted plants and blooming flowers. Wishing she had her triskelion for comfort and luck, Ruth pushes at the large wooden doors facing the street, and is relieved, if slightly confused, to find them unlocked. She walks along a covered entranceway into a shared courtyard. On all sides, individual apartments look down on the cobblestones and the moss-covered fountain at the courtyard's center.

A brass arrow points toward the external staircase leading to Helen's wing of the building, and Ruth follows it. Thinking about young girls and beasts as she passes the water fountain. And reminding herself that it's only going to be a woman on the other side of the door.

Helen Halvorsen is taller than Ruth expected. Almost masculine in her angles, in the sharpness of her features and the thin line of her limbs. The word that comes to Ruth's mind, as they sit across from each other in the woman's light, airy living room, is brittle. As if, one shove, and she'd break. Not that Ruth has any intention of shoving her.

Her introduction in Helen's doorway had been hasty. Delivered all in one breath. She was an American criminology student visiting Oslo for the summer, and her studies had sparked an interest in male serial killers from the 1970s and '80s—or, more specifically, an interest in what she considered these men's silent victims: their wives. If Helen was prepared to give Ruth a few minutes of her time, Ruth would like to explain her concept for a podcast titled *The Other Women*, and perhaps—perhaps Helen might consider participating in some way?

Small truths, big lies, it made no difference now. What mattered was whether Helen slammed the door in her face.

Helen Halvorsen did not slam the door in her face.

Now, Ruth is sitting on a plush, oatmeal-colored couch, set down on a polished wooden floor. Across from her, an exposed brick wall meets a high, coffered ceiling. To her left, a built-in bookshelf is tightly packed with books. More than Ruth's ever seen outside a bookstore; not even her uncles' library of the classics comes close. To her right, a set of French doors lead to one of the picture-perfect balconies she'd noted from the street. Through the glass, Ruth has a glimpse of the Akerselva flowing by as she waits for Helen to speak.

She has no idea if it was politeness or fear that prompted Helen to invite her into her home. As expected, the woman had appeared momentarily stunned at Ruth's sudden appearance and impassioned introduction, but she'd made no attempt to deny her identity, either.

Instead, she simply asked how Ruth had found her.

Ruth explained there were some people who made a sport of doing such things, before assuring Helen that her source was very discreet, as was she. In fact, Ruth declared, she hadn't told a single soul about finding Helen. *Not yet.* It was these two little words that made Helen flinch, then invite her in. Not blackmail, exactly, and not a threat, either. But Ruth had delivered that *Not yet* with just the right amount of ambivalence. As if she could change her mind at any time.

"I suppose I've been quite lucky," Helen says now, "to have flown under the radar for so long. Though you'll need to forgive me for not exactly being thrilled about you turning up here, Ruth-Ann."

She is sitting, ankles neatly crossed, in a cognac leather arm-chair that is angled toward Ruth on the couch. Observing Helen this close, Ruth can't decide if she looks younger or older than her seventy years. It's obvious from Helen's blunt-cut, highlighted hair, the French polish on her nails, and the crisp linen of her pantsuit that she looks after herself. But there is also a fragility to her, something vitreous. The only thing Ruth can say for sure is that Helen Halvorsen is calmer than Amity and less changeable than Rose. Although she, too, gives little away.

Not yet.

"I can understand that your anonymity is important to you," Ruth assures her host from the couch, hoping she sounds sympathetic. "I'm not here to exploit your past, Helen. I'd just like to understand a few things about your life. And if you trust me enough, I'd like to share your experiences with people who want—even need—to hear them."

What was it that Amity had recalled Ethan saying?

"I'm *big* on trust," she adds, keeping eye contact with Helen.

If this phrase resonates in any way, Helen doesn't show it. Instead, she half smiles. "If that's all you want from me, Ruth-Ann, then perhaps we can come to some kind of arrangement. My stories for your . . . discretion."

"Sure," Ruth responds, just as a telephone starts ringing in the next room.

Helen glances briefly toward the sound, then turns her attention back to Ruth.

"Where would you like to start, Ruth-Ann?"

In the other room, the ringing phone stops, then almost immediately starts up again.

"Someone is persistent," Helen says, raising her eyebrows. "If you'll excuse me, I think I had better answer that before we begin."

"Of course," Ruth replies, and Helen stands and strides from the room.

Ruth hears her answer the call, but someone must have a lot to say down the line, because Helen doesn't appear to respond, not for a long while. And when she does finally start talking, it happens simultaneously with the unmistakable click of a shutting door.

Alone in Helen's living room, Ruth looks around, wondering what this place might have to say about its owner. For all the considered detail (and there are many considered details), the room feels conspicuously absent of personal touches. There are no framed portraits on the walls, no photographs among all those books neatly arranged on the shelves. It's the one thing Helen's home has in common with the Mulvaney house, Ruth realizes. The sense of gaps in its history, of things redacted.

But what do you put in a frame when your husband murdered twelve teenage girls? Do you keep the gifts he gave you? The jewelry and the birthday cards? Ruth shivers involuntarily. What about *letters*? From the looks of this apartment, Helen Halvorsen could definitely afford to spend $10,000 on a collection of correspondence, if she wanted those letters badly enough.

Standing up, Ruth wanders over to Helen's wall of books,

trying to shake off the chill that's settled on her skin. Running her finger over the spines of the books at her eye level, Ruth sees they're mostly Nordic titles. She recognizes some of the authors; before her five-year sabbatical from murder, Ruth had been an avid reader of Scandi noir. Helen, it would seem, is also a fan of this genre, and of crime and mystery in general. On the shelf directly above her Scandi noir collection is a row of English-language paperbacks by the likes of Sir Arthur Conan Doyle, Agatha Christie, and Raymond Chandler, mixed in with hardbacks by a host of contemporary crime writers.

Helen's taste in literature does nothing to smooth out the goose bumps on Ruth's arms.

Crouching down, she looks over the titles running along the bottom shelf. Most of this space is taken up by an author she hasn't heard of. Helen must like this Jonas Nilsson's writing, however, because she seems to have more of his books than any other single author's; they take up the entire shelf. Picking up the first one, Ruth turns it over, taking in the cover's cloaked woman running through snow. Above her is the book's title, *Flykte*, in large, black, embossed letters, and Ruth doesn't need to understand the word to imagine its context. Sliding the book back into place, Ruth notices something odd. The next three books appear to be the exact same copy of *Flykte*. In fact, there are multiple copies for each of the Jonas Nilsson titles lined up on this shelf. How many copies of the same book does a person need?

Ruth's eye goes to the last book in Helen's Jonas Nilsson collection. This one, *Nydelig,* is a much slimmer volume than the others. A novella, she figures. Ruth tries saying the title out loud as she pulls a copy from the shelf. The word trips on her tongue, but when she sees the image on the book's cover, she gasps so loud there is no way Helen won't have heard it, even from another room.

Scrambling to get back to the couch, Ruth's hand goes to her throat, feeling for Beth's ring. It has to be a coincidence, she tells herself, heart thumping. The way the tiny forget-me-not ring on that book cover looks exactly the same as the one hanging round her neck.

But Ruth-Ann Baker doesn't believe in coincidences. She never has.

———

Her heart was still beating fast when Helen reentered the room. A young friend was having a small crisis, she'd explained, apologizing for taking so long on the phone.

"It does mean we'll need to postpone this little chat," Helen added, and perhaps she took Ruth's sudden paleness for disappointment, because she'd offered her cell phone number, then suggested they pick up their conversation tomorrow. After that she would be unavailable, as in two days' time she was leaving for a month's vacation to the Atlantic Coast, including a week in New York. Would tomorrow suit Ruth to reconvene?

"Of course," Ruth said. At this point, she only wanted to get out of there.

When Helen escorted Ruth to the apartment's front door, she hadn't seemed worried so much as impatient. Whatever that phone call had been about, it was clear she had matters to attend to.

Still, as she had bid Ruth farewell, she'd paused, her head tilted to one side.

"So pretty," she commented softly, staring directly at Beth's flower ring on its chain around Ruth's neck, before closing the door between them.

And now Ruth is standing on the Fairy Tale Bridge, her heart still pounding. But this irregular drumbeat is no longer in response to seeing the ring on that book cover, or even Helen's strange goodbye. Ruth's heart is all out of rhythm for a very different reason.

Because she might be getting better at telling lies these days, but Ruth-Ann Baker has never been a thief.

Until now.

Reaching into her bag, Ruth takes out the copy of *Nydelig* she stole from Helen's bookshelf before she'd raced back to the couch. She can only hope Helen doesn't do an inventory of her Jonas Nilsson books each day.

But it does seem less and less of a coincidence now. That a replica of Beth's ring features on the cover of this book. Because with the help of her phone, Ruth has just translated the novella's one-word title. *Nydelig.*

And the closest word to *Nydelig* in the English language would be . . . *Lovely*.

TWENTY-FIVE

The next afternoon, Ruth sits, rigid, on Helen's couch once again, watching as her host enters the room, a glass of white wine in each hand.

"Relax," Helen says as she sets one of the glasses down on a side table next to the couch. "I haven't poisoned you, Ruth-Ann. Wine is far too expensive in Norway to waste on such things."

Helen making a joke? Ruth blinks. If anything, Helen appears to be in good spirits. Seemingly unbothered by her guest, no matter what she thinks Ruth is here for.

Ruth is also doing her best to appear unaffected. Confident, despite spending the past twenty-four hours feeling completely lost. Ironically, the more information Ruth uncovered after leaving Helen's apartment yesterday, the more confused she'd become. It seemed that not only had the wife of TBK changed her name and moved countries to preserve her anonymity; Helen Halvorsen was hiding yet another identity, if @RoderickAlleyn is to be believed.

Jonas Nilsson. Author of ten books, published by a Norwegian small press. Successful, if not bestselling, and especially popular with local readers.

This was @RoderickAlleyn's big reveal, in a message that arrived just as Ruth walked into her hotel room after fleeing Helen's apartment, the stolen copy of *Nydelig* in her bag.

> I've had it confirmed by Nilsson's literary agent. Though I've promised her my absolute discretion, so please don't use this information without checking in with me first. It is, as you can imagine, a delicate matter. The wife of a notorious serial killer secretly reinventing herself as a crime writer. And one who writes very dark books, at that!

Very dark indeed. Only half of Nilsson's published books seem to have English-language editions, but of the ones she could download, Ruth was alarmed by the recurring themes. Serial killers. Young girls stalked and brutalized. Filled with such explicit detail, some of the murders depicted read more like anatomy lessons.

If there was a psychology to Helen digging her fingers into the wounds her husband had created, Ruth didn't understand it.

"There's no right way to process trauma," Courtney had said in one of their therapy sessions.

But there are probably better ways, Ruth thought as she read over those scenes, than murdering girls twice over.

Beth, in particular, had been horrified by Helen's writing. Even more so when Ruth admitted she would be going back to her apartment today.

"She's luring you in," Beth protested this morning. As if Helen were a witch in a fairy tale.

Sipping tentatively at her glass of wine, Ruth keeps returning to *Nydelig*, the one Jonas Nilsson book she hadn't found any trace of online. Her eyes keep flicking to Helen's bookshelf, to that bottom row of books, where three copies of the novella remain.

"Do you speak fluent Norwegian?" she asks Helen from her seat on the couch, thinking of her failed efforts to understand the book's back cover last night.

Something had been very much lost in translation, no matter what online tool she used to decipher the blurb.

Girl, serial killer, crime—yes. Very little else made sense.

"I spoke fluent Norwegian as a child, thanks to my maternal grandparents," Helen answers. "And I studied very hard when I first moved here. Turns out you can teach an old dog new tricks. Or at least remind them of what they used to know."

"You were a teacher back in the US, weren't you?" Ruth responds, over the noisy thrum of her heart. (How is it possible Helen cannot hear it?)

"I was, Ruth-Ann. A music teacher. But I gave that up a long time ago."

"Why?"

"I had to leave many things behind when I left America."

"Your children?" Ruth asks.

Helen purses her lips slightly at the baldness of this question, then nods.

"Yes. My children are part of that. Not by choice, however. You might say we haven't seen eye to eye for a long time now."

"How old were they when your husband was apprehended?" Ruth asks, even though she knows the answer.

"The twins had just turned eighteen."

Ruth pretends to do a calculation. "But you didn't move to Norway straightaway."

"No." Helen purses her lips again, and Ruth realizes she's doing it to control her breathing. "We moved to another state so the twins could start university, like we'd always planned."

"Where?" Ruth's voice remains steady. This time, she's not letting a single syllable give her away.

Helen, however, inhales sharply through her nose. "Connecticut," she answers finally. "My children were both accepted at Yale."

"That's a good school," Ruth says.

"Indeed. But neither of them made it to a single class. Magnus was off to California before the semester even started. And Louise, well, she went off on her own version of the Peace Corps. For the next few years, I was lucky if I knew what continent she was on."

"I guess they had a lot to process," Ruth says, her second banal observation in a minute.

"Indeed," Helen repeats. "And after what they'd been through, I had no choice but to let them go."

"Did *you* stay? In Connecticut, I mean. I don't remember reading anything about your family living there?"

Ruth is proud of how (almost) direct she's being now.

"Anonymity was a little easier to maintain back then," Helen says, giving Ruth a pointed look. "We kept the house. I wanted my children to have a home to come back to, should they ever need it. But I was rarely there myself, once they were gone. It's lonely to be in a family home all by yourself."

"Why the move all the way to Norway then? That was . . . years later, wasn't it?"

Ruth tells herself to slow down; she nearly gave away her knowledge of just how long the Torrent family owned that house in Connecticut.

"It was time for a fresh start," Helen answers, after closing her eyes briefly. "In America, I will always be Mrs. Martin Torrent. When it was clear my children were not coming back to me, I decided to leave too."

Does that also include your tenant not coming back to you? Ruth imagines asking. *Because he, too, was arrested for murdering a child?*

"And what did you do once you got here to Norway?" she asks instead. Not missing the way this question causes Helen's eyebrows to rise.

"I taught, Ruth-Ann. English instead of music. And now I am retired."

Ruth can't help herself. She looks over at that shelf of Jonas Nilsson books again. This time, Helen follows her gaze.

"I have a lot of time for reading," she says, sipping at her wine.

"Me, too," Ruth replies, raising her own glass. "Though I don't read nearly enough Scandi noir."

They hold eye contact for a beat too long. And it's obvious, in this moment, that neither woman believes a word the other is saying. The only question now is: Who's going to admit it first?

Ruth knows that she has no right to be mad at Helen for her lies, given how many she herself has told to get here. But she didn't come all this way just to confirm what she already knows about Helen's time in Connecticut. Short of accusing the woman of harboring a criminal, all Ruth can do is revert to what she knows about interviewing reluctant witnesses. Sometimes you have to start them in a different place. Let them tell you a story. It worked for Amity a few weeks ago. Maybe it will for Helen too.

"Do you mind if I record the next part of our conversation?" Ruth asks, bringing her new voice recorder out of her bag.

"May I first have your word that you won't reveal my location?" Helen asks her in return.

Ruth nods her agreement.

And then they begin at the most obvious place for a story.

"What were you like as a girl?"

"I wanted to be a *weather* girl," Helen says, glancing at the voice recorder, before half smiling at the confused tilt of Ruth's head.

"It was the outfits, Ruth-Ann. In the 1950s, weather presenters

197

on television wore the most extraordinary things. Silk night-gowns and fur coats and diamonds. They were beauty queens. In those days, you needn't have a qualification to deliver the weather on the nightly news. You just needed to be pretty. I wasn't at all pretty, even my father said so. It wasn't supposed to matter to me. My father had a Methodist upbringing in Minnesota. Decency was important to him. Hard work, and discipline. Beauty was not something to aspire to or be proud of. As his only daughter, my father drummed that into me, as if it were a sermon. But he couldn't conceal how much he loved those weather girls. And so I knew he wasn't telling me the whole truth. I believed him when he said I was a plain girl, but I never believed him when he said it didn't matter."

"I've seen pictures of you," Ruth volunteers. "Just a couple from when you were young. And I think you were actually quite striking."

Helen shrugs the compliment away. "I wasn't blond, I wasn't feminine. I was tall and angular, and unsure of my own limbs. Handsome, a writer might say, but certainly not beautiful. And it really shouldn't matter. But it does in the end, because if you grow up thinking you are not special, you cling to anyone who suggests you might be."

Enter Martin Torrent.

"I was seventeen. He was twenty-three, from a military family and just out of the navy himself. Good-looking in the way of men who are physically competent. It was a double date with my childhood friend Clarissa. She had begged me to come along as a companion for this friend of her new boyfriend, Hank. She wasn't allowed out with Hank on her own yet, so I was essentially a chaperone. I don't think she or Hank actually thought Martin and I would hit it off. And I'm not sure you could say we did. He barely spoke to me over dinner, though I remember being very impressed that he could speak Italian, or so I thought, because I'd never been to an Italian restaurant before and was in awe of how he could pronounce every foreign thing on the menu. It's funny, isn't it, what captures our attention. The details we fixate on."

At the expense of so many other things, Ruth adds silently.

"I can still see a young Martin sitting there, drinking a glass of wine, ordering food I'd never tried. Even though my grandparents had come out from Norway, my family never traveled, and I wasn't exactly a worldly young woman. Martin's quiet confidence entranced me. Next to him, Hank, who couldn't tell risotto from ravioli, suddenly seemed like such a boy. Martin, who had grown up on naval bases around the world, *became* the world to me that night. I saw him as a spinning globe; I wanted to put my finger on the place he stopped, declare it as my own. By the end of the night, alone in the back seat of Hank's truck while Hank and Clarissa had their moment down by the lake, I was already in love. One of the perils of having had no prior experience of love is how quickly you fall. I see you narrowing your eyes at me, Ruth-Ann, but don't presume I knew at the time just how perilous it was. Our courtship was the happiest I've ever been."

Helen pauses to take another sip of her wine.

"We assume we can spot a psychopath from across the room, and that only the willfully ignorant or easily duped would fall for their charms. But it's not quite that simple. The man I met and fell in love with wasn't trying to take advantage of me. He might have appeared more cosmopolitan than anyone I'd ever met, but he wasn't grandiose about it. At twenty-three, Martin was—and this is what nobody wants to hear—quite normal."

Helen stops, appears to consider something.

"Did you grow up expecting life to be fair, Ruth-Ann? Because I did. There was nothing I had done, nothing I had even thought about doing, that God would want to punish me for. I'm not religious now, not at all, but as a child, I believed what my father told me. That there was a capital-G God, and He knew everything about you, so if you were good, He would be good to you in return. And being good was as much about what you asked for as about what you did. I never coveted wealth or fame or grand adventures. The notion of ending up where I am now was completely outside my realm of expectation. I don't think I even knew to want this kind of life. I wanted kindness. Security. Safety. And that's what Martin offered me. Growing up the way he did, always moving around, he'd already had enough adventures for the both of us. What he really wanted was to settle down, build a home and a family, after years of constant upheaval thanks to his father's career and then his own.

"And we did settle down. We raised our two children, and if it seemed like we were a happy family it's because, in those early days, we were."

Helen allows herself a small sigh.

"We ask a lot of young women, don't we? I was still a teenager when I was expected to know what would be best for the rest of my life. I went straight from my father's house to Martin's, both metaphorically and literally. When I got married, I had never spent a single night on my own. It's different for your generation, but that was life back then. We were our men."

Ruth flinches.

"Is it true," she asks, hardly believing her own boldness, "that Ethan Oswald grew up next door to you and your family in Minnesota?"

"*Ethan.*" Helen breathes out his name as if she hasn't spoken it in years. When she looks at Ruth, her eyes are glittering.

That his name should elicit such a response . . . Ruth feels something white-hot course through her.

"Do you know about the girl?" Ruth asks, staring straight into those glittering eyes. "The one who went missing in *Connecticut*?"

Helen is the one to flinch this time.

"I know that Ethan did a terrible thing," she says softly. "And it broke my heart when it happened."

"And why is that?" Ruth asks through gritted teeth.

Helen frowns. "You've clearly done more research than I gave you credit for, Ruth-Ann. I expect you already know that Ethan was very close to my children. To have them lose their father and then their *brother* like that—it would break any mother's heart."

"You loved him," Ruth says. This sudden realization repulses her.

"I did," Helen answers, wiping away a tear. "I thought of that boy as a son."

Ruth is shaking now.

"You don't think it's strange," she asks, her jaw still clenched, "that he ended up murdering little girls too?"

"Oh, Ruth-Ann," Helen says, sounding sad. "As surprised as I am by all this, I am also quite sure you didn't fly all the way from New Zealand just to ask such a predictable question. I've already told you that I had no idea what my husband was capable of, and he was someone who lived under my own roof. Ethan is a sad footnote in the history of my family's disintegration, but I will not be accused of understanding what motivated that young man's awful behavior."

"But that was *your* house," Ruth starts, her words catching in her throat. And then, because it feels like the walls are closing in on her now, she leaps up, grabs her voice recorder and bag, and runs from Mrs. Martin Torrent as fast as she can.

It's not the small truths she is running from. Or the big lies. It's how little any of it seems to matter. You can tell the truth if you want to or lie through your teeth, and the only thing that ever counts is whether people believe you.

Helen said you couldn't spot a psychopath across the room. But would you ever see one in the mirror? Because Ruth knows that all she's really been doing these past few weeks is manipulating people into believing her own stories too. And she's justified her lies because of the truth at their core: Ethan Oswald did terrible things to more than one girl. Amity alone is proof of that.

But Ruth can barely separate victim from perpetrator now. She's locked everyone in that dyadic dance, including herself.

And worse: she seems to have let Oswald take the lead at every turn. Because, even as a dead man, he remains one step ahead of them all.

TWENTY-SIX

Three blue suns on the wall. They might be the wrong color for the real sun, but if you only have one crayon, it's better than drawing no suns at all.

She's been trying not to cry. It helps to bury her face in the single, musty pillow on the bed and scream. Her mouth gets filled with dust and feathers, but at least he won't be able to hear her. She doesn't want to make him angry.

She can hear him again. That man. Talking to someone, low and muffled, outside the door. If she holds her breath, she can hear actual words he's saying.

She. Her. Move. Today.

She lets out a gasp and then holds her breath.

Had he said her name just now?

Yes—there it is again. Her name!

She forgets about being quiet and tries to shout her name back at him, but she can't make her voice loud anymore. It's just a small, croaky sound, and when she tries again, nothing comes out at all.

If this is being dead, she doesn't like it.

The blue suns go blurry. Her thoughts have gone all wavy too. She is sinking underneath them, too fast.

Disappearing.

And then someone starts shouting and banging on the door. It gets louder and louder, that banging, and that shouting, until the door bursts open, and there he is, standing in the sudden light.

The magician, come to let her out of the box at last.

TWENTY-SEVEN

A wearied Ruth sits at a gate in Oslo's small, efficient international airport, waiting to board her flight home. By the time she lands at JFK, she will have been crisscrossing the globe for nearly two weeks. Watching planes take off for London, for Paris and Rome, she alternates between hot shame at the way she ran from Helen's apartment yesterday and awe at her own gumption.

It took guts, she reminds herself, to embark on this journey. And just because she's flying back to New York today, that doesn't mean it's over. Things will surely be much clearer once she's on home ground. Her strong reaction yesterday at Helen's apartment was only because she was tired. Emotional. And unprepared. She'd blurted out that stuff about Ethan without actually knowing what she wanted to hear from that woman.

Helen, who has at least been honest about how much she cared for Ethan, once upon a time.

Even if she's not been honest about much else.

Ruth pats the copy of *Nydelig* in her bag. She must already be thinking more clearly, because just this morning she went online and found a Norwegian-speaking adjunct instructor at the NYU School of Professional Studies who was willing to create a book report for her. An English-language summary of *Nydelig* for the tidy sum of $2,000, plus $500 more if he could produce it within two weeks.

Ethan Oswald's letters might be lost, but if the cover and title are anything to go by, this little book likely contains its own share of his secrets.

Yesterday, despondent, Ruth had told herself the truth probably didn't matter. Now that she's back on its tail, she understands she was just feeling sorry for herself. Looking only at her failures over these past two weeks instead of tallying all the things she's achieved and seeing them as building blocks. A foundation of her own, for once.

Again—a plan is forming.

A pre-boarding announcement for Ruth's flight comes over the PA system. It's nearly time to go home, where sleep, safety, and sanity await. Her original holy trinity, she thinks, which reminds her of Gideon's missing triskelion. The hotel in Auckland said she hadn't left it behind, and it occurs to her that she should probably check in with Rose too. Maybe she only thought she'd packed it away when she left Marama River. It's possible that the triskelion is still sitting there on Juno's nightstand, now that she's gone back to school.

As if on cue, Ruth's phone pings with a message from none other than Ms. Juno Mulvaney.

Have you seen this???

Juno's *this* is a link to a social media post, with a headline all in caps.

POSSIBLE BREAK IN THE MYSTERIOUS
DISAPPEARANCE OF LITTLE COCO WILSON!

Ruth's hand goes to her throat as she reads the story beneath that headline.

> Unconfirmed sighting alert! A witness has reported seeing a child who matches the description of seven-year-old Coco Wilson, who went missing from her family home in Hoben, Connecticut, on May 25. They describe seeing a young girl wearing a Rangers baseball cap and holding the hand of an older man at a gas station just outside Guntersville, Alabama. She then climbed into the back of a gray sedan. In the front passenger seat was a young woman holding a small, white dog. The man is described as tall, Caucasian, and in his mid-thirties, while the young woman is blond and Caucasian. Anyone with further information should call the FBI hotline number below.

Ruth is still trying to process what this possible sighting means, when a second message from Juno arrives on her phone.

Told you that town was creepy! the text says, followed by another link, this time to a blog post.

When it loads on her phone screen, Ruth finds herself staring at a close-up photograph of a little girl who still has most of her baby teeth, and the kind of grin that doesn't belong anywhere near the headline that leads her story.

THE MURDER THAT HAUNTED HOBEN

A minute later, Ruth's fellow passengers are standing up from their seats, jostling into lines to board their flight. She lets these other passengers pick her up, sweep her along; she's suddenly in no condition to make her own way. Her legs feel hollow, and for a second she worries that she's going to faint.

Because halfway down that blog post about Beth Lovely's abduction and murder is a grainy image of another little girl.

And this girl is clinging to a man in uniform as he shields her from the bright light outside a house on Longview Road. That haunted house, with its papered-over windows and blue crayon, with its chains, and that stinking bed, and those three wrong-colored suns scribbled on the wall.

It wasn't the magician.

It wasn't the man who smelled of mint and hit her hand away, and locked her in that room. When that door burst open, it was someone with a kind face and big soft hands. A man who asked her name, and told her his own name too.

"Everything is going to be okay now," he said.

There were others behind him. They looked and sounded like giant toy soldiers, but she focused on that kind face and those soft hands, and she wanted to believe this stranger. When he broke through those chains. When he lifted her from that stinking bed, and carried her like she was still allowed to be a baby. When the real sun hurt her eyes and she buried her face into the solid warmth of his shoulder, and he said her name, like a lullaby.

"Everything is going to be okay now, Ruthie."

And in that moment, she did believe him.

RUTHIE

TWENTY-EIGHT

Connecticut, May 1996

Beth Lovely is missing.

It takes a couple of hours for her disappearance to be reported to the Hoben Police Department. Important hours. Lost to confusion and doubt hours. Waiting by the door and walking the streets hours. Small knot in the stomach hours, it's probably nothing hours.

It has to be nothing, it's not nothing, what if it's something hours.

She was walking home from school with three of her classmates. They stopped at the playground across from the high school, like they always did.

"When did you last see her?"

"I don't know," they say.

I don't know, I don't know, I don't know.

These other kids, the ones who will be tucked into their beds tonight, the ones whose parents will sleep on the floor next to those beds until they add bolts to their windows and chains to their doors.

These other kids who made it home.

They don't know what happened to Beth Lovely.

She was there at the playground. She was right there with them.

And then she was gone.

———

Twenty-four hours. Forty-eight. Five days. A week. Hope becomes a terrorist. A tyrant, offering small consolations: *We received a tip that she was seen in New Haven yesterday.* Meting out devastating punishments. *We found this charm bracelet by the maple tree, do you recognize it? The remains of a small child have been found in the panhandle. There are one thousand two hundred and seven known sex offenders in our database. The FBI want to talk to you, Mr. and Mrs. Lovely. There's a chance she may have been taken over state lines.*

We're throwing everything at this, Bill. We'll find her, Patty.

They can't find her.

Someone knows where she is. Someone knows who did this. Officer Canton repeats this to Bill and Patty Lovely, every time they see him. They've known him since he was a boy; everyone in this town has. He's now a fine young man whose beloved K-9 buddy, John Douglas, picked up Beth's scent by the playground's swings, followed it to the street, then back again. As if she were in a perpetual loop between the road and the playground. Never making it any farther.

Never making it home.

"Someone knows," Canton reminds her frantic parents over and over.

Someone knows what happened to her.

———

Ruth-Ann has had the talk about strangers.

It seems like every grown-up is talking about them right now.

Because that girl went missing. Ruthie's cat Nala is missing too. She's worried about her cat, but her parents seem more worried about the little girl who none of them have ever met. And they keep saying: *You do know, don't you, pumpkin? Never to talk to strangers.*

Of course she knows. If she could just figure out exactly what—or who—a stranger is supposed to be.

———

When Ruthie goes missing on the morning of Saturday, May 25, 1996, Beth Lovely has been gone ten days. Bill and Patty cling to stories of children showing up months later. Years. They would wait that long. If it meant—

These past ten days, they have learned exactly what grown men can do to a child. Every parent's worst nightmare, the headlines scream. But nightmares are never as bad as knowing. The things Bill and Patty now know about what grown men do.

And still, they wait.

They field calls from national media. Receive letters from parents whose own children are missing. Officer Canton sits with them in the living room, reading through those letters, just in case one contains that missing clue. He shows up every day, even when field officers from the FBI take over the investigation. Encouraged by Officer Canton, Bill and Patty leave the curtains open and the porch light on. So that Beth will know they haven't given up. That her parents will wait as long as it takes for their baby to come home.

Everything changes the morning Ruth-Ann Nelson, Cynthia and Ellis's little Ruthie, disappears.

"He's still here in town," the Lovelys say to each other. "He can't have taken Beth too far."

One day, they'll be ashamed that they found hope in another

family's nightmare. Bill and Patty Lovely will spend the rest of their lives trying to make up for that treacherous feeling. But now, ten days after their daughter disappeared, they think: *We're going to find her.*

If the man who took Beth has already snatched another child, and from a front yard not five blocks from the same playground where Beth disappeared, he must be from around here, Bill and Patty reason. A lot of families live over there on Canyon Road, where Ruthie was taken, including a few from their church. Barb and Mike, with their four kids. Jo and Joseph, with their trio of J-named offspring. Jim and Sally, with their son Chip and that exchange student from New Zealand they've been hosting this year—the girl who did a terrific job as Julie Jordan in the high school musical last month. Patty had wanted to ask if she'd be interested in teaching Beth the piano before she went home.

Is her own daughter ever coming home?

Beth.

Little Ruthie Nelson is all anyone can talk about at church on the Sunday after she, too, has disappeared. Bill's and Patty's hands are red from all the silent, squeezing comfort they receive as people walk by. People who still don't know what to say, even as they can't stop speculating with each other. Is there a serial killer in their town? A pedophile living among them? A monster hiding in plain sight?

Ethan Oswald squeezes Bill Lovely's hand too. He offers his deepest condolences for the Lovely family's loss.

"I can't even imagine the pain you must be feeling," he tells them the morning after Ruthie Nelson disappears.

Cynthia and Ellis Nelson are not religious people, but they have certainly been keeping the Lovely family in their prayers.

When their own daughter goes missing, they understand just how little thoughts and prayers mean. There is no condolence, no invocation or incantation, that can ease their suffering or quell their terrified anger.

The Lovelys are so much more gracious, others will think later, when they compare the two sets of parents and how they each reacted to the loss of their little girl. For now, neighbors leave casseroles at the door, lasagna, a carrot cake. Officer Canton is the one who brings each dish inside.

"It was only five minutes," Cynthia keeps saying. "I only lost sight of her for *five fucking minutes*."

"We'll find her," Officer Canton repeats to yet another grieving parent, but even to his own ears the words sound formulaic. Two little girls in as many weeks. It doesn't look good. Not given what they know about children kidnapped by a stranger. Canton won't even let himself think about the stats on the primary motivation for strangers abducting children in the first place.

By mid–Sunday morning, the young officer has had as little sleep as Ruthie Nelson's parents. He is agitated, drinking his umpteenth cup of coffee at the otherwise empty station. Everyone else is out working on the case. Sitting at his desk, feeling hopelessly ineffective, Canton wants to punch right through the solid wood under his fingers, break something—his own hand would do . . . and that's when the phone starts ringing.

Into the silence of the empty station, the sound is shrill, desperate. Commanding.

Canton is sure, even before he picks up the receiver.

That *this* is the someone who knows.

———

Sunday lunchtime. Ruthie Nelson has been missing for twenty-eight hours, and John Douglas, a bloodhound on the verge of retirement, is the one who is agitated. Twitching, like his handler twitched when he first took that call.

John Douglas knows where she is. The little girl who wore that *Lion King* nightgown they held under his nose. The one her parents took from the wash and handed over to the police yesterday.

He'd lost her smell the first time, after tracking it across the road from the girl's house. Just like that other little girl, the one whose scent seemed to disappear at the curb. But she's been *here*. Six miles away from where John Douglas last sensed her presence.

And the scent of her fear is pointing like an arrow now.

This way, John Douglas says to his handler as best he can. *This way!*

It's never one single blow that cracks a case wide open. But the phone call Officer Canton took was enough to cause a fracture. A fault line that quickly spread all the way to Longview Road. The anonymous woman who made that call hadn't known exactly where the missing girls were.

But she did tell him where to start looking.

For a while after she was rescued, it seemed like every adult Ruthie met wanted to write down what she said. She's done her best to answer their weird questions, make them smile instead of *hmmm*, because she doesn't want to upset anyone, the way she seemed to upset everyone when she climbed into the front seat of the man's van early that Saturday morning, because he said he had found her cat. Months later, and Ruthie's mother is still chewing her fingernails. Crying. Her father still looks like someone has smeared purple chalk under his eyes. And her parents aren't the only ones she's disappointed since that day. All those Clipboards, even the kind ones, say *hmmm* when Ruthie tells them the truth.

When she insists that Beth Lovely was with her, near the end. That she showed Ruthie how to scream into the pillow, and told her not to show the man she was scared. She knows what Beth told her right before she was rescued was real. *She* was real. The actually dead girl, in those photographs all over the news, had stayed with her until Officer Canton burst through the door.

"Beth Lovely died over a week before you were abducted, Ruthie."

It was a child psychologist from New Haven called Susan who told her that. Susan definitely wasn't one of the nice ones. But at least she bothered to explain why everyone with their clipboards and tape recorders and *show me on the doll* toys was so unhappy with her. They all thought she was lying to them.

So, Ruthie has started telling them what they want to hear.

Yes. She understands that Beth was already dead.

Yes. She understands she couldn't possibly have been talking to her that morning.

Yes. She understands she was the only one in the room the whole time Ethan Oswald had her chained to the bed.

It hasn't saved her mother's fingernails or wiped away her father's chalky bruises, but it has stopped the *hmmm*s and the *let's start again*s and all the furious scribbling of notes anytime she talks about Beth.

From the beginning, they've wanted Ruthie to be the only girl.

And so she says she was.

———

Something Ruthie never mentioned to the Clipboards.

The flower ring. They thought it was never recovered. Lost somewhere between the playground and Ethan Oswald's house, after he told Beth her ailing grandfather had been rushed to the hospital. Though a recalcitrant Oswald confessed very little after his arrest, he did share the story he'd used to lure Beth into his van.

"Your parents are waiting for you at the hospital," he told the worried little girl. "We have to get you there as soon as possible, because they're sad, and they don't need any more stress while they're taking care of your poppy. I'll go start the van—see, that blue one over there—and you meet me as quick as you can."

When Oswald said he had no idea what happened to Beth's forget-me-not ring, he meant it. He wasn't one for trinkets.

No one ever thought to ask Ruthie about the ring. And she never said. That she'd been sobbing, and Beth had told her to bury her face in that smelly pillow to silence her screams. How her lips found another solid thing beneath the feathers, much smaller than the crayon she'd retrieved from under the bedcovers. A ring with a blue-and-yellow flower, just the right size for what Ruthie's mother called her wedding finger.

Beth told her the flower was called a forget-me-not and that the ring had been a gift from her grandmother on her seventh birthday.

The last birthday she ever had.

They thought she couldn't hear the debates about her sanity.

But she's gotten good at hearing what is said behind closed doors. This is how Ruthie learns other things too. Like how the man had taken her on a *whim*, whatever that was. Snatched her from her front yard, where she'd gone to collect the Saturday paper for her parents, while her mommy was making pancakes in the house. There were places he had to be that particular day, private singing lessons he had to teach. Then he had to stay overnight in a whole other state for a chorale concert and make it back for church the next morning. He needed to be seen. And this meant Ruthie was lucky; the man who wasn't really a magician didn't have enough time to finish his trick.

Officer Canton was the real magician, anyway. He made sure she was the one who didn't really die.

Because here's another thing she's learned since he carried her from that room: a lot of children *do* die.

There is map of the long-term missing. An online, interactive map that Ruth finds a few years after her rescue. There are tiny pins, dotted all over the United States, representing children who have been missing for years, along with those children whose bodies have been found but their identities have not.

There are so many pins on that map. You have to zoom right out to see them all. Beth's not there. Ruth's not there. Eventually, she almost forgets that she might have been.

But she never forgets what America really looks like.

It is a landscape of the lost.

TWENTY-NINE

New York, June 2015

Summer lands in New York before Ruth-Ann Baker does.

The season is changing, and Coco Wilson is still not home. That sighting in Alabama doesn't seem to have made it further than a couple of crime blogs. Either it has merit, and investigators are keeping it quiet, or someone got a little too enthusiastic with their armchair detective work. Ruth knows that both things are possible.

When she arrives in New York, the heat is unbearable. Back in her apartment, all Ruth's favorite houseplants have turned an accusatory yellow. Oslo was politely warm. Marama River was downright chilly. Melbourne couldn't seem to choose. New York? In her absence, it has started to swelter and sweat. Opening the windows inside the apartment does nothing to cool the place down.

She has over an hour to kill before there's somewhere she needs to be. Restless, Ruth remembers that it's seldom too hot at Sweeney's, because Owen desperately hates the heat. After an attempt to revive a petulant peace lily and a recalcitrant orchid, Ruth puts on the least amount of fabric possible while still remaining decent and heads over to the bar.

"Nancy Drew!" Owen exclaims when she walks in. He has so many portable fans set to their highest settings, Ruth can barely hear him over the din.

"We missed you, kid. Don't kiss me, though—you're too sweaty. But let me get you a cold drink."

"What did *I* miss?" she asks as Owen heads behind the bar to mix two gin and tonics. She's hoping for a little time before the inevitable questions about her trip begin.

Pouring more gin than tonic, Owen points to two Ken dolls sitting up on the bar, one of them wearing a wedding dress.

"Three proposals while you were gone, Ruth. *Three.* It was like Fire Island in here the other night. The gays are going to save marriage, I tell you."

Ruth smiles. "Here's hoping."

Owen nods at the Kill Jar. "Not many murderers while you were gone, though. I reckon your boy scared them off."

"My boy?"

Ruth pretends not to understand, but Owen is having none of that.

"Don't be coy with me, Miss Marple. I know you've been texting each other."

"Do you even know who Miss Marple is, Owen?"

"No. But don't change the subject. That Gabe fella came in every day the first week you were gone."

Ruth can't help but smile. Owen, dramatic, nosy, optimistic Owen, is so far removed from the complications of her life, she can almost forget they exist.

Almost.

But she's done pushing away all the things she was never, ever meant to forget.

On the flight home from Oslo, Ruth had what she can only describe as an epiphany. A tectonic shift that jolted her forward in her seat, and for the first time she could see the cause of the collision. Little Ruthie Nelson's ordeal had always been the fault line she lived on, but ignoring it, ignoring *her*, had only caused these two versions of Ruth to jam up against each other, get stuck. It was no wonder she lived on such shaky ground.

It took seeing Amity, Rose, and Helen, these three women with their erasures and their evasions, for Ruth to fully see her own self-deception. She had been shocked to receive that second blog post link from Juno, but when the plane took off from Oslo, Ruth suddenly felt euphoric. Because she wasn't a manipulative liar, like she'd feared back in Oslo. And she wasn't having another "episode." Ruth-Ann Baker was simply a woman who had never truly confronted her past.

We didn't think to ask where those memories might go, her uncle had said when she last saw him.

Now Ruth could give him the answer to that: "I gave so many of my memories to Beth."

It's not like Ruth never understood what she herself had gone through at seven years old. It's more like those memories had never truly felt like her own. Her name, when it did appear in a story about Ethan Oswald, was always the footnote. Most times, she was simply referred to as *another little girl*.

Ethan Oswald was caught when he abducted another little girl.

Another little girl was found safe and well.

That was a blessing, in its way. It meant she'd only had to take her mother's maiden name, Baker, instead of changing her whole identity. Anonymity, as Helen said in Oslo, was easier back then.

But when Coco Wilson went missing on the same date as

Ruth's own abduction nineteen years earlier, she'd felt exposed in a different way. Like all that sedimentary rock she'd been buried under was suddenly cracking, crumbling. It's taken four countries and three women across two hemispheres for Ruth-Ann Baker to realize what she really wants.

She wants to forgive herself for willingly getting into that van. Because everything that came after, from having to leave Connecticut to her parents' divorce, has felt like her fault.

To have made the worst mistake of your life at seven years old is a terrible weight to carry through your life.

It's always been assumed that Oswald kidnapped her on a whim. But what if he just chose the wrong day? What if he'd targeted her long before that Saturday morning, and someone she'd felt safe with had tricked her into trusting him, *groomed* her, even? Then little Ruthie Nelson stops being another cautionary tale about children and strangers. She stops being an example of what not to do.

The same goes for Coco Wilson.

Prepare your children!

For heaven's sake, parents. Warn your kids about the monsters out there so they don't make a terrible mistake.

Too many people still say that. Not realizing that the monsters are mostly just—men.

Fathers, husbands, teachers. With daughters, wives, students, right there beside them.

If someone did trick Ruth, the most obvious suspect among Ethan's women is the young Annie Whitaker. But if Amity was writing Ethan letters back then, and he was living in Helen's house, did either of them know what he was doing too?

The only round of poker Ruth won against Juno, back in Marama River, was because she had a full house. Two kings. Three queens. She thinks of those cards now, and that singular winning hand.

Maybe it makes sense only if she considers Amity, Rose, and Helen, in it together.

But she still can't see *how*.

Ruth forces her attention back to Sweeney's, and to her boss, so hopeful about the boy. *Her* boy, Gabe.

"I gotta go," she says, setting down her drink and kissing Owen's cheek. "I just wanted to let you know that I'm back."

The adjunct instructor has just finished teaching a class in Norwegian cinema. Cory speaks seven languages, all of them fluently, and he is, he assures Ruth, a very good reader.

They meet at a café near Union Square. Ruth feels like she should be wearing a trench coat and a fedora, so cloak-and-dagger is the exchange, as she hands Cory an envelope of cash as well as her stolen copy of *Nydelig* in a brown paper bag.

She repeats the instructions she sent him from Norway.

"Think high school book report," she reiterates. "Where there might be a test on the metaphors and themes after. Like, *What was the author really saying here?*"

Cory nods. "I get it. Should be interesting, so thanks again for the gig."

He pulls the copy of *Nydelig* out of the bag and turns it over in his hands.

"I don't know anything about this author," he says, frowning.

"Me neither," Ruth responds. A little truth.

Or the biggest one, yet.

The next day, Ressler is so excited to be reunited with Ruth he nearly bowls her over on the street.

"Sorry," Joe and Gideon say in unison, as Ruth attempts to control both her breath and her balance, her giant dog resting his giant paws on her shoulders, like he is telling her to never, ever leave him again.

She knows this means her uncles have been spoiling Ressler, letting him jump all over them. *You gotta show these dogs who's boss*, Office Canton warned her years ago, but when she repeated this to her uncles the first time they'd looked after Ressler on their own, you'd think she'd said children should be put to work cleaning chimneys. But she can only pretend to be annoyed as Ressler stretches his neck and lets out one of his foghorn howls. He has found her, with an instinct that lives in his bones.

"Well," Joe starts as they walk toward the park. "How are you feeling, now that you're back?"

Not: *How was it?* Not: *What did you do?*

How is she feeling?

"Excellent!" Ruth says, with a little too much cheer. "The interview with Rose went really well, and I have so much good material. It's nice to have a purpose again."

"That's fantastic," Gideon says, but Ruth catches the quick glance he and Joe share.

To them, she will always be an unreliable narrator.

"We can't wait to hear what you come up with," Gideon continues, before offering any assistance she might need. With no trace of ego, he tells Ruth that he *knows a few people* who might be able to help with her podcast. Gideon is being modest, as usual. She's seen a photo of him—at an environmental fundraiser, she thinks—standing between Robert Redford and Al Gore.

With her uncles either side of her now, and Ressler a nose

in front, Ruth's mood feels tempered, manageable. The heat has dialed down this morning, and the sky is clear as they enter Central Park at West Ninetieth Street. Behind them, the muted colors of the iconic Eldorado towers somehow make every other hue brighter.

After nineteen years in New York, if Ruth doesn't take certain things for granted, she sometimes forgets to enjoy them. Today, she takes a moment to appreciate the beautiful contradiction of the 843 acres of flora and fauna that is Central Park, this oasis in the midst of a city forever constructing itself. She really did miss New York while she was gone. It is good to be home. And this *is* her home, even if she feels guilty about how her family came to live here.

She's not coping, all those Clipboards said. *Have you considered a change of scene?*

It doesn't surprise Ruth that the Lovelys never moved from the house Beth grew up in. Surviving takes many forms; Bill and Patty made their own survival about maintaining the back-yard where Beth had loved to play. For years now, they have nurtured the flowers and plants and trees that watched Beth grow. They have bird feeders and squirrel houses, and clover to attract deer. They find solace in the various wild animals that visit Beth's garden as the seasons change. They said as much in a television interview once, and it made Ruth's throat ache. How tender Bill and Patty were with their love for their daughter. How soft they were with their grief.

Today, as Ruth's small processional walks along the park's Bridle Path, where her parents used to take her horseback riding in the early days, her thoughts wind their way back to Rose Mul-vaney. Rescuing wild horses, yet refusing to leave the place that makes her own daughter feel so trapped. Ruth has not heard from Juno since she fired her latest arrow, sending that blog post.

Hopefully, Juno has gone back to school and is barely giving her former houseguest another thought. Her mother, however, is another matter. But when it comes to Rose, Ruth hasn't got her so-called ducks in a row just yet.

Crossing over West Drive, Joe announced he wants, or rather needs, another coffee. Their little band exits the park to head over to Milk Bar on Columbus, where they order lattes and three delicious *I shouldn't, but I'm going to* slices of pie. No one is in any hurry today, there's nothing to cram in, because Joe and Gideon will be coming back to the city next week for Pride weekend, anyway. And for what they hope to be an even bigger celebration, with the Supreme Court's ruling on marriage equality due any day now. Ruth has been so preoccupied lately, she hasn't stopped to think how that must feel for her uncles. To have their love, their *family*, up for debate. With no explanation, she pulls Joe and Gideon in for a hug. Ressler, slack on his lead, stares at the trio with his wise, mournful eyes, and the girl behind the counter making their coffees smiles at them. This happy family they make.

Ruth says it out loud this time: "It's good to be home."

To keep herself busy while she waits for Cory the polyglot to translate Helen's book, Ruth refocuses on Coco Wilson. It's not like she hasn't been thinking about the little girl, but there's no denying all those surfaced memories of her own abduction have turned Ruth's head other ways.

But why should looking back prevent her from seeing what is happening in front of her now, when Coco's disappearance from her front yard so eerily mirrors her own? It even happened on the same date, May 25—National Missing Children's Day, which is either a terrible coincidence or someone's sick idea of a joke.

And Ruth *really* doesn't believe in coincidences. To her, it's how people talk themselves out of seeing painful truths. That's why no one ever believed her about the girls. They refused to acknowledge the constellation their disappearances made above Hoben, Connecticut, because it was easier to consider each abduction a terrible, unforeseen tragedy rather than an indictment of their community, their society. Their *men*.

It would seem that others are starting to connect the dots now, though. There's a whole new thread on *Stranger than Fiction* suggesting that Hoben might be the new Hellmouth.

NEW HELLMOUTH ALERT! the thread is not-so-subtly titled. Ruth rolls her eyes, but she reads on all the same. The first post outlines the details of Coco's disappearance and then suggests it *might* link to Beth Lovely's murder. Ruth's own abduction, too, which she is used to skipping over, but she doesn't now. She allows herself to sit with the truth of her name. Her *Known Victim* status. To Ruth's surprise, there's even a brief mention of Rhea and Leila in this thread, though the commenters haven't gotten to little Lori yet. For the first time it seems like Ruth is not the only person seeing that sixty-mile radius. All those pins on the board, so close together.

Reminding herself that this is *Stranger than Fiction*, not the *New York Times*, Ruth reins in her excitement as she reads through the thread's comments so far.

It would seem people are suddenly bursting to talk about Ruth's old hometown.

So, a bunch of girls have gone missing along the I-91 over the years, the first reply says. *And Hoben is right there in the middle? Hmmmm . . .*

That's one weird town, dude, someone adds, and the responses come thick and fast from there.

It's one of those cookie-cutter places where your neighbor probably has bodies in the basement, right.

I used to live there and you nailed it!

Really? So it's not a good place anymore? Sad!! That's where my folks grew up.

It *used* to be safe.

What, like in the 50s?

Yeah, man. I miss small-town America.

Only a white person would say that.

Whatever. I'll tell you who is not white. Coco Wilson's so-called daddy.

Dude. 80% of serial killers are white.

Who said Wilson is a serial killer??

More like a baby killer!!

And so it goes on, as Team Leo (they even call themselves that) throw more and more accusations at Coco's dad. Eventually, Ivy Wilson is pulled into the muck with him. To the comment-ers blithely tapping out their theories, she just doesn't seem *this* enough, *that* enough. She isn't acting the way a mother would act if her child was missing.

Ruth impulsively types out a text message to her own mother. *Mom, what was it like for you when I was kidnapped?*

She knows that Cynthia has recently taken herself to a well-ness retreat in Perugia; her message shows as undelivered.

Returning to the Hoben thread on *Stranger than Fiction*, Ruth pauses over a new comment, posted thirty seconds ago.

My cousin used to live in Hoben. He says Ivy's high school boyfriend had a real temper, and that she kept hooking up with him for years after graduation. Maybe she has a thing for bad boys. Lots of women go from one bad guy to the next.

Maybe the HS boyfriend did it! someone responds as Ruth watches the conversation in real time.

Anyone know his name?

Lemme see if I can find out from my cousin . . .

Don't waste your time, dude. It was the stepdad for sure. I heard he was pimping Coco out to his friends. Hellmouth shit, for sure.

Ruth's stomach lurches as she quickly exits the thread. What does it take to say such things about a person?

"What does it take to *do* those things?" Beth fires back.

"Dad?"

"Who is this? Just joking, pumpkin! Yours was the first number I put in my new phone. How the hell are you, Ruthie?"

A flash of purple bruises. Those tired eyes. In the years since Ruth's kidnapping, Ellis Nelson has remained relentlessly positive with his only child. Exhaustingly so.

Ruth sighs. Repeats the question she asked her mother.

"What was it like for you when I was gone?"

"Jesus, Ruthie—that's a big one," Ellis splutters down the phone, before forcing a laugh. "Should I be lying down on a couch for this conversation?"

"Be serious for a second, Dad."

"Sorry," he says, though he sounds more defensive than apologetic. As if catching himself, his tone goes back to light in an instant.

"I thought we'd agreed to let those sleeping dogs snooze their lives away, Ruthie. It was so long ago. And we've all come so far since then, haven't we."

It's not a question. Ruth realizes there's no point in pushing him further. They finish the call talking about the weather. Joe and Gideon, and whether they're still enjoying life on the farm. And the upcoming Caribbean cruise Ellis is taking with his wife, Brenda.

"We'll do dinner as soon as I'm back," he says, before they hang up. As if he was already gone.

Later that night, checking her messages, Ruth sees that her mother has read the text she sent this afternoon.

And just like her ex-husband Ellis, Cynthia has declined to respond to her daughter's request.

THIRTY

This book is trippy.

Ruth hadn't asked to receive updates on Cory's translation efforts, but he has been sending them almost daily anyway.

Nearly there.

OMG, didn't see that coming.

This would make a GREAT movie.

Ruth can't decide whether she is glad for these unsolicited updates, or if they just make her nervous about what's coming next. Because that book may well be her reckoning. If there really are answers about her own abduction to be found in *Nydelig*, she's going to have to decide what to do with them.

If Officer Canton once told her that ghosts did not count as proof, how likely is he to be swayed by a work of fiction?

"Why not just do the podcast?" Rhea asks. "*How I tricked three women into telling me their darkest secrets*, or something like that." She laughs at her own cleverness, and for a strange, startling moment she looks exactly like Juno Mulvaney.

It has occurred to Ruth. That *The Other Women* could be the best way to share what she finds. She wouldn't even have to point any fingers, herself. She could simply lay out all the facts for her listeners and let them determine who is guilty. A trial in the court of public opinion.

"You're getting ahead of yourself again," Beth reminds her. "We don't even know what that book says."

She's right. Ruth can decide, once she actually has facts to lay out. Cory will be getting back to her next week with his report, and she simply needs to wait.

"And maybe take a break," Beth suggests hopefully. "You haven't stopped since Coco went missing. Maybe use this time to regroup. Get your thoughts in order. And spend some quality time with your uncles and Owen."

"Besides, everyone else is out of commission right now," she adds pointedly.

This is true. Back in Marama River, Rose had essentially told Ruth to leave her alone. Amity is seemingly still in Paris (though her Instagram feed has remained oddly Paris-free). And as for Helen, Ruth presumes the woman is on her vacation here in the US—but they haven't communicated since Ruth's dramatic exit from Helen's apartment in Oslo.

She is still embarrassed about that. She has no idea what Helen thinks of her now. What *any* of them think of her, if she's honest.

A little break from dead and missing girls might be the best thing.

"Not like five years ago," she quickly assures a worried Lori. "I promise."

It'll just be a brief time-out. A sabbatical. She can take one from Gabe too. Because she has no idea what he thinks of her, either. Owen insisted the "boy" was keen, but just yesterday he sent a text saying he was going to be offline—*for a bit*. Ruth knew he was out of town, but out of touch felt different. Like a dismissal.

She'd had to stop herself from sending something snarky back. Eventually, she settled on a (passive-aggressive) thumbs-up emoji.

Just another thing to feel embarrassed about. When it comes to Gabe, Ruth seems to have the emotional maturity of her moody houseplants.

———

Three days later, Owen opens Sweeney's early.

The small crowd that gathers is made up of Sweeney's regular staff and Owen's theater buddies, plus Joe, Gideon, and Ruth. And Ressler, of course, wearing his best rainbow collar. All but the latter sip at Bloody Marys and mimosas as they stare up at the televisions mounted on the back wall of the bar, the three screens tuned to a live feed of the nation's Supreme Court steps, on this Friday morning at the end of June.

Gideon and Joe are sitting at opposite ends of a long table, but Ruth sees the way they constantly find each other, the little nods and smiles, the gaze held, as the minutes tick by.

In contrast to their subtle apprehension, Owen wears his nerves like bright, bold jewelry. Necklaces jangling, bracelets clattering. He is older than everyone else in this room. Knows what it is to be kicked out of your own house, and God's house too. It's clear to Ruth that, for most of Owen's friends, this day is not just about the right to get married. It's about all the ways they've been othered. Misrepresented and mistrusted. *My father used to beat my mother black-and-blue, but we're the ones destroying the sanctity of marriage?* Owen had said last night, bitter in a way Ruth hadn't ever heard him before.

She is determined to push her own issues aside, at least for another twenty-four hours. Today is about Joe, Gideon, and Owen. She wants to be present and supportive for them, as they have been for her.

They watch in awed silence as marriage equality becomes law of the land in these United States. When the decision makes its way down the Supreme Court steps, the roar from the waiting crowd reverberates all the way to this small bar, more than two hundred miles from Washington, DC. Their silence gives way to shouting, hugging, tears. Owen disappears from her side, and Ruth knows to let him be. When he comes back to the group a few minutes later, his eyes are red, but he is carrying a bottle of Dom Pérignon and sashaying to the Donna Summer song he has set to blast throughout the bar.

"Come here, Velma Dinkley!" Owen commands, and for the first time since she was seven years old, Ruth lets herself dance.

By midafternoon, Sweeney's neon *Closed* sign has been turned on in the window, but the doors stay open. Ressler, clearly bemused by all the activity, alternates between sleep and mooching for food and chin scratches. When Ruth checks her phone, she sees separate but identical messages from her parents, asking her to give Joe a big hug from them.

Unexpectedly, the text underneath these messages is from Juno in New Zealand. No actual words. Just a series of rainbow emojis.

There's one from Gabe too. Not completely offline, after all. She smiles at the single rainbow he's sent, accompanied by the word *Yes!*

It is startling for Ruth to realize that, for all her angst about him, she wishes he were here to share this moment with her. They've been in such an odd push-pull routine, but all of a sudden, she can imagine them dancing to Owen's disco tunes together. Getting their arms stuck as they attempt to twirl, finding new ways to be in sync with each other. She sees them laughing and loosening and—

Maybe absence really does make the heart grow fonder.

I want to see you, she messages back.

Buoyed by the joy of this day. And this proof that things *do* get better.

She wants to hold on to that certainty for as long as she can.

———————

The next two days pass in a blur of Pride celebrations. Ruth falls into bed on Sunday night, her feet sore and her head likely to follow suit, once the glow of the weekend fades and the fizz from all that champagne flattens.

She wakes in the middle of the night with a dry throat and a raging headache, dimly aware that she'd been dreaming of a boiled kettle, whistling. Glancing at her bedside clock, Ruth sees a brief, neon flash of 3:33 a.m. Tiptoeing to the bathroom so as not to wake Ressler, she leaves the lights off as she leans over the sink, splashing water over her face, before cupping her hands to gulp it down.

In the mirror over the bathroom sink, Ruth's reflection is hazy. She stares hard at the glass and, for a second, she completely disappears. Blinking her way back into existence, she feels the fog of sleep lift until she is suddenly very much awake.

3:33. The triplicity that is Hecate. Goddess of crossroads and queen of the restless dead.

She might have been taking a break these past few days, but Ruth hasn't entirely left the dead and missing behind. Each night, she's allowed herself entry to the cult of Hecate, discovering as much as she can about this goddess who roamed the earth with her hounds and visited the underworld so freely. Though she might not be as well-known as other ancient goddesses, Ruth learned she did make a couple of brief, haughty appearances in the play *Macbeth*. Ruth is no Shakespeare buff—most of Hecate's speech to the Three Witches on the heath went right over her head—but one particular line had struck her, and it returns to her now.

And you all know, security / Is mortals' chiefest enemy.

People get complacent. Overconfident. They stop looking over their shoulder. Hubris can be the downfall of even the most cunning villain. History—and *fiction*—is full of such examples.

Ruth races back to her bedroom, not caring if she wakes Ressler now. When he does indeed open his eyes, she pats the mattress, encouraging him to jump up onto the bed beside her.

Hecate, with her hound, ready to hunt.

When she opens her laptop, it is there in her inbox, as she'd known it would be. Cory's summary of *Nydelig*, delivered early.

As she reads over the fifteen-page report, Ruth feels as if she might still be dreaming. Her cheeks blaze as she gets to the end, before returning to the first page to start again.

Her finger traces every woman she recognizes in this book.

And every girl. Including Coco Wilson, who can be seen right there in the epilogue. If you know what to look for.

Cory's analysis of *Nydelig* does not offer any neat answers. But it does change one important thing. Or, rather, bring it back into focus.

What Ruth thought before she woke up at 3:33 this morning: Coco's abduction, one so similar to her own, sent her straight back to all those unresolved questions she had about Ethan Oswald.

What she considers now: Coco Wilson's disappearance really might be connected to him.

To *her*.

And it's not just one suspect conceivably linking these cases across decades.

Of course—there are three.

There is a scene in *Nydelig* that so closely mirrors Ruth's buried memories of the events leading up to her abduction, she might have written the pages herself. The animal is different (a rabbit). The setting and country (a skating rink in Norway). The girls' ages, too (thirteen and nine).

But the twist is not.

In his report, Cory used this particular scene to illustrate the MO of Billy, the murderous protagonist. The way an older girl befriended a younger girl over the course of a few weeks. Extracting information from her, like the fact that her rabbit was missing, before passing those details on to her teacher to use as he pleased.

When she was seven years old, Ruth told Officer Canton and all the other uniformed people that she got into that van because the man said he had found her missing cat. He even knew Nala's name. But she never told them about the girl who she'd been crying to the day Nala disappeared. It hadn't seemed important.

Not until a few weeks ago, when Coco went missing.

That girl, the one who'd comforted Ruth, didn't have an accent. But Ruth remembers, now, how seamlessly Rose switched from her own New Zealand accent to an American one when they were sitting at the kitchen table in Marama River. There's no exchange student in *Nydelig*. No Julie Jordan. But Ruth is convinced at least one of Billy's loyal students is based on Annie Whitaker.

Cory called that character a "myrmidon," introducing Ruth to this new word. It meant someone who followed a superior's orders unquestioningly. Someone who did what they were told, even if it was immoral.

And then there was Billy's "muse." An ex-student who wrote her former teacher love letters.

Well, the author calls them love letters, but they're more like twisted little fantasies, Cory explained. *About how she liked it when he hurt her. And then she asks him to do it to another girl, and tell her all about it (yeeesh, this book, Ruth!).*

Impossible not to see Amity Greene, here.

As for Helen, Ruth knows, from the English-language versions of Jonas Nilsson's books, that she is capable of mining her husband's crimes. Had she written this novella—it had been privately printed, Cory had learned, and never published—as a way of exorcising Ethan's crimes . . . or her own? Because the narrator, Billy's surrogate mother, knows all along what he's doing. And she never tries to stop him.

"I don't think she'd just confess like that," Rhea says, wrinkling her nose. "I mean, that would be pretty stupid."

Leila shrugs. "So maybe Helen wasn't as careful as she should be."

"Or maybe she never saw it as a confession," Beth says quietly.

As everyone turns to look at her, she continues, "Maybe Helen was trying to make sense of what Ethan had done, so she made up a fable about it. We might be trying too hard to make it fit our theories, when it's just—a story."

Ruth briefly presses her fingers to her eyes, screwing up her face. There is just so much she's trying to comprehend. She needs to read through Cory's notes again, to see if she's understood them correctly. Especially when it comes to the end of the book. The part that describes another crime that happens years later.

In a town just like Hoben.

"Well, it is the Hellmouth," Leila jokes, but not even she is smiling as Ruth logs back on to *Stranger than Fiction*. She can't think of any other place to go.

"And here we have it," Rhea says dryly, pointing at a new list that has been posted to the Hellmouth thread. It's appears to be a catalog of every man in Hoben who could be considered suspect—in any way. There's a pervy janitor from the high school. A handsy Little League coach. A doctor who recently lost his medical license (*For what???* commenters ask). The weird guy who runs the toy museum, and a too-quiet dentist. The completely subjective list goes on.

"Look," Leila exclaims. "They've even found Ivy Wilson's old boyfriend. The angry one."

His name is Bobby Johnson. Hoben Heights High, Class of 2003, someone has responded under the original comment suggesting Coco's mother had a thing for "bad boys."

Counting back with her fingers, Ruth calculates that Ivy's ex-boyfriend would have been around twelve years old when Beth was killed. The same age Ethan was when his neighbor started murdering young girls.

"You know better than to take anything on this site seriously," Beth warns, as if she can see Ruth's mind ticking over this new information.

"It's just a bunch of bored people throwing shit at the wall to see what sticks," Rhea agrees, but she needn't have bothered backing up Beth.

In an instant, Ruth has been distracted from the Hellmouth. Because she's just received another text message from Gabe. Telling her he's back in New York and wants to see her too.

I've been thinking about you, he says, *the whole time I've been away.*

———————

A few hours later, Owen calls Ruth. Exhausted from the weekend's celebrations, he's made a snap decision to close the bar for three weeks. A summer vacation, effective immediately. He already has plans to leave for the Hamptons tomorrow, and when he asks Ruth to come along, she politely declines.

"Ressler," she says, by way of excuse.

"You can't stay in this pizza oven," Owen says, horrified.

"Maybe I'll take Ressler to the farm," she lies, knowing that Joe and Gideon made their own snap decision after the excitement of Pride weekend. They flew out to Italy this morning to meet up with her mother.

With Ellis and his wife already on their cruise, Ruth is going to be the only one left in New York. Alone in this city, in a way she never has been before. Which suits her just fine, because her break is well and truly over now. She has work to do. And it will be much easier to focus without the watchful eyes of friends and family on her.

Although there is someone *she* wants to see, first.

THIRTY-ONE

Gabe is impressed with the apartment.

Ruth knows this, because after she takes him on a brief tour and they sit down on the couch together with a beer each, he says: "I'm impressed!"

It makes her laugh, despite herself. It's nice to have a break from second-guessing. To have someone think something, then actually say it out loud.

When Gabe asks what's so funny, she tells him as much.

"I just feel like there's so much that people keep to themselves. Even when it's something you'd want to hear them say."

A beat.

Why not? Ruth thinks.

"Are you ever going to kiss me, Gabe?"

He splutters into his beer, causing Ressler, at his feet, to jump.

"Um, okay. That's direct, Ruth."

Oh God.

Ruth wants to bury her face in her hands. Why is it that every time she tries to fire an arrow, the way the Junos of the world do, she always misses so spectacularly?

Resisting the urge to hide, Ruth forces herself to look at Gabe. What she sees is concern, rather than revulsion, which only makes her feel marginally better.

"Seems like you have a lot going on right now," he says, briefly meeting her gaze. "And I didn't want to complicate things."

Ruth bites her lip. Hadn't she thought that very thing about him? It's just that, when she went downstairs to let Gabe into the building tonight—after Owen had spontaneously closed the bar and she had spontaneously invited Gabe to come over—Ruth had felt her knees actually weaken. He was taller in person than she'd remembered. Broader. And he smelled delicious. Like campfires and leather. They had hugged on the street, and she'd wanted to bury her face in his neck. This was swoony, high school stuff. Not that she'd ever let herself swoon in high school.

But she is well and truly mortified now.

"Hey," Gabe says, gently stopping her as she tries to get up from the couch. "*Hey.* I do like you, Ruth. I just figured you might need some space at the moment."

There is pity in his expression. And that is not how she ever wants him to look at her.

"I have a *lot* of space," she protests, waving her arm to take in the room. "And I wouldn't have invited you into that space if I didn't want you here."

Is that doubt she sees flicker across his face now? Ruth feels her cheeks grow even hotter.

"Sorry, forget I said anything," she mumbles. "I clearly need to brush up on my seduction skills."

"You really don't," Gabe says, and then he leans in. Kisses her on the mouth.

It's quick and dry. Chaste. And it makes Ruth want to sink through the couch. Maybe right through the floor.

Ressler's stomach suddenly makes a loud gurgling sound, mercifully saving her from this free fall.

"That's some dog you have," Gabe says, reaching down to pet him.

"The best," Ruth replies with as much dignity as she can muster.

She fetches more beer, and when she returns Gabe changes the subject, asking Ruth how the podcast is coming along.

"Good," she answers stiffly, because things feel strange between them now. Are they really not going to talk about what just happened?

And then, like so many decisions she's made these past five weeks, Ruth swerves from her usual path. The one that says she'll be safe, protected, if she keeps holding those cards of hers close.

"I'm not really doing a podcast, Gabe."

He blinks. "Huh?" Gabe's beer bottle is paused halfway to his mouth.

"I told everyone I was making one, but really it was just an excuse."

"I don't follow."

"Have you read about that little girl Coco Wilson?" Ruth takes a big swig from her own bottle. "The one who went missing last month from Hoben, Connecticut?"

Gabe shakes his head no.

"Well, I'm originally from the same place. And I know a few things about that town. There was another girl, Beth Lovely, who was murdered by a guy named Ethan Oswald back in 1996. Her story got eclipsed by other, more high-profile cases that year. Ones that weren't solved, like the JonBenét Ramsey murder. But the Lovely murder was a big deal in Hoben."

Gabe nods, as if to say, *Go on*. But he looks confused. And perhaps wary.

"The women I said I wanted to interview for my podcast—I chose them deliberately. I think at least one of them had something to do with Beth's murder."

Ruth says this in a rush; if she pauses, she won't be able to start up again. Not with the way Gabe is staring at her.

"You think one of those women killed a *kid*, Ruth?"

"Not exactly." Ruth falters in the face of Gabe's confusion. She remembers Beth, in Oslo, calling him uncomplicated. As if that meant he could never understand her.

Maybe that's the whole point, Ruth had realized, after Gabe texted to say he'd been thinking about her. Maybe she needed someone to look at this whole situation in a way she and Beth never could. They've always been too close to it. But if she explained her thinking to Gabe and he saw the logic of it, then Ruth would know she was on the right track. She wouldn't just be throwing shit at the wall, as Rhea had so charmingly put it earlier today.

"For a start, I think Ethan had an accomplice," she says. "Someone who helped him lure Beth into his van."

"Bloody hell." Gabe looks shocked. "Do you have proof?"

"No. Well, maybe. TBK's wife, Helen—"

"The one from Oslo?"

Ruth recalls her promise to keep quiet about Helen's relocation. "The one we don't *say* is from Oslo, but yeah. Her. She wrote this book under a pseudonym, and I had it translated from Norwegian into English. It's about this series of murders where basically everyone is in on it. They're all guilty, like they're in some murder cult. One that is still thriving today."

This is the part Ruth is still trying to grasp. How Ethan might have had help in more ways than one.

"Wait," she tells Gabe. "I'll try to explain it to you."

Ruth gets up to retrieve her copy of *Nydelig* from her bedroom, along with Cory's notes.

When she returns, Gabe is the one with his head in his hands.

"You know the serial killer gene, right?" she asks, returning to her seat on the couch. "Well, it seems this is the cultural version of that gene. The meme version." That was how Cory had described it. "Ideas and beliefs about murder get passed down, imitated, until it's like they have a life of their own. All they need is the next host, and the next, to survive. So maybe more like a virus, I guess."

According to Cory's analysis, the world Helen describes in *Nydelig* is one where nature and nurture have combined to create a disparate yet connected community of killers (and their enablers), of which Billy was just the latest iteration.

Billy's own MO—including how he used his students as accomplices—was secondary to the main plot, Cory explained in his report (though it didn't feel secondary to Ruth). People didn't have to be inherently evil or predisposed toward violence. They simply had to meet the right person at the right time, and the meme took over from there.

According to Jonas Nilsson (and a bunch of fantasy films!), Cory wrote, *at some point, the apprentice always usurps the master.*

"See this?" Ruth asks Gabe, opening her stolen copy of *Nydelig* to the epigraph Helen had chosen.

"*There is no crime of which I do not deem myself capable,*" Ruth reads out loud. "Goethe."

When she looks at Gabe, she sees that he's gone pale.

"It's not exactly new, though, is it?" she quickly adds, trying to sound more confident than she feels. "The notion that humans are so easily influenced by each other."

"Not exactly," Gabe responds. "But what makes you think this is all connected to that girl you mentioned—Beth? And the other one. Coco, is it?"

Ruth is aware that things are already weird enough. But she's too far along this new path to stop now.

"Well," she answers, "there's the fact that the first set of crimes committed in the book, as narrated by the wife, are basically identical to TBK's murders. The couple have a young boy living next door, Billy, who hangs out with their twins. The kids are really close, but then they have a falling-out."

In his report, Cory translated a particular scene from the book that he thought was illustrative.

An only child relies on his neighbors. And Billy had the double luck of being born next to a set of twins. Sometimes, if the twins were being nice, they let Billy say they were triplets. They even made up another sister, ten minutes younger.

A girl who had died.

"How?" other kids would ask.

Train wreck. Car crash. Rabid dog. The triplets killed off their imaginary sister in any way they could envision.

"I know how I'd do it," Billy said when they were nine or ten, but by then, the other two had lost interest in the game. Moved on to something private, just between them, the way twins so often do.

It bothered Billy that they could discard him like that. But he had a secret that made everything better. Something he carried around like a lucky penny.

The twins' father liked him better.

It was Billy he chose to share his own secrets with. Down by the river. All those pictures of dead girls. Really dead ones, not like that made-up sister.

"How?" Billy asked, like the other kids did.

And this time, he got a grown-up answer.

Ruth describes that scene to Gabe now, and all the others that back up her theory. Including the part of the book where Billy grows up to be a math teacher who shows his young student, Greta, those same images, and generates those same ideas within her. Greta can't bring herself to actually kill anyone, but she does go on to procure victims for him. After Billy dies, she picks a young, worthy man, and shows him how to get away with murder too. And so on, ad infinitum, all over the world. The book finishes with a flash forward to some twenty years later, when another little girl is abducted, on the same day as Billy had kidnapped his final victim. And from the same town.

Billy himself is long dead, but his legacy lives on.

———

That's how Cory ended his report, and how Ruth ends her summary for Gabe now.

"Right." Gabe frowns as he looks at Ruth, before shaking his head. "I don't mean to be rude," he says carefully, "but that just sounds like the plot of any old crime novel, Ruth. Why would it be proof of anything?"

Ruth swallows. It's time to tell him the bit she left out.

"I know it might sound strange," she starts. "But I just have this *feeling*."

"Ruth." Gabe's expression is as serious as his tone. "You need more than just a feeling if you're going to start accusing people of murdering—sorry, *helping* murder—little kids."

Ruth's come too far now. She's had enough of her little truths. It's time to tell the big one.

"The thing is, Gabe, when I was seven years old, I went missing for twenty-eight hours. Well, not 'missing.' I was kidnapped. By Ethan Oswald."

"I . . ."

Gabe looks like he's been punched in the face.

Ruth winces. All her life, she has done everything she can to avoid triggering that look in someone she cares about. But she can't take it back. She doesn't want to.

"It's okay if you don't know how to respond," she says. "It's a lot to take in. But look—I'm fine."

She opens her arms out wide. *See?*

"I might need another drink for this," Gabe responds, offering Ruth a brief moment to collect herself while he goes to the kitchen for another beer.

When Gabe returns to the couch, she tells him about Ethan Oswald. About getting into his van to look for her cat, and knowing as soon as the door clicked shut that she had done something wrong. Made a very, very bad decision. He was still being nice to her then, talking about how excited Nala would be to see her, but then she reached for the passenger-side door handle. She remembers the slap, and the mint gum, and how fast he drove her away.

"When he took me into the house, I didn't fight back, I didn't run away. He wasn't *hurting* me. I had been told to watch out for people who want to hurt you. But he made me a sandwich and gave me a drink of water. He acted so normal. He was wearing jeans. His house was ordinary; the kitchen could have been my parents' kitchen. And then he said we should go get Nala from the other room, and I thought that even if my parents were mad at me for going off with a stranger, they would be so happy when I brought Nala home that it wouldn't matter."

Ruth stops, looks at Gabe. "Are you okay?"

"Fuck, Ruth." He lets out a long breath. "I'm the one who should be asking you that."

She takes a deep breath of her own.

"My memories after that are a bit . . . well, there are things I've obviously blanked out. And others I've had filled in for me by all the investigators and social workers and psychologists I had to talk to."

"You were so little."

"I was. Oswald had a thing for kids. He murdered Beth. But he never actually hurt me. If . . . if you know what I mean."

Any color that had returned to Gabe's face drains away as he nods.

"Beth wasn't so lucky. Although that's a terrible word to use. He assaulted her at his house, and then he killed her."

"Jesus."

Be careful, Ruthie, Beth warns. *Don't—*

"This might sound weird," Ruth rushes on, "but Beth talked me through the last of those twenty-eight hours I was held captive. I thought I was dying, and she comforted me, and she told me not to cry, because when you cried Ethan stopped being a nice person and turned really, really mean. I wasn't nearly old enough to understand the psychology of a man like that. I really think Beth was there with me. Helping me get through it.

"I still see her, Gabe. And sometimes other girls too. Other dead girls, who I think were also Ethan's victims, even if I've never been able to prove it. So, when it comes to Ethan Oswald, it's *more* than just a feeling."

Gabe is no longer looking at her. As he reaches down to scratch Ressler's ears, Ruth can see that his hand is shaking.

It's too much, she realizes. She has stupidly asked him to take on too much.

"Sorry," she says to the back of his head. "That all came out really fast. I'm not even sure why I told you."

Gabe sits up, his skin ashen. "Don't be sorry, Ruth. I'm glad you did."

She can't tell if he means it.

"Can I say something?" he asks, waiting for her nod before he continues. "Why don't you just come out and ask these women what they know about your abduction?"

"That's not how you get the truth out of someone," Ruth answers automatically. "Especially if they're a psychopath."

"So these women are psychopaths now?"

"They could be. Or Helen, at least," she says, thinking about all those Jonas Nilsson books. And the way *Nydelig*'s narrator seemed to absolve herself of any responsibility. She considered herself no match for the meme, was how Cory described it.

Adding that it almost seemed like she was the original host.

"They say fifty percent of psychopathy is inherited," Ruth tells Gabe. "Maybe you get the rest from a marriage."

Ressler's stomach suddenly emits another loud gurgle, and the crassness of the sound brings Ruth back to her senses. How did she go from *it's too much*—to this?

"Anyway," she says with a forced cheeriness that hurts her jaw. "I bet you didn't expect any of this when I invited you over."

"Not exactly," Gabe answers quietly. "But I'm glad you felt you could tell me. Thank you for trusting me enough." Then, clearing his throat, he looks at his watch and makes a show of comprehending the time. "I feel bad for taking off after everything you just told me, Ruth, but I really should get going. I only just got back to the city, and I have something on tonight. We'll definitely do this again, though. For sure."

For sure.

Gabe can't seem to get off the couch fast enough; Ruth almost laughs at his transparency. He's too nice a guy to come out and say it, but what she's told him tonight has obviously changed how he sees her—and now he can't wait to get away from her.

It's not like she doesn't know that feeling.

Waiting in the hall for the elevator to take him down to the lobby, Gabe turns to look back at Ruth, standing in her doorway. His left leg is jiggling furiously.

"I'll see you soon," he says as the elevator doors open and he steps inside.

Before the doors close, Ruth sees Gabe briefly touch his fingers to his lips, as if remembering their kiss.

It feels like a consolation prize. Even if she can't say exactly what it is that she's lost.

THIRTY-TWO

Ruth is miserable.

It's been twenty-four hours since she blurted out everything to Gabe. And twenty-four hours since she's heard from him. She feels exposed. Vulnerable. Mostly, she feels foolish.

Why indeed would *Nydelig* be proof of anything?

It's just like last time. When Ruth got so trapped by her theories, so tangled up in her patterns, she couldn't see her way clear of them.

A witness saw a man wearing a baseball cap hanging around the mobile library on Lori's street. It had to be the Minnesota Twins.

Someone noticed a beat-up old van parked across from the gas station where Rhea disappeared. It had to be dark blue.

A young man in denim jeans was seen hanging around the gates of the local pool right before Leila went missing. "Young man" had to mean twenty years old, Ethan's age in 1985.

"Call him," the girls would say, whenever Ruth found one of these new, tenuous links.

"Call him."

Call him.

Ruth lost count of the number of times she did call Officer Canton. How many times he answered. How many messages she left when he didn't pick up.

"Come to Hoben, and we can talk in person," he'd offered wearily one night. It might have been midnight, or even later.

"I don't ever want to come back to that town," she told him.

"Then I'm not really sure what you want me to do here, Beth."

Beth.

Canton's slipup that night had caught them both by surprise.

By then, she'd told Officer Canton about being able to see the girls. The other girls she kept insisting Ethan had murdered.

"I talk to them all the time," she'd confessed.

"The way you talked to Beth in that room?" he'd asked.

"Ruthie," Canton added gently, the night he accidentally called her Beth, "has anyone tried to help you through this? Have you had *any* therapy since you were a child?"

"I'm not the one who died," she'd whispered down the phone.

What she can remember now is that he laughed. The sound was jagged, a record scratch that was too loud.

"Do you think you had to die to be a victim?" Officer Canton asked her that night.

"No. But I think there are people who've had it far worse than me."

Canton sighed. "Ruthie, trauma is not a pie. We don't carve up slices for the most deserving, then see what's left on the plate. You know the facts about your case better than anyone, kid. You don't need to add a bunch of conspiracies to the mix. There's enough that you *do* know, and if you don't mind me saying, I think you need some help with processing that information. Coming into that money on your birthday might have triggered this particular episode, Ruthie. That's perfectly understandable.

But can I just ask you something? And I want you to really think about the answer. Exactly how long do you want to be locked in that room?"

Is that what she's done all over again with the Coco Wilson case? Put herself back on that bed, back in those chains?

Do not cry, she warns herself now. *Do not cry*.

Not because she's still afraid of Ethan Oswald, but because she knows there is no one around to comfort her.

No single person left in this city who cares.

———

Ruth's despondency lasts into the next morning. She wishes she'd just made an unoriginal mistake, liking sleeping with Gabe when he was clearly so ambivalent about her. She could deal with rejection after *that*. This feeling is so much worse. Knowing she's scared him off, not because of anything that happened between them, but because of who she is. Because of what happened to her.

She is wallowing in her self-pity, deliberately letting it overwhelm her, when Juno shoots another of her arrows.

And everything is upended all over again.

———

The winter holidays in New Zealand officially start next week, but Juno has come home a few days early, because school is just not holding her attention this term.

From her bedroom in New York, Ruth can hear Juno moving around on that little hill outside the farmhouse in Marama River, searching for better reception, as she chatters down the phone.

"You barely changed your name," she'd said accusingly, as soon as Ruth answered her call. "That made it so easy to find who you really are, *Ruthie Nelson*. And I know that's why you've been ignoring me, but honestly it's not like I care about that bit at all."

"Wanna know how I figured it out?" she asks, pride-tinged now.

"Not really."

Juno snorts. "You're not the only one who knows how to find people online. I *knew* something was up with you; you had that whole haunted thing going on. So I did a little investigating, and when I found that blog post about Coco Wilson—*hey presto!* Or whatever it is you're supposed to say when you find what you're looking for."

"I don't think that's it," Ruth tells her glumly. "Does your mom know?"

"God, no! Ruthie, she *needs* to talk to you. Everyone hates us around here, like I told you. I think the podcast would be good for her, and I've been telling her that ever since you left. You can't keep all that stuff bottled up forever, right? But if I told her about *your* past, she might get suspicious of your motives. Think you had an agenda or something. Especially since you kept it from us."

"I should have told you both," Ruth says after a long pause. "But I don't exactly like talking about that time in my life either."

Especially now.

"Yeah, well, I have some news for you about your old hometown," Juno carries on, and Ruth can hear that tinge of pride in her voice again. "I've decided to do my podcast next term on the Coco Wilson case! I have that whole weird link to Hoben, too, you know? I've been doing a ton of research already, and I think I've found something really huge. Like—massive. I'll tell you when I'm sure.

"But Ruthie, I think I might have figured out who took her."

———

There are so many things banging up against each other. *Nydelig*. The Hellmouth. Juno planning a podcast about Coco's disappearance, and her naive confidence that she can find whoever is responsible. Then there're the girls, so hopeful people are now looking for them too. And Gabe, whose rejection still stings. Ruth needs help making sense of everything crashing around in her mind.

Beth was right. Someone as uncomplicated as Gabe could never understand.

Who *would* understand all that jumbled noise in her head? Who might be able to hear it too?

When it comes, the realization is both sudden and obvious. Like the fireworks Ruth can hear out her window most nights. All those people breaking the neighborhood's rules by setting off their cheap, Fourth of July rockets early, the ones that offer a shrill shriek of warning before they explode in a burst of color. They always make Ressler jump, and now it's Ruth who's propelled from her bed.

"Get up, boy," she says to Ressler. "It's time to go home."

Officer Canton is obviously glad to see his former canine buddy, but Ruth cannot be sure this enthusiasm extends to her. (He really did understand why she had been drawn to all those cold cases, he once told her, but she needed to leave that kind of work to professionals. All those cases are still unsolved today, she could tell him now.) But he hugs her warmly, asks if she'd like a drink ("Water, please"), and then he ushers her past a row of desks and curious faces to a glass-walled room at the back of the station, with the blinds pulled down. It is larger than Ruth would expect an interrogation room to be; she's used to the ones on television, dank basements with small tables and metal chairs that scrape on the ground. The ones detectives like to lean back in as they sip coffee and wait for their suspect to slip up and confess.

By contrast, this room is well lit and relatively spacious. There's a couch along one wall, and the oval table in the middle could accommodate a whole team of people. Canton delivers Ruth's water in a tall glass, sipping from his own drink in a *World's Best Dad* mug.

"Not mine," he says as Ruth's eyes go to the mug. "The captain gets a new one every Father's Day. We have a whole shelf full of 'em."

A bowl of water is also set down for Ressler, who gives it a customary lap, before returning to Officer Canton's side, staring at him eagerly. When Canton produces a small treat from his pocket, Ruth understands why her dog has so readily given her up.

Canton sits down next to Ruth, angling their chairs so they're face-to-face. Five years ago, during her episode, most of their interactions were conducted over the phone. Afforded an up-close look at Canton now, Ruth notes his still-boyish good looks, the kindness of his gray eyes. He looks wholesome, safe. Thinner than she remembered, and more furrowed at the brow, but not so different from the young man who burst into that room on Longview Road, a blur of dogs and uniforms behind him.

"Thank you for coming," she supposedly said to him that day.

"To what do I owe this pleasure, Ruthie?" he asks her now.

She might as well come straight out with it. "I wanted to talk to you about Coco Wilson."

"Ah."

Taking a sip from that *World's Best Dad* mug, Canton's expression is briefly masked. When he sets the mug down, it is equally opaque.

"I'm not on that task force, Ruthie. But it's certainly an interesting case."

He's not shutting her down. Ruth presses forward.

"I just wondered . . . well, because she was taken on the exact same date as me, if there's been any connection made between her case and mine?"

"Your case?" For a second, Canton looks confused. Ruth watches as he quickly comprehends what she's alluding to.

"You think this could be connected to Oswald."

It's not a question.

"It's possible, isn't it?"

"No, Ruthie, it's not. Given that he's been dead for years."

Ressler moves from Officer Canton's side now. He comes to Ruth and lies beside her, his front paws resting on her feet. She concentrates on this grounding. Reminding herself that Canton, of all people, understands those terrible things people are capable of.

"It could be possible," she asserts. "If Oswald wasn't working alone back then. If he had an accomplice."

"Ruth—"

"Coco's disappearance has stirred up a lot of things for me," she interjects. "And I'm conscious it might seem like we've been here before. But every time I come close to letting it go, something else—*someone* else—comes up."

She thinks of how the revelations, big and small, have been relentless this past month.

"Officer Canton, did you know that Ethan was abusing a young girl in Ohio before he came to Hoben? Amity Greene. She was fourteen."

"I did know that, yes."

"She told me that Ethan wanted her to hand over her little sister."

Ruth sees Canton flinch.

"Amity didn't do it, or so she told me," she continues. "Maybe she was more savvy, I don't know. But there was another girl after that."

Ruth feels emboldened now, as if her confession to Gabe was a trial run.

"And there's something I never told you. It's about that other girl. I think I remember her asking me questions in the playground a few days before I was kidnapped. About my cat. Things that Ethan knew when he came up to me at my house. I maybe even heard her singing, through the wall. When I was in that room. I'm not even sure these memories are real, but if they are . . . if they are, I think that girl was someone named Annie Whitaker."

Canton, who has remained silent throughout this monologue, is now looking at Ruth with undeniable compassion.

"You did tell us that," he says, back to that firm voice he'd used with Ruth on the day he came to her apartment in New York. "You might not remember it, but we have all this on record, Ruthie."

Ruth shakes her head. "That's *not* possible. I kept it a secret from everyone. From myself, even."

"You were seven years old," Canton says. "I wouldn't expect anyone to clearly remember everything that happened nineteen years ago, let alone someone who was a child at the time."

"No."

"I could get you the case notes," he says, "but that might take a while. The archiving system is not the greatest around here."

He has no reason to lie to her. Ruth knows this.

"I was so sure I never said anything about her," she says, looking down at her hands. At least she knows that her memories of Annie, of Rose, are real now. But she's not sure if that makes her feel better or worse.

"Did you actually investigate her?" she asks finally.

"Of course we did, Ruthie. Annie Whitaker was very forthcoming with information about her time with Oswald. They spent a lot of time together when she was his student, and he was very controlling with her. She was a young girl, and she had no idea what he was truly capable of. Fully grown adults missed the signs. Across multiple states."

But I banged on the wall.

Even as she thinks it, Ruth wonders if she really did that. Perhaps she invented her resistance to manage her guilt.

"What about Helen Torrent, the wife of TBK?" Ruth can hear the scramble in her voice. "She used to be Ethan's neighbor when he was a kid. And she owned that horrible house in Hoben."

"That she did," Canton says. "Yet another manipulated woman, Ruthie. To tell you the truth, I've always felt a bit sorry for her."

"Why?" she asks, bordering on petulant now. Realizing, as the word catches in her throat, that she is close to tears.

"Like many wives of serial killers, Helen was a woman who had the rug completely pulled out from under her," Canton answers, after appearing to weigh the question carefully. "She'll forever be associated with her husband's crimes. It taints you, that proximity. People cannot believe you didn't know what was going on, right under your nose. But as I think I've said to you before, Ruthie, sometimes you can be *too* close to the truth. You don't see it because you don't want to. Who *would* want to?"

"That's not an excuse," Ruth says, hating how her voice wavers.

"Nope, it's not. But it might be a reason. You know, more than a few people had their suspicions about Helen back then. Her relationship with Oswald was thoroughly explored. But evidence of anything untoward just wasn't there. Turns out she was just a sad, lonely woman trying to hold on to the few relationships she had left."

Ruth begins to wonder if it's actually Officer Canton who has been too close to this case. Only seeing what he wants to. Which doesn't include the possibility that women can be every bit as deadly as men. Like Mrs. Lovett, encouraging Sweeney Todd.

Ruth knows Canton would not get the reference.

"Helen wrote a book about my abduction," she says instead.

"Did she now?" Officer Canton doesn't seem bothered by this. Or curious, even.

"Yes! A whole, awful book about a community of serial killers who passed on their ... their *trade* ... to other people. It's basically a confession."

"Interesting," he responds, not sounding interested at all.

Ruth realizes that he's humoring her, and barely.

"You never believe me," she whispers.

"I'm sorry, Ruthie," Canton replies, and this time his expression matches his words. "I don't mean to be dismissive, I promise you. Send me the book, if you want to. I'll read it."

"You can't. It's in Norwegian."

There is a distinct pause, and then they both start to laugh. They've gone through too much to be mad at each other now.

"Listen, Ruthie," Officer Canton says, once they've pulled themselves together. "For everything I've learned about trauma, there are twice as many things I don't know—and I could be completely wrong here, but it does seem like you get pulled back to your, ah, investigative work, anytime something reminds you of Ethan Oswald. It's no surprise that the Coco Wilson case—the coincidence of her going missing on the same date you were kidnapped—stirred up a lot of unresolved issues for you. Hell, that case has shaken us all.

"But," Canton continues, "sometimes a coincidence is just a coincidence. We're hardwired to look for a pattern, but that doesn't mean there is one."

"Do they have any idea who might have taken her?" Ruth asks, ignoring the rest of his sermon. "Because there's this whole list of men who—"

"You know I can't discuss specifics with you, Ruthie," Officer Canton cuts her off. "I will say that it's not the same as your case, though. Not by a long shot."

He checks his watch.

"I need to get going," he says. "But I'm free after my shift, if you're sticking around?"

"I have an appointment back in New York," Ruth lies, and she can't tell if Canton is disappointed or relieved by the brevity of her visit.

When they walk outside together, the bright, uninterrupted sunlight of the summer day causes them both to squint as they say goodbye. The hug between them is tighter this time, and Ruth allows herself a brief collapse into the security of Officer Canton's arms. This was once her safest place in the world.

"Don't be a stranger, okay?" he says as they break apart, and Ruth doesn't have to wonder about his expression now. She can see it clearly in his eyes: the deep, still waters of their bond, underneath all those layers of disagreement and frustration. After all they have shared, they could never actually be strangers to each other.

Ruth watches as Canton shifts his attention to Ressler. This time, his eyes actually water.

"Take care, buddy. I hope I get to see you again."

He knows even better than Ruth that her hound dog's clock is ticking down.

She is walking back to the car when Canton calls her name. She turns back to face him across the parking lot.

"Do you see her?" he asks. "Is Coco one of your dead girls?"

Ruth shakes her head. "She's not dead."

Even from a distance, she can see the look on Canton's face when she says this.

When it comes to Coco Wilson, they appear to have found the one thing they can agree on today.

―――――――

Ruth has one more stop to make in Hoben.

Bill and Patty Lovely live in a beautifully maintained home, with a well-tended front garden. It's easy enough to find their address; Hoben is even smaller than Ruth imagined it to be. *Imagined*, because she has so few sure memories of this place. Earlier, as she'd driven along the town's main street, she felt a flicker of recognition at the redbrick buildings, the awnings, and the American flags. But it could have been a main street she'd seen in a television show.

If she had felt nervous pulling into the parking lot of the Hoben Police Department, turning into the Lovelys' driveway makes Ruth feel outright nauseous. She has a fervent moment of hoping Beth's parents are not home today, but then she sees a figure step onto the porch at the front of the house. A short, ample woman, wearing a brightly colored caftan. The sound of the car has brought Patty Lovely to the door.

"Stay here," Ruth tells Ressler, winding the windows half-down for him, before locking him in the car.

Stepping onto the driveway, into Patty Lovely's view, Ruth can only hope that her legs continue to hold her up. Right now, they are refusing to move her a single step toward Beth Lovely's mother.

This woman Ruth has never actually met.

THIRTY-THREE

It started early. Pretending that she'd always known Beth Lovely. And that Beth's parents, Bill and Patty, had always been her friends. When she was old enough, Ruth would watch TV interviews the Lovelys had done, and read the many essays they'd penned as they advocated tirelessly for better victim support services. This was how she'd learned about the programs Beth's parents helped develop to offer other grieving parents some form of solace when their child never came home. It was easy for Ruth to feel that she knew them, and not much of a stretch to imagine they might return her affection, given the money they'd gifted to her on her twenty-first birthday. That Bill and Patty Lovely forgave her for being the one who didn't die. This has been the constant in Ruth's life, for nineteen years.

And now she's about to discover if her fantasy holds. Forcing her feet to move along the driveway, Ruth reaches out her hand, feels for the pads of Beth's fingers brushing against hers. It is the closest thing she has to prayer.

"Hi," she says, approaching the porch. "I'm Ruth Bak—Ruthie *Nelson*. I've been wanting to meet you for such a long time."

She has been fed an array of sandwiches and sweets. Had her glass filled and refilled with homemade lemonade. Ressler sits beside her, waiting for crumbs.

"You can't leave that beautiful boy in the car," Patty had said, insisting he accompany Ruth inside. The hospitality of this house is everything Ruth had ever dreamed.

Beth's mother had cried when she realized who it was walking up her driveway. Patty Lovely's hug, after she flew from the porch, the wings of her caftan nearly lifting her from the ground, was fierce. Delivered with the strength of someone twice her size.

"My darling," she kept saying. "My darling girl. We've thought about you every day."

A little over an hour later, Bill is on his way home from the golf club. Out on the course, he'd initially missed the barrage of messages from his wife telling him to come home *immediately*.

"Are you sure he won't mind that I'm here?" Ruth asks from her perch on the coziest chintz couch she's ever encountered. Her whole life in New York, the furniture has felt temporary. Perpetually removed or replaced. Even Joe and Gideon's farmhouse has a sense of presentation to it. The decor could be—has been—featured in design magazines. But this living room feels like it has earned its name. Ruth feels a pang for all the years missed, all the times she could have sunk into this couch and been taken care of by Patty Lovely.

"Your parents wanted a clean break for you, and we respected that," Patty told her when they first sat down. "We would've dearly loved to have a relationship with you, Ruthie. But we needed to respect your parents' wishes, and that's not something many people are good at doing, as Bill and I learned the hard way."

"Darling, he will be beside himself to meet you," Patty reassures Ruth now. "There really hasn't been a day that we haven't wondered how you are."

All around the room, there are pictures of Beth. For Ruth, who has only ever had the same four or five images to look at, those photographs given to the press, and the few grainy home videos featured in television interviews she's seen, this is a wonder. To see Beth riding a bike with streamers tied to the handlebars. Feeding deer in the backyard, still in her *My Little Pony* nightgown. A family portrait where the three Lovelys are wearing matching Christmas sweaters. Pictures of Beth hard at work in the garden at her elementary school. Beth went to the Montessori three blocks over from Hoben Elementary; had she gone to Ruth's own school, they would likely have been in the same class.

What Ruth sees in every photograph is the joy little Beth radiated. All that beautiful potential, a child nurtured by loving parents, and a learning environment where she had thrived. It is obvious to Ruth that Beth would have gone on to make the world a better place. Through her parents, she already has. Patty has been telling Ruth about the work she and Bill still do with families who have lost a child, how they turned the wilderness they found themselves lost within into a journey.

"We still put one foot in front of the other every day, Ruthie. It's not that it gets easier, so much as we simply know what to do now. What we *can* do. And if we can carry others along with us, so much the better."

Ruth learns that her own parents had been invited to the support sessions Bill and Patty started running for families who were dealing with trauma and loss, but they had always declined, just as they had asked for their daughter to be left alone to heal. Though they still saw fit to accept Beth's death money, Ruth thinks, with a rare jolt of bitterness. She would've much preferred having the Lovelys in her life. Especially Patty, who eventually got a degree in child psychology, before adding another credential and another. Ruth knows this from reading about her, but in her presence, surrounded by all these reminders of Beth, Patty's resilience is even more special.

It's no wonder, Ruth thinks, that Beth has always tried to be her better angel.

When Bill Lovely walks through the door, Ruth finds herself swept up into another hug, softer this time, as if Beth's tall, slight father leaves the ferocity to his wife.

"Sit, sit," he says when he releases her. "Let me look at you."

Of course. She is the same age as Beth. Bill's coffee-colored eyes fill with tears, and Ruth knows that he is thinking about what he and Patty have missed out on. The chance to keep moving their daughter from frame to frame, capturing her life as she grew up; there is still so much space left on the walls of the Lovely home.

The next half hour is spent catching Bill up on Ruth's life in New York; Patty has already heard the basic details. Ruth talks about Ressler and her job at the bar. Her uncles and their farm. She does not mention the podcast or the episode that was triggered when she came into the money they gifted to her.

Or the fact that she can see Beth quietly watching the three of them from the other side of the room.

It's not until Bill asks what brings her to Hoben after all this time—something Patty, in her excitement, had not yet asked—that Ruth remembers the purpose of her visit. What she came here to find out.

"I came to see Officer Canton," she answers truthfully. "I had some questions for him about my—about *our* case."

Not a lie. But a very small truth at best. For the only other two people she could think of who might understand just how terrible people can be.

"What a lovely young man he is," Patty says of Canton, though he must be in his mid-forties by now. "We were very lucky to have him back then. Did you know he's a sergeant now?"

Ruth nods.

"And he doesn't work with the K-9 team directly anymore, but he's never lost his love for those dogs."

Ruth learns that the Lovelys often have Sergeant Canton over for dinner. But while Patty sings his praises, Bill stays silent, his brow slightly furrowed.

"What did you want to know about the case?" he asks, when Patty finally takes a breath. Ruth is sure she sees his wife shoot him a warning glance as he says this.

"I suppose, with the Coco Wilson case, it got me thinking about what happened to Beth and me. There are a few gaps in my understanding that I thought he might be able to fill in."

Again, a small truth. Ruth is not ready to mention the women to Beth's parents. Her wide-ranging suspicions about them. She wants to see if the Lovelys have their own suspicions, first.

"As you know, my parents don't like to talk about what happened," Ruth continues. "And my own memories are hazy. I'm really sorry if this makes you uncomfortable, especially since we've just met, but I was wondering if you'd ever heard that he—that Ethan Oswald—had someone helping him?"

"Oh, darling, we've heard every rumor under the sun," Patty responds with a rueful smile. "If you can think it, it's been said. There's even a lunatic group who think Bill and I were in cahoots with that man. Twenty years later, they remain convinced that we practice child sacrifice in the backyard."

"Thank goodness there was no social media back then," Bill adds. "Coco Wilson's parents are getting crucified."

Patty sighs. "Oh, those poor darlings. We're doing our best to help them, but they've been absolutely crushed by the weight of this thing."

"You know them?" Ruth is startled, even as she realizes she should have assumed this. Hoben is a very small town.

"We didn't," Patty clarifies. "But since little Coco went missing, we've gotten to know Ivy and Leo very well, along with their older daughter, Maya. They are a wonderful family, and the hate directed their way has been so devastating to witness. There's an unkindness in people that really seems unashamed of itself at the moment. And it worries me that it's only going to get worse."

"Everything worries Patty," Bill tells Ruth, with his own rueful smile. "But yes, the attitudes of some people toward Leo Wilson have shocked me too."

Ruth doesn't need to ask; both Patty and Bill appear certain that Leo Wilson had nothing to do with Coco's disappearance.

"Do you ever wonder," Ruth starts tentatively, "if Coco's disappearance might be connected in some way to us? She was taken on the same day as me."

Sitting across from Ruth in a plush armchair, Patty blinks her confusion. In a matching chair positioned alongside, Bill's expression is closer to consternation.

"Where on earth did you get that idea?" he asks, causing Patty to reach out, squeeze his arm.

"Sorry, Ruthie, I didn't mean to sound abrupt there," he says hastily. "Let me rephrase that. Has something happened to make you think that might be a possibility?"

"No."

This lie makes Ruth feel miserable. It suddenly seems that all she ever does is lie. Especially to people she cares about.

She immediately corrects herself. "It *is* possible he had help."

Synchronized sighs. Bill and Patty exchange a look, that wordless language Ruth has never spoken with anybody. A slight nod from Patty, and Bill clears his throat.

"I met Ethan," he says. "Not long before he died."

"*What?*"

Ruth feels as if she has been pinned to the back of the couch. Her jaw drops, but this is the only movement her body will allow.

"It was part of a reconciliation trial the state was running," Bill explains. "A rather controversial one, but I—we—wanted to see if Ethan's remorse was genuine. We'd had some correspondence to suggest he might have turned over a new leaf, so to speak, and I went along to see for myself."

Mint gum. The slap of his hand. Being guided into that room. The utter incomprehension as Oswald commanded her to sit, and the hot metal stink of that chain as he clipped the cuff around her little wrist. Suddenly Ruth can't breathe.

Patty is at her side on the couch in an instant. Instinctively, Ruth tries to move away, but Patty clasps her hand, doesn't let go.

"We were so angry at that man, Ruthie," she says. "And for so long. But that rage, that desire for vengeance, was eating us both up from the inside. It took us dangerously close to understanding just how easily a person could really hurt another human being. So we decided to hold on to our humanity by participating in the program. Right up till the minute Bill walked into that room, he wasn't sure he could do it."

"He murdered your daughter."

Ruth has started to cry. This is a betrayal she never, ever saw coming.

"Yes, darling. And when Ethan made the decision to do that, he destroyed life as we knew it. This was not an attempt to excuse what he did to Beth, and certainly not what he did to you. But,

Ruthie, if there was any chance he was a man and not a monster, we needed to know it."

Patty is weeping now too.

"Do you want me to tell you what happened?" Bill asks gently from his chair.

Ruth goes to shake her head, then nods. Understanding that if he doesn't tell her, she will wonder endlessly. She might as well know the truth of it.

"We spoke to each other for an hour that day. I found him to be articulate, thoughtful, contrite. And very, very cunning. Not so much a monster as a young man who had no sense of himself. Which meant he could only mimic that contrition. I don't think he knew *how* to be sorry. He'd had a terrifically violent upbringing in Minnesota, physically and emotionally abused by people he should have been able to trust. It's a familiar enough story, unfortunately. But while most people find a way to break the cycle of abuse, I came away certain Ethan would do it again, if given the chance. This was a man who needed no motivation other than his impulses. There were advocates, people in his corner, who did believe in him. Who saw something I just couldn't. We'll never know if he was truly sorry for what he did."

"*The evil that men do lives after them; the good is oft interred with their bones*," Patty says softly. "As Shakespeare so eloquently put it."

Beth's mother releases Ruth's hand. "This has been an afternoon of surprises," she says. "I hope this won't put you off coming back to see us again?"

Ruth raises her freed hand to her damp cheeks, feels the startle of those tears, when she hasn't cried for so long. She shakes her head. Of course it won't.

"I still don't understand how that makes you so sure he did

all that damage on his own," she manages to say finally. "If he was so manipulative, couldn't he also have convinced someone less savvy to help him? Someone like that exchange student he used to drive home?"

"Annie Whitaker? That poor wee mouse?" Patty knows exactly who Ruth is referring to. "Just another cruel rumor, darling. Picking on an easy target. She was a lonely girl, that one, if you remember."

"How would *I* remember?" Ruth asks.

"Well, she was your neighbor, darling. But given all that happened, it's no wonder you've forgotten that."

Ruth is not sure she should be driving. Her head is so full of everything Bill and Patty told her this afternoon, she can barely see the road in front of her. She keeps asking her thoughts to wait until she's back in New York, but they insist on coming, one jostling another for space. Each one of those thoughts is equally alarming.

Ruth managed to hold it together long enough to say goodbye to Beth's parents. There had been hugs, promises to return, and only when she'd pulled out of the driveway and onto the road did Ruth let her breath jag, all that air she couldn't catch, every single thing she couldn't process, as it turned into hyperventilation. As soon as she was sure she was out of sight, she pulled over. Head against the steering wheel, Ruth's breathing finally slowed, but her heart was still marking double time. How had she forgotten that Annie Whitaker was her *neighbor*?

More importantly, how had Annie Whitaker forgotten her? Ruth was only seven in 1996, but Annie was seventeen. Her teacher had just kidnapped the kid next door and been charged with murdering another little girl. That's not the kind of thing a teenager would just gloss over or forget. Like Rose's own daughter said, Ruth had barely changed her name. Hadn't her presence in Marama River stirred things up?

Perhaps it had.

This became the loudest drumbeat as Ruth drove south toward the highway, before suddenly swerving left and heading for Canyon Road.

There it was. Her parents' old house, and the front lawn she'd been standing on when Ethan Oswald pulled up in his van on the other side of the road. Next door, at a considerable distance, was the former Johnson residence. Patty said that Jim and Sally had moved down to Florida some years ago. Both houses appeared to be occupied by families once again. The overturned bikes and assortment of toys on their front lawns suggested as much. In the gap between the two houses, Ruth could see through to the shared backyard. Closest to her old house were the bones of an old swing set, chains dangling where a seat used to be. She had no memory of ever using that swing, but she wondered if this might be where she'd talked to Annie about her cat. Not the playground, after all.

Helen's book said you didn't have to be inherently evil to commit terrible acts. You just had to meet the right person.

Or live next door to them.

Ruth had pulled away from the curb so suddenly that Ressler, sitting in the back seat, had given her a reproachful look, visible in her rearview mirror.

And now she is nearly home. Everything she's learned today has started to clamor again. The constant din almost causes her to miss a red light; she just manages to stop in time.

Breathing hard at this near miss, it occurs to Ruth that ever since Amity, Rose, and Helen came into her life, she's felt like she was losing control. Careening toward something inevitable.

But she's no longer bouncing off the wall.

She's ready to crash right through it.

And find out exactly who is on the other side.

THIRTY-FOUR

Juno Mulvaney hasn't stopped grinning since she walked into Ruth's apartment.

"I can't believe I'm really here," she keeps saying. "Really, really here in New York City. I feel like I'm in a movie. And your apartment is everything I imagined. Minnie would *die*."

"She did know she was welcome to come, too, right?" Ruth checked, when she found out Minnie wasn't coming with her mother and sister to New York. That she would be spending the New Zealand winter holidays in Queenstown with her friend's family, instead.

"Of course," Juno assured Ruth. "Trust me, it's better for all of us if the baby stays home."

"It's not exactly the Plaza," Ruth says now as Juno looks through the guest room window. The view is unremarkable, though Juno declares it very New York: a narrow alleyway and the scaffolded wall of the building next door.

If Juno is uncharacteristically enthusiastic, Rose appears as remote as ever. Standing in the doorway of the guest room, she tells Ruth that she feels as if she could sleep for days.

Wanting to appear hospitable, Ruth points Rose toward the bathroom, telling her there are fresh towels in the cabinet under the sink.

"A shower and drinking lots of water will help," she says.

What she's thinking: *Do you recognize me now?*

And this thought, a persistent niggle: *Am I safe with you here?*

There's no denying Ruth flinches now any time her old neighbor comes too close.

Thankfully, Juno doesn't seem to have noticed this new tension in Ruth. And Rose appears too tired to have noticed anything at all.

Willing her body not to betray her, Ruth forces a smile as Juno turns to face her, expectant.

"Can we go out now? I don't even care if we just ride around on the subway. You know I've never even been on a train?"

"Maybe we should let your mom rest tonight," Ruth suggests, and receives a classic Juno eye roll in return.

"I don't mean go out with *her*. She's probably too scared to ride the subway, anyway. She can go to bed if she wants, but I'm not tired, Ruthie. Besides, we have loads to talk about."

("I'll tell you when I get there," Juno has kept saying, anytime Ruth's asked about her planned podcast on Coco Wilson.)

"We can take Ressler for a walk around the neighborhood and pick up some takeout," Ruth relents. "If you're still buzzing after that, we can discuss options from there."

At this, Juno looks as eager as the tail-wagging Ressler, who, upon hearing the *w* word, has gone to sit at the front door.

"Your dog is so cool," Juno says as she kneels down beside him to scratch his ears. "Hey, beautiful boy," she whispers, before turning to Ruth with narrowed eyes. "How did you get yourself a hound dog, anyway?"

"It's a long story," Ruth answers.

And it's going to be a long few days, she can tell.

Ruth just needs to remember that she is in control here. It was all her idea, and it's been executed perfectly so far. In fact, the biggest sticking point—getting Rose Mulvaney to New York on such short notice—has turned out to be surprisingly easy.

"I can convince her," Juno said, when Ruth first proposed the idea. "Leave it to me."

True to her word, within twenty-four hours Rose had accepted Ruth's offer of round-trip flights to New York, along with a cash stipend that Ruth hastily dubbed an "appearance fee."

"I wasn't going to let her say no to New York," Juno asserted when she called to confirm they were coming. "My bags are already packed."

Juno had also insisted she and Rose stay with Ruth instead of at a hotel. "I want to feel like an actual New Yorker," she'd said. "Not some cheesy tourist."

Ruth had reluctantly agreed, mostly because she felt a kind of anticipatory guilt. Because if everything went to plan on Friday, Juno might very well lose her love for this city.

The realization Ruth had, when driving back from Hoben last week, was that she needed to bring everyone together.

She'd been dancing around the idea for a while now, and then *Nydelig* took it up a notch. That book might have been a fable, but weren't fables a way of imparting life's lessons? Like the fact that it takes a village. Not just to raise a child, but to protect a murderer too.

The myrmidon, the muse, and the mother. Billy's women all had their parts to play.

With Helen already on the East Coast, Ruth had sent her a message that night. This time, *blackmail* was the only word for what that message contained.

If you don't agree to meet with me, I'll blow your cover as Jonas Nilsson. And not in a way that will be good for sales.

Ruth can only think she'd seen someone say something similarly awful on TV.

She'd messaged Amity after that, saying she had a feeling her Paris trip was over, which was *great*, because she had some important things to discuss with her. For the podcast, of course.

And now, Ethan's women will be in the same place for the first time since—well, maybe since the pages of *Nydelig*. Ruth's three queens from her winning poker round. She intends to play her hand when Helen arrives on Friday, the day after tomorrow. Gather everyone together and insist they tell her the truth.

Exactly how did Beth, and then Ruth, end up in that room? And what do they know about Coco Wilson's disappearance, all these years later?

Three girls. Three women.

It's time to snap that triskelion. And see which piece she's left holding in her hand.

———

"They found a body."

Thursday morning, and Ruth and Juno are sitting in a diner on Broadway, the latter already on her third mug of coffee, while Rose continues to sleep off her jet lag at the apartment. When they walked into the restaurant, Juno had exclaimed over the black-and-white-checked linoleum, the red vinyl seats at the counter—and the promise of bottomless cups of coffee.

Now Juno is holding out her cell phone to Ruth.

"They found a body," she repeats, her cat eyes narrowing as she waits for Ruth's reaction. "And they think it might be Coco Wilson."

An ornithologist wading through a salt marsh just less than fifty miles from Hoben had come across the skeletal remains while searching for the elusive clapper rail. The fragments were clearly human. Clearly small. In temperate climates it can take as little as three weeks for a body to reach the final stage of decomposition. Soft tissue gone. Hard bone left behind.

Coco Wilson has been missing for well over a month now.

"It's not a murder until there's a body. I read that once."

Juno might be trying to sound blasé, but Ruth hears her voice wobble as she says this. Last night, on their walk with Ressler, they'd discussed the case. Juno was clearly very invested, but she remained vague about who she'd identified as the potential kidnapper. Ruth didn't hold much stock in her claim, given how many theories (and how many supposed suspects) were out there. But she was curious about what Juno thought she'd uncovered. A little nervous too. Because Juno might very well know the perpetrator, thanks to her mother. And what would happen if she discovered that before Ruth did?

"I'm almost there," she'd said, when they got back to the apartment. Ruth might very well have told her the same thing.

She reaches out her hand to squeeze Juno's arm. "It doesn't have to be Coco," she says.

"Yeah," Juno responds. "But it's *someone*. Someone whose body shouldn't be there."

She puts down her phone, making a show of looking serious.

"I found something too. Mum's host parents from Hoben."

Ruth blinks. "What?"

"Yup. Old people never lock their social media accounts, right? They were surprised to hear from me, but they seemed nice enough. A bit sad about their estranged son. They used to call him Chip, like that little teacup from *Beauty and the Beast*, because he was such a cute kid. I guess he stopped being cute one day, and they started using his real name again."

Juno looks so proud of herself.

"That's the thing I've been working on, Ruthie. Tracking him down. And it turns out I was right. Because his *real* name is Bobby. Bobby Johnson. The guy who used to date Ivy Wilson."

Ruth's jaw drops, which makes Juno grin.

"You're not the only Nancy Drew around here," she says, before turning serious again. "But you can't tell Mum, okay? She'd be so mad at me for digging around in her past like that. And she's mad enough at me already."

"Why is she mad at you?" Ruth manages weakly. She's still trying to comprehend Juno's startling news.

"Because of what I did to get us here," Juno answers, with a customary shrug.

"But that's not important right now, Ruthie. I have an idea, and I reckon you're going to love it."

———

Juno knows where Bobby Johnson lives.

"Sunset Park is not far, right?" Juno asks, clearly excited. "We could go see him tonight. Leave Mum to her beauty sleep. She's been to New York before. She won't mind if we go off without her."

"Juno, we can't—"

But Ruth doesn't finish her own sentence.

What *is* stopping her from checking out Rose's former host brother for herself? This lead she's unfathomably missed, when it was right there in front of her.

"You *know* what," Beth warns, and this time she's got the other girls on her side too. Silently reproaching Ruth for even considering taking Juno to meet him.

You're supposed to protect girls like us, they seem to be saying. *Not lead us right into the lion's den.*

Ruth would never harm Juno. Surely the girls know that? But how can she pass up this opportunity to meet a man who might not only be Ivy Wilson's ex-boyfriend? If he lived with Annie Whitaker in 1996, there's a chance he might also be Ethan Oswald's "worthy" successor.

———

Brooklyn bound, they transfer to the R train at Fourteenth Street–Union Square around 7:30 p.m.

"You have to admit," Juno says as they pass a purple-haired saxophonist jamming with a drummer dressed as a fox, "this is pretty fucking cool, what we're doing."

The knot in Ruth's stomach tightens. They'd told Rose they were heading to Times Square to see it all lit up for the evening. Juno had guessed correctly that her mother would not want to join them, tired from an afternoon spent wandering through Central Park and up and down Fifth Avenue.

"I'll be more myself tomorrow," Rose had promised, not looking entirely certain of this. "Then we'll have the whole weekend to explore."

The Mulvaneys are not booked to return to New Zealand until next Wednesday, but Ruth wonders if things will look different after tonight. Let alone tomorrow, which was meant to be the main event.

Right now, Ruth wishes she could go back in time to when she agreed to go along with Juno's plan to hunt down Bobby Johnson. As they near Sunset Park, guilt has come at Ruth full force. She knows she is being irresponsible. It doesn't matter if it was all Juno's idea; Ruth is the grown-up here, and she could be putting the teenager in real danger. That's what Beth and the girls had tried to tell her this morning, and she'd stubbornly ignored them.

Ruth closes her eyes, takes a few deep breaths as Juno babbles about all the things she can't wait to ask Bobby. And when she opens her eyes again, she has made up her mind.

"Juno, you know you can't come in with me."

"Huh?"

"Your accent," Ruth says, trying to sound like this is obvious. "Bobby will know in a second you're from New Zealand."

"So what if he does?" Juno is looking at Ruth like she has suddenly grown Hecate's three heads.

"If he knows you're the daughter of his old host sister, I think he'll get suspicious of our motives."

"Why would he?"

"Because it's too much of a coincidence, Juno. Too personal. It'll put him off."

When they reach their stop and exit the train, Juno looks like she could murder someone herself.

"There are more than five people in New Zealand, you know," she hisses as she follows Ruth up the subway station's stairs into the dim light of early evening aboveground. "You're being ridiculous, Ruthie."

"You have no idea what his relationship with your mom was like was back then," she tells Juno over her shoulder. "You're the one who said he was a little psychopath, and I'm not putting you at risk two days after you landed in New York. And I'm not going to waste this opportunity to talk to him about Coco, either. Not with a rookie error like that."

Juno looks positively incensed now.

"This was *my* idea. You can't just sweep in and take over like this."

They have emerged onto the street corner opposite Bobby

Johnson's apartment. It sits above a laundromat and next to a sprawling church. Looking left and right, Ruth can see at least three sharp spires stabbing at the sky; this row of God's houses gives her no comfort right now.

"I'm sorry," she says, reaching out her arm to stop the younger girl from crossing the street without her. And then Ruth says the thing she knows will get through to Juno. "If you won't listen, I'll change your flight home. You and your mom will have to leave tomorrow."

She watches as a whole army of emotions battle their way across Juno's face. Rage. Incredulity. Disappointment. The briefest surge of defiance, and then the hardest to witness: betrayal.

Juno gestures to the near-empty street, dotted with delis and 99-cent stores and all those churches. "What am I supposed to do then?" she asks, her face like thunder. "Stand here like a target and wait for someone to drag me into their van?"

She is clearly too angry to realize the insensitivity of that comment; Ruth lets it slide.

"Wait for me right here," she says, indicating a metal bench just down from the subway entrance. It sits directly across from a brightly lit Mexican restaurant that seems to be the one bustling place on this block. "I'll be back in ten minutes tops. And if I'm not—well, hopefully you still like me enough to call for help."

"I hate you," Juno calls after her as Ruth crosses the street toward Bobby Johnson's apartment.

In this moment, Ruth doesn't doubt it.

Alone, Ruth pushes through the unlocked main doors to Bobby Johnson's building (does anyone else care about security? she wonders) and takes the two flights of stairs to his apartment. She knocks with as much faux confidence as she had in Oslo.

When he opens the door, Bobby Johnson doesn't look suspicious so much as annoyed by this unexpected intrusion into his evening. Ruth can hear a baseball game playing loudly on a TV behind him.

"Who are you?" he asks, looking her up and down.

He is tall, broad-shouldered. Wearing gray sweatpants and a Brooklyn Cyclones tank that reveals tanned, muscular arms. The kind of arms that could pin you down, Ruth thinks, as she tries to concentrate on his face, focus on the could-be-anybody-ness of his features. The barely there eyebrows. A nicely shaped bottom lip sitting above a thick but neatly trimmed goatee. A few acne marks, but not many. Ruth has no doubt Bobby is assessing her in this moment too.

But they don't seem to recognize anything in each other; Ruth definitely doesn't see a boy next door.

"I'm Nancy," she lies. "I'm working on a podcast about a series of murders and kidnappings in Connecticut, and I wanted to ask you some questions."

She finally sees recognition flicker in Bobby's eyes, but his face stays neutral.

"Not sure what you'd want from me."

Ruth takes it as a good sign that Bobby hasn't shut the door in her face. But she doesn't want to provoke him by mentioning Ivy Wilson, or her missing daughter, too soon.

"I think you knew Annie Whitaker," she says, holding his gaze. "I'm not looking for anything on the record. I just wondered if there was anything you might be able to share about your relationship with her?"

Bobby looks puzzled now.

"Look, I know this seems random," Ruth pushes, "but you were Annie's host brother, weren't you? So you knew her back in 1996."

"Yeah, I knew her," Bobby says, after a quick glance over his shoulder toward his blaring TV. "She was a total freak. Not sure what my parents were thinking, bringing her to live with us, but they probably thought God was calling them to save her or something."

"Save her?"

Bobby's expression darkens. "Yeah, whatever. My parents liked to help people. Charity begins at home and all that. But they weren't sorry to see her go."

Ruth knows she needs to get back to Juno; she said she'd be gone only ten minutes. But she still can't bring herself to say Coco's name.

"So you weren't sorry to see her go back to New Zealand either?" she confirms, instead.

"Shit, man." Bobby scratches at his goatee. "It was a long time ago. I was an angry kid back then, and she was so sad and mopey. It made her an easy target, you know?"

Then, as if he really sees Ruth for the first time, he asks her if she wants to come inside.

When she tells him that she can't stay long, he reaches out a hand as if to pull her through the doorway. Instinctively, Ruth rears back.

"You had a bug on your shirt," Bobby says, dropping his arm. In the darkening hallway, he is suddenly more shadow than light.

"Do you think Annie had anything to do with Beth Lovely's murder back in 1996?" she blurts out, her heart thumping now.

"Fuck do I know, Nancy? I was a kid. She was weird. She was friends with that little girl, for sure. She hung out with lots of little kids at the park, which used to embarrass me. Like, get some friends your own age. But I couldn't tell you if she was a murderer. Maybe. I mean, haven't we all got it in us?"

That little girl.

"What do you know about Coco Wilson, then?" Ruth whispers.

That's when Bobby Johnson does shut the door in her face.

Juno doesn't say a word the whole journey home.

Ruth had been relieved to find her still sitting on the bench by the subway entrance, texting someone at double speed on her phone.

"He's got nothing," Ruth said with an exaggerated groan as she approached her. "So you didn't miss out."

Forget the Peabody. Ruth figured she deserved a Tony Award for that live performance. Acting like her encounter with Bobby had been no big deal, when she was still shaking from the impact. Not that this mattered, because Juno wouldn't look up from her phone. And she hasn't so much as glanced at Ruth since then. Only when they're transferring to the 1 train, heading back to Ruth's apartment, does she deign to say something. It's when Ruth tries to reiterate that she was only trying to protect Juno tonight.

"Whatever."

That's as much as Ruth is going to get from her.

Back at the apartment, Rose is on the couch, watching a middle season of an old comedy series, a half-empty bottle of red wine on the coffee table in front of her.

"How was it?" she asks as Juno silently stalks past on her way to their shared guest room. She turns to Ruth. "Did something happen?"

Ruth is trying to decide how to answer when Juno comes back into the living room.

"I'm taking Ressler for a walk," she announces.

When Ruth goes to protest, Juno gives her an icy look.

"I grew up on a farm, Ruth. We may not have had *bears*, but I know how to take care of a dog."

Juno keeps Ressler out for almost half an hour, and Ruth's anxiety increases with every minute they're gone.

"He's not himself," Juno says when she finally returns. "I had to practically drag him down the street. You might want to keep an eye on him, Ruth. If you're not too busy thinking about yourself."

The comment is mean, but it works, because Ruth immediately feels guilty all over again.

Kneeling down to check Ressler over, she vows to do better from now on.

"I won't ever let anything happen to you," Ruth tells her dog, holding his sad, beautiful face in her hands.

"That's what my dad used to say to me," Juno says from behind her. "And look how that turned out."

———

It wasn't that he had "nothing." It's just that Ruth can't say for sure what she learned from Bobby Johnson tonight. He had seemed bewildered by her questions about his old host sister. But he'd also slammed the door shut when she asked about Coco. That wasn't exactly a subtle move, when Ruth thinks about it. Not quite the reaction of a criminal mastermind, or an apprentice usurping his master, as *Nydelig* might put it. It was a sign Bobby had something to hide. But what? Remembering the way he'd reached for her in that dim hallway, Ruth is not sure she wants to go back and ask.

Getting into bed, she can only hope tomorrow brings her the answers she's so desperately been seeking.

"It has to," Rhea says from the doorway. Reminding Ruth just how long they've all been waiting.

———

Friday morning, Juno is up first. When Ruth walks into the kitchen, she finds her at the counter, drinking a coffee and staring at the yellowing houseplants.

"Do you know why my mum agreed to come here after saying she wasn't going to do your podcast?" Juno asks, without turning from those plants.

When Ruth doesn't answer, Juno turns to face her. "I broke a kid's leg, Ruthie." She says this flatly, before continuing in that same monotone. "He was a bully. And he was harassing Minnie. Dick pics, rape threats. Links to shitty porn. Getting his friends to join in. There's a reason Minnie doesn't go back to Marama River anymore. I warned him to leave her alone. And when he didn't listen, I had to make him. It was an accident, but no one was very happy with me, 'cause he's on the rugby team and finals are next week. The timing definitely worked in your favor, though. Mum desperately wanted to get me out of there."

Juno makes a little popping sound with her lips now. "Did you know there's a way to kick at the side of a knee that makes a person's leg buckle?" she asks, her expression unreadable. "If they're not expecting the impact, the bone just—snaps."

Ruth flinches. "Are you in trouble, Juno?"

"It was an *accident*," the teenager repeats, then her expression hardens. "Anyway, Ruthie, I'm just saying you don't need to protect me. I can take care of myself."

Juno squares her shoulders and leaves the kitchen.

What have you done? Ruth wants to call after her.

Knowing the real question is: What has *she* done? She knows that Juno watches her. Maybe even looks up to her. Has Ruth inadvertently taught this young girl that it's okay to hurt someone to get what you want from them?

Or has Rose Mulvaney already passed on that life lesson to her daughter?

THIRTY-FIVE

Sit down. Stand up. Pace. Sit down again. Ruth can't stay still. It's Friday morning and she's at Sweeney's, grateful for the spare key Owen left her, because this shuttered bar is the perfect setting for today's gathering. If only because it's Ruth's own territory. She knows every inch, every corner.

And where the security alarm is.

It's not like she's scared. But she does know this day is going to change things, for better or worse.

Ruth has set up her voice recorder and its accompanying tripod on one of Sweeney's main tables. The instruction booklet and corresponding video tutorials that came with her purchase had assured her the device was guaranteed to offer "the world's best" sound quality in a group setting.

Her reasons for setting up for the podcast are twofold. If the women think they've been brought together for *The Other Women*, they might be less likely to turn and leave the moment they see they're not alone. More importantly—assuming they all stay—Ruth will have a record of whatever they confess. To her or each other.

She'd left Juno and Rose back at the apartment, Juno—who was back to ignoring Ruth—growing increasingly frustrated at how long her mother was taking to get ready.

"It's a *podcast*," she'd seethed. "It's not like anyone is actually going to *see* you."

Ruth can only assume Amity and Helen are also getting ready, if not on their way.

The official format for the morning, Ruth has decided, will be to get the women talking freely on uncontroversial topics. She won't ambush them; Bobby Johnson slamming that door in her face is proof of what happens when you shoot unexpected arrows, the way Juno likes to.

Ruth has been reading up on the differences between conducting source and suspect interviews. Under the PEACE model of interrogation (not an intentional oxymoron, Ruth assumes), you build rapport with your suspect before you call out their contradictions. You let them sit with their story a little before you take it apart. So that's what she'll do. Instead of allowing all the lies to build up between them, she'll topple the tower when it gets too tall.

Unpacking the deli sandwiches she intends to serve for lunch (if they make it that far), Ruth is considering pouring herself a shot of something from behind the bar for liquid courage—when a message comes through on her phone.

Gabe.

It's more than a week since he left her apartment in such a hurry. More than a week since she's heard from him. And here he is, with his bad timing yet again.

Sorry I've been MIA. A bit going on. Just wanted to say I think you're ace, Nancy D. And I know you'll do amazing things in your life xx Gabe.

There's nothing Ruth can do but laugh, even if the sound

cracks when it meets the air. Gabe's kiss-off is so spectacularly bland, she doesn't even have the energy to be offended. Shaking thoughts of him away, she sets her phone face down on the table, next to the voice recorder on its tripod, and heads over to the bar.

A shot of tequila ought to do it. Maybe two.

Amity is the first to arrive, looking deceptively refined in capris and a white shirt. Worn as an actual shirt, this time.

She air-kisses Ruth on both cheeks, then plops down at the table Ruth has set the tripod on.

"I have sooooooo much to tell you," she is saying when the door to Sweeney's opens, and Helen walks in.

Stopping when she sees Amity, Helen frowns slightly, but nothing in her expression suggests fear or reticence. At best, she looks mildly confused. Before Ruth has a chance to explain herself, Juno comes barreling through the door, almost running into the stationary Helen.

"What the—" Juno's confusion is worn more broadly. She looks from Helen to Amity to Ruth. Then back at her mother, who has entered Sweeney's behind her daughter.

"Surprise," Ruth says weakly, watching any confidence she'd thought she possessed walk right out the still-open door.

To her immense relief, none of the women immediately follow.

It was too good an opportunity to miss, Ruth explains, as she guides Helen and Rose to the table where Amity is already seated. Having all her "other women" in the same town, at the same time. There is just so much they have in common. And she completely understands if they want to back out, now that they know it's to be a shared session today, but really, nothing will be so different from the one-on-one interviews they've already done. Only this time, they'll get to hear each other's stories.

This all comes out in a rush, not unlike the way Ruth introduced herself back in Oslo, when she first showed up at Helen's door.

Of course, Helen knows at least part of what Ruth told her that day was a lie; she wasn't really spending the summer in Oslo. Who knows if the woman is going to believe her now? If the look on the older woman's face is anything to go by, she's not expecting the truth from Ruth anyway. Not after she was blackmailed to get here. In fact, Helen almost seems amused at what she, more than the others, must surely suspect is a farce.

Amity, glancing from Helen to Rose, appears confused, while Rose's expression is blank. Like she's just wiped her face clean.

Juno has retreated to a bar stool and is watching them all from across the room, her expression as blank as her mother's. Only when she meets Ruth's gaze does she raise her eyebrows slightly, as if to say, *What the hell is this?*

Ruth shifts her attention back to the women seated around the table. Grateful no one has fled. She clenches her back teeth. Hoping her strained smile doesn't look as grotesque as it feels.

"Shall we begin?" she asks, and when she receives three nods, Ruth switches on her voice recorder.

At first, she gets them talking about love.

And when you start with love, control is seldom far behind.

"I wanted to be the girl who says yes," Amity says about her physical relationship with Eric Coulter. "I wanted to be the girl who got to choose.

"He liked to strangle me. When we were having sex. You could play connect the dots with his finger marks, some nights. I had a big collection of concealers. And scarves. And I said yes every time, because then it's only a game, right? You can't really hurt someone if you're just playing around."

"I understand that concept of turning it into a game, Amity," Helen says. "Martin might not have been violent, but he certainly liked to be the man of the house. I never ate unless he said so. Never laughed unless he was telling the joke, or spent money unless he approved it. I had to stay one step ahead of his needs at all times if I wanted peace in my home."

"You don't always have to hit a person to wound them," Rose says, looking down at her hands. "Even when we were engaged, I knew Peter had another girlfriend. One that he actually liked to touch. After the babies, he would never even kiss me. It was the same as being starved."

If Ruth were not so impatient to get to Ethan, she'd find this conversation, and the way these women so clearly relate to each other, fascinating. And she has to admit, she'd find it heart-wrenching. No matter what they did before or after their relationships with those men, it's painful to consider what all three of them experienced in their marriages.

(If only things were different, she really could have done something with *The Other Women*.)

"We sacrifice so much of our own freedom to protect our children, don't we, Rose?" Helen says, as kind as Ruth has ever heard her.

Ruth glances at Juno, listening from her perch on the bar stool. Her face remains impassive.

"I accidentally got pregnant," Amity blurts out. "Smartest thing I ever did was to get an abortion. But can you imagine how people would respond if they knew I thought *that*."

"You do seem rather obsessed with what people think of you, Amity."

Helen again, after a long pause. Not so kind this time.

Ruth looks back to check Juno's reaction, half expecting her to laugh. Which is when she notices the girl is gone from her stool.

"Let's take a lunch break," she suggests as everyone at the table follows her gaze.

"She probably just needed some air," Ruth assures Rose, leaning over to click off the voice recorder. "There are some sandwiches over on the bar. Help yourselves, and I'll go find her."

Stepping outside, Ruth is relieved to see Juno sitting on the stoop of a well-preserved brownstone diagonally across from Sweeney's. She is texting someone furiously; Ruth briefly wonders about the kind of friend a girl like Juno might have on call.

"Hey."

The greeting makes Juno jump. She puts her phone in her pocket but doesn't get up or move over for Ruth to join her on the stoop.

"You doing okay?" Ruth asks, not sure she'll get an answer.

"Just dandy."

Right. She's angry, still.

"You're full of surprises these days, aren't you?" Juno continues, looking up at her now. Ruth can see her cheeks are blotched with red.

A distant memory, like hearing a phone ringing in another room. On the beach, Ruth promising to tell Juno about the other women as soon as she could. Today's "surprise" must feel like a brand-new betrayal.

"I'm sorry, Juno," she says. "This all happened so quickly, and—"

"Spare me," Juno interrupts, getting up from the stoop. "This podcast is obviously *very* important to you. Probably the only thing you've *got*, right? So let's get it done."

She starts to turn from Ruth and then stops.

"It's not her, by the way. That body they found in the marsh. Those bones must have been there for years, apparently. They don't know who it is yet, but it's a girl. So maybe you missed something with Bobby Johnson last night after all, *Ruthie*."

With that, Juno crosses the street and strides into Sweeney's without a backward glance. Watching her go, Ruth gets a flash of the young girl stalking that boy in Marama River. The one whose leg she says she broke.

Ruth waits a full minute before following her.

Stepping into the bar, she can hear the women talking over their sandwiches. They are sitting in their same spots at the table, and Amity is asking Helen if it upsets her that her children cut her out of their lives. Ruth can't tell if Amity is actually curious or making a clumsy attempt to be mean.

"It bothered me for a long time," Helen says, dabbing her mouth with a napkin. "But there's nothing more Sisyphean than a mother trying to persuade her children to understand her."

Amity blinks. "Sure."

"Where are they now, Helen?" This comes from Juno, back on her bar stool.

"My son, Magnus, passed away three years ago. And my daughter, Louise, could be anywhere. She is—what's the correct term these days? Something of a wanderer. She never married, but she has a man in every port, as they say."

"Cool," Amity says, before catching herself. "Like, good for her," she mumbles, twisting at the diamond on her engagement finger. After a small, deliberate sigh, she turns the conversation back to herself. "Eric and I weren't *actually* married, you know. It was just a Vegas thing that we never made official. I just said we were married so people would understand how serious it was. So they'd understand what happened to me. Because I was a victim too."

As Ruth returns to the table and resumes her seat, she suddenly understands how Amity's name ended up on *What Happened to Her*, under that list of Ethan's known victims. In fact, she can't believe she hadn't seen it before now.

Amity is the one who had her own name added to that list.

A second realization immediately follows. If Amity has been a member of *What Happened to Her* this whole time, there's no way she hasn't at least considered the real identity of @DrBurgess96. That "Friend" so interested in Ethan Oswald and his *other* victims.

And if she's kept all this from Ruth, is it possible she's kept Ethan's letters from her too? What are the chances Amity never sold them at all? Highly likely, Ruth concedes.

She is confused to find she's not only angry at this thought—she's hurt.

"Do you know the names of your husband's victims, Amity?" she asks, letting that hurt leak into her question, because she doesn't know where else to put it.

Amity blinks again. "I donate money to the Sex Workers Project whenever I can," she says defensively.

"So the answer is no?"

From across the room, Ruth can see Juno sit up straighter on her stool. She has obviously noted this new, sharp edge to Ruth's tone.

"Mia Alvarez," Ruth says slowly, mixing in anger with her hurt now. "Shana Washington. Dee Jordan. Charise. It took four of them, Amity. Before anyone cared what happened to those girls.

"And you . . ." Ruth is blazing now as she turns to Helen. "Can you name your husband's victims?"

Emily and Natalie. Both fourteen years old. Babysitters who had posted ads in their local diners, three counties apart. Their bodies found together. Karen. Jane. Sarah. Leah, Summer, Lucy. A Louise like Torrent's own daughter. Two Kates. One Anne.

Ruth doesn't wait for Helen to recite their names.

"Kelly Parker and Nichole Morley," Rose says quietly, before Ruth can get to her.

"What is the point of this, Ruth?"

It could be any of the women who ask her this, but it's Helen. No longer looking amused.

The point is all that loss. The staggering *pointlessness* of it. Every one of those names belonged to a real person. A girl who should be a woman now. Living out whatever life she chose for herself. Not forever suspended in time. Not kept—a girl.

Like Beth.

Ruth says her name out loud now. She adds Beth Lovely to that damning list of dead girls.

What does she expect from these women at the table, now that it's out there? Gasps, denials, anger? Another kind of confession? What she gets, after all this time, is nothing. Silence. The three women say nothing at all.

It is Juno who finally speaks. "She thinks you killed her friend."

"Juno!"

Rose, finding her voice, says her daughter's name loudly, like a warning, though it seems to have the opposite effect.

"What, *Mom*?"

Juno gets up from her stool, her whole face a sneer. "How long are we going to pretend, ladies? That Ruth doesn't have it in for you. That she isn't trying to get you to confess. That's what this podcast is actually about, right? Making you think she's on your side, that she actually cares about you. When all she wants is to trap you!"

Juno's head jerks toward Ruth, her words accompanied by a spray of spit.

If they're not expecting the impact.

Ruth feels as if Juno has taken her legs out from under her too. And still, the women remain silent.

"Don't any of you care?" Juno is now close to tears as she looks at her mother imploringly.

When Rose doesn't respond, Juno lets out a strangled sob, before reaching into her pocket and hurling something small and hard at Ruth.

"Take your stupid talisman and your stupid dead girls, Ruthie. And leave the rest of us alone."

The triskelion hits the corner of the table, clattering to the floor at Ruth's feet, as Juno turns and runs out the door.

———

"Leave her."

Helen has reached out a hand to Rose, who is halfway out of her chair. Juno's mother looks at the older woman, bewildered. But she sits back down.

"Have I missed something?" Amity asks.

"Quite often," Helen says. She stands up herself now. "I think we're done for today, Ruth-Ann. Perhaps we can reconvene tomorrow."

None of what Juno said can be a surprise to Helen. Not after the way that conversation ended in Oslo. And the lengths Ruth went to just to get her to come here today. Still, the woman's calmness is unnerving. Like Juno's pain made no impression on her at all.

Ruth can only watch, open-mouthed, as Rose and Amity silently pack up their things and follow Helen out the door.

She stays at the table, alone and stupefied, for at least five minutes. Eventually, she gets up to leave, but it feels like she's walking through tar.

The only thought she can hold on to as she heads for the door: *They definitely know each other*. It was there in the way Helen touched Rose's arm. The way both Rose and Amity followed her out of the bar. As if they were used to doing what she said.

Ruth arrives back at her apartment with no conscious memory of how she got home. Too many other things were pushing through on her walk, little earthquakes of realization.

Helen, in Oslo, saying Ruth surely hadn't come all the way from New Zealand just to ask her a "predictable" question. But Ruth had only told her she was an American student in Oslo for the summer; she'd never once mentioned New Zealand.

Amity calling and asking her out for a drink, after she'd gone to Sweeney's looking for her. Ruth had never mentioned her job to any of these women. Not until she invited them to meet her here today.

And Amity correctly "guessing" her star sign that night. Was that only so she could drop Ted Bundy, that most infamous of serial killers, into the conversation? Did she want to toy with Ruth a little?

Have they *all* been playing her?

Supine on her bed, Ruth lets another traitorous thought in, one that she's been willfully ignoring for weeks. It's all been so easy. Too easy, a reasonable person might say. Rose inviting her to stay at the farmhouse, then dropping everything to come to New York. Helen *not* slamming the door in her face, when it should have been a terrible shock to have someone find her after all this time. Amity, with her "secret" recordings. All those drunken confessions. Had she known *exactly* what she was saying?

And was it all because these women have always known that little Ruthie Nelson was on their tail? Have they spent the last nineteen years waiting for her to catch up to them? This girl who *survived*.

How foolish has Ruth been to think she'd actually wrested control from them? Lying on her bed, she feels as if she's on that riverbed in Marama River. As she stares at the ceiling, it becomes that sky, her wet eyelashes the water, making everything above her blur. Digging her hands into the quilt beneath her, Ruth feels those fine fragments of stone and shell and bone. The scattered remains of a girl, slipping through her fingers.

She stifles a sob. It's all been for nothing. She went traipsing around the world on a ridiculous quest, careening from one deluded situation to the next. And for what? She can't ever go far enough to come back around to that van. To that moment she stepped up into the front passenger seat, when she should have run away. She'll never run fast enough, or far enough, now. To not go missing that day.

The way Coco went missing, and her girls went missing. And Ruth has never been able to find them.

She's failed them, and she's failed herself. Which means she's failed Beth Lovely too.

Beth.

Ruth sits up, panicked.

She can't hear Beth. When was the last time? Yesterday, when she told Ruth not to go to Bobby Johnson's apartment? Trying desperately to remember, she hears a choking sound. It takes her a moment to realize that this terrible noise is coming from Ressler. Racing to the living room, she discovers her dog, her beautiful boy, lying in what looks like a bloody pool of entrails.

You came, he seems to say as he lifts his head briefly, before dropping it back down to the floor.

Through the hot haze of her panic, Ruth knows she needs to get him to the vet as soon as possible. But there's no one she can call. And there's no way she can get him to the vet hospital on her own. It's a full seven blocks away, and Ressler is already too weak to walk.

She can't carry him all that way, though she tries as hard as she can, getting them as far as the front door, before she collapses beside him.

Sitting there on the floor, her beloved dog's head in her hands, Ruth cries as loudly as she did when she was seven years old. She doesn't care who can hear her pain, or that they'll know how scared she is. She is alone, and Ressler is dying, and she really has failed in every way.

"I'm so sorry," she sobs, letting the grief wash over her.

Thinking, if he dies right now, she wants to die too.

"Get up."

"Get up, Ruthie."

"Get *up*."

It's not just Beth's voice that suddenly fills the entranceway. It's all of them. All her girls. Firm, encouraging. Insistent, as they remind her that giving up is never, *not ever*, an option.

"You survived," they tell her over and over as she cries. "That is enough, Ruthie. For all of us."

Enough.

Covered in Ressler's blood, that word ringing in her ears, Ruth feels the girls lift her back to her feet. Then they release her, and she springs into action. As if her life depends on it.

THIRTY-SIX

In the end, Ruth tipped an Uber driver $300. To help carry Ressler downstairs, then let her sit with him in the back seat of his clean little Mazda, the dog wrapped in the quilt from her bed.

"You got him here just in time," the emergency vet said, assuring Ruth that Ressler was going to be just fine. Hemorrhagic gastroenteritis, the doctor called it. Not exactly common in larger breeds, she said. But not unheard of, either.

"It's likely he ate something he shouldn't have," she explained to a still-shaking Ruth. "Which can happen with these greedy fellows. We've got him on a drip to rehydrate him, and we'll monitor him overnight, if that's okay with you. You should be able to pick him up in the morning."

For the second time today, Ruth walks back to her apartment building in a daze. It's midevening now; she's been at the vet hospital for hours. As she wearily exits the elevator on her floor, Ruth is startled to see Rose Mulvaney sitting, head in her hands, outside her front door.

"Have you seen her?"

It takes a moment for Ruth to comprehend the question. She stares at Rose, who is now on her feet.

"Juno," the woman says, urgent now. "We can't find her. *Please*, Ruth—have you seen her?"

———————

How many times have these words been spoken to a worried parent?

She'll be fine.

We'll find her.

Don't panic.

We'll find *her.*

Juno Mulvaney. Seventeen years old. Missing since early Friday afternoon. Last seen at Sweeney Todd's Sports Bar on the Upper West Side.

Did she seem agitated?

Yes.

Had there been a fight?

Yes.

With her mother?

Not exactly.

Ruth imagines how that questioning might go, if Rose had agreed to call the police. But she is refusing to do so right now. She says Juno doesn't trust cops and that she'd never forgive her for involving them too soon.

Sitting on the couch, an agitated Rose continually checks her phone, shifting it from hand to hand. But still—nothing. Juno, forever furiously texting someone, has not responded to any of her mother's messages. Has not answered any of her calls.

Rose had wandered the neighborhood after Juno ran from the bar, certain her daughter just needed to walk things off. She was used to having space, after all. Back home, she had a whole farm to roam when she needed to be alone. When she couldn't find her daughter in the streets surrounding Sweeney's, Rose had come back to the apartment, realizing too late that Juno had Ruth's spare key. She managed to walk into the building with another resident, a neighbor of Ruth's who recognized Rose from the day before. This got her as far as Ruth's front door.

But with Ruth missing in action, too, Rose could only sit outside in the hallway. And wait.

Ruth sits down on the couch beside her. This time, the proximity doesn't make her flinch.

"She was really angry today," Rose says miserably.

Ruth bites her lip. There's something she's been thinking about ever since the vet examined Ressler.

"She was mostly angry at me, yes?"

Rose nods.

"Please don't be offended by this, Rose, but would Juno ever hurt my dog?"

"Ressler?" Rose looks genuinely confused.

"It's just that I had to rush him to the vet this afternoon. She said he might have eaten something he wasn't supposed to, and Juno took him for a walk on her own last night, so . . ."

Ruth backs out of this sentence halfway through it. It already sounds obscene.

"No," Rose says firmly. "Juno *loves* animals. She would never do anything to harm Ressler. Or you, for that matter."

"But if she's mad at me?"

"For God's sake, Ruth. She's a teenager. That's all teenagers ever are: mad at something or someone. Or the whole bloody world. That doesn't mean Juno is going around poisoning dogs."

Rose looks closer to weary than offended, as she shakes her head, before pressing her fingers to her eyes. Ruth recognizes the gesture, the effort to comprehend exactly what's happening to her right now.

"I'm sorry," she says quickly. "I guess I'm just a bit confused about what Juno's capable of when she's mad. After she told me about breaking that kid's leg . . ."

Rose lowers her fingers. Opens her eyes. "What are you talking about now, Ruth?"

"Juno told me about how she hurt that boy who was harassing Minnie—" she starts to explain, but even as Ruth says it, something feels wrong with the story.

"Juno hasn't broken anyone's leg," Rose interrupts, sounding annoyed now. "There was a boy who was giving Minnie some trouble over the summer, but I spoke to the parents and we dealt with it. The *adults* dealt with it. I can't believe she would tell you something like that." Rose sighs. "Juno seems to have given you the wrong idea about her entirely. And I'm beginning to think she did that on purpose. Why? So you wouldn't be able to hurt her, I'm guessing."

"I would never hurt her!" Ruth exclaims.

"Weren't you listening at all today?" Rose's frustration is now undeniable. "There are so many ways to hurt someone, especially when they're already vulnerable. Rejection is right up there. She admires you, Ruth. And I think she was afraid you'd judge her if you uncovered her secret. The thing she's most ashamed of."

Rose checks her phone again and shakes her head before she continues.

"I still can't get her to talk about it. Anytime I try, she clams up. But I'm convinced she thinks it was her fault."

"Her fault?"

Ruth is struggling to keep up.

"I think she feels responsible for Nichole's death," Rose says. "Juno told Nichole to go after Peter that night. She'd been having trouble sleeping. None of us knew she was fully aware of what was going on between her father and Kelly. That night, for whatever reason, she woke up and told Nichole she'd seen Peter doing things to Kelly, and the girl went off after her cousin. Nichole was never meant to be down there at the river. If Juno had kept quiet, there's a chance that terrible night would have ended very differently."

"Jesus."

Ruth's hand has gone to her chest. All these years burdened by a split-second decision she made as a child. And here was Juno, similarly weighed down.

"That's too much for a little kid to carry," she whispers.

The two women stare at each other.

"I know who you are," Rose says quietly. "And I know what happened to you when you were a child. I'm very sorry for all *you* had to carry at that age. I also know who you think *I* am. But I can assure you that you have the wrong idea about me too."

"I think I know where she is," Ruth says suddenly. The answer is so blindingly obvious, now that she knows Juno's secret. The guilt she must have been living with after sending Nichole down to the river. The desire to go back and make it right.

When you *can't* make it right, you look for other girls to save.

"Stay here," Ruth tells Rose. "In case she comes back."

On the way out of the apartment, she grabs her bag. The one with the mace and the lipstick stun gun.

"I'll find her, Rose," Ruth says, before she adds the triskelion to that bag of weapons. "I promise."

Then, commanding her restless dead to follow, she sweeps out the door.

———————

It's only thirteen miles, but in the staccato traffic from the Upper West Side to Sunset Park, it takes Ruth thirty-three minutes to arrive outside Bobby Johnson's apartment for the second time in as many nights. The doors to the building are still unlocked, and she heads up the stairs more confidently this time, feeling the safety of those weapons against her hip. Especially since her recently retrieved triskelion is there too. She imagines it flashing like a beacon.

"Remember this address," Ruth had said to the Uber driver, when he dropped her off right out front. "Just in case you see me on the news tomorrow."

He'd shrugged and said, "Sure." Like passengers had said this to him many times before.

Now, rapping her knuckles against Bobby's door, Ruth once again feels comforted by the fact that someone knows where she is. Even if it's a stranger this time around.

When he opens the door and sees Ruth standing there, Bobby grins.

"I knew you'd be back," he says. "You wanna come in?"

Just like little Ruthie Nelson, she walks willingly through the door.

———

Bobby's apartment is compact, neat. The walls of the open-plan kitchen and living area are made of exposed brick. The wooden floor needs a sweep. There are dishes in the sink; not too many. A rowing machine and set of weights in the corner, next to the TV. Baseball still playing. Bobby mutes it as he guides Ruth to a brown couch.

"Make yourself at home, Nancy," he says.

Ruth had forgotten that she lied about her name.

Without asking if she wants one, Bobby goes to the fridge. Comes back with two beers.

"Sorry about last night," he says, handing her one of the bottles, already opened. "I've had a few people nosing around about that Coco kid, and I wasn't in the mood."

"And now?" Ruth tries for a smile.

"Now—I'm in the mood."

Bobby clinks the top of his bottle against hers. Sits down next to her. Too close.

"Besides, they don't usually look like you."

"Ah."

A bubble of panic escapes her. Ruth takes a sip of her drink. Struggles to keep the beer down.

"People have got it in their heads that I have something going on with Ivy still. That I might be that kid's dad or something. No thank you. Not me. I haven't seen anyone from Hoben since high school, thank fuck."

Bobby leans back, beer bottle at his lips.

Ruth strains for sounds of anyone else in the apartment. A girl. Hidden away.

"Did anyone else come see you tonight?" she asks.

"Just the pizza delivery guy." Bobby grins. "And you."

"No one else? You sure?"

He gives her a strange look now. "Nah. Why? You jealous? Think I've got some other girl here?"

It took nothing, Ruth understands, for this guy to think she is here because she wants him. She gave him no signal, no sign. But he's already acting like she's coming on to him.

"No," she says evenly, more annoyed than alarmed. "It's just that my friend is missing, and I wondered if she might have come to see you tonight."

Bobby pauses with his beer halfway to his mouth. "What's this about? Why would your friend . . . I just met you, Nancy."

"No, you didn't. We used to be neighbors, *Chip*. My real name is Ruth. I was the little girl who lived next door to you in Hoben.

I went missing around the same time as Beth Lovely. And then my family moved me out of town."

Bobby tilts his head in confusion. "I don't remember you?"

The way he frames this as a question makes her believe him.

"I don't remember you either. But hey, we must have blocked a lot of shit out from back then."

Ruth feels her confidence building back up again. It's as if the girls are right behind her, egging her on.

"My friend is called Juno," she continues. "She's Annie Whitaker's daughter. Let me ask you again: Did she come here tonight? Is she here?"

"What the actual fuck?"

The muscles in Bobby's jaw pulse as he gets up from the couch, his eyes wide.

"I haven't seen Annie Whitaker since I was twelve years old. I don't even *think* about her. And now you're accusing me of— what? Kidnapping her daughter? You're crazy, Nancy. Or whatever your fucking name is."

She should have been prepared for what happens next. The switch. The way Bobby suddenly throws himself at her, pinning her against the back of the couch with his full, considerable weight.

"You got some sick fantasies going on, hey?" he growls, his breath hot against Ruth's face. "Is that what this is all about? 'Cause I can dig that. Help you out a little."

Ruth feels Bobby's pelvis press against her. The shift of his legs as he pins her tighter.

"Get off me," she says through gritted teeth.

"Nah, you know you want it," Bobby starts to say, when she shoves at him with the force of every girl who never got that chance to fight back. Seven-year-old Ruthie Nelson, the fiercest of them all.

"Get *off* me," she repeats, as if her voice is made of steel.

She sees it. The way she's ruined the game for him now. Bobby's face twists as he spits at her, the gob hitting her cheek. But he lets her go.

"Get the fuck out of here, you crazy bitch," he says, wiping at his mouth. "And don't ever come back."

Ruth is out the door, down the stairs, before Bobby Johnson has a chance to change the rules on her.

Doubled over, Ruth can see a Friday-night crowd at the well-lit Mexican restaurant down the block. She is safe. She got out. All on her own. Still, she moves closer to the safety of that busy restaurant as she takes her phone from the bag she was quick-witted enough to grab before she ran out the door.

There's a message waiting. From Rose.

We found Juno. She's safe. A friend brought her back to your apartment.

Ruth doesn't know whether to laugh or cry as she shakily books her Uber ride home.

—————

On the road back to Manhattan, her Uber driver has a musical theater playlist going.

"Do you mind?" he asks, and Ruth shakes her head, grateful the old man would rather listen to a succession of divas than try to make conversation with her.

Leaning back, the seat belt tight across her chest, Ruth half listens to the song that's just started playing. "No Good Deed" from *Wicked*, a musical Joe took her to when she was fourteen years old. She knows—from Owen, of course—that this song is called an eleven o'clock number. A showstopper that comes late in the second act, when the protagonist has a big, dramatic realization. One that propels them toward the finale.

The neon clock on the driver's dash says it's just after 10 p.m.

Ruth closes her eyes and tries to breathe. Juno is safe. That's all that matters.

Some deeds *do* go unpunished.

Silly girl. Thinking it was over now. Letting her defenses down as she unlocks her front door and walks into her apartment.

To find Rose, Juno—and Gabe.

Run.

Standing on the threshold. Frozen.

Run.

He knew exactly what to tell her. Exactly want she wanted to hear.

Ruthie, run.

How do you know if they're a stranger?

"Gabe."

Ruth hears the rumble before she feels it. The fault line in her lithosphere. The collision as her worlds crash into each other yet again.

Then: collapse.

THIRTY-SEVEN

D id I faint?"

Ruth comes to on the couch, Rose kneeling in front of her with a wet cloth. Fighting her way back to the surface, Ruth sees Juno sitting in the armchair opposite.

And Gabe, standing in the corner of her living room.

The instinct to run kicks in all over again, but Rose moves to sit beside her. She puts her hand on Ruth's arm. Reminding her, oddly, of Patty Lovely.

"Not exactly," Juno says from her chair. "You just sort of staggered."

Ruth looks from Juno to Gabe, but he won't meet her eyes.

"Will someone please tell me what's going on?" she begs weakly.

"Gabe knew where to find me." Juno shrugs, as if it is the simplest thing. "And he brought me home."

"Juno, you know what she means."

Gabe, now. He steps out from the corner, but doesn't come too close.

"Juno and I know each other, Ruth," he says, still not meeting her eyes. "We have for a long time now. We're friends, you might say. Though she's making that a little hard right this minute."

Juno sticks her tongue out at Gabe, who sighs.

"I'll just come out with it, I guess," he continues, looking miserable at the prospect. "Helen is my grandmother. I only found out about my grandparents a few years ago, after my uncle died. And not long after that, I met Juno online. We, ah . . . we suddenly had a lot in common."

At this point, Ruth is beyond surprise. She closes her eyes, but there is nothing that needs to be steadied. Her body is completely numb.

"Go on," is all she can say, her mouth moving just enough to let the words out.

"There's a group of us. A secret group, I guess. Invite only and all that. It's for the families of men like Juno's dad, and my . . . ah . . . men like TBK. And that's where Juno and I found each other."

Something clicks.

"You didn't come into Sweeney's that night by accident."

"No. No, I didn't, Ruth."

Gabe meets her eyes for the briefest moment, then looks back down at the floor.

Rose, who has stayed silent until now, turns to face Ruth on the couch. She removes her hand.

"When I told Juno someone had contacted me about doing a podcast, she was concerned. We've had so many people poking around in our lives, looking for even more things to hold against us. My daughter is very protective of what little family she has left. She's very protective of *me*."

"And when I told Gabe about the podcast," Juno picks up, so much louder than the others, "it turns out he was worried about his grandmother being bothered by you too. From what we can tell, you started looking for both of them at the same time.

Asking around and all that. And when you've been through what people like us have—well, you learn there are no coincidences. Just what you know. And what you don't know yet."

"So this whole time . . ." Another sentence Ruth cannot bring herself to complete.

"We were just trying to figure out what you were up to," Gabe says. "But as you would know, that got a little tricky."

Tricky. Ruth almost wants to laugh.

"I wouldn't make a good Nancy Drew," Gabe adds forlornly. "You're not supposed to fall for the villain."

The villain.

They think *she* is the villain.

And now Ruth does laugh. The sound so wounded, so like a wrenching sob, that even Juno looks away.

———

They've all gone.

Rose and Juno to a hotel for the night. Gabe to his apartment in Brooklyn. His *grandmother's* apartment.

"Sorry to hear about Ressler," Juno said as she walked out the door with Gabe and Rose, wheeling her hastily repacked suitcase behind her.

When the door clicks shut, Ruth is too stunned to cry.

"Help," she says to her girls. "*Help.*"

But she knows this mess she's created has nothing to do with them.

She's going to have to work it out with the living this time.

———

The next afternoon, a still-reeling Ruth walks toward Sheep Meadow in Central Park. Wondering if she's supposed to be the wolf or the lamb in this situation.

When she'd picked up Ressler from the vet this morning, the doctor reminded Ruth that most dogs have little sense of self-preservation when it comes to food. If he'd eaten something he shouldn't, there was no guarantee he wouldn't do it again. The doctor was smiling as she said this, but also firm. Ruth would need to stay vigilant if she wanted to keep her boy safe.

She clearly needs to be more vigilant with herself too. But self-preservation can come later. There is no way Ruth is going to let everyone leave New York without hearing what they have to say. What they *want* to say, now that it's clear they know who she really is.

What would a show be without a spectacular finale? she asks herself as the meadow comes into view. Shouldn't everyone get to take their bows?

Helen has instructed her to meet them at the Roc d'Ercé. Scanning the dapples of people lounging and laughing around the large rock, Ruth soon sees the trio she is looking for. She tries not to feel disappointed that Juno hasn't come along (reminding herself that she's furious with the girl, anyway) as she takes in the women, sitting arm's length apart on a large rug. Nearby, a small child is celebrating his birthday with a giant Spider-Man cake and a menagerie of balloon animals, shaped by a vaguely terrifying clown.

Giving the clown a wide berth, Ruth exhales.

Curtain up.

It's quite the scene. Helen reclining in summer linens, as unnervingly calm as she was yesterday. Rose sitting stiffly in a sundress and sneakers, as if she were off to a matinee at Lincoln Center. Amity lying on her back, wearing her white dress that's a shirt and a pair of tortoiseshell shades, Holly Golightly–style. Various opened tubs of food are dotted around the blanket.

They are having a *picnic*. Ruth suddenly thinks of Owen's

Mrs. Lovett, and she can't help it: she looks around for a slice of meat pie.

"Sit," Helen says, patting at the blanket as Ruth approaches.

Ruth eases herself down, as distanced from each of the women as she can manage.

"We're glad you came," Helen says, while the other two simply stare.

When Ruth doesn't respond, the older woman lets out a small sigh.

"We find ourselves in an unusual position, don't we, Ruth-Ann? I imagine you feel a great deal of distrust right now, and yet you've hardly been honest with us either. Where does that leave us? Or, rather, where should we begin?"

Ruth opens her mouth to speak, but nothing comes out.

"Fine, I'll start then," Helen says. "This podcast. *The Other Women*. It would seem Gabe and Juno are correct in believing it was just a tactic to persuade us to meet with you?"

Ruth looks at Helen. "Yes."

"You'll be dropping it then? The podcast?"

Ruth nods. Just.

"Good! Then we can move on. What would you like to know, Ruth-Ann? All cards on the table now."

Three queens. Truly, the only hand she ever won against Juno.

Ruth takes a deep breath. "Which one of you helped Ethan Oswald kidnap me?"

She might have asked them about the weather for all the women react. Nobody gasps or recoils or even blinks. They merely glance at each other, and then Rose lets out her own short breath.

"I never procured girls for Ethan, Ruth. I know you think I did, but I was just a kid from New Zealand who knew nothing about the world back then. And when he was kind to me, I liked it."

One minute in, and Ruth already feels like screaming.

Rose continues her monologue. "Ethan knew I was struggling to make friends. I'd been so silent for most of that year, I'd almost forgotten how to speak. And then I got the lead in the musical, and I had to find my voice again, somehow. *Practice on little kids*, he used to say to me. *They'll talk to you about anything, Annie.* We used to go to the playground, and I'd chat to all the cute kids from the elementary school. They thought it was cool that I was from somewhere else. I *liked* talking to them. That's how this whole dreadful mix-up started."

This whole dreadful mix-up. Where Annie Whitaker mined children for information about their lives so she could pass those insights on to Ethan. Isn't this the confirmation Ruth has been seeking?

She reminds herself to stay calm.

"You told him about my cat."

"Your cat?"

Rose shoots a look at the other women, before turning back to Ruth.

"Nala," Ruth insists, her voice catching on the name. "You told him about Nala, and Ethan used that to trick me into getting into his van."

"I'm so sorry," Rose says. "I honestly have no memory of that. I used to see you on the swings behind your house sometimes. But that's all I remember about you. I should have paid more attention to what he was like, I do know that. We *all* should have."

This prompts Amity to sit up.

"I was only a kid," she says defensively, shaking some grass from her hair. "How was I supposed to know how huge the consequences would be?"

"The consequences of changing your story?" Rose asks, looking at Amity intently.

"The consequences of wanting him to *like* me. Even after he hurt me. You get it, right? He could make you feel like the most important person in the world."

Rose shifts her gaze to Helen. "And then the worst person one minute later."

"He was like that even as a little boy," Helen concurs. "He had such an intensity. Something my own children lacked, and I was drawn to it, I'll admit."

Amity watches her, wide-eyed, as if listening to a sage.

"I deeply regret not raising the alarm about Ethan's behavior sooner." Helen turns to Ruth now. "For years, I told myself that his . . . proclivities . . . were simply the markings of a genius.

"I don't mean his interest in little girls," she clarifies, after catching the look of horror on Ruth's face. "I mean his desire to control a situation. Ethan was a perfectionist, which I liked to think came from me. Of course, I missed all the ways in which he was like my husband."

"I've been drawn to men like him ever since," Amity admits. "You're the one who made me see that, Ruth. Like, he made nice guys seem *boring*."

Rose shakes her head. "You can get therapy for that, Amity. Believe me."

"I probably need it," Amity says. "Because I miss him sometimes."

"So do I."

Helen and Rose, together. Ruth remembers what it was like, back in Oslo, to realize Helen had *loved* Ethan. In triplicate, it makes her dizzy with rage.

"I don't understand any of you," she snaps, scrambling to stand. "Have you forgotten what he *did*?"

"Never for a second," Helen answers, reaching out her hand to stop Ruth.

"Sit down, please, Ruth-Ann. I know this must be very painful for you. Though I must say, this is exactly what you asked for. Would you prefer that we were dishonest?"

Ruth hesitates. Part of her wants to run. But she can also hear Officer Canton's voice from five years ago. Asking her how long she wanted to stay locked in that room.

She sits back down and fixes Helen with what she hopes is an icy stare.

"Did Ethan ever visit you at your house in Hoben?" she asks. "When he was younger?"

"He did."

"And did he ever hurt anyone while he was staying there?"

Helen meets Ruth's stare. "If I knew the answer to that, I would tell you."

"Then what was he doing there?"

"Keeping a grieving mother company," Helen answers, still maintaining eye contact with Ruth. "Or that's how I saw it at the time. He would come and visit me, drive for hours sometimes, when my own children wouldn't even pick up the phone."

"Am I supposed to feel *sorry* for you?" Ruth asks, incredulous.

"I would hope just a little," Helen says. "The same way I feel sorry for you. You have been through things I would wish on no one, Ruth-Ann."

At this, Ruth feels the fight drain out of her. The woman doesn't falter.

She plays the only card she has left up her sleeve.

"What about *Nydelig*, Helen? Or should I call you Jonas? Because that book seemed to tell a very different story."

Amity and Rose look from Ruth to Helen, expectant. Evidently they're just as interested in what her answer might be.

Infuriatingly, Helen smiles.

"Gabe told me you took a copy, Ruth-Ann. That book was never meant for an audience."

"So why did you write it?"

"To find meaning in the incomprehensible," Helen says. "I was devastated by what my husband had done, and Ethan utterly destroyed what little sense of self I had left. I wrote *Nydelig*, with all its little tropes and clumsy attempts to grasp memetics, to make sense of the world I suddenly found myself in. I had thought it might help my children make sense of their lives too. They wanted nothing to do with it, of course. But the process of writing healed something in me. Or began to, at least. And so I wrote more books, *better* books, from there."

This sounds a lot like what Beth had been trying to tell Ruth when they'd first tried to understand the meaning of that book.

Ruth frowns, still not convinced it's as simple as that.

"But you don't want people to know about your writing. If it's just fiction, then why hide it?"

"Ah, yes. Your little blackmail attempt. I must confess, when my agent phoned to say someone was threatening to spill the beans, I never imagined you were involved. A blind spot, you might say, given you were sitting right there in my living room. Juno set me straight, as that girl so often does. But I digress. Why do I write under a pseudonym? Because I *like* my anonymity, Ruth-Ann. You could even say I need it. Serial killers might be considered a type of celebrity these days, but their wives and families are seldom treated with the same reverence, I assure you."

"It's not like you were treating us very nicely, Ruth," Amity points out. "All I wanted to do was tell my story for once. But it seems like you had an idea of how that should go."

Ruth is surprised that Amity is being so direct.

"If you knew who I was, why did you agree to speak to me?" she asks her. She's still not sure how Amity fits into this whole spiral of betrayals.

"I *didn't* know who you were," Amity protests. "Not at the start. The first two times we met, I just thought you were some intense chick who . . . who got me."

"But you still checked me out."

Amity pulls a face.

"Not really. That old waiter guy at the restaurant told me where you worked. And it seemed legit, because I don't know a bartender in this city who doesn't have creative . . . aspirations. I thought your podcast was for real, Ruth."

Amity glances at Helen and pouts.

"Then they told me you weren't who you said you were. And that I should disappear for a bit while they figured out what you were up to."

"You never went to Paris."

"Nope," Amity answers, still pouting. "By then, I was doing what I was told."

"What Amity means by that," Helen jumps in, "is that we three women quickly realized we had something in common. And how easily our shared interests could be misrepresented."

Ruth narrows her eyes. It's almost too neat. The answers that Helen, especially, has for seemingly everything. But if she *is* lying, how would Ruth know? The only person who might tell her for sure is dead and buried. Not even his words remain.

"Did you really sell Ethan's letters to a collector?" Ruth asks Amity, though she already knows the answer.

"No," Amity confirms. "I burned them, mostly because I was so embarrassed about his responses to all the dumb things I'd said to him. But I figured you'd get suspicious if I told you that. So . . . I lied."

Looking at Amity's forlorn expression, Ruth feels a traitorous sense of understanding. She'd prefer to stay mad at her. Especially when it's now obvious that Amity—inadvertently or otherwise—is the one who started all this. All because of a mistake she'd made at fourteen years old.

Nothing, Ruth realizes, gets buried deeper—or surfaces more destructively—than our own sense of shame.

She stands up, just as the little boy from the birthday party kicks a soccer ball their way. It stops just short of the picnic blanket, and an older boy, maybe ten or twelve, comes to retrieve it. He smiles shyly at the women before turning and hard-kicking the ball away.

"Rose," Ruth says abruptly, watching as the boy runs back to the party, "did you ever introduce Ethan to your host brother?"

"Why would I do that?" Rose looks disgusted at the thought. "I hated that kid."

"No reason," Ruth says, feeling one last shred of loyalty toward Juno.

"I'm going now," she quietly declares. "And I'm going to leave you all alone from here. No more questions. No more dredging up the past. You have my word on that."

It's obvious she can't take this any further. She's never going to fully trust these women, and it's unlikely they'll ever trust her. This trinity of women, with her at the center, binding them all together.

Another realization. The real reason Ruth needed to break that triskelion into pieces was to free herself from these women orbiting her.

She doesn't wait for their response as she turns and walks away. But she hasn't made it a hundred feet when she looks down and sees a small, discarded sandal on the ground. A little girl's shoe, left behind after a playdate in the park.

Ruth spins back around. Sometimes the universe does put you in exactly the right place.

"Which one of you was it?" she calls out across the meadow. "Who phoned in that anonymous tip?"

Which one of you saved me?

From a distance, they answer.

"I did."

Three women. Saying the same thing. At the very same time.

Curtain down.

This time, Ruth really does walk away.

THIRTY-EIGHT

Him?"

"Nah."

"How about him, then?"

"God, no!" Ruth laughs. "He was here the other night, and he knew all the words to 'Everybody Says Don't.'"

"Hmmmm." Owen puts a finger to his chin. "You're probably right, Nancy D. I guess all the murderers have stayed home."

"How nice of them," Ruth says, rolling her eyes. "Looks like no one's going into the Kill Jar tonight then, boss."

It's been three weeks since Sweeney's reopened. A month since that afternoon in Central Park. It's taken time, but Ruth is feeling considerably lighter. Able to sleep at least a few hours in her bed each night. And less likely to hover over Ressler like a helicopter parent, although she has insisted on bringing him to work with her. He sleeps out back on his oversize pillow, an arrangement that Owen has agreed to as long as it never becomes "a situation."

Ruth's boss has no idea of what she did while he was in the Hamptons. And though she's decided it really is time to tell

Owen (over many, many drinks) about her past, Ruth is not yet ready to discuss what happened these past few months. At the very least, Joe and Gideon need to know first. She'll talk to them when they get back from Italy. If they get ever back from Italy, because her uncles are having so much fun, they keep extending their trip.

Courtney has just finished her maternity leave, so Ruth will be back to her therapy sessions next week. But for now, there are only two people she's been able to confide in. About just how far she took things this summer.

Beth's parents, Bill and Patty Lovely.

Their relationship is fast becoming everything Ruth had spent so long hoping it would be. She and Ressler have been back to see them in Hoben three times now. Last week, while Bill was golfing, Patty took Ruth to visit Beth's grave for the first time. Sitting on the grass in front of Elizabeth Grace Lovely's heart-shaped, pink granite headstone, Patty recounted sweet, funny stories about her little girl, and cried as she shared her aching loss for the woman she might have become.

"Do you ever see her?" Ruth asked tentatively.

"I see her every day," Patty answered, closing her eyes. And Ruth knew not to ask in what ways.

On the drive back to the Lovely house, where Ruth and Ressler were staying for dinner, they'd talked about her "adventures" over the summer, as Patty now so generously called Ruth's race around the world. Beth's parents had been gentle with her confessions; they said they'd been worried, back when they first met Ruth, about how intent she'd seemed on proving Ethan hadn't acted alone. Not because they couldn't understand Ruth having questions, both Bill and Patty were quick to assure her. Because they knew how torturous it could be to pursue the kind of relief you were never actually going to get.

It was a race she could never finish, let alone win.

"Believe me"—Patty returned to the subject, on their car ride home from the cemetery—"I understand that it *does* offer temporary solace, Ruthie. When you're that fixated on something, you can stay one step ahead of your pain. You don't have to sit with it. So you'll do all sorts of . . . *interesting* . . . things to stay busy."

She reached over to squeeze Ruth's hand. "There's a quote from Dr. Jung that resonated with me when I first started my psychology studies. He wrote: *People will do anything, no matter how absurd, in order to avoid facing their own souls.* It's something to consider, don't you think? Because—and this aphorism is often misattributed to Jung, but I expect he'd agree with it, Ruthie—what we resist very much persists."

Sitting down together back at the house, Patty said something Ruth has thought about every day since.

"I could tell you a thousand times that you didn't do anything wrong. But what I most wish for you, darling, is that you let yourself grieve."

There on the couch, Ruth had cried in Patty Lovely's arms. For Beth and the woman she never got to be. For the little girl *Ruth* never got to be. That dance-loving, geology-loving, curious and happy kid who got stopped in her tracks the day she was abducted. It was like she really had died in that room.

When Ruth told Patty this, Beth's mother said she understood how she might feel that way.

"But listen, darling: we've all got versions of ourselves we never became. And who's to say that person would have been better?"

Bill Lovely had coughed from the doorway then. Cleared his throat.

"And we think you're pretty great just the way you are," he said, his eyes wet.

Supportive as Bill and Patty have been, they're also steadfast when it comes to the women. To Amity, Rose, and Helen. They do not believe any of them could or should be held responsible for Ethan Oswald's actions. Not unless, Bill clarified, something new came to light.

"Just don't go booking an airline ticket if you're the one to find it," he'd joked, and Ruth had never felt more seen in her life.

Not surprisingly, Ruth hasn't heard from any of her "other women" since she walked away from them in the park. When they all said they'd called in that anonymous tip. And at least two of them must have been lying. She has to try very hard not to think about what that means. Patty says they each probably wanted to believe it.

Ruth hasn't heard from Juno either. Which is also no surprise. But it stings, just a little. She really did care for that girl. At times, she almost admires her for the double cross she pulled off.

Almost.

Back behind the bar at Sweeney's, Ruth is making a round of cosmopolitans for a group who have just finished a *Sex and the City* walking tour when Owen lets out a low whistle.

"Look who's back," he says, nudging Ruth so that she slops cranberry juice everywhere.

Gabe. Walking up to her at the bar with a sheepish look on his face.

"I'm sorry," he says, stopping directly in front of her.

All the ruminating in the world. All the things she's imagined saying to him, and Ruth simply ducks her head and sighs.

"Yeah, well. Get in line, Gabe."

"I'm sorry," he repeats. And then he tells her that he knows she might not want to see him after what he did, and he's here only because he's leaving tomorrow. Not for Melbourne, however. There are some things he needs to work out, so he's heading on a road trip out west, in that time-honored tradition of tortured souls trying to find themselves (Ruth does not smile at this). He just wanted to say—sorry. And goodbye.

A plaintive recording of Mandy Patinkin singing "Finishing the Hat" is playing in the background as Gabe makes this earnest speech. Ruth knows, because this is the Sondheim song Owen loves most, that Patinkin is singing about the consequences of personal obsession. Of single-mindedly pursuing something, no matter the damage you cause.

"Damn it," she whispers, as her eyes fill with tears.

Owen has been watching the two of them like he's at the US Open, eyes darting from Ruth to Gabe and back again.

"Go," he says to Ruth now. "I'll take care of this cluster of Carries and their cosmos. You two go for a walk and sort out whatever is going on between you."

Ruth is practically pushed out from behind the bar, but not before Owen instructs her to take that dog of hers along too.

"He's becoming a *situation* back there," he insists.

"Fine," Ruth concedes, searching for a cloth to wipe her sticky hands. "But just ten minutes, okay?"

"I'll take it!" Gabe responds, grinning with relief.

From the corner of her eye, Ruth sees the Kill Jar gleaming.

"I'll go get Ressler," she says.

Owen understands. That nothing bad can happen to Ruth-Ann Baker when she has her hound dog by her side.

They walk in silence for half a block, until Gabe stops.

"So."

"So."

"I really am sorry, Ruth. Things just escalated really fast."

She stops. "You said I was the *villain*, Gabe."

"Not my finest moment, for sure," he admits. "But that night was a real trip, Ruth. Juno had run away, and then she showed up at my place, and it was like all my worlds were colliding."

"I know that feeling," she says, trying not to get distracted by those sea-glass eyes, watching her so intently.

"I felt like I had to protect Juno, and my grandmother, of course," Gabe continues. "But I didn't want to hurt you. Especially after you were brave enough to tell me what happened to you."

"Or stupid enough."

"Please don't think that," Gabe says, a stricken look on his face. "I'm surrounded by people who don't talk about their pain. It was a relief to find someone willing to look it square in the face for once." He pauses. "Even if I didn't handle it so well that night."

"When I tried to kiss you," Ruth says.

"Yeah, when you tried to kiss me, and I tried not to kiss you back."

They stare at each other for a long time after that. In another life, this is when they *would* kiss.

Instead, Ruth asks if Gabe has heard from Juno.

"Yeah," he answers, but not before letting out a slow, shaky breath. "Not as much as usual, because she's got some big project she's working on this term at school. A podcast, would you believe. She seems really into it, which is probably good for all of us."

"Unless we're in it," Ruth suggests, not sure if her alarm is feigned or real.

"Lord help us then." Gabe laughs. "The wrath of Juno is something to behold."

Ruth rolls her eyes in tribute. "Tell me about it."

"She's a good kid," Gabe says, his face serious now. "I don't think any of us realized just how hard it was for her, growing up in that town. She was terrified all this stuff about her mum would stir everything up again."

"And you?" Ruth asks. "Why did you go along with her, Gabe?"

"I was terrified of losing my inheritance."

"Ha-ha."

"Truthfully, Ruth? My grandmother was afraid that this would get in the way of her reconciliation with my mother. Which, let's be honest, it totally would. My mum is still furious about my grandfather, and a whole lot of other things I don't fully understand.

"Anyway." Gabe is looking sheepish again. "One man's reason is another man's excuse. I should have come right out and told you, back when we started getting close. And now it seems like it's too late."

Ruth looks up at the night's starless sky, imagining all the clear skies waiting for Gabe on his road trip. All those constellations glittering over Arizona and Colorado and California, the patterns he'll get to trace with his fingers. The meaning he'll get to make of his life.

In another life, she might have asked to go with him.

But they do not belong together.

Ruth turns from that absence of stars to sea-glass eyes. Smiles.

"Don't be a stranger," she says.

Side by side, they walk back to Sweeney's, Ressler leading the way.

————

Two days later, Ruth wakes to the news that Coco Wilson has been found.

Safe and well.

It was indeed Coco those witnesses saw in Alabama, back in

June, after being abducted by her biological father, a man named Carter Collins.

Turns out, Ivy Wilson never told Carter about Coco, and she'd never told anyone but her closest girlfriends about Carter. They'd had a brief, tempestuous relationship while they were both in grad school at LSU, where Carter already had a serious girlfriend and a serious temper (just like her high school boyfriend, Ruth thinks). By the time Ivy found out she was pregnant, Carter had transferred to a school in Texas; his serious girlfriend had moved there the year before.

Ivy saw no reason to let Carter know about the daughter he would not have wanted with her anyway. Except when one of Ivy's old friends spilled her secret, he *did* want Coco. Enough to track her down in Hoben and whisk her away in a borrowed van, with the help of his new, very young girlfriend, Katie. That was the woman the old neighbor had seen Coco talking to at 3:33 p.m. the day she disappeared. Katie had offered to let Coco walk her dog, Milo, down the block, and if that neighbor had stayed looking out that window a minute longer, she would have seen Coco proudly leading Milo away. Or, rather, Katie leading Coco away, right into the arms of the father she'd never met, never even knew existed.

"You can't kidnap someone if they're already your child," Katie kept wailing in her police interviews, after a state trooper had pulled over the gray sedan, just over the Texas border. Coco, bewildered, had been sitting in the back seat, Milo asleep in her lap.

Of course, it will take time for these details to come out. For now, it's all breathless, breaking news about the kidnapping and Coco's safe return. Later, there will be many, many people who seem to agree with young Katie. Money and moral support will flow to Carter as he becomes the new poster "dad" for parental alienation and the reasons why men might feel forced to take the law into their own hands.

When a man gets pushed too far . . .

And no one ever apologizes to Leo Wilson for all that finger-pointing.

The space made for Carter Collins will make Ruth think of those sisters, Gina and Ari, who were murdered by their father in Melbourne. From across the world, as she follows the inquest into their murders, it will strike Ruth that the focus seems to have shifted. Online, it's no longer a small faction blaming the girls' mother for their father's actions. Even in mainstream media, when it comes to Brant Mitchell's crimes, the word *tragedy* has started to replace the word *murder*. As if the girls had been struck down by the gods, not by a vengeful father bent on hurting their mother in the most calculated, devastating way.

When a man gets pushed too far . . .

Patty Lovely was right when she said it seemed like things were getting worse these days.

But in August 2015, all of that is still out there, simmering. Today, processing the news about Coco's safe return, Ruth weeps with relief, for both the child and her family. And yet she also knows that *safe and well* is just the beginning. Ruth has no doubt Coco Wilson has many difficult days, and even harder nights, ahead of her.

Perhaps this is how she can finally help. She could be someone for Coco to talk to, someone who understands even a little of what she went through when she was abducted. Ruth decides to talk to Bill and Patty the next time she sees them. Ask them if they can connect her to the Wilson family when the time is right.

"I think that's a great idea," Beth says. "It was never a good thing that you only had me."

———

Ruth calls Officer Canton.

"You knew, didn't you?" she says, sitting up on her bed. "That it was probably the biological father."

He tells her that he can't discuss such things, but she can hear the kindness in his tone.

Next, just as she did with Bill and Patty a few weeks ago, Ruth admits to the full extent of her recent obsessions. The overseas trips, the podcast, even going to see Bobby Johnson at his apartment, which makes Canton let out a long, loud exhale.

"Why didn't you tell me what you were up to?" he asks, sounding more worried than frustrated.

"I guess I was a little embarrassed. Like, deep down, I knew I was acting crazy."

"You're not crazy, Ruthie."

Canton lets out a shorter breath this time.

"I've seen things in this job, kid. Things that have nearly made me lose my faith in the human race. But you—you've always brought me back from the brink. Finding you safe, bringing you home to your folks, that was the proudest moment of my career. Hell, Ruthie, it was the proudest moment of my life. Anytime I've ever considered giving up, it's your face I see. The way you never give up. You might try my patience sometimes, but the way you've pushed for those girls of yours, it's something special."

"Oh."

What she means to say: *I will never, ever be able to thank you for everything you've done for me.*

"I may not see what you can," Canton continues, "but I do know they are lucky to have you on their side, Ruthie. Their cases would have stayed cold, if it wasn't for you."

"*Stayed* cold?" Ruth sits up straighter.

"I'm not supposed to discuss this with you either, but what the hell—it'll be all over the news soon enough, and you deserve to know. That little body they found in the salt marsh a while back? That little girl? It's Lori. *Your* Lori. The samples were very degraded, so it took a long while, but forensics were eventually able to get what they needed. And they were able to make the match so quickly because we already had DNA from Lori's grandmother on file."

"How is that thanks to me?" Ruth asks, confused.

"Well, you caused such a fuss when you started poking around those cold cases five years ago, a few extra resources were quietly thrown their way. Part of that involved collecting DNA samples from close relatives of the girls, given we've never had DNA from the girls themselves. People are still looking for them, Ruthie, I promise."

"Why didn't you tell me?" She doesn't mean this as an accusation.

"I'm telling you now," Canton says simply. "I always hoped to come back to you with good news one day."

They both fall silent after that.

Can the discovery of a child's body ever really be considered *good* news? It is a bittersweet victory at best, knowing they are one step closer to finding whoever harmed sweet little bookworm Lori. She disappeared in 1991. Twenty-four years of secrets are closer to the surface now.

Whoever buried those secrets is closer too.

Ruth thinks of that map. The one with all the pins representing missing and unidentified children across the United States. She imagines zooming out even farther, so that you could see the shadow pins. All the people who know what happened, forming their own constellations. Able to be traced with the finger too. If you keep looking for what others can't see.

If you never give up on the restless dead.

"Thank you," she manages to say as the girls crowd around her, solemn with awe, and gratitude.

After finishing the call with Officer Canton, Ruth's fingers go to her neck, to the place Beth's flower ring used to hang. She'd lost it the night she dragged Ressler to the vet. The chain on the necklace must have snapped when she was lifting him into or out of the Uber. If it had happened in the apartment, she would have found it by now, because she turned the place upside down when she realized it was missing. She was devastated, but she's had to accept that the ring is long gone now.

Still. Nothing is ever truly lost. Someone in this city is going to stumble across it one day. Pick it up from the ground and turn it over in their palm.

Lovely, they'll say, slipping that forget-me-not into their pocket.

Lovely.

JUNO

THIRTY-NINE

Marama River, August 2015

Juno Mulvaney doesn't believe in regret.

Mostly, she doesn't believe in mistakes. People get so hung up on right and wrong, good and bad. They're always going on about *consequences*. But really, who gets to decide?

Even juries get it wrong.

Besides, people rarely consider why you do something. Who you do it for. Take Ruth-Ann Baker, for example. All those questions she was asking about her "other women" these past few months, she never saw how simple the answer really was.

A man gave them attention. That's all.

See, some women understand they need a man to make them feel whole. Her mother is that kind of woman. Amity Greene is *definitely* that kind of woman. They want lives bigger than the ones they were given, but they don't know how to get those lives for themselves, so they find men who will make them extraordinary by association. And then they play the victim when that doesn't work out for them. What a surprise!

Juno can't relate, but she tries not to judge. Because she knows that she's not like most other girls.

"That Juno is quite something," people would often say to her bewildered father.

"It's like she came from someone else entirely," he'd always reply.

If only, she thinks now. The one interesting thing her father ever did was sleep with a teenage girl, which was more stupid than interesting. And gross. He was messing around with a girl who was only a year older than Minnie is now. This is not something Juno likes to think about.

Sometimes, she does let herself think about that night. Sometimes, she imagines sitting in front of one of those juries, looking earnest and demure, as she tells them it's not like she knew what was going to happen.

It's not like she wanted anyone to *die*.

Is that what her mother would have said in front of a jury too?

Juno was only ten when she found the secret love notes Ethan Oswald left in Annie Whitaker's locker each day, back when she was an exchange student. The romance, the melodrama! He might have been her teacher, but he was the one who seemed like a teenager.

No one understands me like you do, Annie. I've finally found my Julie Jordan!

"Who's Julie Jordan?" Juno asked her mother that night, which caused Rose to burst into tears.

That's how Juno knew those notes were important.

She's read them over and over since then. There are some she can quote verbatim.

Like the one where Oswald told her mother that he didn't need her to die for him, which makes Juno think she must have offered.

I don't need you to die for me, Annie. Stop saying such things, please! If you really want to prove that you love me, you know what to do. It won't be bad, I promise. Nothing between us could ever be bad.

That note made it seem like Oswald was just a regular old creep, pressuring the teenage Annie to have sex with him.

But Ethan Oswald didn't like teenage girls. Not in that way.

"Why didn't I see it?" her mother asked, when Ruth had started sticking her nose into the past and they had to get their stories straight.

"You *did* see it," Juno said, the next time Rose cried about it. "You just prefer to forget that part of the story."

Even now, her mother insists she had no idea he'd actually go through with it. Kidnapping little Beth Lovely like that. When he talked to her about it, she thought it was a fantasy. At seventeen, her mother had so few fantasies of her own, she'd assumed this was what some grown men thought about. So that, when Beth disappeared, she said, she thought it was some kind of terrible coincidence.

She said.

But she never said anything to stop him.

"What did you do?" she had the nerve to ask her daughter, when Juno came back from Marama Bend six years ago, dripping wet. "What did you do?"

"What did *you* do, Mama?"

The truth is, Annie Whitaker just wanted to be special. She was willing to do anything for the man who made her feel important. The star of the show. She wanted to be a better Julie Jordan than that other girl. The one back in Ohio who wrote pathetic, "pick me" letters to Ethan, while he was writing his own love notes to Annie.

I like what you did to me, that other girl kept saying. Unaware he'd already moved on.

At least, that's how Helen explained it. That woman ended up with all of Ethan's personal belongings, including his letters from Amity Greene. She has the notes Annie Whitaker wrote him too.

Giving him all that information about those little girls.

If Juno had long had her suspicions about what her mother did when she was seventeen years old, Helen filled in the blanks.

Sometimes you just need to hear someone else say it.

And sometimes you need to keep your mouth shut. Her father gets so sad about things, still. But it's not like Juno set out to hurt Nichole that night. She simply followed her down to the river after sending her off in a panic. And when her dad realized he had an audience, he panicked too.

Really panicked.

He probably should have, given what he was doing to Kelly at the time.

When Nichole went at him like that, all Juno did was stop her. She simply turned all that anger back on the girl. That has always been Juno's superpower.

She *told* Ruth that.

She also told Ruth that she would do anything to protect her family. So it's definitely not her fault that things got a bit messy in New York too.

No regrets. Not one.

Even if she found herself liking Ruth-Ann Baker. Even if there were times it felt like they could be great friends.

Juno Mulvaney doesn't care.

She goes to her bedside drawer, takes out the necklace with the blue flower ring dangling at its center. How many times had she seen Ruth reach for that ring? It feels nice to have brought this tangible part of her back to Marama River, at least. To be able to close her eyes and hold that flower, the way Ruth always did.

One, two, three. *Twist.*

The ring almost makes up for having to give that cool talisman back. Juno would have preferred to keep it for herself, but it was a nice touch, she thinks: throwing it across the room like that. Even if Helen said it was too much. What did she know, anyway? Ever since Gabe introduced them a few years back, his grandmother has acted like she is the boss of everyone, just because she knew Ethan first. As far as Juno is concerned, the old lady cares way too much for a dead guy. She's always trying to sweep up his secrets anytime they spill over.

But keeping secrets for a boy is different from burying them for a man. Things are going to get very interesting for Helen, Juno predicts, thanks to the bones of that little girl. They know who she is, that was in the news the other day. If any more of those girls show up—well, Helen can keep saying it was only a *book*, but if Ruth hadn't been so fixated on her own case, she might have seen what Juno did from the start.

Helen Torrent doesn't lie. She simply omits the most important parts of the story.

She's passed on that skill to Juno, no doubt.

But to use one of Helen's favorite quotes: *At some point, the apprentice always usurps the master.*

Honestly, Helen wouldn't even have known what Ruth was up to, if Juno hadn't clicked to who she really was. All because she paid more attention to online chatter than sweet, trusting Gabe did.

Poor Gabe, wallowing around their hokey little support group, trying to come to terms with the fact that he was related to a cold-blooded murderer. *Try having a guy like that for your dad!* Juno said, when they first started talking about their families.

But Gabe never found the things she said funny. He could be so serious sometimes.

Like a big brother, she supposes. And everyone says brothers can be annoying.

This makes her think of Bobby Johnson. *Chip*. Bringing him into the mix had been a masterstroke. He'd basically tortured her mum when they lived together as kids. And he never let up about her relationship with Ethan.

"Oooooh, *lovers*," Chip used to snark, when Rose—well, Annie—was dropped home by her teacher. After Ethan was arrested, Chip was even worse.

"Your husband is a murderer," he used to hiss as he walked past Annie's bedroom, where she was mostly crying and waiting to go home. And then he would laugh.

Yeah, well, now who's laughing, Bobby Johnson! After Juno went off script, as Helen called it, and started sharing hints about him and Ivy Wilson online, it was never just going to be Ruth who showed up at his door. Something Juno knows very well: once people have you in their sights, they'll find all sorts of ways to convict you. A bully like Bobby—his time will surely come. Because the internet hounds won't give up their hunt, now that she's set them onto him. Whatever shitty things he's done to women, and there will no doubt be many, many shitty things that he's done, someone is going to find out. Juno can only sit back and wait.

At least little Coco made it home safely. Juno really hopes she's doing okay. The things that happen to you when you're a kid can really mess you up. Besides, Coco is the reason these last few months have been so interesting. And pretty exciting, she has to admit. Because there's no denying how much fun she's had, staying one step ahead of Ruth-Ann Baker, citizen detective and damaged soul.

Before Coco Wilson went missing, Rose always said the past

would come back to haunt her one day. Her mother might fear ghosts, but that's another thing Juno doesn't believe in. If you really could be haunted, surely Nichole, if not Kelly, would have shown up by now. But not even a swooping tūī or jittery pīwakawaka when Juno goes down to the river or to the girls' graves in that little old cemetery. She tried a summoning ceremony there once, all crystals and candles, but ultimately Juno is more goddess than witch.

Vigilant Juno, protector of women.

Or the ones who need protecting, at least.

And no woman needs protecting more than her mother, these days. With all those confused confessions frothing at her mouth. She can be such a doormat sometimes. Juno had to remind her, just the other day, that the bully husband died in *Carousel*.

It was Julie Jordan who was left standing at the end. With her daughter.

So, no. Juno has no regrets about the tiki tour she took Ruth on. She prefers to think of it more like a scavenger hunt, anyway. All the red herrings she deliberately left after @DrBurgess96 (Friend) suddenly reactivated their account and started leaving a trail of questions all over the internet. It's not like Juno ever lied to Ruth. Credit where credit is due—this was the genius of Helen's original plan. After it became clear to them that Amity Greene, that vapid, fame-hungry loser, was going to blab to anyone who listened about her relationship with Ethan. Muddy up the waters, Helen said, when Rose was so worried about what Amity might unwittingly reveal. Overwhelm Ruth with so much information, she'd drown in it. Metaphorically, of course. No one actually wanted to harm her.

They really could have been friends.

Maybe Juno will go back to New York one day. Surprise Ruth in a better way. Gabe said she mostly hangs out with a bunch of dead girls—it might be nice for her to have a real-life partner in crime.

It'll happen if it's meant to happen. Ruth is not going any-where, and neither is Juno. They're survivors, both of them. Not like her father, crumbling into the sea.

That was one of Juno's favorite days, in fact. When she took Ruth down to the beach. It was nice to see the wild beauty of that place through someone else's eyes. And there was a moment when Ruth had really seemed to care about her. As if she wasn't just using Juno to get information about her mother.

But then the tide started coming in, and they had to leave.

No regrets. Not one.

Sometimes, a moment of truth is all you're going to get.

ACKNOWLEDGMENTS

We made it!

Family, friends, strangers who stopped me to ask how the new book was going: your support and generosity means so much to me. As does the expertise, patience, and care offered by every single member of my publishing team(s). Thank you all for making this grand adventure possible.

With special thanks to:

Emily Bestler and Libby McGuire—thank you for inviting me in. You have truly made my dreams come true.

My real-life Hecates, Cara Lee Simpson and Jane Palfreyman. Thank you for trusting me to start over when my restless girls wouldn't wait.

My North American team who make me feel right at home, especially: Dana Trocker, Megan Rudloff, Maudee Genao, Paige Lytle, Shelby Pumphrey, Morgan Pager, Claire Sullivan, and Hydia Scott-Riley (thank you for only ever being an email away!).

My UK bookends, Darcy Nicholson and Molly Walker-Sharp.

My earliest readers: Aaron, Caitlin, Conrad, Jodee, Karen,

Karena (aka my eagle-eyed editor), Laura, Lindsay (forever "LKB"), Sophie, and Stef. And my chief vintner and printer, Keith. Thank you all so much for spending time with the girls before anyone else did. You truly kept me going.

My trusted sources who helped map a story that covers three continents: Michael "Beth" Buttrey, Sue Hoben, and Sarah Coogan. My experts in the field, Christopher Arciero and Coralea Craw, who helped this amateur detective understand how things really work. And Jacqueline Frawley, who IS New York to me.

My New Zealand squad, led by Sonya, Bridget, and Simone. Teams Mawson and Allan. The Hour Glass gang. Kerry and the Chaos crew, who kept me caffeinated. My Tuesday night (Aqua) Therapists. Amie, who reminded me to breathe. And every local who so generously offered a couch, bar stool, kitchen table, or an ear, as the book progressed.

My whānau, who are the biggest cheer squad of them all.

My Melbourne family, especially Bron, Chris and Penelope, Con and Clinton, Stacey, and Paw Paw. How far we have come together, my loves.

Scarecrow, who helped set me on this path.

Ms. Sharrow and Mr. Hamilton, who took this Kiwi kid under their wing. And all my fellow Broadway babies from the Flushing High School Class of '94.

The goodest of dogs, Ruby, Raffy, Derek, Buffy, and Albus. Actually: ALL dogs.

The kidlets, who bring me back to the real world in all the best ways. I love being your (great) aunt.

Booksellers and librarians in the US and across the globe, and my beloved readers—you!! I'm so glad we get to do this together.

All the writers, past and present, who strive to make this world a little easier to live in—thank you for showing me the way.

ACKNOWLEDGMENTS

Lastly, my deepest gratitude to my parents. Mum, you are my very favorite reader. And Dad, thank you for teaching me how to finish strong, and for *always* cheering me home. As I wrote this book, you served as the ultimate reminder that death does not end love—it expands it.